Also by Reid Matthias

The Amicable Circle Novels

Butcher

Baker

Candlestickmaker

Son of a Butcher

And
Historical Fiction

Blank Spaces: The Legend of Jerusalem Walker

Visit the author at reidmatthias.com and

Facebook.com/Apostle 13

ISBN paperback: 978-0-6456882-0-7
           ebook: 978-0-6456882-1-4

This edition first published by A13 in June 2023

Typesetting by Ben Morton

Publication assistance from Immortalise

Front and back cover through Unsplash by Daniel Jensen

THE SICK HOUSE

A Novel
By
Reid Matthias

For truly spectacular people who have shown me what life means. Firstly Christine, my extraordinary wife; and my daughters, Josephine, Greta, and Elsa.

List of Characters:

Residents of Cloud End

Owner of Cloud End	Claire St. Croix
Owner of Cloud End	Donald St. Croix
Grandchildren	McKayla Ashford
	Oswald Ashford
Cleaning Woman	Nancy Harper
House Manager	Carl Van der Hoven
Cook	Esther Fields
Housekeeper	Radiance Morrison
House doctor	Swithin Chandruth
House psychotherapist	Jane Boeder-Mankins
Nurse	Kylie Carlson
Nurse	Jack Walters

Guests of Cloud End

Priest	Father Lawrence Haskins
Prostitute	Chantelle Ingram
Police officer	Gavin Matthews
Speeder	Monica Xiao
Businesswoman	Jacquelyn Archer
Gravedigger	Alonzo Turner
Divorcing man	Damian Bellows
Divorcing woman	Sydney (Tauchman) Bellows
Divorce lawyer	Wallis Takamoto
Drug addict	Seraphim Wyman
Politician	Winston Faraday III
Draper family	Sam Draper
	Dorothy Draper
	Gina Draper
	Pasqual Draper
	Titus Draper

Herzfeldians

Mayor	Gemma Cranmere
Tavern owner	Steve Cranmere
Tavern owner	Edgar Post
Grocer	Elizabeth Happel
Constable	Robert (Igor) Kovschenko
Hotelier	Bridgette Priveto
Parish Rector	Magnus Falkirk
Banker	Renata Lerner
Paramedics	Tom Bolstrud
	Albert Kampman
Baker	Selina Lomiller

Government Politicians

National Health Officer	Emery Donaldson
Senator	Allen Membree
Senator	Quentin Forsythe
Intelligence Director	Stella Reed-Conway
Infectious Disease	Monica Portney
Director of United Psychology	Dylan Renfroe
Capitol Socialite	Isolde Howard

Fear again. If you want to control someone, all you have to do is make them feel afraid.

Paolo Coehlo

If you tell a big enough lie and tell it frequently enough, it will be believed.

Adolf Hitler

(Reuters) The Hague

In a stunning turn, World Health Secretary Vidas Gausman announced that instead of relaxing restrictions, further measures would be taken to stem the effects of Halovirus 29. Due to increased pressure from world governments, Secretary Gausman hinted that various Convalescent Centers were being created to take in those infected with Halo 29. Increased testing has revealed that almost ten percent of the world's population currently has the virus, thus increasing the level of worry that Halovirus would be COVID 19 redux. While the mortality rate hovers at less than two percent of those infected, generally killing those who are obese or suffering from other chronic health conditions, scientists at the World Health Organization warn that the virus could quickly mutate and become a civilization killer.

Proponents of the Convalescent Center plan, including most Western nations, state that the 'Safety of the majority is of utmost importance' and that 'those required to move to Convalescent Centers do so with haste and calmness for the sake of the greater good.'

Detractors of the plan have immediately likened Convalescent Centers to internment camps, and that those who are taken there would have no timeline for their stay. Kelly Norman, spokesperson for Humane Humanity, demanded that '...there be significant communication about those who are moved to Convalescent Centers and how long they would be separated from the rest of society.'

Requests for interviews concerning Convalescent Centers have not been granted, but rumors persist that those who are locked down will have no connection with the outer world.

Sep. 3, 2031

Communication 3BZ890
24 August, 2031

From: ██████████████████████████████████
To: ██████████████████████

████████████████,

After weeks of thorough searching of dossiers, ████████████, ██████████
██████████████████████, has selected a diverse cross-section of people
with whom to begin Project Green Light.

Over the course of the next six weeks, sixteen people will be subjected
to various psychological manipulations, not limited to ████████████
████████, ████████████████, and ██████████████████, and also constant
surveillance by ██████████████ at the Cloud End Convalescent Center near
Herzfeld.

The objectives of testing will be, but are not limited to:

Group psychological manipulation. Can the Government actively control a
small group of people? And if so, can the results be used large scale?

To see if ██████████████████████████████.

To test the effectiveness of ██████ to sway public opinion.

To form effective strategies for the next pandemic.

Please advise for go-ahead.

Communication 2AA415
26 August, 2031

From: ██████████████████████████

To: ██████████████████████████████████████

████████████████████,

After liaising with ██████████████████, be advised: Project Green Light
is approved.

Against the pale grey sky, a large, two-story resort loomed beneath clouds that threatened to consume it. Flecks of paint peeled back from siding like curlicued pigs' tails; shutters, previously painted blue, had succumbed to the power of the sun turning them a strained cornflower color, and the land on which the house sat was devoid of trees save two large oaks which stood guard twenty paces from the front, wraparound porch. The grass was splotchy; numerous weeds had infested the lawn giving its face a freckled look. Where once was a flower bed, a toy graveyard sat in its place: a tricycle and plastic earthmover, sand shovels and a basketball which bared a black rubber hernia, were muddied by sporadic rains and lay abandoned on their sides waiting for new life.

A large wooden sign in the shape of a cumulonimbus had been nailed above the porch.

CLOUD END

The owners, Donald and Claire St. Croix, were a gentle couple who loved both the home and its history, but nothing could have prepared them for the manic darkness that was the Halovirus. The St. Croix's had dwelt at Cloud End for more than two decades entertaining countless guests for a modest rate as they overnighted towards more exciting and exotic places. When they first arrived, they were stunned by Cloud End's vista. Though the promotional photographs showed the resort with an overlooking view of the cliff as it tumbled down to the ocean, they did it no justice. From Faucini Cliff to the roaring water below was two hundred feet. The website proclaimed that the cliff was 'one hundred breathtaking steps away,' but those would have been a giant's steps. The reality was closer to two hundred. And the path was through thick, oatey grass, which left irksome prickles on their clothes as they strolled to take in the precipitous drop.

Claire and Donald purchased Cloud End as a downpayment on their fairytale retirement happiness, but it had been decidedly less happy than they had hoped. As the Halovirus turned off reservations like a corroding tap, their tolerance for each other dripped into the sink of their dreams. When their daughter Blanca took her own life (after her useless husband ran away with another woman), Claire and Donald found themselves as guardians of their two grandchildren, McKayla and Oswald. The children were happy to be living on the edge, but the pinched look around their eyes and the way they floated to their bedrooms each night made them seem more like adolescent ghosts than grandchildren. Claire and Donald wanted them to put their phones down to emerge into the wonders of Cloud End, to embrace the indoor waterfall and small library by the front door, maybe even pitch in with serving meals, but their words fell on deaf ears.

On the day of the public Convo announcement, the St. Croix's felt honored to be part of the World Health Recovery Effort. A senator had called them personally, asking for complete confidentiality, to request Cloud End's assistance for use by the Government as a Convalescent Center.

'Of course,' Claire had responded as she held her hand over the receiver to tell Donald to sit down. 'We would be honored to help.' Nodding, she listened intently to what the senator said, took a few notes with a partially chewed pencil, added a few more *mm hmm's* and *yes-of-courses*, then disconnected the line. Before speaking to her husband, she stared at the ancient device, an Apple iPhone 19. Oswald and McKayla had tried to convince her to upgrade to the newest version of the AutoCom, a next generation mobile phone technology, which surgically embedded components in the forearm, eardrum and temple. The AutoCom automatically updated the Artificial Intelligence for the best and brightest streaming and messaging service. Claire had refused, stating that she wouldn't know the first thing about how to use it. 'And besides that,' Claire added with a raised eyebrow, 'we're not quite sure what those things are doing to us anyway. Why, they could be uploading viruses into us!' McKayla had rolled her eyes and told her grandmother to *Chill* back. But Claire didn't know what that meant, either. When the children begged for AutoComs, Claire told them they'd have to wait until they were at least fifteen. Even as they complained, Claire did not give in.

2

1

'Who was that?' Donald asked.

'A senator.'

'Of what?'

Claire frowned and set the phone on the benchtop which was littered with bills and documents they'd been working through regarding the viability of Cloud End. 'Of the Government.'

'What did he want?'

'*She* wants to use the End.'

Donald, his eyes puffy with lack of sleep and darkened by worry, studied his wife of forty years. As she leaned against the counter with one hand hitched up on her hip and a loose floral dress draped over her sagging body, she appeared tense, like a cobra preparing to strike.

'She's coming to stay?'

'Heaven's no. She asked if Cloud End could be used as a Convalescent Center.'

His face twisted into a frown. 'What's that?'

'Haven't you been watching the news?'

He shook his head and grumbled, 'The only thing they do is report on Halovirus.' His voice faded off until he tapped the table lightly. 'Just fearmongering if you ask me.'

'No one's asking you, Donald.' He gritted his teeth while she picked up notes and continued, 'The senator,' she stressed, shaking the paper, 'wants to know if we'll house Halovirus cases until they have recuperated.'

'How long will that be?'

'She didn't say, but after the last pandemic, it could be a while.'

'Sounds like a recipe for disaster.'

Claire looked over her reading glasses at him. 'It could be our salvation. We haven't had guests for weeks. People are afraid to travel.'

'Not really a news flash, that.'

'Which is why,' Claire drew out the word, 'we need to accept the invitation to be part of the solution.'

Donald snorted. 'The solution to what?'

'To help the world get better.'

3

Donald walked to the kitchen window where he peered through the dusted glass in the direction of Faucini Cliff. Neglected weeds waved in the wind unheeding the storm swirling through the human world.

'I don't know, Claire. Bringing active cases into the End would be risky. Think of the grandchildren.'

Claire made a *psh* sound. 'It's not a risk for the children. It's not even a risk for us. Halovirus kills fat people.'

Donald stared at his wife. 'So far, but what if it mutates?'

'What if it doesn't?'

His eyes followed a pair of seagulls winging delicately in the updrafts. Wistfully, he wondered what their freedom would be like, to float above and beyond the chaos of viruses and shrinking retirement accounts and business transactions and cleaning Cloud End toilets. If only they could go back to the time when Blanca was little and they were younger, when things were simpler and...

'Donald?'

'Hmm?'

'I asked if you wanted to do this. What should I say to the senator?'

'You should turn her down.'

'How will we pay our bills?'

'Something will come up. It always does.'

At that moment, a whirlwind of activity spun into the kitchen. McKayla, red-faced and angry, her crimson hair caked to her face with sweat, was chasing her younger brother, a smaller blonde version of her, who had an impish grin on his face while holding something in his hands.

'Hold on, what's going on?' Claire asked.

McKayla pointed at her brother. 'Os let that thing into my room, and it started chasing me.'

'I did not!' Oswald shouted. 'I didn't *let* him into your room. Caspar *chose* to go in there.'

'If you can't control it, we should get rid of it!' she screamed. 'It's disgusting!'

4

Oswald clutched the rat to his face where it wriggled next to his cheek. 'No! He's my pet!'

'Children,' Claire interrupted their argument, 'aren't you supposed to be in class?'

Approaching his grandfather, Oswald continued to nuzzle his rat and spoke through his fur. 'We are, but the teacher said she needed a break, so she told us to watch a video about climate change.'

'That sounds interesting,' Claire responded.

'Can I go outside and play?' Oswald asked.

'If you take your sister with you.'

'Do I have to?'

'I don't want to go outside,' McKayla grumbled. 'I want to talk to my friends.'

Claire made a brushing movement with her hands. 'Later. Go outside and get some fresh air.'

'Do you want to come outside, Grandpa?' Os asked.

'Maybe some other time.'

The children bustled out of the room while Donald refocused his attention on the freewheeling seagulls.

'I'm going to tell the senator we'll do it,' Claire said authoritatively.

He sighed. 'Do whatever you think is best.'

A lonely man, clad entirely in black, trudged disconsolately along the gravel road towards the foreboding residence perched near the cliff. When the World Health Police rapped on his door, he felt a peculiar roiling in his gut, and it wasn't from the Halovirus. He had a feeling they'd come. Like an indignant parasite twisting inside his stomach, the feeling squirmed through the inner coils as he stared at the box in his living room. Installed in every home, by mandate of the National Health Office, was a World Health Approved Halo Detector, a screening monitor which took daily readings of temperature, blood pressure, oxygen levels and weight. In addition, the monitor filtered the air for traces of the Halovirus, and if found, well... *Hi ho, hi ho, it's off to the Convo we go.*

News broadcasts had been strangely devoid of information regarding Convos (Convalescent Centers), but rumors persisted about what occurred inside the walls. To be a Halo - as social media sites like BeMe, PhotoBend and Shitzoo were calling those unfortunates who contracted the virus - was to be shunned and shamed by the rest of the healthy world. Though Lawrence Haskins, Father Lawrence to his parishioners, was designated as one of these outcasts, he was quite used to being an outcast. Faith in a higher power, considered fairytale sentimentality, along with the atrocities of the past, left only a remnant of faithful elderly. To be certain, he was alone and lonely most of the time.

Lawrence was not entirely sure how he'd contracted the Halovirus. Possibly, it happened in the grocery store or perhaps in the drive-through café line. He thought he had taken precautions: World Health approved mask, World Health approved gloves and glasses, World Health approved hand sanitizer. Yet when his screening monitor blipped a positive result, the sinking feeling he felt (exacerbated by the frustration that all precautions had not kept him from becoming infected) was disheartening.

Thus was his sense of dread when the heavily shielded World Health Police rapped on his door. Father Lawrence was directed to pack a bag, (just a few necessities - the Convo would provide everything else) cover himself in World Health approved gear (which didn't work the last time) and exit the front door where grey-uniformed officers would accompany him to the World Heath van. Once locked behind the mesh wall, one courageous officer drove him to the depot whereas the other officers took a separate car to minimize the danger of transmission.

Once at the depot, Father Lawrence was escorted onto a small train (also with mesh caging) which would deposit him and the other Halos on the outskirts of a small village called Herzfeld. There they would be ushered to a dusty road that would lead them to a place called Cloud End.

After boarding the train, the officers separated the infected Halos into mesh cubicles where they were monitored for health emergencies along the way. Like animals, the Halos alternated between pacing or staring morosely out the barred windows at the passing landscape. The view, verdant hills dotted with farmhouses, rickety fences penning sad-eyed cows, and sparsely forested hills covered by grey clouds, was disorienting, even ironic. The world seemed far too beautiful to be so sad.

Joining him on the Halo-train was a menagerie of people: a family with three children, a wary woman, and a couple who faced away from each other. There was a heavily made-up woman, eyes smeared with shadow and liner, with pouting lips covered by red lipstick. She was dressed in a short skirt and fishnet stockings.

Isolated from the others was a wealthy looking man in a suit and tie. As opposed to the small cases the other Halos had brought, this man had a different interpretation of 'basic necessities' based on the steamer-trunk positioned on the seat opposite him. Although he was similarly imprisoned, he appeared relaxed. He had the appearance of an aristocrat; lean limbed with erect posture, his prematurely silver hair cut and styled perfectly. Leaning back in his seat with one leg crossed over the other, the man checked his AutoCom and typed in a response. Then the man touched his ear to activate his implanted receiver and began talking to someone on the outside. His face displayed both power and boredom, but also immense irritation.

Once the train unceremoniously dumped them at Herzfeld, the World Health Police herded them to the path on which they now walked. As they passed through the village, Lawrence noticed the wary faces of the residents peering contemptuously behind darkened glass. Very few stood the prescribed five feet apart, but all of them wore their fear behind their masks. *Terrible thing*, they might have been thinking, *to have these kinds of people so close to us.*

The officers, decked out in virus-resistant gear, with batons and tasers at the ready, stood at a distance watching the Halos separate and begin their trudge to Cloud End. As the last one off the train, Father Lawrence sighed and hefted his small carry-on suitcase in one hand while shouldering his brown satchel containing his books and writing utensils on the other side.

The walk was not entirely devoid of beauty. Even as he coughed delicately into his elbow (much to the disgust of the other Halos), he could hear the sound of crickets and cicadas hiding somewhere in the grasses. Above them, soft clouds floated past the sun, a slide show of shadow and light. To his right, not too far away, past a barbwire fence and expanse of wheat-like grass, was the cliff and endless steely-grey sea. It would not be the last time Father Lawrence wished that he was on holidays rather than internment.

Halfway to Cloud End, its foreboding façade appearing like a larger version of the house behind the Bates' Hotel, the priest paused to catch his breath. He noticed a well-dressed woman wearing stilettos (one of which had just broken) muttering angrily under her breath and removing her shoes.

'Are you alright?' he asked, his voice deep and gravelly.

Seeing his outfit, the white tab collar under his throat and the black suit which seemed inappropriately undertakerish, she recoiled slightly and grimaced. 'What do you think?'

'No, I suppose not.'

Reaching into her suitcase, the woman produced another pair of expensive shoes. With a harrumph, she pulled the right shoe up and over her heel and turned away from Father Lawrence.

'Do you mind if I walk with you?' he asked.

Jacquelyn Archer, of Archer Business Solutions, 2028 Businesswoman of the Year, was not impressed by the priest. His bushy eyebrows and his sallow cheeks, the greasy hair plastered over his skull, even the way he wore his filmy glasses halfway down his nose, gave her the creeps.

'I prefer to walk alone.'

Feeling the familiar sting of rejection, he motioned with his hand for her to lead the way. As she stumbled forward, her most recently donned shoes not much better than the broken ones, which she left on the side of the path like discarded flowers, Lawrence watched her catch up to the besuited man and his large steamer-trunk suitcase.

It was Winston Faraday III whose father had been a lifelong member of the Right Party. Faraday II had worked diligently to promote traditional values and considerations for the working class. Faraday II had blasted businesses and media alike for tearing down the societal mores which had served the country so well for generations. Faraday III was the polar opposite of his father and had opposed everything he had stood for. Although claiming to be equally ethical, he pandered to social media and big business. The son railed against institutions and identities which subjugated the future to the past and ran on a platform of tolerance and progress. Eventually, the son defeated the father in one of the most widely watched, and what some called 'entertaining,' elections in history. As the father extended the hand of congratulations to the son, the younger Winston sneered derisively in his victory. In his mind, the victory was one of validation about ideology as well as a directive for the way the world should be run.

Faraday heard the woman and turned. They had met socially at benefits and through mutual friendships, but Faraday and Jacquelyn Archer were certainly not well acquainted. At the very least, though, they were of similar social class.

'Ms. Archer.'

'Senator Faraday.'

'Mildly unfortunate, isn't it?'

'*Mildly* would be under-representative of what is happening to us?'

'When did you test positive?' He studied her profile as she pulled in alongside him. She had a strong face, jutting chin and prominent forehead. Dark hair, recently dyed, hung loosely over her cheeks, and was cut severely at the jawline. Jacquelyn was four or five inches shorter than the senator.

'What difference does it make? I tried to explain to them that I felt fine: I had no symptoms - I didn't even know I had it. I was willing to isolate at home. But there's no arguing with the Government,' she responded bitterly.

Faraday's jaw tightened. 'The Government's response was one of keeping people safe.'

She snorted. 'Do you feel safer?'

He pondered her question but remained silent.

Feeling as if she had scored a point, she pressed, speaking through clenched teeth. 'What were they thinking? It's one thing to attempt to contain a disease, but another to approach the edge of financial destruction.'

'For the good of the nation, we thought it best...'

'Until it happened to you.' The Halovirus was the great equalizer. Faraday could no more escape the Government's incessant power-mongering than the cleric she'd just left behind.

'Things will get better. We just need to get control of this virus. As soon as the Government institutes more...'

'Do you even listen to your own propaganda?'

'What do you mean?'

'You can't control a virus. Period. By shutting borders and limiting the distance to which people move from their houses, you just frighten them. You can't be constantly monitoring them and then be surprised when they turn against each other.'

'What are you saying?'

'The Government can't control a virus because it can't control people. No matter how many police you put into place, people will rebel. Even the police don't want to be rounding up people and sending them here.' Jacquelyn jerked a finger back at Herzfeld where the World Health Police guarded the path with arms crossed.

Minutes later, after she walked in silence, a sign appeared on the side of the road.

CLOUD END

'It's a beautiful name for a prison, don't you think?' she said.

Faraday's irritation rose. 'Don't you think you're being slightly dramatic? As soon as we test negative, we'll be released.'

'Will we?'

'Of course,' his voice quavered. 'They can't keep us here forever.'

1

'They might not keep us here in prison,' she responded while picking up speed to pull away from him, 'but the prison most certainly will follow us. Once a Halo, always a Halo.'

As Jacquelyn Archer finished speaking, Faraday looked up to see a family of five standing on the railed porch to the right of the front door. The mother, Dorothy Draper, a tired woman in her early forties with prematurely greying hair and prematurely decaying spirit, watched the wealthy people ascend the stairs. Unsure as to how these rich people contracted the Halovirus, usually rich people could avoid things like this, Dorothy disconsolately sat down in a chair. Turning to her right where her husband, Sam, clutched a small suitcase on his lap, his chin resting on the handle, she spoke, her voice low, slightly more audible than the breeze which blew across the porch.

'It's quite a collection of people.'

'Seems like a lot,' Sam agreed.

'See that lady over there,' she pointed surreptitiously, 'the one picking her fingernails?' He nodded. 'She looks like a prostitute.'

Sam studied the cross-legged woman in a miniskirt and stockings. 'Maybe.'

'I can see why she'd get the Halo.'

He said nothing.

'And the Asian lady over there.' A woman in a matching sweatsuit, stripe running down the outside of the pants, danced nervously from foot to foot as she stared down at her arm. 'I wonder how many people she's infected.'

'Maybe none.'

'Yeah, maybe.'

After the noncommittal answer, Titus, their youngest child, a boy of six, sidled up close to his father. Sam put an arm around him. 'What's up, T?'

'Can I go play?'

'Sure, pal.'

Dorothy stopped him. 'Titus, we don't know anything about this place yet. It might not be safe. Just sit over by the railing and play on your computer.'

'I don't want to. I want to explore.'

'There will be plenty of time...'

'Just let him go,' Sam said softly.

'Oh, all right. But check in with us every ten minutes.' Dorothy watched her son bound off the step. 'Pasqual. Go with your brother.'

'I don't want to. I want to play my game.' He pointed at his phone.

'You can do that later.'

'Gina can go.' He nudged his sister with his arm. She frowned.

'Pas is better with him. Titus drives me nuts.'

'Please, Pas. Just go.'

Sighing loudly, Pasqual logged out and stood melodramatically to follow his brother down the steps and into the deepening grass.

Above the recently arrived rabble, inside an overlooking bedroom, four faces watched with curiosity and trepidation. Wearing uniforms with Cloud End's logo, the employees studied the Halos beneath them in the yard and entering the porch.

'They don't look sick to me,' said Radiance Morrison, one of the cleaners, as she pressed her forehead to the glass.

Nancy, the other cleaner, copied Radiance's posture against another pane. 'That's what the deniers say about the disease. It's subtle in how it destroys.'

'I thought it was something fat people got?'

'Careful,' Esther Fields, Cloud End's cook warned. Esther was not petite in the least.

'I didn't mean anything by it,' Radiance responded into the windowpane. Her breath fogged up the lower half of the window. 'That's just what I heard.'

'I heard that it attacks fat people's lungs,' Nancy said. 'Are you worried?'

Esther snorted and shuffled towards the door. Karl, the house manager, smiled at her as she walked past.

'Don't worry,' he assured. 'We'll take plenty of precautions...' His voice trailed off as if disbelieving his own assurance.

The employees were still uneasy with the thought of tending Halos. Although the virus had not spread significantly, or as easily as predicted, there was something perverse about inviting the Devil to dinner and then asking him to set his pitchfork down while they conversed about anything but him.

Radiance, the newest (and youngest) member of the house staff was not particularly nervous about doing her job. In fact, she felt that tending to these people, was a virtuous thing to do. If possible, Radiance wanted to interview them about their experiences of contracting the Halovirus and, if possible, video log her journey as junior cleaner at Cloud End. Already, Radiance had a mildly successful BeMe channel. She had the looks and body for the screen. It was just a matter of being discovered by the right producer. A television personality once told her that. With her blonde hair and her figure, those luminous brown eyes and full lips, why, there was nowhere she wouldn't be watched.

When word filtered to the staff that Cloud End was to be a Convalescent Center, Nancy felt a constricting sense of dread. During the Coronavirus, she remembered the devastating effects of lockdowns, restrictions and pervasive sense of fear. Radiance had grown up during these anxious times, but Nancy had ministered to others, her children and parents included. No one on staff had known anyone who had died from the Halovirus, but there were plenty of news outlets and social media sites to remind them that they were never safe.

Never ever ever.

Whenever Nancy spoke to Karl regarding her unease, Karl's response was always the same: the St. Croix's would do everything in their power to take care of them. Including paying the staff overtime. The Government had been extraordinarily generous during these pandemics doling out money hand over fist. If you wanted to work and earn some extra cash, they were happy to have you take care of sick people.

Nancy stifled the karmic glee she felt when Winston Faraday III appeared. He appeared regularly in front of cameras, microphones propped in front of his face like metal ice cream cones, serene and above-it-all, reminding viewers and voters that the Government was working hard, working so hard, for the common man, woman or genderless person. As his colleagues explained the necessity for Convalescent Centers, describing the opportunity to help people recover while simultaneously SPEARING THE SPREAD, Nancy believed that no self-respecting public servant would ever be caught with the disease. She was happily disappointed.

Nancy exited the room behind Esther, Radiance and Karl. Karl led a brisk pace to the central staircase. The twelve second-floor rooms were prepped carefully for the Halos. They had done everything they could to help them feel comfortable during their extended stay. Each room had been fitted with the most modern, World Health HEPA filters. Every banister support held a mounted World Health-approved bottle of hand sanitizer. Staff would wear the latest protective cover and hopefully, fingers crossed, the Halovirus would get bored of this generation and move on to extinction.

Included in these safety precautions were compulsory Halo Detectors - black boxes the size of dinner plates affixed to walls - which would ultimately determine the length of guests' stays. Positive results for the Halo would turn the unblinking light red, and, for negative results, green to go. Theoretically, there would be an exit interview and a signed non-disclosure agreement. Nancy had overheard this bit of information while cleaning the cinema one afternoon.

When the staff finished descending the central stairs, they waited patiently, albeit nervously, for the Halos to enter Cloud End and huddle into the atrium. The central atrium, which held the primary dining area, was lit from above by a large skylight, and on the eastern wall, running beneath the stairs, was a small, gently cascading waterfall, which finished up behind the dining tables. To the north end of the house was a cinema (which also would double as the group meeting area), to the west, the library and gift shop. Cloud End's front door, a solid wooden fixture with a brass knocker, was at the end of the hallway next to the library. To the south, past the bar, was the kitchen, and, further on, the staff quarters. Included in the Convalescent Center's carers was Dr. Swithin Chandruth, two nurses, plus a staff psychologist, Dr. Jane Boeder-Mankins. All in all, they were a cohesive unit with specific responsibilities.

When Donald appeared from the kitchen, dressed in his full World Health protective gear - orange suit, gloves and boots - he seemed nervous. As of yet, he'd not donned his helmet and mask. Claire followed soon after. Her grey hair was pulled back from her face and her eyes darted between Donald and the staff.

'It's an important day,' she began as she moved in front of Donald and pulled at a fleck of dirt on his sleeve. 'Not only for our future, but for our country also.

'For your own safety, please wear your full protective gear at all times unless in your quarters. In the worst-case scenario that you contract the disease, our insurance will fully cover you during your own convalescence, here.'

'I feel so much better now,' Nancy mumbled.

Claire silenced her with a glare. 'We believe we've done all that we can to keep you safe.' As almost an afterthought, Claire thanked them. 'For your service to your country, we are grateful. Please help our guests enjoy their stay.'

The words seemed ironic. It would be like saying to a cancer patient, *'Enjoy your surroundings while we pump you full of poison.'* Nancy bit her lip to keep from responding.

'Any questions?'

Their eyes were drawn to the moving shadows in the window drapes. Like wraiths they passed back and forth, pacing, pausing, stopping to stare at something, anything but the house behind them.

'I have a question.' Radiance's voice squeaked. 'What are the limits of interaction with them? I mean, do we talk to them?'

Claire was about to respond when Donald spoke first. 'They are guests, Radiance. If they ask you a question, you answer. If they need something, you respond.'

'But aren't they dangerous?'

The question hung in the air.

'No more dangerous than you or I.'

'I think I'm dangerous,' Radiance countered. The rest of the staff snickered.

'Be that as it may, we'll assume that our guests have no interest in passing anything on to you.'

As the guests milled just outside the front door, Donald St. Croix straightened his orange suit and set his helmet.

It was 5:43 in the evening on October 17.

Encoded message #2484093

17 October, 2031

Government device sent: CVH4580387

Government device received: SRC9022289

Be advised, study participants have arrived at Cloud End Convalescent
Center (CECC). They appear haggard and dejected. Only one piece of
luggage per participant. Each appears to have a mobile device and are
actively communicating with the outside world. Connections with ████
████████████ have been made. Psychological manipulations will proceed
in two days, beginning 19 October.

Halo Detectors have been installed in all rooms.

2

Alonzo Turner was thrilled by his accommodation. As he set his small bag on top of the thick, down-filled quilt, he scanned the room. Certainly, Alonzo was not used to carpet, and the feel under his sock-covered feet was wonderful. Neither was he conditioned to so much light in his home. Walking toward the window, he threw back the drapes and smiled broadly at the outlook. From this position, he could see a rickety wooden shed with a sliding door listing slightly on its rail. Various rusted tools, rakes and shovels, a moldy length of rope and a wheelbarrow lay forlornly around the shed. Two lonely trees seemed to be commiserating with the shed as its branches reached downwards as if offering a tender embrace.

Beyond the shed, tall grass waved delicately in the sea breezes coming up and over the cliff. This undulating motion was mesmerizing. It wasn't until there was a knock at the door, that Alonzo was torn from his vista.

'Come in.'

'Good afternoon,' the housekeeper said with muffled voice as she paused in the doorway. 'Is there anything special you require to make your stay more comfortable.'

He shook his head. 'That's very kind of you, miss.' He pointed behind him out the window. 'The view is fantastic.'

Radiance's gaze followed his hand and she nodded. 'I'm glad you like it. Please feel free to ring for whatever you might need.'

'How do I do that?'

She pointed to a buzzer beside his bed.

'You mean I just ring that and you come?'

'No, not necessarily. When you buzz, I will answer through the speaker on the wall, and you will tell me what you need.'

'Aah.'

'Will that be all, sir?'

'You can call me Alonzo.'

Radiance smiled. 'As you wish, Alonzo.' He had a clean white smile and kind eyes. His brown skin shimmered in the dim light. His hands were rough and cracked. Alonzo had the appearance of a contented man whose life was a continuous set of rebounds. From good to bad. Up to down. Healthy, sick.

'What's your name?'

'I'm Radiance.'

Alonzo nodded and turned back to the window to pay particular attention to the slow drifting clouds kissing the horizon. 'Nice to meet you, Radiance. Stay safe.'

The housekeeper nodded and left the room to attend to the next guest.

Radiance found Alonzo's neighbor less friendly. 'Look, I don't think you understand who I am,' an angry voice shouted at her. 'Senator Winston Faraday. What I REQUIRE, is not to be interrupted. I have important political business to attend to and I don't need you imbeciles knocking on my door.'

Alonzo heard the outburst and stuck his head out of the room. His first instinct was to come to the young woman's assistance, but she seemed unperturbed. When his tirade finished (a good deal about his stature in the Government and important contacts overseas with whom he was making important decisions), she nodded slightly. 'As you wish,' she repeated and turned to her right. Three steps from Winston Faraday III's door, she flipped him the bird through the wall and kept walking.

Stepping outside his room, Alonzo approached the wooden railing and grasped it. It felt solid. He was standing precariously fifteen feet above the ground floor. From this heightened perspective, Alonzo spotted an Asian woman standing in her doorway across the second floor nervously chewing her fingernails.

Waving, Alonzo caught her attention. She looked surprised and pointed to her chest.

'Yes, you!' he laughed.

'Are you talking to me?'

19

'Yes! What's your name?'

'Monica.'

'I'm Alonzo.'

'Nice to meet you.'

Their voices rang out over the empty space below. Suddenly, Winston Faraday III's door slammed shut.

'He's a little testy, that one.'

Monica made a face and returned her fingers to her mouth.

'Do you mind if I come over?' Alonzo asked.

Scanning side to side, Monica raised her eyebrows. 'Do you think it's safe?'

'I don't think we're going to catch the Halo again, if that's what you mean?'

'I suppose.'

Leaving his door open, Alonzo strolled past multiple guestrooms in various states of unpacking and disarray. The noise seemed one of preoccupation and frustration.

'I can see you now,' he said when he reached her room.

Fidgeting with her hands, Monica nodded. 'How did you get it?'

'Halo?' She nodded again. 'Oh, I'm pretty sure it was at a funeral. One of the mourners stumbled against me. She'd been sniffling.'

'Was it someone close to you?'

'What? The woman who fell into me? No.'

'I meant the person that died.'

This was the juncture in every conversation where Alonzo wrestled with telling people about his occupation (gravedigging - which generally led to a shocked look, an unconscious step backwards, and a sometimes-polite goodbye). Generally, Alonzo told people he was in earth management, which was close enough to the truth to be pseudo-truthful without scaring people.

'No, I wasn't that close. Just in attendance.' Alonzo returned serve. 'How did you end up here?'

Monica's face disintegrated into a full-blown frown. 'Let's just say a routine traffic stop turned into a life-changing experience.'

'What happened?'

Monica pointed across the hallway. 'Officer Matthews,' she responded in a sing-song voice, 'wrote me a speeding ticket, and after handing me a summons to court, he gifted me the Halovirus from the same ticket.'

'That's unfortunate.'

'A double-whammy as they say.'

Alonzo glanced behind him. 'Are you telling me that the police officer who gave you the ticket and the virus is staying here too?'

'Afraid so.'

'Nothing like rubbing a little salt in the wound.'

Monica had been shocked to see Officer Matthews appear on the train. When their eyes met, he frowned, attempting to place where he'd seen her before, but she could tell he couldn't remember her. Just another ticket. Just another fine. Just another ten-miles-per-hour-over fundraiser for the men and women in blue. She was sure she'd been profiled: a young, attractive Asian woman, driving just a smidge over the limit. Since COVID, all Asians had been persecuted, or so she thought.

An uncomfortable silence straddled the fence between Alonzo and Monica. When their initial source of connection finished, Alonzo nodded to her and swiveled back towards his room – number 6.

When he entered his room, Monica's attention was drawn to the pert, young housekeeper who was making her way along the south side of the balcony. A man and a woman stood in consecutive doorways, rooms 4 and 5. Strangely, they seemed to know each other, but most certainly did not like each other. Their frosty voices startled the housekeeper.

'Why did you put us next door to each other?' the man asked loudly.

'I'm sorry, sir, but I wasn't part of assigning the rooms.'

He gesticulated wildly to her and then to the woman next door. 'Obviously, they could have asked questions. This is *not* going to work.' He grabbed his hair with his hands, exasperated.

'He always does this,' the woman said. 'He gets completely bent out of shape about the smallest things, and then the big ones, he deposits on my doorstep like a paper bag full of dog turds, which he then sets on fire.'

'Very mature, Sydney. Very mature.'

Monica studied the man. He was in his mid-thirties, muscular, with a determined jaw. Black hair, parted to the side, and the makings of a very distracting, thin moustache added to Monica's jumbled first impression of him. He was wearing khaki pants and a polo shirt that stretched slightly over his pre-middle-aged manbelly. From this distance, Monica could still see the wild look in his eyes and the disgust he felt towards the woman next door whom Monica assumed to be his wife (or ex-wife, more probably).

'Damian, please. You're embarrassing yourself. It's just a room. We can close our doors.'

'But I'll hear you breathing. Or showering. Or going to bathroom! It will be like we are still living together.'

Sydney rolled her eyes. 'I don't know how you'll survive,' she said sarcastically.

'You see what I have to put up with?' Damian asked Radiance.

'Sir, I am simply here to see if there is anything...'

'I know! I know! How about you march yourself back downstairs and get us rooms on opposite sides of this god-forsaken place! How about you do that!'

Radiance, with months of patience-practice under her belt, lowered her voice. 'Sir, we are currently fully occupied. Perhaps if one of the other guests recovers quickly and...'

'We're not going to recover!' he shouted loudly. 'They've sent us here to die!'

Taking a step back, Radiance moved slightly closer to Sydney's door. 'Now you can see why we're getting divorced,' Sydney said to Radiance. 'Everything is drama. Regular MacBeth this guy.'

Enraged, Damian made a face at Sydney and slammed the door behind him. One second later, he reopened the door. 'I'll take a bottle of scotch. That's what you can get me.' Then, he slammed it again.

Sydney looked over Radiance's shoulder to see the Asian woman close her room door behind her. Then, Sydney smiled at Radiance. 'I'm sorry about that. It's been a difficult time for us. It was our anniversary the day we found out we were infected. We weren't even together. We haven't been for months, except when we're at court.' Her voice lowered. 'Damian and I are getting divorced. He's insufferable.'

Radiance did not respond.

'I think we actually got it from our lawyer. She's here, too, you know.' Sydney pointed across the courtyard. 'Wallis Takamoto, a quality lawyer, but I'll be happy when I don't have to see her again.'

'Life moves on, I guess,' Radiance said lamely.

'Let's hope so.'

The door to Room 3 opened and a bony woman exited. Blue jeans emphasized long legs and a shapeless top covered milky white skin. Her lank hair hadn't been washed recently, and it covered a thin, pinched face exaggerated by murky eyes. Sydney unconsciously touched her face. This woman's sultry appearance reminded Sydney of her younger days when she used to be beautiful. Or that's what Damian said when they were first married. With silky brown hair and a curvaceous body, Sydney had caught the eye of many men before Damian. But Damian had been the one for her. He had been witty and charming, handsome, and he bought her things, things she liked, things to show off. But not anymore. Not any of it. No beauty, no things, no Damian.

The skinny woman from Room 3 avoided all eye-contact as she walked to the central staircase where she placed a trembling hand on the banister and began her descent.

In the dining area, at one of the tables backdropped by ferns and the dripping splash of the waterfall, Jacquelyn Archer reclined in a chair, one leg crossed over the other. She held a book in one hand and a glass of water in the other. She had not been reading. Her focus was hazy. The words were inkblots to her eyes, mashed jumbles of periods and question marks, semicolons and exclamations. As the descending girl finished the last steps, Jacquelyn was thankful to have something, or someone else draw her attention. There was something off-center about the girl; the quaking hand, the throbbing temple. Thin hair and pale skin. She'd seen the look before. A hopeless woman.

Jacquelyn watched her pause at the bottom of the stairs, look to her right and left, then opt for the entrance to Cloud End. Just as she was about to reach for the door, a man appeared to her right. The young woman recoiled.

Jacquelyn strained her ears.

'My apologies, miss,' the man said. 'It is not time to go outside.'

'But I want to go. I need some fresh air.'

The man pointed to the inner courtyard. 'We can open the skylights for a breeze,' he suggested.

'No,' she insisted, 'I want to go outside.'

'It is not time.'

'What? Is this a prison?'

The man's face hardened. 'Government regulations specify that to keep our neighbors safe, guests at Cloud End must remain in...'

'Our neighbors? Who is that?'

'Those who live in Herzfeld.'

'You must be joking. The town is a kilometer back up the road. How can we possibly spread the virus from here?'

'I'm very sorry, Miss...'

'My name is Chantelle.'

'Thank you. I'm sorry, Chantelle, but we'd be happy to open some windows for you.'

Her mouth twisted into anger. 'I just want to go outside.'

At that moment, Jacquelyn appeared behind Chantelle. 'I couldn't help but overhear. Are you saying that we are all trapped here?'

'Trapped is not the right word. You are guests here. We'd like to make you feel...'

'Excuse me,' Jacquelyn responded brusquely. 'What is your name?'

He straightened. 'My name is Van der Hoven.'

'First name?'

'It is not our practice to give out that information,' Carl stated.

'And yet somehow, you are privy to all of our personal information?'

'There are privacy measures in place.' Carl's red face deepened behind his mask.

'I feel so much better.' Chantelle glanced at Jacquelyn and smiled.

'If you would be so kind as to return to the atrium, I can bring you some refreshments, or something to eat?' Carl's plaintive voice was enough to shift Jacquelyn's demands.

The women turned to walk back. Carl emitted an audible sigh. They sat down opposite each other. Chantelle fidgeted with the table in front of her.

'Your name is Chantelle. That's pretty.'

'It's not my real name.'

Jacquelyn pondered her. 'Then why did you tell Van der Hoven it was your name?'

'Because he made me angry.'

'What is your name?'

Chantelle had been asked that question hundreds of times over. Every man wanted to know her name before they took advantage of her. So, she gave them a name, any name that came to mind. That way, though they paid for her body, they did not own her soul.

'I don't know you yet.'

'I'm Jacquelyn. Jacquelyn Archer.' She reached out a hand. Chantelle studied it before shaking it limply.

'And you are...?'

Chantelle bit her lower lip. 'Let's stick with Chantelle.'

At that moment, Carl returned wearing an apron over his protective suit and a symbolic towel draped over his forearm. 'Now, is there anything I can get for you?'

'I'll have a burger and a glass of red wine,' Jacquelyn said with a flick of her wrist as if sending him away.

'And for you, miss?'

'The same.' As Carl turned, Chantelle stopped him. 'Actually, I'll have three fingers of scotch.' He nodded.

'And I'll have a bowl of ice cream,' a voice came from the stairway behind the woman.

It was the priest.

'Anything else, sir?' Carl asked.

'Perhaps later, you could bring me a cup of coffee?'

Carl nodded and left.

'Do you mind if I join you?' Father Lawrence asked.

Appearing uncomfortable, Chantelle didn't know how to respond. Jacquelyn, noticing Chantelle's unease, held up her hand. 'Maybe next time. We're having a private conversation.'

With a slight bow, he moved to another table and sat down by himself.

As Chantelle and Jacquelyn returned to their stilted conversation, Father Lawrence waited for his ice cream. This isolation had become all too normal for him. Many times, in the last few years, the last twenty actually, as story after story of clergy indiscretions, parish mismanagement, and the moldy cherry on top of the rotten cake, Halovirus, Father Lawrence wanted to renege on his ordination vows and enter the world in which everyone else lived. A world of selfishness, of greed, of wild despair, love, joy and blissful ignorance. To find a partner in life – hell, even a friend – would have taken the edge off the dismal feeling he so often awoke with in the morning.

Father Lawrence thought of his small domicile next to the church, a musty, three-bedroom house purchased at the turn of the *last* century when it had been a modern home with a fireplace and wood banisters. Those were the days when humanity took religion seriously. Those were the days when people looked to the church for guidance and hope. Those were the days when priests were sought for counseling and wisdom. In those days, people would stop by the parsonage looking to the priest for a blessing.

But that manse had become a lonely jail cell. No longer did parishioners look to him for confidence and hope. No, they saw him and his religion as an artifact. And him personally, they looked on with suspicion. In that manse, he spent many nights praying for the people who passed by. They might point to the lonely yellow light in his study where he knelt, pleading for God to change the world, to deliver them from the evils that had blanketed them.

Now that he had been interned at Cloud End, Father Lawrence felt slightly guilty about his happiness to be out of the manse and living with people. Even though their wary glances were disheartening, quiet whispers were better than no sound at all.

As Lawrence received his ice cream bowl, cupping it gently, the ceramic bowl cooling his hands, a voice floated over his shoulder.

'Do you mind if we sit with you, Padre?'

Turning, Father Lawrence saw the young man and woman, dissimilar but for the wry smiles on their faces. 'Why, that would be wonderful.' He pointed to two of the chairs beside him.

'This is a nice spot,' the man said, 'right near the waterfall.'

'Peaceful, certainly.'

The man stuck out his hand. 'I'm Alonzo. Alonzo Turner and this is Monica... uh, I forgot your last name.' Alonzo's face scrunched up with embarrassment.

'Xiao.' She pronounced it *zhow*.

'What are you in for?' Father Lawrence asked.

Alonzo laughed. 'Wrong place. Wrong time.'

'Which was?'

'A funeral.'

'I'm sorry.'

'At least it wasn't my own.' Alonzo paused. 'At least not yet.'

'Have you had any symptoms?'

'A cough here and there. Nothing serious.' Alonzo focussed on Monica. 'What about you?'

'I had a fever for a few days. But on the news, it seems like a lot of people are dying.'

Alonzo shrugged. 'Everybody dies of something.'

'That's kind of callous,' said Monica. She touched at the side of her mouth where her lipstick had clotted.

'It's part of the job, I guess.'

'Which is?' Lawrence asked.

'I'm a gravedigger.'

'You're joking.'

Alonzo shook his head.

Monica recoiled from him slightly. 'Are you... do you have to... touch a lot of dead bodies?'

'No, not since that exhumation in '24. Whooee, that was a smelly one.'

Monica grimaced. 'Maybe we should change the subject. Maybe we'll talk about the Halo?'

'Don't you ever get tired of talking about that?' Alonzo leaned back in his chair and put his hands behind his head. 'How'd you get it? What precautions were you taking? How are you feeling? Do you have enough hand sanitizer? Jeesh,' he whooshed out of his mouth, 'I'll talk about anything but that.'

'I'm just trying to be polite,' Monica exclaimed. 'It's morbid enough being in this place, surrounded by the thought of death, but sitting at a table with a gravedigger and a priest? It's like the beginning of a bad joke.' She held out a hand to Father Lawrence. 'No offense.'

Alonzo snorted and smiled. 'What's wrong with talking about death?'

'It's... it's creepy. Like talking about vomit while you're eating.'

'And yet you want to talk about the virus? You know, the thing that is sweeping the planet, indiscriminately murdering people left and right?'

'I get your point.'

'What about you, Monica,' Father Lawrence interjected, 'tell us about yourself.'

She touched the side of her hair and smiled coyly. 'I'm just your average citizen, upholding the laws of the land, and made a mistake.'

'What did you do?' Lawrence asked.

'No, no, nothing like that. I was speeding. A couple of miles over the limit. No biggie.'

'What?'

'I was driving down a street at night, no one was coming from the other direction, and at a yellow light, mind you, I simply sped up, but this copper was sitting just up the road waiting. They're predators, you know. Cops sit in the shadows lurking like great white sharks, waiting for the opportunity to wreck someone's life.'

'It feels like that sometimes,' Alonzo agreed. 'Why, I got a ticket for...'

'Anyway, back to my story,' Monica interrupted with a nail-flashing tap on her fashionable white blouse and pearl necklace. 'So, the stupid cop gives me a ticket, thrusts it through my window like he's stabbing me with it, and not only did he give me a fine, but he gave me the Halo, too.'

'You're kidding,' Lawrence responded pityingly.

'Talk about a bad traffic stop.' Once again, she drew attention to her looks, this time crossing her legs slowly. The grey sweats hiked up over her defined calves. Monica was proud of her physique after three-day-per-week sessions with a personal trainer. She leaned forward. 'And the bastard is here, too. They sent him to this Convo.'

'Which room is he in?' Lawrence peered above him.

She pointed to the second floor. 'Room 5. I saw him when we were walking up the trail. Ooh, it makes me so mad. In some wicked way, though, I'm happy that he's stuck here too.'

A bell rang above them. Seconds later, a voice came over the internal sound system.

'All Cloud End guests are cordially invited to attend an information session in the dining area in fifteen minutes. All questions will be answered to the greatest extent possible.'

3

The village of Herzfeld was nestled in the valley alongside a sparkling, meandering stream, which wended its way through the center of town, past shopping stores, what few remained open, and dodged between immaculate two-story houses. Even to its citizens, Herzfeld's history was not well known, not because of any callous disregard for the past or their foreparents, but the citizens did not really need to know.

Until the Halovirus showed up. Then, Herzfeld was at the center of everything.

On October 17th, when the Halo train paused at Herzfeld station, many of the town's shop owners gathered across the street standing cross-armed and claw-footed to watch the miserable arrivals be vomited onto the dirty cement by the dust-streaked Government train. Some Halos appeared confused and bedraggled while others seemed quite content, certainly un-sick. The cross-armed Herzfeldians frowned at these last ones, the smug, self-satisfied infected, who obviously had not followed health protocols. They didn't care in the least about restrictions or caring for other people. They'd just kept living their lives and everyone else was paying the price. The news told them that most people caught the Halovirus because they'd been in the wrong place, doing the wrong thing at the exact wrong time. These people had become infected because... well, they deserved it. Social media was good at reminding who were the righteous and who were not.

Yet, as they had tumbled out of the train, one hand above their brow shading their eyes from the merciless sun, and the other hand grasping a small suitcase full of whatever meagre belongings they could bring to the Convo at Herzfeld, there were a few who felt sorry for them. Certainly, Bridgette Priveto, the hotelier, felt a sense of empathy while at the same time wrestled with resentment. These people would be the death of her business and lifestyle. No one was going to come to Herzfeld if Halos were nearby.

Just over five feet from her, Steve Cranmere and Edgar Post, owners of the local tavern, the Lagoon Saloon, a decrepit dive on the eastern edge of town, enjoyed having something new to talk about. As they pulled their masks down and slurped up an afternoon beer or two, they judged the Halos on their appearances.

The prostitute.

The rich, snobby ones, especially the well-dressed man with his large, rolling suitcase and thousand-dollar threads.

The military man with the crewcut.

On and on, they took mental notes subconsciously thanking their lucky stars they weren't like *those* miserable people.

After the party stumbled towards Cloud End, a few Herzfeldians perched themselves at the bar holding up their empty mugs to Steve and Edgar. Even though the Halovirus had stripped the Lagoon of a year's worth of income, when the restrictions had eased, the locals, moneyed up from Government shellouts, made up for their thirst the next year. Distanced, of course.

It was just like last time; except they knew what to expect from the Government. Even though the measures taken were barbaric and manipulative (weaponized, some believed), they walked a similar path with the Halovirus as they did Corona. At the beginning of the pandemic, Steve remembered sitting at home, feet up in front of the television, when he got the call to tell him he was an 'essential' worker. He snorted at that. He ran a bar. Obviously, 'essential' had many definitions.

Elizabeth Happel walked the same line as Steve and Edgar. While empathetic to the trials of the common man, Elizabeth was secretly overjoyed by the common Herzfeldian's desperate need to hoard. Her convenience shop, *Icho Veggies*, had never done a better business. And because she had also been deemed essential by the Government, not once had Elizabeth had to stay home. Every day she drove happily to the store, masked and content, never needing to worry about the overhead. Elizabeth had never been so wealthy.

Yet when the Halos arrived, she felt a niggling discomfort. What would it be like if she was one of them? How would she react to being torn from her home, solitary bag in hand, and condemned to a sty like Cloud End. Oh, yes, she'd seen how the hotel, if that was what it could be called, had fallen into disrepair. Elizabeth and her husband Ken had trekked up the rock-strewn path one afternoon. They wanted to stand on the cliff's edge, to gain a better perspective than that from the valley, but no sooner had they seen the broken shutters and the cracking deck when they tsk tsked their way back home.

Most Herzfeldians felt uncomfortable with the idea of bringing a trainload of infected vectors from God-knows-where. Why couldn't they ship them to the city where there were more resources? Why Herzfeld? It was a semi-thriving community with shops, gas stations, even a cinema. Just because it was socially distanced from the Capitol didn't mean that the Government should infest it with the Halovirus. When Elizabeth chatted with Magnus Falkirk, rector of the local Protestant Parish, he was quick to remind her that God could use bad things for good ends.

'What could God possibly bring about for good with regards to the Halovirus?' she asked him.

On the other hand, Robert Kovschenko, the town constable, was primed to make life miserable for any who would mix with the Halos. Or, if he had his way, anyone disregarding Government restrictions would pay the price. Igor, as he was nicknamed as a semi-racist play on his surname, had a penchant for the pedantic. Because of his badge, he was free to fine those who didn't wear masks, didn't follow the rules, didn't fall down in fear at the thought of Igor and his Government-ordained righteousness. More than one Herzfeldian wanted to protest the rigidity of Igor's pedanticism, but most had learned to keep their mouth shut as tight as home quarantine.

As the Halo rabble staggered from the train, the proprietors of tavern and veggie store, along with a slightly nervous hotelier and interested rector, stood side by side with the banker of National Bank of Herzfeld, Renata Lerner. Renata, a shade over six feet tall, with ebony hair and thin fingers that looked like bleached coral, stood with one hip cocked and arms folded across her chest. Her hair, piled on top of her head, reflected the mid-morning sunlight.

As the Herzfeldians paused their activities to watch the Halos trudge away from the train onto the dusty track, Steve and Edgar stood next to each other just inside the swinging doors of the tavern.

'Terrible thing that they had to come here, don't you think?' Steve said.

Edgar nodded. 'The Government doesn't know its head from its ass if you ask me. Why Herzfeld? Better to keep them in the Capitol and wipe out the politicians.'

Steve snorted. 'Did you hear about Elizabeth? She's rationing toilet paper again. Said something about supply chain issues.'

Ed shook his head. 'People never cease to amaze me. Of all the things you're going to hoard, and you go for TP. Do they actually shit more during a pandemic?'

'Must.'

'She's done pretty well. Bought a house out on the river. Nice big one. Used to belong to some rock star, I think.'

'Yeah,' Steve agreed, 'I wish we would have invested in a grocery store instead of a tavern. We'd be millionaires by now.'

Edgar punched his partner on the arm. 'You can't drink beer in a grocery store.'

'But what about them? What happens when they recover? Are they going to want to live in Herzfeld? I'm not sure I trust having their kind here, even if the Government says they're 'clean.''

Edgar shrugged. 'We'll have to have a town meeting or something, I'm sure.'

As the wind blew bits of sand and grass across the street, the tavern owners noticed Bridgette retreat from her gazing spot in front of the hotel to the darkened interior. She nodded coolly before entering. The front desk was deserted. Even though Bridgette was the hotel's owner, she also worked the desk on slower days. Frankly, since the announcement of the Convo at Cloud End, tourism in Herzfeld had not so much slowed as come to a crashing halt.

She moved behind the counter to await a phone call – or anything, really – that might signal an end to this horror. Frankly, as Bridgette pondered the current predicament, she wanted to go back to the way things used to be. The old normal. But there was a lot of wishing going on nowadays – a wish for more Government money (at least that helped with paying the bills, or for Bridgette, buying a bigger boat); a wish for more travel; a wish that the Halos would be shipped away (or die *en masse*, but that sounded so selfish). In every case, wishes were helium balloons, easily popped by whatever sharp, dream-wrecker cloud that floated nearby.

The phone rang.

'Good afternoon, Hideaway Hotel. Bridgette speaking.'

A second passed before a metallic sounding voice, not a recording, per se, but a person reading from a card filtered down the line. Scammer.

'Don't you have anything better to do?' she yelled into the phone as she slammed it down.

When she looked up, Reverend Falkirk was standing in the doorway. 'You sound frustrated.'

'I'm sorry, Reverend. There have been so many scammers.'

'I get them, too.'

After a pause, Bridgette pondered the clergyman. Fleshy described him, with his thick neck and passively muscular arms which filled out his shirt sleeves. He tended to wear black, or brown, which was very much like his colorless personality. Although generally tolerated, Reverend Falkirk would not have been considered popular, but the town was content to have him, even if they paid little attention to him, his words or his faith.

'What are we going to do, Reverend?'

He fixed his beady eyes on her. 'About what?'

'Them,' she gestured out the door and up the road. 'The Halos.'

'I suppose they'll take care of themselves. From what I understand, they have to stay there for the duration of the plague, or whatever it is that we're calling this one. Plague seems kind of ruthless, like ripping your skin off with a Band-Aid. Perhaps pandemic really is the most compassionate word?' His voice was a question, much like the rest of his life.

'I don't care what they call it,' Bridgette responded. 'I just want them to go somewhere else so I can get my business back.'

34

3

Certainly, the reverend wanted to say something particularly religious, a wholesome platitude, something about looking out for the sick and the poor and the prisoner, but all that he could do was to let his mouth flap up and down.

'And another thing,' Bridgette continued as the reverend spluttered, 'the Government better keep my Compassion checks coming, or I'm liable to do anything.'

'Such as what?'

'Anything.'

4

Donald and Claire, clad identically in their World Health approved hazmat suits, stood uncomfortably on the dais in front of the Halos. As they peered out over their guests, they could see a flustered, frustrated menagerie of sick people. The children, especially, seemed nervous. Although they fidgeted with their phones, the teenage girl constantly also worried with her hair. If it were up to Donald, they would not have gone to such extremes of protective measures, but Claire agreed with the Government's perspective. It was better to be safe than sick.

As the St. Croix's prepared to make a formal welcome to Cloud End, their grandchildren, similarly clad in protective gear, were amazed by what was transpiring in front of them. Oswald waved shyly at the Draper boys who smiled back at him in return.

'Greetings, guests.' Donald noticed a few of the better dressed folks roll their eyes at the term. 'It must be disconcerting to be sitting in this place. I'm sorry we had to meet like this. I wish you could have come to vacation here instead of this...' his amplified voice trailed off.

'My name is Donald St. Croix and this is my wife, Claire. These are our grandchildren McKayla and Oswald.' Donald gestured to them. Oswald clutched his pet rat closer to his chest.

Donald had held these welcoming sessions many times in the past. Whenever a new cohort of guests had arrived, fresh-faced and rosy-cheeked, he had greeted them with all the exciting things to do while staying at Cloud End. They would have swiveled their heads to study the skylight or leaned to the side to spot the library or cinema, but never would they have stared with such daggers about spending time away from home.

'It is not necessary for me to recap why you are here, but allow me to describe what you can expect while you convalesce at Cloud End.' He cleared his throat. 'Two months ago, the Government imposed a quarantine on those testing positive for the Halovirus. The Government's final solution was to gather you to provide the opportunity not to be alone, and to heal together.'

4

The crowd grumbled. Donald's words were slightly disingenuous. Home quarantine was deemed too dangerous because many were not capable of 'doing the right thing.' Thus, the Government felt it had to step in – to strong arm those Halos who couldn't control themselves, or those who considered their own personal freedoms of more importance than the greater good of society.

He spread his arms. 'As was explained to me in the Governmental letter, isolation creates mental health issues. Instead, the Government concluded you should be brought here where you can be taken care of.'

Donald's double entendre caused a stir.

'As health and safety is our greatest priority, each of your rooms has been fitted with World Health approved air filters, hand sanitizer, personal masks, if you desire them, call buttons, and, of course, Halo detectors. As you all know, when they finally blink green, you will be on your way back to civilization. Until then, feel welcome at Cloud End.'

A few hands shot up, but Donald held them at bay. 'Before I take your questions, let me explain the boundaries of the property. When you came up the path and through the gate, you would have noticed that Cloud End is perched on the edge of a cliff, Faucini Cliff. This cliff drops roughly two hundred feet to the rocky ocean below. For your protection, fences have been installed. Feel free to approach them carefully. At the appropriate times, make use of the outdoors here at Cloud End, but please do not leave the property.'

'And what if we do?' Damian Bellows asked.

'I'd prefer not to talk about consequences, Mr. Bellows.'

'And I'd prefer not to be *here*,' he retorted belligerently. 'You choose to live here, but I have been imprisoned with her.' Bellows jerked a finger at the table behind him, to his soon-to-be-ex-wife dressed in a body-sucking dress with high heels and large hoop earrings.

'Oh, shut up, Damian. You're being annoying.'

Wallis touched her arm. Ironically, the three contracted the Halovirus after a particularly vigorous and spiteful exchange outside the courthouse. Now they were stuck together for the long haul.

'Now,' Donald continued, 'during your Convo stay, we hope to keep you comfortable and, if at all possible, entertained. To your right is a fifty-seat theater with a stage. Down that hallway is an exercise room with weights and stationary bicycles. A small library is located near the front entrance. If there are other things we can provide to make your stay more comfortable, please let us know.' He took a deep breath and the microphone inside his suit echoed in the room outside. 'Now. Questions.'

Gavin was the first. 'How much is this going to cost? I tried contacting my insurance company, but they seemed a little hazy on the details. Even using my sick leave for this is bad enough.'

'The Government will be footing the entire costs.'

'Really?' Gavin's astonishment was reflected in the murmuring. 'Does that mean we can eat and drink whatever we want?'

Donald waggled his hand. 'To a point. We are not in the business of perpetuating drunkenness, but everything will be paid for, yes.'

Seraphim Wyman's face paled. Since her late teens, Seraphim's drug habit had worsened. To hear that alcohol was free and easily accessible was her best dream and worst possible nightmare. Already, she was feeling the gentle squeeze of her addiction. If only she could get some heroine – or, at the very least, Vicodin. She would need it if she was going to survive the gauntlet of the Convo's buffeting restrictions.

More questions about timing, health facilities, isolation, quiet hours, came and went and Donald answered them in turn. Finally, when all were answered to the best of his ability, Donald spotted the smallest hand in the back. It was Titus Draper.

'Are we going to die?'

Donald was unable to craft a response to the startling question. Donald and Claire both wanted to say, *You'll be fine. We'll all be fine. We'll take care of you*, and yet they couldn't. Promises made of air. But they couldn't promise anything.

Finally, when the silence grew too heavy, Father Lawrence turned to the family. 'What's your name?'

4

The boy pressed into his mother's arms and spoke from their protection. 'Titus.'

'That's an excellent biblical name, Titus. How old are you?'

'Six.'

'When I was nine, there were lots of things happening in the world that scared me. Wars and angry people and diseases, too. And yet here I am, Titus. How old do you think I am?'

'One hundred.'

Father Lawrence laughed which broke some of the tension. 'Almost. I'm sixty-one. And I want you to know, that even though all those bad things happened all those years ago, I'm still here.'

The little boy smiled.

'And you'll be a bright star in the world, I bet.' Father Lawrence nodded to the boy and turned back in his seat. Dorothy, Titus' mother, smiled gratefully.

'Now,' Donald said, 'maybe we should get to know each other.'

'Just a second,' Alonzo, raised his hand. 'You said we could go to the movie theater, and the gym and all that, wander the grounds, but can we do that at any time we want? Or are we supposed to be confined to our rooms?

Donald inhaled deeply. 'In general, you are free. There are Government guidelines to the amount of time you can spend outdoors, but we'll stretch it if we can.'

'A lot, I hope,' Alonzo responded.

'Lockdowns only occur if there is an emergency.'

'Such as?' Alonzo's eyebrows were arched.

'A fire, or... or... a health emergency.' Donald glanced at Titus who had ceased paying attention.

'What about if we're freed? When we go home? What does that look like?' Alonzo pressed.

'We'll cross that bridge when we get to it.'

'I prefer to at least step on that bridge already,'' Alonzo said.

'It's not that I don't want to tell you,' Donald said slowly, 'it's just that I don't know what the timeline looks like yet. I – we,' he paused to gesture towards Claire, 'haven't been briefed on that scenario yet.'

'You said that the light in our room just needs to turn green, right?'

Donald's pause was deafening. 'Yes,' he responded slowly, 'that green light is your ticket out, but we'll still need to do an exit interview.'

'An exit interview?'

'It's just a debrief, really. I'm sure that you won't be...'

'We just want to go home.' Seraphim intoned from far in the back. 'I just want to go home.'

'That is our ultimate goal,' Donald said. 'Everyone wants to get better.'

Minutes: Joint Pandemic Committee
18 October, 2031

Attendance:

████████████████ opened the meeting asking the question, 'How far can society be pushed before breaking?'

Research description of 'Lemming Syndrome.' During COVID 19, effects of media consumption, news, social media platforms, encouraged mass hysteria and drastic reactions of 'leaping from the cliff' to be followed by family and friends.

Followed by discussion on how fear and panic can be used as impetus for Governmental control and society's need for stability.

████████████████████ reminded the group of the installation of Halo Detectors in every household in the country to understand how quickly and widely the Halovirus is being spread. Once testing positive, those infected are asked to move to CCs where they will stay until their Halo Detector turns green.

After further conversation, a vote was taken for final approval of Project Green Light. ████████████████ reminded the committee on the ethical nature of what Green Light represented and was hesitant to continue, but ████████████████ reminded him of the greater good of humankind.

Unanimously carried.

Project Green light approved.

Encoded message #6348611
Govt device sent: SRC9022289
Govt device received: CVH4580387
18 October, 2031
Proceed.

5

Winston Faraday III yawned broadly as he lay in bed. When his eyes popped open at 8:30, he first checked his Halo Detector – still red – and then scanned his AutoCom for messages and news. Once satisfied that everything outside Cloud End was understandable, he pondered the ceiling replaying parts of his life, as he always did, on the spackled screen above.

When he helped his father pack up his office, Winston noticed the photos of his mother and other mementos of people Winston II had helped along the way. There were ticket stubs to fundraising dinners for the less fortunate; trips to underfunded and underprivileged schools; photos of hospital visits to constituents who wanted to know their politician cared for them. The elder Faraday did not publicize these opportunities to which the younger thought an incredible waste of a media opportunity. Any time a politician was out and about being seen helping people, it should be recorded – not simply for posterity's sake, but for the polls. The power of polls, both goad and lash on their backs.

His father, a humble man, nauseatingly so according to the son, was beloved by many. Winston II was notoriously protective of his privacy and unwilling to publicly respond negatively to criticism. He was a man of his constituency – a true fighter for human rights. Contrarily, the son waged his campaign battle in front of cameras and defeated the father soundly. Winston III would never have chalked up his victory to the media – he was much too vain for that.

On his first day in office, Winston Faraday III proudly took his place at the podium and proclaimed his fight for the 'common man,' the downtrodden and outcast. Strategically, he placed behind him people of different races, different cultures, religions and sexual orientations. They clapped wildly, faces alight with a manic fury, sweat glistening on their lips, that Faraday III was a step into the future of tolerance and self-expression.

It may have been the last moment he spent any time with these people. Yes, he felt sorry for them. Yes, they carried a heavy burden. To live in a constantly changing world – which if right wing opinion was correct, they were a subset of humanity who needed to be given a platform for victimization – was entirely confusing and exhausting. So, Winston Faraday III made himself too busy telling people how hard he was working, how much he was doing for his district, to actually interact with them. 'Working hard' attending $10,000/plate fundraisers and flying across the globe to understand global social issues seemed much more important than listening to the resentful people in his district whine about their circumstances.

Certainly, his importance to his own party was apparent. He was the handsome face of progress, of tolerance and the future. Winston knew his ability to control the camera irritated many in the Party – perhaps the Government in general – but he didn't care. He had a role to play, and the world needed to see it.

Which was why it was devastating for Winston III to be unfairly laid up by this horrible disease. Granted, when the virus finally got to him, he felt strangely exhilarated by the thought of posting about the trials and tribulations of his illness. Though he only had a sniffle and a sore throat (perhaps a touch of a fever?), his first post was:

Unfortunately, I have contracted the Halovirus. Currently, I'm feeling quite ill. Some serious effects, but I'm being taken care of. I have to tell you, the Halovirus is not a joke. But I want you to know I'll continue to work hard for you even as I get better. #persevere #fightingthehalo #keepingyousafe

As he scanned his feed in the following days, Faraday was grateful for the well-wishes and thoughts during his recuperation. Each time one of these messages arrived, his forearm vibrated.

Faraday scratched his nose and put a crooked elbow behind his head as he pondered the moment when his Halo Detector had turned red. Once his nose started running, he assumed it would turn color, but still, it was disheartening. Yet, Faraday also felt an odd sense of relief that he would get some time off from his busy schedule. Working from home sounded kind of nice. But then, the news of being transported to Cloud End. Instead of putting his feet up on his plush, living room furniture, he was ensconced in a second-rate resort, with tattered armchairs and a kitsch indoor waterfall, where every other resident seemed to be on the wrong side of insane.

Faraday checked his arm again for any new messages. A few social media feeds had dropped into his arm and a message from his father to tell him that he was praying for him. Winston frowned. He didn't need prayer. He needed to get healthy.

A knock at the door startled him and he drew the covers up over his chest.

'Who is it?'

'Housekeeping.' The voice echoed in the morning stillness outside his door.

'I'm still in bed.'

'Would you like me to come back later?'

'Yes, later. Much later.' His terse voice was perhaps too harsh, but these people needed to leave him alone.

'Of course.'

Much later, Faraday pulled himself from bed. He stood in front of the mirror reflecting on the face which stared back at him. It was the face of his father. Long nose, prominent cheek bones, intense blue eyes. His forehead was prematurely lined with three wrinkles, but Winston thought these made him look wiser – certainly more handsome. Many of his social media followers thought so, too.

Winston studied his toned body. He frowned at the hair on his chest. It had been a few months since he'd had it waxed. Normally, he would do this every three or four weeks, but the optics of going to a waxing salon during a pandemic would not have been good. Polls didn't take kindly to politicians breaking restrictions. Instead, he suffered undo trauma from an itchy triangle between his pecs.

While he studied himself in the mirror, his arm buzzed, and he touched his ear.

'Senator Faraday.'

'Winston!' a voice shouted happily. 'How are you?'

Isolde Howard was a congressional socialite who took pride in attending events with attractive politicians. Notoriously callous, Isolde bounced from congressperson to congressperson, district to district, gleaning information and making it profitable.

'I'm sick.'

'Yeah, I saw that. That's rough.'

To Winston's ears, she sounded distracted.

'What do you need, Isolde?'

'Where are you? I've been around to your apartment and the doorman said he hadn't seen you for a few days. Are you off on a junket somewhere in your sickness?' Her voice displayed a sarcasm that Winston found irksome.

'I'm working.'

'You're not at your office. I checked there too.'

'Of course I'm not there,' he responded testily, 'I have the Halo. But I have highly confidential business meetings which need attention, so I've holed up,' he lied. 'You don't have to know everything, you know.'

'Yes, I do,' she laughed.

'I can't tell you where I am.'

'You know, when people get Halo, they get sent away,' she poked slyly.

'Faraday glanced around at his apartment noticing the frayed carpet and the chipped edges of the bedside table. He shook his head with irritation. 'I've *chosen* the place where I will recuperate.'

'Oh.'

'Were you just checking up on my health, or was there something you needed?'

'I was worried about you,' Isolde pouted. 'It sounds like Halo is picking up steam. So many cases everywhere. People dying.'

'Where do you hear that?' he asked.

'It's everywhere. News. Social media.' She paused. 'I hope you don't die, Winnie.'

He hated that moniker, but he tolerated it because of her immense usefulness to him.

'I won't.' Faraday continued to study his face in the mirror as he spoke. He dabbed at a spot on his cheek. *Age spot?* 'Listen, I need you to do something for me. Can you place yourself in the same circle as Senator Forsythe? I need more information about *Convalescent Centers*. Can you do that for me?'

'Convos? Everyone knows about those. Bad places. Basically mortuaries, or at least that's what I've heard. Why Forsythe?'

'Because I've got this sneaking suspicion he is up to something and I want to know what it is.'

'Okay, Winnie. You take care of yourself.'

'Thank you, Isolde.'

'Oh, one more thing, Winston. There's a rumor on the street you're going to have to hand over your powers to...'

His face reddened. 'That's ridiculous, Isolde. Now get to work.'

Winston Faraday wondered why rumors moved faster than the internet itself.

While a politician studied his ageing appearance, another face, ravaged by years of addiction, avoided the mirror. Seraphim Wyman had not slept for two days. She shook with chills. Her body felt as if it was being assaulted by an invisible assailant. During the middle of the night, she began to see things. Terrible things. Spiders scrabbling across the headboard, clicking across the wood, spinning their webs, awful, gossamer strings preparing to wrap her up and suck her dry. Seraphim could only stare in horror as they crawled closer and closer.

She did not want to tell anyone about her battle. Judgement was already a horrible reality in her life. It always had been. From parents to teachers, her friends and ultimately the law, Seraphim had continuously felt the weight of others' expectations and the failure to develop her own. When she tried marijuana for the first time, Seraphim encountered a blessed retreat from the stress of this world into the blissful realm of pharmaceutical ignorance.

As her perceived judgement from others deepened, so did her dive into the cesspool of harder drugs. Once she'd worked her way through the rainbow of painkillers, a 'friend' let her try methamphetamines. It was withdrawal from these that now wracked Seraphim.

Huddled under a blanket, Seraphim wondered how she would survive the day, much less the night. While the owner of Cloud End told them they need only push the button to summon room service, she highly doubted they would bring her meth on a crystal platter.

Seraphim attempted to get up from the bed. Quickly, she became lightheaded and stumbled, crashing into the wall. With a cry of pain, she crumpled at the base and curled up into a fetal position.

There was a knock at the door.

'Ms. Wyman? Is everything okay?'

Unable to respond, Seraphim coiled farther into herself willing the pain to go away.

'Ms. Wyman? I'm going to come in, all right?'

Seraphim did not care, and when the door opened and one of the housekeepers entered, she sighed.

'Ms. Wyman!' Rushing to Seraphim's side, Nancy Harper knelt on the floor next to her. Nancy's full protective gear crinkled noisily as she reached out. 'Are you injured?'

Seraphim could only grunt.

'Is it the Halo?'

Cracking her eyes, Seraphim regarded the hidden face of the housekeeper. Of course, she would be worried about the virus first. God forbid that anyone would care enough about her. God forbid that they might enquire about her recent tumble, but no – just their own safety with this damned virus.

'Leave me alone.'

'We have to get Dr. Chandruth. He'll know what to do.'

'Leave me alone,' Seraphim insisted.

Ignoring her, Nancy stood and pressed the call button. At the front desk, Carl answered. 'Carl, I need Dr. Chandruth immediately. Room 10.'

Nancy repositioned herself next to Seraphim and waited for Dr. Chandruth to arrive. When he did, he carried a small bag with a gun-thermometer and other diagnostic tools.

'Doctor, it might be the virus...'

Chandruth checked Seraphim's vital signs. She was febrile, but not dangerously so. His worry was the emaciation, the shallow breathing and weak pulse. He turned her hands over. *There...* he saw the trail. Needle marks running up the side of her arm. Cloud End was not the place to be drying out.

'When is the last time you had your drugs?' he asked quietly.

'Don't you judge me,' Seraphim retorted as strongly as she could.

'I'm here to help you, Ms. Wyman. When was the last time?'

'Two days ago.'

'What was it?'

'What difference does it make? You can't get it for me anyway.' She rolled slightly away from him.

'But I can help you make it through the withdrawal.'

'I want to die,' she whispered. 'I'm starting to see things. I haven't slept for a while.'

'Those are side-effects of withdrawal, Ms. Wyman. We have to get you down to the infirmary. I may have something to help you.'

A glimmer of hope sparked for Seraphim. She tried to pull herself up from the floor and winced. 'I can't move. Something's wrong with my leg.'

Dr. Chandruth reached down to the leg she indicated and touched it. He manipulated it slightly but stopped when she cried out.

'You've sprained your ankle.' He glanced up at Nancy. 'We'll need some help.'

She nodded and left the room. Walking down the hallway quickly, she checked inside open-doored rooms where most guests were either reclining on their beds watching television or sitting on chairs staring at their devices. Asking each one for help, they shook their heads or ignored her. The rich man, Damian Bellows even shut the door in her face. Finally, she glanced over the railing to the floor below where three men were having coffee. The family of five were engaged with their devices.

'Can someone help me, please? There's been an accident.'

'What kind of accident?' Sam Draper called out.

'One of the guests has fallen and we need to carry her to the infirmary.'

'Is she sick?'

Nancy wanted to be snarky. *Of course she's sick, dummy. She's got the Halovirus.* 'No, she's not sick, but yes, she's hurt herself.'

'Aren't there other nurses here? Why not call them?' Sam's plaintive voice begged for Nancy to move to someone else.

'They were on night shift. They need to sleep. We only need help carrying her down the stairs.'

'I've got my family to think about,' Sam said and smiled at his wife and children. 'I'm sorry.'

Alonzo raised his hand. 'I'll help.'

'And I,' the priest said. As they stood, the policeman grunted and followed them to the stairs.

When they entered the room, Dr. Chandruth crouched near the floor. Nancy and the three men entered, but when Gavin Matthews, the police officer took one look at Seraphim, he shook his head. 'Junkie.'

'What?' Alonzo asked.

'She's in withdrawal. I've seen it a million times before. I wouldn't go near her,' he pointed. 'She's liable to try to rip your throat out.' He turned to leave.

'Wait,' Alonzo called after him, but it was too late.

'Please, help me,' Chandruth said.

Alonzo and Father Lawrence approached. 'She is... having difficulty. We need to gently lift her and help her down to the infirmary. Do you think you could do that? With these suits on, Nancy and I are hopeless.'

Now deputized as orderlies, Alonzo and Lawrence reached under Seraphim's arms and gently lifted her from the ground. She was surprisingly light.

'Don't worry,' Father Lawrence said. 'We've got you. We won't let you fall.'

While they carried Seraphim out the door and around the balcony, the rich man reopened his door to watch the three people stagger to the stairway. Damian's soon-to-be ex-wife, and current-next-door-neighbor, recorded the scene on her AutoCom. The politician's door was still closed. Across the hall, Wallis and Chantelle looked on with curiosity.

Finally, they reached the infirmary where Dr. Chandruth opened the door and led the trio to an examination bed with a paper runner on top. 'Lay her there, please.' They did.

Father Lawrence spoke to Seraphim. 'If you need anything, I'll help if I can.'

'I don't need anything from you,' she snarled.

'Nevertheless,' he responded with a wry smile, 'I will be here if there is ever a need.'

He left the room leaving a shivering Seraphim wrapped up in her misery to be tended by a fully protected doctor.

Encoded message #8924517
19 October, 2031

Government device sent: RBM1347763
Government device received: SRC9022289

Due to foreseen issues of dependency, subject 13 is in drug withdrawal.
███████████ has taken subject 13 to the infirmary where she is
currently undergoing treatment. ████████████████ requests timeline to
be moved forward to mitigate against subject 13 affecting other
subjects. Please advise.

Encoded message #892492
19 October, 2031

Government device sent: SRC9022289
Government device received: RBM1347763

Be advised. ████████████████ is to proceed when ready. Safety
protocols as first stage. The greatest caution should be displayed when
in contact with subjects.

6

Renata Lerner opened the office door where she found four patrons standing behind shielded glass waiting for tellers' assistance. Renata sighed. She'd been in the banking business for over thirty years. It used to be that people would come to the bank for a check and a chat. Exchange of money and information. But now, the bank building sat mostly empty, and what little cash was kept in teller's tills seemed like toy money. Thus, Renata drove to an empty bank every day, put in her eight hours of staring at a computer screen, and returned home to an even emptier house.

As Renata watched the elderly patrons passively accept their receipts and tuck them into archaic purses strapped over their ancient, bony shoulders, Renata renewed her sigh and pondered her Gen X past. Gone were the 90's and its rebellious, flannel-wearing, Birkenstock shod generational music. In Renata's mind, they worked uncomplainingly, bearing the burden of the Boomers' oversized consumerisms and the painfully complacent Millennials. Yet the Xers were not innocent. As they rolled their eyes and stuck their heads in the sand, they allowed the world to float down the muddy stream of resentment and intolerance. What had once been a future full of Utopian idealism, Nirvana studded tires and Stone Temples piloted by a generation which had thrown off the suit and tie, was now dystopian at best and downright hellish at worst.

At least once per day, Renata wished that she had pulled up stakes and moved to the suburbs with the rest of the traitors and taken up life as a day-trader.

It was not as if there weren't positives, though. Removing the constant in-person complaints, combined with happier loan officers working from home, the building seemed lighter. Renata wasn't sure how much work was being done, but if she didn't have to put up with their moaning about being burned-out, this was a good thing.

Renata paused by the water cooler near the teller's rack and saw the front door open. Steve Cranmere looked worried and excited. When he spotted her, he strode quickly to the swinging door and motioned for Renata to speak with him.

He was wearing his traditional pub attire: blue jeans, boots, a wide belt, and blue shirt with the pub's logo on it. His thinning hair was mussed, and it was apparent he hadn't shaved for a few days.

'What can I do for you, Steve?'

'Is there a place we can talk in private?'

'That depends.'

'On what?'

'Is this a business conversation?'

'No.'

'Then we can't talk in private.'

'Then, yes, this is a business conversation.'

Renata sighed. 'Steve, I've got a busy day. Perhaps this can wait until...'

Steve noticed an aging woman, Della Finstrom, who was arguing with a teller regarding the denomination of bills she required for her withdrawal. 'Overwhelming,' he responded sarcastically.

'What is this about, Steve?'

He lowered his voice. 'I've been hearing things.'

'You mean voices in your head, or rumors?'

'Don't condescend me, Renata. We went to the same high school.'

Renata Lerner felt an irritation. People like Steve were a dime a dozen: know-it-alls, with no knowledge. Pretentious and overbearing because of his longevity in Herzfeld, Steve carried himself like a king among knaves.

'I've got some information which might interest you.'

Renata checked her AutoCom for the time. 'All right, Steve, let's talk. I've got ten minutes.' She ushered him through the gate to a meeting room where they sat across from each other.

'Now, what is this about?'

'It's about the Halos.'

'What about them?'

'Aren't you worried? They're just up the road!' He waved his hand behind his head in the general direction of Cloud End.

'I don't see what we should be worried about. They're locked up, convalescing, you know.'

'But what if one of them gets out? What if one of them brings the Halo to town? What do we do then?'

'They're not wild dogs, Steve.'

Frustratedly, he tapped on the table. 'When you go down to the river and you see people fishing there, what do they catch?'

'I don't go to the river.'

'They catch carp, Renata. Carp. Have you ever eaten a carp?'

'Not that I know of.'

'That's right, because no one eats carp, not even the Japanese and they'll eat anything.'

'Steve, don't be racist. And I don't know what this has to do with our current topic.'

Steve shook his head. 'Carp are not native to the river. They were brought in by some careless aquarium owner who thought that dumping a lonely carp in the river would be more humane than flushing it down the toilet. Well, that one lonely carp produced hundreds of thousands of other not-so-lonely carp, and now, twenty years on, basically the only fish that live in the river are carp.'

'Still haven't grasped what you're getting at.' Renata leaned back in her chair and crossed her arms.

'Halos are *not* native to Herzfeld. In fact, they could destroy our delicate ecosystem. The Government thought it would be more humane to put them all together, but if one of them is released and they make their way into town, we could all get it and then...' He held his palms up and shrugged as if to say, *We're done for.*

'Don't you think you're being a little melodramatic. Those poor people have been ripped from their homes and...'

'Blah, blah, blah. Poor people. Yakkity yakkity. Once they spread it here, you'll be the poor person, Renata,' he pointed at her face.

'Be that as it may, I'm not sure what we can do about it. The Government has decided. One doesn't dicker with the Government.'

'We need to petition our politicians. Tell them we want these people moved on. Send them to an island somewhere.'

'That's ridiculous.'

'I'm serious,' he said as he tapped his hand on the table. 'Just off the coast. That will keep everyone safe.'

There was some sense to his argument, but Renata momentarily put herself in the Halos' shoes.

'Well, you do what you think best,' she responded.

'Will you sign the letter with us?'

'You've already drafted it?'

'Yes.'

'I'd have to read it first. Who else has signed it?'

'Edgar, Beth, Igor... Bridgette. Begrudgingly, but she signed it. And even Rector Falkirk.'

'Hmm. Let me look at it.'

Steve smiled as if he'd already won. 'You got it.' He pulled a copy from his shirt pocket and placed it in front of her. Then, he strutted from the room and out the bank.

Renata opened the letter and frowned as she read.

To whom it may concern,

And it should concern you, esteemed politicians, that some people who voted for you, are not happy.

At all.

Our frustrations are numerous, but we will concentrate on the most pertinent and direst which threaten our very existence. We recognise that in Government circles, towns like Herzfeld do not garner the same level of attention as New York, London, Buenos Aires or Tokyo. Nevertheless, Herzfeld has its own value to this country. As a well-regarded tourist village, we receive visitors from near and far. We pay our taxes faithfully and yet the Government has, with its immense power, without consultation or collaboration, decided to place a Convalescent Center on the outskirts of Herzfeld.

We realize that you, the Government, are stuck, but certainly, there are more remote places than Herzfeld to position a Convo.

Because of your actions, we worry for our town, and we are already seeing the effects of a disease factory situated so close to us. Tourist numbers are down. Supplies are arriving late. People are afraid of these infected people, who, if in a moment of insanity, succeed in escaping Cloud End would most certainly enter Herzfeld first. If any of our citizens would be infected and, as every news outlet tells us, succumb to the ever-increasing threat of the Halovirus, their deaths, as well as our financial fate, are on your heads.

We beg you consider the removal of Cloud End so we can get on with our post-virus, safe lives.

Sincerely,

Citizens of Herzfeld.

Renata read the letter twice before rubbing her chin with thumb and forefinger. While the letter had merit, it certainly had not been written by an ignoramus like Steve. Probably Gemma or even Reverend Falkirk. Whoever wrote it got at least a few things right.

People were scared.

People were nervous about loss of life and money.

People were saddened by the sudden leeching of neighborliness. Where there used to be a true sense of camaraderie, now was suspicion and genuine distrust of each other. Those who would smile and greet their neighbors had now become amateur epidemiologists, pointing fingers and casting aspersions at those who didn't wear their masks correctly or stood inside the magic boundaries of sixteen square feet.

But Herzfeld had had no cases of Halovirus. In fact, the disease's absence was startlingly suspicious. Some town leaders had smiled smugly that this was due to their protective restrictions and preventative measures.

Others, not quite ready to swallow the isolationist pill, simply assumed that the virus was not anywhere near as contagious as what the media was telling them.

In Renata's mind, the truth lay somewhere in the middle.

There was something about the letter that resonated deeply with her, something which tapped into a dark well of her own fear. Why shouldn't these kind of people be moved on? Why did they have to be placed in Herzfeld? Obviously, they had been in the wrong place at the wrong time. They should have stayed home. Safe.

As she pondered what the Herzfeldians had written, Renata's AutoCom buzzed. After scrolling past the advertising, (amazingly, much of it was a reflection of recent conversations she'd had with other Herzfeldians – number of cases of Halovirus, a new book, travel, some pain she'd been having in her back) Renata saw that she was needed in front. Sighing, Renata gripped the letter and returned to her life.

7

Day three.

It might have been day three hundred as far as Sydney Bellows was concerned. Although there were supposedly many things to do at Cloud End, Sydney struggled to summon the power to leave her room. She knew that next door, Damian was plotting to publicly shame her. The reason she knew this was because she'd been stalking his social media feeds. While none of them were overtly libelous, Sydney could read between the lines. Oh, yes, she could. She'd been doing it for years with him, starting with the way the lines of his forehead crinkled, and the way he sniffled when he was annoyed, and that irritating arch of the upper lip when he condescended. Her least favorite was how he cracked his knuckles when he was about to give her the 'lowdown on truth.'

For Sydney Bellows, Damian was an ungrateful wretch. Everything she did for him, from managing the household staff, to decorating their properties, to keeping up to date on fashion, he overlooked. Damian was far too concerned about himself and his own desires to care that she was lonely. Desperately lonely. Locked up in her castles with no one to talk to except her online followers.

Sydney scrolled through his most recent posts and videos. Her mouth pinched at the second-to-last where he wrote, 'I suppose life could be worse, but not sure how.'

Uh-huh, Damian. Struggling with everything. Especially your wife in the room next door? How dare you.

The comments underneath were typical. 'Thoughts and prayers,' 'Great attitude.' Sydney's eyes stumbled on one in particular, a woman, Sheena Davidson... *Who was Sheena Davidson? She must be one of his mistresses. Look at her.* Sheena's profile was rife with airbrushed, activewear photos, generous curves and large, Botoxed lips. *I see what you've done, Damian.* Sheena's comment was, 'Take care of yourself.'

I know what you're thinking, Sheena. You want him to take care of himself so he can take care of you!

Frustratedly, she continued to snark her way through his other posts. Almost maniacally, she felt the urge to respond, but Wallis had been adamant that she refrain. Nothing good came from online discourse. Especially when Sydney was requiring half of Damian's estate as part of their divorce proceedings.

Damian was apoplectic when he heard Sydney's terms. *What have you done to earn any of this money? Half? Why, you don't deserve a tenth. You sit around all day staring at your nails, attempting social media challenges, and shopping. You've already spent half my estate!*

Money, of course, was where it hurt him the most. The fact that he had made a fortune in shady investments didn't seem to bother either one of them. Money was a useful tool, but the rebounding hammer hurt even more.

As she finished her online stalking, Sydney glanced at the red light of her Halo detector and sighed as the unblinking eye reminded her that she was not well. Just as she was about to get up from her bed, there was a knock at the door.

'Who is it?'

'Wallis.'

Sydney opened the door to find Wallis checking her AutoCom.

'Anything new in the world?' It was a useless question. Sydney received constant updates on her own AutoCom 4. The Auto 5 was about to come out. Sydney was going to use some of her divorce proceedings to upgrade.

'It turns,' Wallis answered with a wry smile. 'Still here.'

'Would you like to come in?' Sydney asked.

'If you're up for it, I thought instead we could go for a walk.'

'What? Like a stroll around the balcony?'

'I was thinking about something more refreshing. Maybe outside – to the cliff.'

A spasm of anxiety crossed Sydney's face. 'Outside?'

'The owners were explicit that we were free – encouraged – to leave our rooms and explore. Come on. It's a beautiful day and the sun will do us some good.'

Sydney nodded reluctantly. After grabbing a light jacket, she checked her hair, then AutoCom, and followed Wallis onto the balcony. Passing Damian's closed door, Sydney flipped his room the finger and laughed derisively.

Wallis frowned. 'You really hate him, don't you?'

'He brought this on himself.'

Wallis wasn't quite so sure. As the months of her attorney's fees piled up, and the stories of irreconcilable difference were stacked one on top of another, Wallis wondered where everything went wrong. The common factors between divorcing couples were similar, but also different: money (most of the time), selfishness, (all of the time) affairs, abuse, disinterest... Frankly, Wallis wondered why anyone got married.

Wallis had never been married and never intended to. Working with couples for the last twenty years had dislocated her matrimonial urge. Though she had dated a few men, online interest which had turned into dinner and drinks, always in the back of her mind were the men and women who hired her every day, biting and devouring each other as if they'd never been in love in the first place.

In the late 90's, as Wallis was finishing the last days of college, she watched couple after couple hooking up, holding hands, holding on to a perfect life their parents had peddled: get a job, get married, get a house, pop out a few kids, fly to Disneyland and, right after they celebrate their 60th wedding anniversary, while cuddling their nineteenth great-grandchild, suffer a mutual coronary and die in bed. It sounded good, but most of the college couples had popped out a couple of kids and grown bored with each other. The second decade of marriage – the Great Yawn, as one of her colleagues called it – was when Wallis began to see the Xers show up en masse at her office door. It was their arrival when Wallis thanked her lucky stars for never falling that far.

But it had been a lonely life. Married to her work, divorced from the social scene, people came and went, just as the years did. Now that Wallis was in her forties (two years before, she celebrated the advent of her fifth decade by standing in front of a stern-faced, bored judge, in a decidedly bitter court case where the couple wanted to divide up the kids as well as the money), she heard the clock ticking a little more loudly. She always assumed she had more time.

Sydney and Wallis descended the staircase. Like the last two mornings, Father Lawrence and Gavin sat at opposite tables staring into their coffees to portend the future from the sediment. The haggard looking mother and father (Wallis couldn't remember their names) were eating a light breakfast and checking the news on their phones. Unconsciously, both Sydney and Wallis checked their AutoComs.

The brisk morning chilled Sydney's arms and she donned her light jacket. As they allowed the morning air to wash over their cheeks, Sydney noticed the rusty shed door was slightly ajar. An abused, herniated basketball looked dismal on the dewy morning grass next to it.

'Aren't you cold?' she asked Wallis.

'Once we get moving, I'll be fine.'

The lawyer opened her bag and produced a set of designer tennis shoes. Smiling, she sat on the bench and replaced the footwear before moving off the porch. They strolled out over the grass towards the cliff. At this time of morning, the fog had mostly lifted, but the sun's power had not yet intensified to show them the entire path to Faucini Cliff.

Striding briskly, the women felt the gravel crunch under their feet. Tall grass along the unpaved path, still wet with morning dew, dampened their spirits. Soon, their shoes were soaked, and clothes replete with stowaway seeds, but the exercise felt good.

Halfway up the slight rise towards the cliff, Sydney paused at a small outcropping of rocks. Breathing deeply, she saw that Wallis was not struggling but had stopped with her.

'How are you doing with all this?' Sydney asked as she pointed at Cloud End.

'I can't say it's a welcome addition to my life.'

Sydney snorted. 'You can say that again.' As she regained her breath, she pointed at Wallis. 'You know, it's strange. We've spent a lot of time together, but I don't really know anything about you.'

Wallis smiled and nodded.

'Uh, that was an invitation for you to share a little bit about yourself.'

Wallis laughed. 'I never really get the chance. I meet with divorcing people five days per week, fifty weeks per year. I ask questions. They answer. So, I listen and take notes. There's probably nothing I haven't heard before.'

'What's the weirdest thing a couple has divorced for?'

Wallis laughed. 'A man decided he'd rather have an inflatable doll for a partner than his wife.'

'What a weirdo!'

'Yes, humans can be tough to get along with.'

A strange semi-quietness settled over them. A slight breeze picked up and began to carry away the misty fog which hovered over the grass. Seagulls twirled aloft above their heads in the shy sunshine. Thankfully, the warmth began to soak in.

'You still haven't told me anything about yourself.'

Wallis touched her hair, then the side of her face. In this younger woman she saw passion and frustration, a touch of recklessness. Wallis used to have that – to feel that.

'I was born in Japan.'

'With a name like Takamoto, I would have assumed that.'

'My parents are actually Canadian, but my grandparents are Japanese.'

'How interesting.'

'While my dad was working in Europe, my mother took me to her parents for my birth. My dad didn't actually see me until I was three weeks old.'

Sydney studied her nails while Wallis recounted her story. Although she wanted to know something about Wallis, her ability to listen did not match her desire.

Strangely, though, Wallis found the storytelling cathartic. 'My parents still live in Canada. I haven't visited in a few years.'

'Why not?' A butterfly captured Sydney's attention and she touched her eyebrow three times to photograph it and capture it on the hard drive of her AutoCom. 'Hey, look!' she pointed at the butterfly taking flight.

Irritated, Wallis felt like walking off, but she still had a conversation that needed to take place. 'I got busy with my work. They got busy with their traveling. We speak to each other a few times via AutoCom – they say they're proud of me – but I think I'm just an interruption.'

'Hmmm.' Sydney stood up. 'Isn't that a great photo?' She held up her arm in front of Wallis' face who politely smiled and swallowed the rest of her story. If Sydney would have been an interested and invested listener, Wallis might have told her about her struggles growing up, her listlessness at school, her inability to concentrate because of... well, other things. But Sydney was not a good listener.

'Alright, let's keep walking,' Wallis said as she made a move to continue along the path and up the rise.

After ten minutes of slow silence, they turned when they heard voices behind them. Coming up the track were four small heads. The Ashford grandchildren and the two Draper boys, Pasqual and Titus.

Moments later, Oswald burst from the tall grass, his face covered with a mask embedded with grass seeds and dirt, a few bugs, but his eyes were alight. Behind him were his similarly masked sister and the bare faces of the Drapers.

'Look out!' Oswald shouted as they overtook the women on the trail.

'Don't be so rude, children!' Sydney shouted at their heads as the last of the kids brushed by them.

'Sorry!' McKayla called out over her shoulder. They were not even breathing heavily.

'Kids these days are so rude,' Sydney grumbled.

Alternatively, Wallis watched the tousled hair and bouncing curls as they turned the corner ahead. *Tick tock. Tick tock.*

'... and they should not be playing together anyway,' Sydney finished up her diatribe. 'Those house kids are going to get the Halo and then we'll see how frisky they are.'

'They're just kids, Sydney.'

'It's no excuse.'

Wallis sighed and forged ahead.

Oswald stopped just short of the fence.

He'd never been on the other side. His grandparents had warned him that there were loose rocks and a precipitous drop, but Oswald felt he was a good climber. Even though it was a long way to the bottom, he was pretty sure he could make it.

Someday.

The breeze was strong coming up from below. The long grass in front of the fence bent in half at the force of it. Above him, seagulls floated on the breeze and turned their heads sideways to study the intruders at land's edge.

Because Oswald was faster than the other three, and McKayla kindly insisted on waiting for Titus, he was there a minute before them. As the wind whistled around him, he closed his eyes and spread his arms. This was one of his favorite places, just here on the edge, on the cusp of danger in a place of safety. Here he could throw things over the edge, talk to the wind, spit upwards and watch it sail back over his head. It was here that his grandparents couldn't follow him, at least not easily.

They'd gotten older. Really old since Oswald's mother had tragically died. Oswald missed his parents fiercely, but the missing was getting easier. Now that he was moving on in school and finding other distractions, he felt like he could move again. His grandparents were generous and decent people, but Oswald needed friends.

And now, Halovirus had supplied them. Yes, they were a few years younger; Oswald was eleven and Pasqual and Titus nine and six, but they were kids. Living breathing kids who wanted to run and jump, throw things, look at things, discover, explore.

Oswald took off his mask. He knew the rules: any time he was around Halos he needed to wear it, but everything Oswald heard about the Halovirus suggested that kids were mostly immune *and* the virus was ineffective outdoors – the sun, or something, probably the wind, too.

Finally, Pasqual squirted through the last tall grass and hunched over next to Oswald. When he looked up again, he raised an eyebrow quizzically.

'You've got freckles.'

Oswald grinned. 'So do you.'

'Aren't you supposed to be wearing your 'helmet'?'

'Aren't you supposed to shut up?'

Pasqual laughed loudly and approached the fence. 'Holy crap!' he exclaimed into the wind. 'It's loud up here!'

'Pretty cool, huh?'

Leaning out over the fence, Pasqual attempted to see the cliff face, but it was just beyond his vision. 'How far down is it?'

'About a mile.'

Pasqual whistled. 'I bet that would be one exciting swan dive.'

'Are you going to try?' Oswald asked.

'No way! Are you crazy?'

'A little.'

They both climbed the white fence. It was smeared with gull droppings, but the boys didn't seem to care. Because the wind blew them away from the cliff's edge, they took one more step up onto the second board. At this height, their knees shakily balanced them. As Pasqual looked out over the empty space out over the ocean, he felt slightly disoriented. Because Oswald wasn't stepping down, he stayed, but he was afraid.

Behind them, McKayla's voice rang out. 'Get down, you two! That's not safe!'

Startled, Pasqual almost toppled over, but the wind pushed him back to the grassy side of the cliff. Oswald waited one extra moment to show his sister that she couldn't tell him what to do, and then slowly climbed down after Pasqual.

'And where is your head covering, Oswald Ashford?'

Oswald thrust his jaw forward. 'You're not my boss, McKayla.'

'You know the rules. We are to wear our masks at all times to avoid being infected.' She glanced nervously at Pasqual who didn't seem to know what to do.

'Infected by what?'

'You know,' she said with threatening voice. 'Put it on, or I'll tell Grandpa and Grandma.'

'Go ahead. I don't care.'

'Then you might have sentenced them to death.' She picked up his helmet and tossed it to him. 'If you get the virus and pass it on, old people will die. It's certain.'

Oswald wasn't certain of that. As he stared at the covering in his hands, he desperately wanted to chuck it over the edge and watch it bounce down to the rocks below. 'I'll put it on when I feel like it. And if you tell Grandpa and Grandma, I'll tell them that you've been crying at night. And then you'll have to talk to Mrs. Bowel Movement.'

Mrs. Bowel Movement was Dr. Jane Boeder-Mankins, a Government-assigned psychotherapist and a wraith who moved stealthily around the grounds. Oswald had never seen her smile.

'You wouldn't,' McKayla said.

'I'd say it's an even trade,' Oswald replied as he dropped it back on the ground.

McKayla did not remove hers. Titus placed his head on her arm. Unlike his own sister, Gina, McKayla did not seem to mind his presence.

For the next few minutes, the boys threw rocks at the laughing seagulls while McKayla sternly watched with intense disapproval.

'What are you kids doing?'

McKayla wheeled to find the well-dressed Wallis and Sydney, who was sucking in large gulps of air, nearing them.

'We're playing,' Titus responded while chucking a small stone into the air. The strong wind plucked the stone from its trajectory and hurled it towards the women. Sydney felt the small stone sting her arm.

'Hey! That hurts!'

Titus covered his mouth and giggled.

'How would you like it if I threw something at you?'

'You couldn't hit me, I bet.' His laughter rankled Sydney, but they both knew he was right.

Wallis eyed Oswald. 'Where's your mask?'

His eyes narrowed. This game of chicken was a little different than the one he played with his sister. Adults were weird like that. They liked to follow the rules so long as the rules didn't apply to them.

He pointed at the ground.

'You should put it on,' she said.

'*You* should put it on. You're the one that's sick. I'm healthy, so why am I the one being punished.'

Wallis had to admit that his line of reasoning was pretty good. He might make a good lawyer someday. 'I agree with you...'

'Os.'

'...Os,' she continued, 'but to keep us all...'

'Safe,' he tossed his hands in the air. 'Safe! I'm so tired of that word. When do we get to do anything dangerous?'

'Just put your mask on, Os.'

Sighing, he reached down and grabbed it and stuffed it onto his face. Wallis saw that his sister was smugly satisfied by this turn of events.

'What are we going to do now?' Pasqual asked.

Oswald pointed along the fence. 'Up a little ways is a break in the fence. Maybe we can find some other things to chuck over.'

The Draper boys seemed pleased by the suggestion, and they tore off. McKayla crossed her arms.

'Are you going with them?' Sydney asked.

'Do I have a choice?'

'There's always a choice when it comes to men.'

'My grandparents might get upset if I wasn't there watching them.' Behind the mask, McKayla's eyes shifted between the women.

'What about the other two boys, the maskless ones?'

McKayla shrugged. 'If I'm watching one, it doesn't make much difference if there are others.'

'That's very mature of you,' Wallis said.

The girl blushed at the compliment.

'But very immature of the boys' parents,' Sydney added.

'Well, I suppose I'd better follow them.' McKayla lifted a hand as she began her trudge to where the boys had scampered off.

'She's a good girl,' Wallis said.

'She shouldn't have to be watching them.'

'Maybe she doesn't mind it? Maybe she simply likes being out of the house.'

Sydney thought about it, then crossed her arms to stare out over the edge, beyond the fence, to the crenulated water far below them. 'How far down is it?'

'I believe the literature in the foyer said it was roughly two hundred feet to the rocks.'

'Quite the drop.'

'Yes.'

'Wallis, what did you want to talk to me about?'

Wallis had been dreading the thought of this conversation. During her career, Wallis had been fighting for women and men (usually women), to get the best divorce settlement. It was her job to find the chinks in the opponent's armor, to insinuate and infer, question, find idiosyncrasies to put doubt into the judge's mind. Normally, Wallis would have pushed on to the bitter end for top dollar, but she was afraid. Sydney's quirks threatened to undo much of the territory they'd gained. If she said something, or worse, did something to Damian while here at Cloud End, everything could unravel quickly.

'We're in a strange place, Sydney, and I don't just mean at Cloud End.'

'Then what do you mean?'

'You've made progress. Damian is on the ropes, and if you play your cards right, as soon as we're out of here, you'll have half of his assets.'

'I know. That's so exciting!'

'But you need to... behave.'

Frowning, Sydney turned towards Wallis who was now staring out over the same sea. 'Don't start with me, Wallis.'

While placing her hands on the fence, Wallis turned her head. 'Don't provoke Damian. At all costs, you must not do this.'

'I haven't said anything at all to him,' she pouted. This wasn't entirely the truth. On the bus, Sydney had told him to move to another seat because his odor offended her.

'This includes,' Wallis ignored her little white lie, 'online provocation. No offhand comments on his feeds. No blogging or vlogging about your time here and your proximity to him.'

'It's just online. It doesn't matter. You'd have to be pretty insecure to be offended by a few words on a computer screen.'

'Sydney...' Wallis warned. More than once, Sydney had been outraged by seemingly innocuous comments Damian had posted, things that did not have double meanings until she doubled them. Tripled them. Escalated them until a war of words ensued, complete with atomic phrases designed to level entire blocks of history.

'Ok, fine. I won't write anything.'

'Or video.'

'Yes! Yes! I hear you, mother!' Sydney exclaimed exasperatedly.

Wallis bit her tongue. It truly was unfortunate that she was locked away for the foreseeable future with a woman like Sydney Bellows.

Half a mile away from the people standing on top of Faucini Cliff, and far below on the rolling sea, two men sat in a fishing boat. It was a day of briny air and fresh wind. Waves slapped the side of the boat which echoed through the hull. A canopy shaded the steering wheel and bench, but neither man was in the shade. One held a fishing rod. He hadn't caught anything for the hour they'd been stationed there. To be fair, they'd never caught a fish in that location. The water was far too deep. Yet neither man cared whether they caught fish or not.

The non-fishing man stood in the stern of the boat, binoculars held to his eyes. He stared up at the cliff. Far above him, two women were engaged in conversation.

Steve squinted into the binoculars then adjusted them slightly. 'Two women, Ed.'

'What are they doing?'

'Talking.'

'Is that a problem?'

'No,' Steve said as he put the binoculars down, 'but they're out of the house.' He pointed up the coastline, down the hill to where Herzfeld was nestled in the bay.

'I'm sure they're given explicit instructions that they cannot leave the premises.'

'Or what?' Steve's face was angry. 'What are they going to do to them? They can't throw them in jail. They can't put them under house arrest in town. They'd only ship them back.' He tapped the edge of the boat. 'Edgar, these people are dangerous. They need to be removed.'

Edgar Post shook his head. 'You've got to dial in your animosity, Steve.'

'Just you wait, Ed. When I'm right about these people, I'll try not to say I-told-you-so, but it will be difficult.'

Edgar set the fishing pole down. 'Now that you've satisfied your curiosity, can we go home?'

Steve nodded. He was ready to be in his own home, feet up on his recliner, watching television. He needed to talk to Gemma, too.

From: ██████████████████████

To: ███████████████

Week 1. Two group sessions have occurred. During the first, only three people attended. Subjects 2, 9 and 11. The first session was awkward. ████████████████████ brought up topics of Halovirus concerns, safety protocols and the Government's responsibility to keeping citizens safe. By the end of the session, Subject 2 and 9 were conversing directly. Subject 11 watched without speaking.

The second session was attended by subjects 2, 6, 9, 11 and 15. Most of the conversation dealt with issues of comfort and personal safety. Subject 6 remained quiet while 15 was animated and spoke at length about her marriage and her developmental years. █████████████████ unsuccessfully attempted to steer the conversation back to safety protocols and dismissed the group time fifteen minutes early.

8

The television numbed Claire's sense of reality. News, ferocious and fearful, played 24/7, in the living and sleeping areas. As she stared over her cup of evening tea, images depicting a malevolent reproduction of the Halovirus rotated in the background behind a stern-faced newscaster. As happened every night of the week for the last eighteen months, the anchorperson gave the dire state of affairs, the exponential increases in cases, the current tally of deaths, and the prediction for what would happen in the next months.

To be quite honest, Claire was both morbidly fascinated and more-than-slightly tired of these daily updates. To fixate on the tally of deaths was insensitive at best and offensive at worst. Transposing victims' names to death numbers was shameful, but the constant reports allowed Claire some space to breathe a little easier that she and Donald had not contracted it.

Yet.

Opening up their Edenic residence to the diseased couldn't end well, but their reasoning was sound. No one was vacationing at Cloud End. No one was coming to the café or the small restaurant. If the finances didn't turn around soon, the bank would foreclose. The gossip hounds had already yelped at their door letting them know that the bank wanted to subdivide the estate and put up 'condos on the cliff.'

Envisioning condominiums on their land, destroying the serenity and beauty, set Claire's teeth on edge.

Claire attempted to remember the last time she felt unworried. She smiled ruefully at the thought that it might have been before the internet, before cable TV, before cell phones and AutoComs. The next thing might be phones implanted directly into brains...

The night before, Claire woke up in a pool of sweat, breathing heavily. She had dreamed of ageing; a clock chased her, ticking louder and louder. Unable to see, she groped in the enveloping blackness trying to grasp anything solid until she felt something reach out and grab her ankle. She looked down to see the clock's hands clawing at her legs, latching on, pulling her to her knees and then dragging her to the edge of a cliff. To go over was death. Fighting against the clock, she scrabbled forwards, fingernails scratching against the smooth surface, unable to gain purchase. She screamed. There was no one to save her. *Donald!* She had called out. *Donald.*

When she awoke, Donald was there, lying on his side, snoring softly. Claire dabbed at her forehead and willed her breathing to return to normal. She placed a hand on his shoulder. He grunted, but she was thankful he was solid. Real.

Forty-one years ago, Donald had asked Claire out on a date. They went to the movies. Claire couldn't remember what it was, only that Donald had held her hand in the dark. They ate popcorn and leaned back in their creaking chairs. She glanced over at him multiple times as the reflected light from the screen illuminated his smiling face. He had a piece of popcorn perched in the corner of his mouth.

But simple things like that had been hard to come by since their Blanca's death. Each day, Claire felt herself pulled down into the abyss of guilt only to drag herself back up to the top. It was mentally taxing, and the exhaustion she felt at raising her grandchildren in this cowardly new world was overwhelming at times. Claire wanted that simple world, the one of half-eaten popcorn and greasy fingers, pithy movies and intertwined fingers. She wanted that world where their daughter was alive and their grandchildren were being raised in another home.

To have no worries was what Claire most desired. She wanted to be like the children streaking towards the cliff, uncaring of its potential danger. That cliff was very much like Claire's life: a beautiful outlook, but untouchable. Too much unsafety to approach it well.

After donning her safety gear, Claire pushed open the kitchen door to see the dining area sparsely populated with guests. The priest was in his normal chair near the water feature; the gravedigger was reading a book from the Cloud End library; the waif, Chantelle, chewed her fingernails as she perused her phone. Like prey, she sat near the edge of the room, her back to the wall, intently watching the comings and goings of perceived predators.

Claire felt a pitiful envy of these people and their freedom. Now that *they* were sick, *they* were unrestricted. No masks. No boundaries except the walls of Cloud End. No conversational barriers. Everything was open to them.

Except going home.

'Hello,' Claire greeted Chantelle who, startled from her phone scrolling, glanced up quickly. 'Is there something I can get you before I turn in for the night.'

'No, no thank you.'

'Okay. Have a nice night.'

Chantelle put her head back down, but suddenly brought it up again as Claire began to turn away. 'Actually, do you think you could talk to me for a little bit.'

Claire was tired, but she decided to stay. 'Of course.'

'Are you allowed to sit down with me?'

Claire sat, careful not to tear any part of her protective gear.

'You're Claire.'

'Yes.'

'Have you always lived here?'

'No. Donald and I bought the place many years ago as a retirement investment, but the investment...' She smiled but wasn't sure if Chantelle could see it.

'Why here?'

'We visited Cloud End back in the 80's for our honeymoon. We stayed in room 8.' She pointed towards it, the room in which Sydney Bellows was living. 'There was something fresh and exciting about Cloud End. So near the cliff. So far from civilization. We spent the week enjoying the outdoors and,' she blushed, 'each other's company.'

Chantelle's jaw twitched.

'Then, not too long before the Coronavirus, we bought it. We had a couple of good years. But then, as every business in the tourism industry experienced, fear killed it. Whispers of new germs or worse, poor reviews sucked the life from this place. We've hung on until this opportunity.'

'Opportunity...' Chantelle repeated derisively under her breath.

'I'm sorry if that sounded callous.'

'I don't hold it against you, only... nevermind.'

'You were going to say something?' Claire asked.

'No. Please, go on with your story. Why are your grandchildren staying with you? Do their parents have the Halovirus?'

Claire's face dropped. 'Not a virus,' she responded softly. 'Blanca, our daughter, just couldn't cope with the world as it had become, and her husband Michael was, how shall we say, unsupportive.'

Chantelle waited.

'One night, about three years ago, we got a call from the police that Blanca was found in her garage.' Claire was surprised at the resurfacing of emotion. 'When the police call, and they use the word 'found' it can only mean...'

'Dead.'

Claire nodded. 'It's hard for me to say that word. Still.'

'I'm sorry for your loss. Why aren't the children with their father?'

Claire pondered her gloved hands.

'I hope I'm not prying too much.'

'No. No, it's okay. Donald and I don't speak of it – of her – of them. Even the children have stopped asking.' Claire attempted to cross her legs, but the suit proved prohibitive, so she stopped. 'Michael's disinterest was not limited to his wife. His children receive an even shorter end of the stick. He hasn't spoken to them in a year.'

'That's tragic.'

Claire shrugged. 'In an ideal world, it would be tragic when a father doesn't speak to his children. But we don't live in that world, and Michael's absence has allowed the children something a little more normal.'

'With their grandparents.'

'That's us.'

'Do you think about her a lot?'

'Blanca?' Chantelle nodded. 'Yes, most days. It's mostly guilt. I wish I could have done more for her, been there for her, you know? But she pushed us away. We were fortunate that she let us see the children, so they were used to us.'

'Are they happy?'

'As much as they can be in a world that keeps producing pandemics.'

'Are you happy?' Chantelle asked.

Claire St. Croix couldn't answer the question. It was not a matter of happiness, but one of survival. 'I keep busy, if that's an answer.'

'It's not,' Chantelle responded.

Claire smirked at her forwardness. 'What about you? How are you doing?'

No one ever asked her how she was doing. Some had asked if 'it' felt good, as if somehow their transaction was satisfying for her, so she lied to them. *Of course, this feels great. So glad you popped by. No, you are the best ever.* That's what they wanted to hear. They didn't want to hear her say, 'I hate my life. I hate what I'm doing. I hate you.' There's no money in *that* truth.

'It's a relief to be here,' she said truthfully.

'A relief?'

Pausing, unsure and unwilling to reveal everything regarding her ancient occupation, the walking, the begging, the horrifying sights and smells of strangers, the washing and the troubled sleep, Chantelle leaned forward, elbows on the table. 'Let's just say my life did not turn out how it was supposed to.'

'How was it supposed to turn out?'

Chantelle was prepared for the opposite question, *How did it turn out?* but this one threw her. 'My mom used to tell me that I could do whatever I wanted in life. Parents shouldn't tell their kids that. It's unrealistic.'

'What do you mean?' Claire told her grandkids the same thing: if they worked hard, kept their noses clean, saved up some money, they could do whatever they wanted and be happy. Happiness, an elusive mirage.

'My mother took me to the ballet when I was twelve. Swan Lake. I was transfixed by the music, the dancing, the elegance.' Her eyes misted over. 'Those long, lithe limbs combined with the power of those boys in the tight outfits. I was mesmerized. When the ballet finished, I told my mom I wanted to be a ballerina.'

'What happened?'

'She laughed. After all those pep talks about, 'You can do anything if you put your mind to it.' But what she really meant was, 'If you just find the right guy, you'll be a perfect housewife.'' Chantelle sighed.

Claire waited. 'And then I kept waiting for my Prince Siegfried.'

'Is that a character in Swan Lake?'

'Yes. He enters the woods to hunt for swan, but as he's about to shoot, the swan transforms into a beautiful maiden who tells him that the spell can only be broken by a man who's never fallen in love before. Everyone knows that's a fairytale.'

Claire thought of Donald and nodded.

'To spite my mother, I went through a series of ugly ducklings never finding my prince, and now...'

'You no longer look for a prince.'

'I no longer look for a prince.'

'You said it was a relief to be here. Do you have no other place to go? Your parent's house?'

Chantelle's jaw hardened. 'They disowned me after I... hit the streets. I haven't seen them in a few years.'

'How old are you?' Claire asked, assuming that the girl was perhaps in her early 30's.

'I'm twenty-three.' Claire's shocked face caused her to burn with embarrassment. 'I know. I look much older. Living on the streets, trying to find my next... meal. It's taken a toll.'

Inside the mask, Claire took a deep breath. 'Well, you're here now. And you are a guest.'

'Thank you, I guess. But I feel strange, nonetheless. You have to wear a spacesuit even to talk to me.'

It was Claire's turn to burn with shame. 'I'm sorry. I wish I could take it off.'

'I wish that too.'

'What will you do when you're out?'

Chantelle transferred her eyes back to her phone and shrugged. 'I hope I don't get out any time soon. The more people stay away from me, the better, I guess.'

'I'm sad to hear that.'

'Yeah, well, that little red light is my best friend.'

Dylan Renfroe, Director of United Psychology, paced nervously in the board room. Sitting at the table, arms crossed, leaning back in a chair, was the Intelligence Director, Stella Reed-Conway. Stella's blue eyes bemusedly followed the psychologist's frantic marching.

'Relax, Dylan. Everything is going well.'

'Relax? Did you say relax? Stella, you do realize that what we're doing is highly illegal and unethical. I can't believe I agreed to this.'

'Don't get cold feet now, Dylan. Much of this was your idea.'

He continued to mutter under his breath until the door opened. Two senators, a National Health Officer and the Infectious Disease Liaison entered the room and took their seats.

'It's about time,' Dylan said, testily.

'We have other business to attend to than listening to crazy people all day long,' Senator Membree responded as he took his seat at the head of the table.

Renfroe wanted to respond sarcastically that the 'work' of a politician *was* listening to crazy people all day, but he held his tongue.

Senator Membree nodded to Senator Forsythe to begin.

'Project Green Light is ready for Stage II. Thanks to Emery,' he nodded to the National Health Officer, 'one hundred and fifty Convalescent Centers have been established across the country. One hundred and forty-nine are legitimately regulated as emergency pandemic hospitals. The sickest of the sick are taken there to recover.'

'At the measly cost of 1.2 billion dollars,' Membree interjected.

'Thankfully, our federal budget can absorb the cost. A small rise in taxes spread over the next ten years should cover this expense.' Quentin added.

'But Cloud End...' Reed-Conway prodded.

'Yes, Dylan has thoroughly vetted the subjects. As we all know, each was selected for psychological, age, gender and economic variances.'

'It was not easy,' Dylan responded. He still had not sat down, but instead leaned against the back wall, arms crossed. His face was partly shrouded in shadow.

'Be that as it may,' Senator Forsythe continued, 'we all agreed that they will be a perfect representative group.'

'I just want to go on the record that not all of us were pleased by the choices,' Monica Portney, the Infectious Disease Liaison added. 'A prostitute and a drug addict? How can we possibly get any reliable information from them?'

'Not to mention a priest and a gravedigger,' Donaldson snickered. 'It sounds like the beginning of a joke.'

'But it's not,' Senator Membree urged. 'It's not at all. This is at the very pinnacle of the highest interests of science and of the nation. Don't forget that.'

'Stage II,' Senator Forsythe stepped in, 'is a barrage of subliminal messaging. In our initial briefing, we discussed what these might look like. Dylan.'

Renfroe pulled himself from the wall and brought up the presentation on his computer. Using the remote on his AutoCom, he pointed the laser light at the screen. 'Through brain imaging, science has documented the effects of subliminal and subtle background messaging for the past seventy years. Although results have been conflicting, there has been some traction where product placement, or even flashed words, have registered with viewers.'

'In the early days, subliminal messaging was limited to a two-hour movie, or a half hour television episode. When the screen shut off, the messages faded away. Generally, they had little effect on the viewer. But,' he raised a finger, 'with today's technology, robotic advertising, the rise of the AutoCom, people can be manipulated twenty-four hours a day, seven days a week.'

'Now, we know that businesses have been monitoring cell phone conversations for years. Social media has almost perfected algorithms for advertising and targets individuals for financial purposes. The question arises: why are social media companies allowed to spy on people, and governments are supposed to keep their noses out?'

Renfroe scanned the room and saw the nods, except for Monica Portney who remained closed. 'This is our justification. Where capitalism succeeds, so does the Government.' He cleared his throat and continued. 'Statistically speaking, every person on the planet is connected to the internet in some way, shape or form – most through a cell phone or AutoCom. Green Light is about targeting a specific group of people to study the effects of our propaganda.'

'What exactly is our propaganda?' Portney asked.

He changed the slide. 'In two days, Director Reed-Conway has a team of computer specialists who will hijack both the Wi-Fi and mobile data at Cloud End. Each person's phone will flash messages on their social media accounts, advertise on search browsers and even at night, sub-audio phrases will be repeated over and over. In two weeks, we should begin to see results.'

'What kind of results?' Donaldson asked.

'Changes in behavior. Changes in web searches. Changes in the way they interact with each other.'

'What are these messages?' Portney insisted again.

Next slide. 'On social media, irrespective of their browsing searches, every person will receive ads regarding the positive role of the Government in keeping people 'safe' during the Halovirus pandemic. This word, 'safe,' will be seen and heard hundreds of times per day. We should begin seeing a lessening of anxiety within a week.'

'Safe? You're going to play a message that tells people they're safe? That's the plan? How does that help us?' Monica was unconvinced.

'It's been proven that once people feel safe, they are much more open to the influence of risk. Guards are let down. Safe minds are open minds.'

'Okay, then what?' she asked.

'After a week of social media propagandizing, of making them feel safe, we'll do the reverse. We'll turn their psyches in different directions.' His eyes hardened and his mouth pinched at the sight of his colleagues squirming. 'The average person spends nine hours per day online. Studies have shown that when people, especially kids, are disconnected from the internet, their first reaction is anxiety, so they go back to it, whether music, streaming services, or scrolling. It is now a reality that humans will spend more time surfing the web than they do sleeping. If we can simply manipulate this addiction, we can see if the contemporary mind will turn against the community. Nine hours per day.'

'Wow,' Senator Forsythe was impressed.

Renfroe pushed onwards. 'Nine hours of unlimited access to influencing people's behaviors. Once they feel safe, then we will bombard their screens with messages such as, 'The Government needs help...' clickbait material. The Government needs help finding those who would be anarchists – those who, when infected, move about in the community. What this means is, we want to see if we can turn those sixteen people against each other. Snitch.'

Portney shook her head. 'These people are under enough strain as it is. Are you sure we want to turn them paranoid? Bad things could happen. Very bad things.'

'Ms. Portney,' Senator Membree pointed a finger at the Infectious Diseases Liaison, 'you've known all along what our ultimate goal has been. To actively help the nation understand...'

'You mean 'control,'' she butted in.

'Semantics, Ms. Portney.' Membree's chastisement caused her face to redden. 'What Director Renfroe is trying to help us understand is: How is it that we can best serve our country? We can't do this unless we know what makes people tick.'

'But it's not their idea? It's *your* idea.'

'Get on board,' he warned.

'I *am* on board,' she insisted, 'I just want to know that what happens at Cloud End is not going to put us all in jail.'

'Nothing we are doing right now,' Renfroe assured, 'is any different than what Facebook, Instagram, Tik Tok, BeMe, Photobend or any other social media empire hasn't been doing for decades. We're simply targeting a few rather than all.'

'Finish your presentation,' Senator Forsythe said as he glanced at his AutoCom. 'I've got a meeting with the Department of Defense in half an hour.'

Renfroe flicked to the last slide. 'Once the second week of messaging has finished, we'll start with the subliminal messaging at night.'

'What's *that* message? Strangle your next-door neighbor?' Portney's sarcasm was not appreciated.

'No, Monica, nothing quite so dramatic. The message is this; *The Government can be trusted explicitly.*'

'But why do we need that message? Shouldn't the Government be trusted explicitly without the subliminals?'

Renfroe's gaze spoke the opposite.

'Remind me again how the subliminal night messaging works?' Donaldson asked.

Senator Membree's eyes glowed. 'Technology and psychology, Mr. Donaldson. The world is changed by both.'

```
Text Intercept
27 October, 2031
07:23
Subject 9 #0597433 to #0534444
```

I miss u
I miss you too.
It's terrible in here - locked away. I just want to come home
How are you feeling?
Miserable
Any symptoms?
Scratchy throat - but don't know if from Halo or crying :(
How long do you think you'll have to stay?
Until the light turns green - hopefully only a few weeks
Then we can get back to normal
Yeah. Can u give the kids a hug for me? Tell them I love them
Will do
Do u want to call me?
Maybe later. I've got to get to work
Okay bye

```
Social Media Intercept - (BeMe)
27 October, 2031
Subject 15
```

```
19 photos attached. Subject stands by fence overlooking cliff. 3 videos
of wind blowing through subject 15's hair. All taken from above. No
other subjects in photo. Subject has pursed lips with red lipstick.
Fake eyelashes. Wearing exercise gear. Photos have been manipulated.
Post proceeds:
```

Day 10 @ Convo. So many things to post for my followers, but mostly not
happy that @DamianBellows is here also. Of all the bad luck. Trying to get on
with life. struggling with captivity, but at least the view is good. I'm staying
strong. #Halosucks #Girlpower #Cantwaitfordivorce

9

Monica Xiao sighed deeply. She missed her family.

Kind of.

Although they'd only been separated ten days, it felt like a month. Guiltily, Monica remembered in the months before the Halovirus how she would have loved to have had some 'me' time, to do self-care, maybe daily yoga or pottery classes, how she would have loved not to have to fix dinner and bathe the kids afterwards.

But now, with only a tenuous connection to the outer world via the internet, Monica felt lonely. There were people cooped up with her at Cloud End, but they weren't really her kind. The gravedigger was nice, but...

ALL GUESTS ARE INVITED TO ATTEND THE GROUP SESSION LED BY DR. BOEDER-MANKINS IN THE THEATER. THIS WILL BEGIN IN FIFTEEN MINUTES.

This was the third meeting they'd had in ten days.

During the first two sessions, Dr. Boeder-Mankins sat behind a glass wall at the front of the theater. From there, she took notes and asked how people were feeling.

Monica was used to talking about her issues. Ken said that talking to someone else besides him might be good. Get things off her chest. Thus, she met regularly with a counselor. Monica felt enlivened by informing her friends that 'her' counselor was helping her work through her issues. *Those things*, Ken said, would be good to deal with.

Those *things*, as he called them, were obstacles to enjoying her best life. Having been brought up by perfectionists - her father, a concert pianist and her mother, a classical violinist - Monica found herself constantly nagged about things out of place: her room, her makeup, the way she drove a car. Eventually, Monica rebelled, and found herself with a messy room, overblown makeup, and a downright terrible driving record. It was this last rebellion which sent her to Cloud End. With the stupid policeman, to boot.

Sure, she'd been driving too fast, and if truth be told, she was checking her lipstick in the pulldown mirror above the steering wheel. But she had to get to the market. Her entire day had been chock full of other things. With fifteen minutes left, she raced down the road for some necessities.

At first, she hadn't seen the flashing lights. Maybe he would have let her go. She'd never know, but once he saw who she was, Monica Xiao was sure that the racist cop was giving her a ticket because he didn't like Asians.

He knocked on her window. He was wearing a mask. 'Can you put on your mask?' he asked pointing to her face.

'What do you want?'

'I need you to roll down your window, but first you need to put on your mask.'

'I need to get to the store.'

'Ma'am...'

With great frustration, Monica reached into the console and produced a black mask. Strapping it over her ears, she rolled down the window.

'I need to get to the store,' she repeated.

'You'll be out of here in just a few minutes.'

'You don't understand...'

The police officer stopped writing and rubbed his eyes with his rubber gloves. His eyes looked tired, frustrated. They were red with irritation. 'As soon as I write this ticket, you can be on your way.'

'Ticket? For what?'

'Speeding. Distracted driving. Crossing lanes.' His voice was muffled.

'I was doing no such thing,' she responded angrily.

'Look, ma'am...'

'My name is 'Mrs. Xiao,' if you please.'

'Driver's license and registration.'

Grabbing her handbag, she dug through the contents with frustration. If only she'd gotten one of those AutoCom's. She could have put her license and everything else on there. Instead, she had to excavate her messy bag for the racist cop. Finally, she found it and shoved it out the window at him. 'There,' she said testily.

He clipped it to his iPad and began to fill out her digital fine. Cars were humming slowly past. A few masked drivers stared while some passengers pointed. They were all laughing at her.

Finally, he finished, but not before coughing through his mask.

'If you give me the Halo, I swear, I'm going to sue the entire city.'

The cop stared over her car with dead eyes. 'Have a nice day, Mrs. Xiao.'

'You pronounced my name wrong.'

He didn't respond but handed the license back to her.

She grabbed it and threw it into the passenger seat. After she rolled up the window again, she checked her makeup in the mirror before driving off. There was a slight chunk of mascara on her right eye. With the hand that received the license, she rubbed at it.

It must have been then.

When Monica Xiao opened the door to the theater, the carpeted
walls muffled most of the sound of her entrance. The muted noises, as well as lights, made the room feel like a womb.

Or tomb, Monica thought.

Scattered through the small auditorium were the same guests as before, but also a few others. Unfortunately, the police officer was sitting next to the priest and Alonzo. Monica thought twice about staying. The police officer's face - that arrogant, square-jawed look, five o'clock shadow, as if he was some kind of movie star - turned her stomach. Taking a deep breath, Monica steadied herself. *You can do this, Monica Xiao. What's past is past. Let it go.*

Tossing her hair haughtily, Monica held her head high and took a seat leaving two spaces between her and Wallis Takamoto. Nodding to her, Monica retrieved her phone and scrolled through her social media feeds until Dr. Boeder-Mankins arrived.

Which she did, shortly. The lights went on behind the glass. The squat, light-skinned woman with large glasses and black hair so thick and luminous it seemed to be white from reflecting the lights, perched on a stool behind the glass and held a microphone to her mouth. Dr. Boeder-Mankins was allowed to go un-suited as long as she stayed enclosed in the glass case. She flashed a smile, something which had been absent on the first occasions, showcasing glitteringly white teeth. Oddly, and distractingly, her eyebrows almost met over her nose.

'Hello, guests. How are we today?'

Alonzo clapped multiple times but fell silent when no one else joined him.

'Okay,' Dr. Boeder-Mankins' voice came from multiple directions through the theater's speakers, 'I'll assume that we are okay. Okay?'

Monica nodded, wanting to encourage her, but as she glanced around at the rest of the room, arms were crossed. Faces were tense.

'It's been three days since our last session. Would anyone like to share how they are feeling?'

No one raised a hand. A few played games on their devices. Finally, Monica cleared her throat. 'I'll go first, Dr. Boeder-Mankins.'

'Oh, that's good. Thank you, Monica. Please call me Jane. All of you.' She spread her arms magnanimously, yet somehow it came across as condescension.

'It's strange, Doctor. Over the last few days, I've felt kind of... well, I don't know how to put it... perhaps, 'secure,' is the correct word?' She turned to her right to see the others staring at her. At least a few were nodding, the police officer was too.

'Tell us more about that,' she encouraged.

'Well, when we first got here, it was overwhelming, like being hit by a tidal wave. I was scared and lonely. I didn't know anyone. Everything seemed so stark and brutal, but now that we've been here for ten days, it's begun to feel like home. Does anyone else feel that?'

'I feel that too,' Damian agreed. 'I'd actually be enjoying myself if my soon-to-be ex-wife wasn't here also.'

'I'm pretty sure I'd rather not be here,' Sam Draper stated before Sydney's outrage could begin. 'Cramming the five of us into one room, albeit a suite, is not ideal, even if we were on vacation. This is anything but.'

'I know what you mean.' Monica agreed. 'If my family was here, I'm not sure how well it would go.'

'That's very honest of you,' Jane said.

'I wish I had a family,' Alonzo Turner's voice was strangely exuberant. His youthful face radiated an energy that seemed vacant elsewhere. 'I was just getting to know this lady, very fashionable, nicely dressed, silky hair. But then I got sent here. She hasn't really reached out to me.'

'You're lucky,' Damian called out.

'Let's get back to your first statement, Monica,' Jane interrupted. 'Tell me more about the word 'secure.' How do you think you came to feel this?'

'I don't know. But just in the last few days, I've felt at peace. Like everything is going to be fine. It will just take time.'

'Have you been doing anything different?'

'No, not really. Maybe I just needed some time away.'

'Time away from what? From your family?'

Monica touched her hair. 'I don't think it's that. Life was slightly stressful, like this dark shadow was always hovering over my head. Maybe it's the clean air or the blue sky here, but something about Cloud End is rejuvenating me.'

Dr. Boeder-Mankins wrote something down on her pad of paper then turned on the screen behind her. 'I thought we could do something different today. I'm going to put some images on the screen behind me, images of what's happening out there in the world, and I want you to tell me what first comes to mind.'

'I didn't realize this was going to be a psychological testing site,' Wallis Takamoto interjected. 'Have you sought permission from everyone to do this?'

Jane's face darkened. 'I was simply thinking of a way we could pass the time. I'm sorry if you feel that this is about tests or psychological manipulation.'

'I didn't say manipulation. You did.'

'Just let her do her job, Wallis,' Damian said. 'She's just trying to help.'

Wallis Takamoto's inner monologue warred. Ultimately, she stood and decided that leaving the room would be the best course of action. Pushing past Monica Xiao's legs, she exited the theater quickly and quietly.

Tension filled the air.

'We're not doing any psychological tests,' Dr. Boeder-Mankins assured them. 'I simply wanted to keep you all updated, as much as I can, with what's going on out there. I know that most of you pay attention to news feeds, but I've got some clips from Government News Source, that might help us make sense of the world around us. How does that sound?'

They begrudgingly nodded. Spooked by Wallis' insinuation, they did not feel quite as safe. Father Lawrence tented his hands in front of his face and watched with hooded eyes.

The first image flashed on the screen. A crowded street in London. Free Life protestors, dressed in their oddly matched purple and orange gear, carrying flapping flags with the *FL* symbol, a large white Pegasus charging forward. They were standing in front of Buckingham Palace. None of the protestors wore protective gear.

'What do you see?' Jane asked.

Damian rose his hand. 'I see free people doing what free people ought to be doing! Standing up for themselves!' He looked around for support but found little.

Jacquelyn Archer spoke next. 'It's an obvious demonstration for human rights. But those people are destructive. What can they possibly hope to gain by tearing things down and burning them? It's shameful.'

'I don't know,' Alonzo responded. 'Some part of me thinks they should be wearing masks to protect vulnerable people from the Halo, but another part of me thinks, hey, if they want to blow a couple holes in their oil pans, go for it. It's a free world, or it used to be,' his voice fell off.

'Which is more important: personal freedoms or societal protections?' Jacquelyn asked.

'Isn't that why we're here?' Alonzo asked the room. 'Weren't we placed here because our personal freedoms are less important to society in general?'

'Is that why you're here?' Jacquelyn asked.

'I don't get you.' Alonzo's face scrunched up.

'It feels like *I'm* here because *I'm* being punished.'

'Punished for what?'

Jacquelyn threw her head back. 'For being a successful businesswoman.'

'That's ridiculous,' Damian interrupted. 'Do you hear any of the other women blaming this on gender, or race?' his eyes fell on Monica.

'I'm assuming, Dr. Boeder-Mankins, that all opinions in the space of this theater, are considered equally valid, is that right?'

'Yes, yes, of course. Mr. Bellows, Ms. Archer is sharing how she feels. That's a good thing.'

'Yeah, but why does everything have to be about race and gender? Why can't it just be – that's the way life happens, so let's tough it out.'

Jacquelyn's jaw clenched. 'Easy for you to say. You look like someone who has had everything handed to you on a silver platter. Rich, smug. Once you get out of here, business will return to normal. But for me? My company's stock figures are down two percent over the last ten days since I've been incarcerated.'

'But you're keeping people safe,' Monica stated.

'What about *me*? What about *you*? Who's keeping you safe?'

'The Government, of course. Things could be a lot worse. We could be in some hotel, trapped in a room battling claustrophobia, like during the Coronavirus pandemic. No, we get to be in this place, mask free; we get to use the gym and the theater and go for walks outside...'

'I agree with her,' Damian nodded and crossed his arms. 'That's a great attitude to have, Ms...'

'I'm Monica. Monica Xiao. Room 12.'

At the sound of her name, the police officer's eyebrows pinched. Suddenly, it dawned on him who she was. His eyes widened.

'I'm Damian Bellows. Room 9.'

'This isn't hook up hour,' Sam protested.

'No, it's not,' Jacquelyn agreed.

The psychologist pulled them back. 'Let's return to the picture one more time. Tell me when you want me to interpret for you.'

These last words made Father Lawrence lean farther forward in his seat. 'What do you mean by that?' Father Lawrence asked.

'By what?'

'That you're going to interpret the picture for us.'

Jane stood and approached the window with her microphone. 'My apologies. What I meant was, I will shed some light on things we might have missed as a group.'

Still not entirely satisfied, Father Lawrence leaned back again.

When no one else spoke, the psychologist used the laser pointer to illuminate other symbols in the background. 'You'll notice behind the scene, a few Free Lifers are being detained by army personnel. But what you may not see is the Government's mobile National Health vehicle administering both vaccines and directions for people in need. This is regardless of their status, race, gender or creed.' His eyes alit on Monica and Jacquelyn, then a frowning Damian. 'Sometimes, the Government takes a lot of flak, but in this case, they are doing everything in their power to keep people safe.'

A hush settled over the theater. The word 'safe' seemed to have a numbing effect on those gathered. All but the priest. His eyes noticed a few other hidden objects.

On the ground near the protestors was a newspaper with a barely legible headline reading, 'Halovirus cases soar into the millions.' On the other side of the scene was a billboard with half the words blotted out by heads, but a close observer could read the words, 'Government: ...rking har... to ...eep ...i..izens... afe.'

Hmmm.

Alonzo, Jacquelyn and Gavin Matthews huddled around a café table sipping coffee after the group session. To close, Dr. Boeder-Mankins had thanked them for attending and hoped they were feeling better by talking things out in the group. Once she bowed to them, the screen went blank, the lights turned off behind the glass, and she faded into the folds of the curtains like the Wizard of Oz.

'What was all that in there?' Gavin asked. 'Sounded like a bunch of psychobabble to me.'

'It was,' Jacquelyn said as she furiously scanned the messages on her AutoCom.

'What was the purpose?'

At last, she turned her arm to silent. 'When people are in strife, they need to find connection and assurance. Dr. Jane's work here is to help us connect and to be assured that we won't be forgotten.'

'What's wrong with that?'

Jacquelyn struggled to put it into words. 'I'm not sure. But I feel slightly uneasy about the whole thing, as if it's a setup.'

'You're not making any sense,' Gavin said as he sipped his coffee. 'This isn't a conspiracy. It can't be.'

Jacquelyn leaned into the middle of the table as if worried someone might overhear them. 'Don't you think it's strange that we've been invited to take part in group therapy when none of us, as far as I know, were brought here for mental health reasons?'

'Maybe they're just wanting people to stay...'

'Safe?' Jacquelyn raised an eyebrow.

'What's wrong with that?'

'Nothing,' she said with voice still lowered. 'There's nothing wrong with safety, but I'm beginning to wonder if the St. Croix's have been given a directive to control the Halos. It wouldn't be the first time a group of people had been tested on.'

'That can't be right, can it?' Gavin turned to Father Lawrence who was following the conversation with interest. 'Padre?'

Lawrence caught Jacquelyn's eye and motioned toward her arm. 'Is that off?'

She nodded.

'Why does that matter?' Gavin asked.

'Let's just say that technology without controls can be a dangerous thing. That AutoCom,' he pointed again, 'is an amazing gadget. So handy, accessible, entertaining. But put into the wrong hands, lots of things could go haywire.'

'Are you saying that Jacquelyn doesn't know what she's doing?'

'No,' Lawrence said slowly, 'but there have always been whispers that mobile technology can be used for monitoring purposes. *That* information is dangerous.'

'What could possibly be dangerous about a bunch of Halos sitting in a café in one of the remote parts of the world having a discussion?'

'All dangerous ideas begin with discussions.'

Gavin's eyes widened. 'What's the danger?' he whispered.

'It started with Dr. Boeder-Mankins throwaway comment about interpreting the picture for us.'

'Yes, I heard you call her on that. Thank you,' Jacquelyn said.

'Was that inappropriate?' Gavin asked.

Lawrence's jaw twitched. 'I don't know yet. But when someone implies that I can't interpret the world around me, and they must show me what I need to see, I'm very aware of how that can be a bad thing.'

'I'm not following yet.'

Lawrence pointed to another table, one situated underneath the skylight, where Wallis Takamoto and Sydney Bellows were sitting. 'Do you see Sydney over there?' He pointed at her, and Gavin nodded. 'What do you think of her sunglasses?'

'Huh? How does that help?'

'Do you have sunglasses?' Lawrence asked Gavin.

'Sure. When I go outside, I don't like to squint.'

'Would you say that sunglasses allow you to see the world as it is, or as you want it to be?'

Gavin thought about that. 'I suppose as I want it to be. Not so painful.'

'So, you buy sunglasses. Tinted lenses.' He paused and sipped. 'Sydney has red-tinted lenses meaning everything she sees in this world is literally rose-colored. But that isn't reality, is it? The world is not rose-colored. In fact, it has an infinite amount of colors which shouldn't be filtered out, but interpreted by our own brains, our own minds to decide what to do with that information.'

'Okay...' Gavin said slowly.

'Now imagine you want to interpret the light, the shadows, the movements and everything good and evil about this reality, but someone shoves a pair of glasses in your hand and says, 'Put these on. Then you won't have to feel the pain anymore.' You take the sunglasses, nice reflective blue ones, that actually tint the world an ocean blue, and prescription, to boot, not necessarily your prescription, but one that this person wants you to *think* you need, and you put them on. Suddenly, you feel cool, you feel calm, you feel as if you are... safe.'

Jacquelyn caught on. 'Not only is someone purposefully giving us sunglasses, but they want us to wear them and see only what they see.'

Father Lawrence smiled at her. 'I think we should be careful about which glasses we're putting on around here.'

'You mean you don't want anyone else interpreting reality for you?' Gavin asked.

'Bingo.'

```
From:  ███████████████████
To:  ████████████████
28 October, 2031
```

Session three incorporated both mental health checks, group conversation and the use of technology to understand subjects' perspectives on current events. ████████████████ made a small verbal faux pas suggesting that she needed to 'interpret' the image for the group which caused at least two subjects, 6 and 10 to question the legitimacy of the session.

Though this was a small hiccup, the group expressed their pleasant surprise at feeling 'safe' and a genuine sense of well-being. When asked about any effects of Halo 29, no serious symptoms were named. The subliminals seem to be working. Suggest the onset of nighttime messaging.

```
Text Intercept
28 October, 2031
13:34
Subject 10 #0512168 to #0590902
```

David - need files regarding acquisitions for domestic priority.

Can do. How are you feeling?

Can't talk now but feeling good. Ready to get back to work.

Maybe you should take a break, you know?

At a Convo? What do you expect me to do? Twiddle?

Read a book.

Very funny.

I'm serious. Stop thinking about work for a while.

I can't. Shareholders won't be happy. Stock prices have already dipped.

Does you no good if you aren't healthy.

I am healthy. Just can't get the green light quite yet.

Whatever you do, take care of yourself.

If I don't, nobody else will. Bye David.

Bye.

```
Social media intercept (BeMe)
Subject 3
28 October, 2031
```

Subject 3 photos and text, filtered out facial imperfections, lighting filter. Video. 14 seconds in room. Post proceeds:

Trapped for a while. Supposedly I have the halo, but not wearing it well. (laughs) Hopefully will be out soon to see you. Message me. #Halobaby #inthedungeon #stupidbrothers

Mayor Gemma Cranmere stared out over the masked faces huddled inside the church hall. Although there were larger spaces to gather, Magnus Falkirk, the Evangelical Church rector, had flung open the doors with a hearty welcome. Restricted to one person every sixteen square feet (unless, of course they were part of the same family), the people spread out across the room. Some, who didn't arrive early enough, were required to stand outside and watch the proceedings on livestream television. These unfortunates were given plastic stackable chairs on which to suffer, while those indoors had at the very least small, padded cushions on their pews.

The front of the church was similar to a movie theater. All resemblances and symbols of traditional church had been removed: no altar, no crosses, no offering baskets. Rector Falkirk believed that this portrayal of faith was much more palatable, less offensive, than previous iterations of church buildings. This contemporary version, scrubbed of suffering, loss, pain and sacrifice, seemed the much safer way into the future.

Magnus Falkirk stood to the side, hands divinely molded in Trinity at his waist, nodding politely to the who's who of town members. Gemma Cranmere's husband, Steve, sat in the middle next to Edgar.

Near the back, Renata Lerner's eyes were darkened by worry. The hubbub about tonight's meeting, a gathering to ensure Herzfeld's future, was troubling to say the least. Once the letter went to the Government, Renata had a sneaking suspicion that things weren't going to necessarily change for the better.

Bridgette caught Renata's eye and waved slightly. Bridgette, too, carried the same concerns. Unlike Renata, Bridgette's livelihood was being threatened by another tourist-less season. Bridgette's family, her husband and two sons, were finding themselves in alternating states of anxiety. Guiltily, Bridgette knew the boys shouldn't be spending so much time online, whether violent video games or pornography (yes, she knew about her teenagers' habits but had been unwilling to confront them) were destabilizing them and their futures. Added to their own mental health issues was their father who spent more time at the Tavern than he did at home. The last few nights, her husband had come home in a drunken stupor ranting about laying siege to Cloud End and dumping Halos into the sea.

Keeping watch over the proceedings was a sombre Igor Kovschenko dressed out in police uniform and a protective facemask. Normally, Igor would have come in civvies, but he'd received a threat that Free Lifers were in the area. One couldn't be too careful with those rabble rousers.

'Thank you, Rector Falkirk, for welcoming us tonight. What an exceptional building to host our discussions.'

'It is a pleasure to have you tonight,' he spread his hands and returned them to their holy position.

Gemma nodded towards the crowd. 'And thank you all for coming. Tonight, will be an informative one, and hopefully we can answer a few questions about what the future might hold.'

Gemma pushed a button on her remote and a three-dimensional picture of Herzfeld appeared behind them. 'This was a picture taken four years ago during summer.' The drone photo showed the town bursting with visitors. Some were at the markets, others in the park. The tavern's parking lot was overflowing with cars. Though not close enough to see faces or hear voices, the picture showed Herzfeld in the blossom of good health.

'Here is a picture from last week.'

The drone photo was taken from the same spot. Herzfeld was essentially empty, a ghost town, lying in the valley between cliffs bisected by a river. The road leading into town was bereft of cars. Everything was dead or dying. 'Up on the cliff, you'll see Cloud End. Is there anything interesting in this picture?'

The audience struggled to understand what Gemma was getting at.

'Let me interpret for you. What you see is the simmering town of Herzfeld, little income, people staying away. Why? Because the Government, in its infinite wisdom, has decided to put a virus processing plant on the cliff, full of people who need to be carefully watched by health professionals, not an older couple and their grandkids. The Government is playing with fire. The Halovirus will send our livelihoods down the toilet. Look!' she laser pointed Cloud End dotting the number of people outdoors.

'Notice how many people are outside. I count eleven, and none of them are wearing masks. Look at Herzfeld. How many do you count outside? I see three and all of them are wearing masks. Stan, you're right here. I can tell by your hair.' The audience laughed through their disposable masks. 'I would guess you hadn't seen many customers that day, and certainly not any without their masks.'

'Wouldn't let them in, even if they showed up.' Polite clapping. 'Gotta keep people safe.'

'It frustrates me to no end that Halos at Cloud End are free range chickens while we're stuck to the chicken coop,' Gemma continued, pressing her advantage.

'What are we going to do?' Edgar asked. He had been primed to ask this question at this exact moment.

'I think it's time to take more assertive action,' Gemma responded with a slight pound on the podium. 'The council believes we have not been listened to. Thus, *we* believe,' she continued to stress the word 'we,' 'that *we* need to send a delegation to speak with the country's leadership to *remind* them,' she continued to emphasize the words with her fist, 'that there are many other lives at stake than just Halos on the hill.'

'Who is going to be in this delegation and what are you going to say?'

Gemma tapped her chest. 'I will go, as well as Rector Falkirk and Selina Lomiller.'

Bridgette caught Renata's eye. The exchange was brief but questioning. Renata tapped a message into her AutoCom. *I'll meet you at the hotel after the assembly.* Bridgette nodded and agreed.

'What will you say?' the concerned citizen pushed.

'In no uncertain terms will this abomination continue. Herzfeld is a sleepy, tourist town in the land between cliffs. Proudly, we have served the region, the country, and the world by offering a place of respite for the weak and weary. If the Government does not listen to us, we'll be withholding our taxes until they bend to our will.'

Bridgette thought Gemma was exaggerating slightly about serving the world, but she was more concerned with the latter half of her statement. 'Withholding taxes?' she said. 'Not only is that illegal, but what good will it do? So they miss out on a few dollars from, how did you put it, 'a sleepy tourist town.' We need something vastly different.'

'The town council disagrees. The Government's primary concern is money in the coffers. We need to rearrange their priorities to put people first.'

Bridgette couldn't stop frowning.

Alonzo sat near the bar where Radiance Morrison, housekeeper and part time barkeep, waited patiently for Alonzo to select something to drink. It was 9:45 p.m. and, according to house rules, the bar was about to close. Alonzo had come down from his room in need of a change of scenery. He was tired of watching television and uninterested in surfing the web.

'I think I'll have a whiskey,' he pointed to the shelf above the bar.

Radiance reached up for the bottle and a snifter and poured a finger's worth of scotch. Alonzo laughed and moved his fingers apart indicating one more shot. Radiance nodded and then poured a little bit more.

'Are you having trouble sleeping?' she asked, her voice muffled by the mask.

'Pardon?'

She touched the voice enhancer on the neck of the suit and repeated her question.

'Yeah, I am.'

'What's the problem?'

'Aw, just the bed... and the room... and the glowing red light above the tv.' He chuckled. 'But it's a very nice place here. I just wish I was on vacation.'

Radiance leaned against the back bar and pondered the man. He was thin, but not skinny, with black hair and a pencil moustache. In the bar's light, his eyes appeared hazel. They were kind and jovial; the eyes of an impish child. Rough hands held the snifter, but they looked strong and steady. Perhaps that was the aura he gave off: Alonzo was a steady man.

'It must be hard,' she said.

'I miss my home, yes, but you know what's really strange? I miss my job.'

'What do you do?'

'I dig graves.'

Radiance choked out a laugh but covered it in case he was serious. He was.

'It sounds morbid, especially when I say I enjoy it.'

'I can't see why?' Radiance said with a smile.

Alonzo grinned as he took another sip. 'You're laughing at me.'

'No, I just don't think I've ever met a gravedigger before. What... how... I mean, how do you do your job?'

'Well, most people buy a plot beforehand, so I can check on the map of the cemetery where they're supposed to be buried. And then I dig.'

'Do your arms get really tired?' Radiance didn't think his arms looked big enough to dig graves, but some people were sneaky strong.

Alonzo laughed again and leaned farther back on his stool. 'I don't use a shovel. Backhoe. Goes a lot faster and a lot less painful. Although,' he held up a finger, 'I did dig a dog's grave one time.'

'Aw, that's sad.'

'Anyway... the digging isn't the best part of my job, it's the stories. Man, I've got some stories.'

'Tell me some. Are they from the funerals?'

Alonzo twirled the amber liquid in his hand. 'Yeah, some of them. But the best ones come from the undertakers. Those guys, I don't know how they keep a straight face sometimes.'

'Now you've got me intrigued.'

'One time,' Alonzo snickered, 'I was standing where I normally do, way off in the back, out of sight, waiting for the service to conclude, and the undertaker finds me. We're standing there in the shade, the coffin is being lowered into the ground, when all the sudden, one of the rollers gets stuck. So, the undertaker's intern, reaches out for the lever but he pulls it the wrong way and one side of the mechanism unlatches and the casket goes crashing to the bottom of the grave – upside down.'

'Oh dear! Did the body come out?'

'No, not at first, but after the mourners got over their shock, the undertaker and his intern run a couple of ropes underneath to lift the casket out. As they haul it up and flip it over, it was only then that they noticed the latches on the coffin were broken and only then did Grandma Gladys make her reappearance to the family. And only then!' he punctuated this emphatically, 'did Grandma Gladys' family get a full view of Grandma Gladys' knickers.'

Radiance burst out laughing. 'Oh, that's awful and awesome at the same time.'

'I know! Nobody realizes that death is funny sometimes.'

At that moment, Father Lawrence pulled up at the stool next to Alonzo. 'Howdy, Padre. How are you doing?'

'Good. And you?'

'Great!' He motioned to Radiance. 'Me and the bartender are just sharing some work stories. Funeral stuff. You've probably had a few of those.'

'Yes,' Lawrence smiled. 'Quite a few. Can't seem to figure out how to get people to stop dying.'

'That's right. You got any funny stories from funerals?'

Lawrence nodded. Dozens of people flashed through his mind. Wonderful, beautiful people who had ceased to be. 'Can I have a beer, please?'

'Yes, Father, but we're closing in five minutes.'

'Can we take our drinks over by the waterfall?' Alonzo asked.

'Yes, of course,' Radiance responded. 'Shall I pour you two, Father?'

'Please, please, enough of the 'father' stuff. While we're here, can we make a pact to simply call me Lawrence?'

Radiance and Alonzo nodded.

She poured two beers for Lawrence and then prepped the bar area for the next day. 'Keep going with the stories. I'm intrigued. And, you can call me Radiance.'

Lawrence continued his story. 'I was riding in a hearse with the funeral director, and we had about a half hour ride to the cemetery, when he told me, 'There was this lady, a cat lady. She was in her 60's, kind of large, fleshy, you know? And one day, she was walking out to the garden, or something, and the cat got tangled between her feet. So she goes down hard, cracks her head on the sidewalk and before her neighbors can get there, she dies of a brain hemorrhage, right there on the sidewalk.'

'Why is that funny?' Radiance dried the last glasses and placed them on the rack.

Lawrence swigged his beer leaving a small ring of foam on his upper lip. He wiped it with a napkin before continuing. 'The family decided that the cat, though unintentionally the cause of their mother's death, should be euthanized and placed in the coffin with the cat-mother.'

'You would have thought they'd killed the cat themselves,' Alonzo said.

'The undertaker said he thought they were secretly happy about their mother's untimely death. She was loaded.'

Radiance sighed and tugged on the chain to shut off the light. The bar was suddenly cast in shadow. What had been a bright, stained-glass room, was transformed into a depressing, echoing place.

'Well, Lawrence, should we adjourn to the other room?'

'Why, yes, Alonzo. I would like that.'

As they moved to the next room, Alonzo stopped and turned. 'Would you like to join us, Radiance?'

She checked the clock on the wall. 'Okay, for a few minutes.'

'Grab yourself a drink,' Alonzo suggested.

'I would love to, but drinking is quite hard with...' she ran her hands over the protective gear.

'Too bad you can't stick a straw through there,' Alonzo said.

'Yes, too bad.'

They walked into the dining area and found a table near the water feature. The only other person in the room was Dorothy Draper. She was reading a book in a small, well-lit alcove near the library. Above them, lights had been dimmed and a few of the brightest stars could be seen through the skylight.

After they sat down, Radiance adjusted her protective gear and leaned back in her chair.

'People don't talk about death much, do they?' Radiance asked.

'Not to you, anyway,' Lawrence responded. 'When people come to a bar, they talk about all sorts of things, I suppose, but not usually death.'

'You got that right. Most people come in to get happy or forget sad. It's the sad ones you gotta watch out for. Alcohol does them no favors.'

Both Lawrence and Alonzo glanced guiltily at their drinks. 'I'm not sad,' Alonzo said.

'Me neither.'

'Good!' Radiance exclaimed. 'Now what can we talk about? No Halovirus, no restrictions, no amateur epidemiology, please!'

Alonzo laughed. 'Tell us about you, Radiance. How did you get that name?'

She shifted in her seat. 'My mother was a closet hippie, but her parents were strict, you know, clean-up-your-plate, make-your-bed-everyday kind of people. Under their intolerant thumbs, my mother wrestled with tradition and structures which provided boundaries. When she left home, she caught on with a vagabond. They traveled through Europe following this pair of famous pianists. Along the adventure, my mother got pregnant. Her vagabond boyfriend left, so she was stuck in Sweden. As the story goes, after my birth, my mother looked at me and said, 'You're the only light left in my life.' So, she named me Radiance.'

'Have you ever met your father?' Lawrence asked.

'No.'

'How did you get here?' Alonzo asked.

'I saw an ad for serving staff near a resort town. I'd worked on visas in other countries, but something about Cloud End appealed to me. I never expected that I'd be doing this during a pandemic with non-tourists wearing an outfit like this.'

'What do you look like in real life?' Alonzo asked.

Lawrence glanced quickly at Alonzo. He'd been wondering the same thing.

'I'm just a girl with hazel eyes and brown hair, some nice cheekbones, and a decent personality, as one boy told me a long time ago. But these outfits wreck my skin. I'm pasty white and feel like a mole. I'd give anything to shed these and go outside for a while.'

'Can't you go outside?'

'I do, sometimes. At night, when the wind is just right and the stars are out, I'll walk over to the cliff and enjoy. But most nights, I'm dog tired and just want to go to bed.'

'What about on your day off?'

She snorted. 'Where am I going to go? We're locked in here just like you. I saw some leaflets somebody put in the mailbox yesterday. 'You are not welcome. Signed, Herzfeld.'

'Wow, that's harsh.'

'The world is full of unwelcoming people. I've grown used to it.'

Alonzo was just about to reply when his words were stopped short by a blood-curdling scream ringing in the atrium.

It sounded as if someone was dying.

II

Throughout the early evening, Jack Walters, the night nurse, had noticed a change in Ms. Wyman's vital signs. Her blood pressure was going through the roof, and she had a fever. After injecting medication into her port, Jack stepped back to study her appearance. Haggard and drawn, her face appeared caved in, as if its supporting columns had crumbled. Even though this woman should have the capacity to recover, Jack wasn't so sure. He woke Dr. Chandruth by calling his emergency phone.

Dr. Chandruth answered the phone groggily. 'Doctor, this is Jack. I hate to call you at this time of night, but I think you need to come down.'

Just as Chandruth agreed and was about to punch off his phone, a scream rang out. The scream was loud enough that he could hear it not only through the phone, but also the muffled ring outside his room in the staff quarters. It was a sound he had heard many times growing up.

Swithin Chandruth grew up in Sri Lanka. Living near the shore, Swithin and his friends would pick through the rocks searching for lost treasure. Sometimes they would find shells or pieces of wood which they used for storytelling. The boys would gather around a fire at night and speak of Muslim pirates or Christian marauders. The shells were used as grenades and the wood made handy swords to beat off the invaders.

On one adventure, Swithin's best friend, Jeewana, broke his leg. The bone was sticking out through his skin, and it made Swithin very afraid, but not so afraid as the other friends. They all ran away while Swithin took care of Jeewana. Swithin did his best. They waited for almost two hours until the medics arrived. By that time, Jeewana had gone into shock, but the paramedics patted Swithin on the head and told him that he'd been a good doctor.

Unfortunately, Jeewana died from an infection in the hospital.

From that moment on, though, Swithin wanted to be a doctor to save people like Jeewana.

And now he was working at Cloud End, a stranger in an uncommonly strange land, where people seemed much more interested in looking after their money than they did their families and friends. Swithin was not prone to making immediate judgements, but when he'd accepted the role at Cloud End, he couldn't help thinking that some of these people might have deserved the virus.

Every time he thought that he chided himself to stay impartial. Except it was so difficult with rich people. Entitled people. Egocentrics.

Thus, Dr. Chandruth treated them as cases, not people. Clinically, he healed them, but he suffered little when they were in pain or sick. His lack of empathy was apparent at times, but in general, Dr. Swithin Chandruth got the job done.

Even with drug addicts.

By the time he opened the doors to the atrium, the din was frightening. Seraphim Wyman was standing in the dining area, hospital gown splayed at the back exposing everything from heels to neck. Her wild eyes scanned the room. Standing opposite her were nurse Walters, Radiance Morrison and three guests, the same ones who had helped carry Seraphim to the infirmary the last time.

With a sudden movement, Seraphim grabbed a serrated steak knife from one of the tables and wheeled on the suited Cloud End staff. Both Jack and Radiance took a few steps backward.

'Jack! What happened?' Chandruth shouted.

'She's out!'

'Yes, I can see that.' The doctor circled in closer to Seraphim who wheeled on the staff and guests. 'Easy, Seraphim. This will pass. We have to get you back into bed.'

'I'm not going back there,' she snarled. 'He's trying to kill me.' Seraphim thrust the knife in Jack's direction.

'Listen to what you are saying, Seraphim. Nurse Walters is here to help. To keep you safe.'

'He's not a nurse! He's a demon!' Unexpectedly, Seraphim rushed the frightened nurse. Jack, unsure of what to do, turned to run but the suit prohibited speed. Within a few steps, she was at his heels staggering through tables, knocking chairs to the side and scattering dishes to the left and right.

Just as she was about to slash him, Radiance caught Seraphim from the side. As they tumbled to the floor, Alonzo and Lawrence joined the fray. With supernatural strength, Seraphim thrashed from side to side.

'Get a hold of that knife!' Chandruth shouted. He looked through Jack's facemask at eyes widened in fear.

'No way! I'm not getting the Halo for the sake of a druggie!' Jack shouted as he backed farther into the corner of the room into the shadows, far away from the danger.

'Put her in a headlock!' a man shouted from above.

'Shut up, Damian,' Sydney yelled at him.

'Why don't you go help them?'

'You're the big tough guy!'

Meanwhile, Seraphim struggled against her real and imagined demons. The withdrawal was ripping her apart, and yet she fought. Fought for her life. For her future. Fought against all the things which were wrong with her world. She slashed and stabbed, foes fell, shadows toppled, and when the last of her drug-induced strength failed, she was left with blood on her hands.

When Seraphim Wyman passed out, Dr. Chandruth cautiously rushed in, avoiding the sharp edge of the knife, and hauled the woman off the other three people.

Alonzo Turner had lacerations across his arm.

Father Lawrence Haskins was bleeding profusely from his abdomen.

And Radiance Morrison's protective gear had been slashed to ribbons. Her face was white with fear.

'Jack! Jack!' Chandruth called out. 'Get over here! This man needs attention!' he pointed at Lawrence who was groaning as his hands covered the hole. Shaken from his reverie, Nurse Walters rushed in, grabbed some cloth napkins and jammed them into to the stab wound.

'Radiance,' Chandruth focussed on her momentarily. 'Are you okay?'

'I'm not hurt,' she whimpered, 'but my suit...' she held out the holes in her sleeves, in her chest and mask. 'I'm going to get sick.'

'We'll deal with that later. Go to your room. I'll find you as soon as I take care of these people.'

Numbly, she nodded and crawled away from the mess. Dr. Chandruth spoke to Alonzo next. 'Can you move?'

'Yes.' His face was wrenched with pain. His forearms would need stitches and his shirt was full of blood.

'Have you been stabbed?'

'I don't know.' He lifted his shirt. The knife had glanced off his ribs and the skin was bleeding.

'That's good. That's good.' Dr. Chandruth helped him to his feet. If you can, find your way to the infirmary. I'll be there as soon as I can to get you bandaged up.' Scanning the watchers above him, Chandruth yelled. 'I need three people. I don't care who you are! Right now!'

Gavin Matthews was the first to run to the stairs, then Chantelle Ingram. Finally, Sam Draper quickly asked Monica Xiao to make sure his kids didn't go anywhere. Monica, thankful not to be going downstairs, stood in front of the Draper's door while he chased after Chantelle and the police officer.

'Jack, you and this man... what's your name?' Gavin told him. 'Gavin, take Seraphim to the infirmary and strap her down. She has to be strapped down. Do you understand, Jack?'

He nodded and left his position when Chantelle took his place providing pressure on Lawrence's stab wound.

'Now...'

'Sam.'

'Sam. I need you to go to the infirmary. In the cabinet above the examination bench, to the right, are bandages. Can you find that?'

Sam's face blanched. 'Can you handle blood?'

'I guess I'll have to after tonight.' He stared down at Lawrence who was lying in a puddle of it.

'Good. Now, go.'

Dashing off, passing Gavin, Jack and Chantelle, Sam hurried into the infirmary.

Kneeling beside Chantelle, Dr. Chandruth looked into her eyes. 'You're a brave woman.'

'It's not my first rodeo.' Her face was a mask of fear and anger.

'This man needs surgery, and we shouldn't do it here. I need to call the hospital in Herzfeld. Can you handle this while I talk to them?'

'Do it,' Chantelle said while grabbing another cloth from the table to her right and then applying more pressure. When she looked up, she saw the other guests, (even the politician) in their lofty heights. Chantelle had the odd feeling that she was in surgery theater. But she was angry, too.

'COWARDS!' she shouted upwards, her voice reverberating in the rafters. 'YOU SHOULD BE ASHAMED OF YOURSELVES!'

Slowly, one by one, they turned back from their supervisory positions and went back to their rooms. Winston Faraday III was the first, and he was already on his AutoCom by the time he reached the door.

Chantelle felt a presence by her side. Dorothy Draper.

'How can I help?'

'I don't know,' Chantelle said testily. 'Talk to him, or something. Tell him he's not going to die. That's what they do in the movies, right?'

Dorothy nodded and situated herself on her knees by Lawrence's head. His eyes were half closed, and he looked pale. 'I think you're going to be all right,' she said unsurely. 'Actually, I don't know if that's true, but believe it, if it helps.'

'Wow, nice work,' Chantelle spoke sarcastically.

'I've never done this before,' Dorothy bit back. She tucked some stray, bleached blond hair behind her ear.

'Not surprising.'

'And I suppose you've been around stabbings all the time?'

Chantelle's piercing look was enough to stop the question from continuing. 'Say something a little more encouraging. Tell him a story. Get his mind off the pain.'

'A story? A story! Are you kidding?'

'You wanted to know what you could do, so tell a story.'

Dorothy took a deep, shuddering breath. 'Once upon a time... there were three bears.'

'Oh, for heaven's sake!' Chantelle groaned.

'I don't know any frickin' stories except children's stories, okay? I'm surrounded by kids all the time. That's what they like.'

'Describe your best day ever, or something like that. Something real.'

'Why don't you do it?' Dorothy pleaded.

'Would you like to hold the tablecloth over his stab wound?' Chantelle asked.

Dorothy blanched. 'No, I'll... I'll think of something. Best day ever...' Her thoughts went backwards. So many to choose from. What about the time...

'Hurry up, woman!'

Dorothy took a deep breath. 'One time, a long time ago, a man wore a blue suit. He was handsome in an entirely average kind of way, and he asked a girl out. She was plain and lonely, not at home in the ways of the world. Naïve, would be the best way to put it.'

As Chantelle listened to the story, she coveted this woman and her background. If only Chantelle could have been plain and lonely, maybe naïve.

Dr. Chandruth rushed up to them again. Dorothy breathed a sigh of relief. 'Thank God,' she muttered.

'The ambulance is on its way.' He knelt next to the three of them. 'Hold on, Lawrence. Help is on the way.'

If Edgar Post wouldn't have had an upset stomach that night, many things might have turned out differently. But as it was, he got up for a teaspoon of Milk of Magnesia and heard the police scanner go off in his living room. Because Edgar was morbidly interested in accidents, domestics and unfortunate deaths, he left his scanner on during the night.

On the night Seraphim Wyman went crazy, Edgar heard about the stab wounds and where the ambulance was headed almost before the ambulance drivers did. Knowing full well that any entry into Cloud End, and more importantly, any import to Herzfeld could mean the end of the town, Edgar quickly rang Steve. 'Did you hear?'

'What?' Steve's voice was annoyed, and slightly slurred. He'd been drinking.

'The police scanner.' Edgar put the phone on speaker and wandered over to the window which had a bird's eye view of the Herzfeld hospital. The ambulance had not left yet. Maybe the emergency personnel were sleeping.

'I'm not into that like you.'

'Well, you should be. There's an ambulance heading out soon.'

'So?'

'It's going to Cloud End. Someone got stabbed.

'What? Stabbed?'

'The inmates must be getting restless. And if one of those disease infested Halos gets taken to the hospital, we could all be done for. That's what you said.'

Steve Cranmere's slightly inebriated mind whirled furiously.

'Steve.'

'I'm thinking.'

'What are we going to do?'

'Get your boots on. I'll be at your house in five minutes.'

Edgar smiled. Tonight was going to be more exciting than he thought.

Steve arrived in four minutes. Knocking was unnecessary as Edgar was already on the porch waiting for him. Edgar had not changed out of his pajamas but simply donned work boots and a stocking cap. As Steve's headlights illuminated him, he shielded his eyes. 'Do I need a mask?' he shouted.

'Bring one just in case.'

Edgar hurried down the steps to the passenger door and climbed in. Steve's hands gripped the steering wheel tight as he backed out of the driveway quickly.

'Have you decided what we're going to do?' Edgar asked.

Steve's face was dimly lit by the dashboard lights. There was a wild look in his eyes. 'Some of this is going to have to be improvised.'

'Where are we going?'

Steve's face hardened. 'Cloud End.'

'Are you crazy! We'll get the Halo.'

'Not *inside* Cloud End, stupid. Just to the gate. When the ambulance shows up, we'll convince them to turn around.'

'How will we do that?'

'Not sure yet.'

'What if they don't?'

Steve turned to his partner. 'They will. They have to.'

Screaming through the streets of Herzfeld, Steve Cranmere raced against the sound and sight of the ambulance. To his right, Steve saw the blue and red lights reflecting off buildings. *Just a few more seconds.* Turning left, they saw the gate to Cloud End Road.

It was open.

Opening the engine up, Steve pushed his pickup to sixty miles an hour. They had twenty seconds. Once at the entrance to Cloud End, Steve's brakes tossed up gravel and dust and he pulled to a stop.

'Get out!' Steve shouted as he put the car in park and popped the hood.

'What are we doing?' Edgar was grinning madly.

'They can't get through if there's a broken-down car.'

'Good thinking.'

Edgar went around to the front of the car and lifted the hood. Reaching in, he yanked on a battery cable.

'Hurry!' Steve shouted.

'I'm trying.' Finally, the cable came off in his hand.

With only seconds to spare.

The ambulance suddenly made an appearance. As the bright flashing lights swirled in their faces, the ambulance driver honked his horn. Steve waved him down and walked to the driver's window.

'We're broken down!'

'You need to move that truck, now!'

'I can't. I can't. It's stalled. I tried everything.'

The paramedics looked at each other and hurried from their seats toward the stalled pickup. 'Is it a manual?'

'No, unfortunately,' Steve said.

The medicos stared at each other. 'We need to get a tow truck up here now!'

'What's going on? What's happening up at Cloud End?'

Suspiciously, the paramedic's eyes narrowed. 'What are you guys doing out here anyway? Why is your truck stopped?'

Steve had not thought about his alibi. 'We... uh...'

Edgar jumped in. 'We're going for a walk.'

'At this time of night?'

Edgar pointed to the stars. 'Beautiful, isn't it?' he responded lamely.

'Tom, use the radio and call that tow truck out here. We have to get there as fast as possible before...' He stopped.

'Is someone dying up there?'

'You know that's none of your business, Steve.'

'You also know, Albert, that if you go up there, you put yourself and everyone else in this town in danger.'

The paramedic's eyes narrowed. 'It's our job. We have to go.'

'No. No you don't. Just call up there and say that the road is impassable.'

The proposition sounded entirely reasonable and good. For Albert, it was a good excuse. He did not want to enter the Convo, nor did he want to put his community at risk. Certainly, they had a doctor up there, and he should be able to...

The radio squawked. 'Unit 2, have you made contact yet?'

Tom raced for the radio. 'No. There's a car blocking the path. We can't get there.'

Silence. 'Unit 2, repeat.'

114

'It's impossible. Someone has blocked the path with a vehicle and we can't get up there.'

'Copy. Please hold.'

After a moment, dispatch came over the radio again. 'Unit 2, return to base. Helicopter is on its way. Over.'

Steve and Edgar hadn't thought about that. 'Copy that. Returning to base. Over.'

Tom and Albert, relieved and frustrated, turned back to the ambulance. Removing their protective hoods, Albert stared down Steve Cranmere. 'Be careful, Steve. You're playing with fire.'

'I'm only looking out for the greater good of the town. We need to keep Herzfeldians safe.'

Moments later the ambulance left, lights off, like a whipped dog running from a fight. Edgar watched them go, then asked, 'What are we going to do about the helicopter?'

Steve returned to his pickup and pulled an object from it. 'Sacrifices need to be made. Everybody knows that.' Cranmere opened a box from the back seat of his pickup and inserted five rounds of ammunition into his rifle.

12

When Swithin Chandruth heard the beating rotors
approaching Cloud End, he sucked in a lungful of relief. Thankfully, they'd
staunched the flow from the priest's wound, but he still had lost a lot of
blood. A pillow had been brought from his room and placed under his head,
but the pain was unbearable for him. After a brief examination, it wouldn't
have surprised Chandruth if his intestines had been compromised. Worst
case scenario, a kidney, too. Either way, the man was in critical shape and
likely needed surgery very soon.

The helicopter would come from the Government hospital thirty
miles away. By the time the flight left, it would take fifteen minutes to get
here. Chandruth had been furious after finding out that the ambulance
couldn't make it up the path because of a broken-down vehicle.

Thirteen minutes later, the helicopter would be coming over the cliff
towards Cloud End. He checked his AutoCom. 10:42.

At 10:43, Chandruth heard something strange. Like firecrackers. Five
in rapid succession. Chandruth thought they sounded very much like
gunshots. From his youthful time in Sri Lanka, he'd heard them before, but
not here at Cloud End. Suddenly, the helicopter's motor changed, and it
didn't sound like it was landing. It sounded like it was turning away.

Chandruth ran to the window and saw the lights of the helicopter
spinning madly. Struggling to maintain altitude, the helicopter lurched to
the left. Swithin Chandruth watched in horror as the rescue helicopter
faltered below the cliff's horizon and then, moments later, he felt the sonic
thud of an explosion.

The helicopter had crashed.

He turned his eyes towards the south, towards the road. Strangely,
Chandruth thought he saw two forms fleeing, but it could have been
anything: animals, shadows, his imagination.

But that didn't matter now.

Swithin Chandruth was going to have to do something he hadn't
done since his residency.

Emergency surgery.

A Convalescent Center was not a great place to do it.

While Cloud End's doctor prepped for the most dangerous surgery of his professional career, and Igor Kovschenko was rushing madly to the helicopter crash site, Senator Winston Faraday III was frantically tapping into his arm, communicating with the one person who had influence. I NEED HELP!

When Isolde read Winston's message, a more than small part of her smirked. Not that she believed in Karma, but certainly in this case, Winston was reaping some of what he had sown. Over their years together, their relationship existed in the shadows of the Government. The partnership had been useful for both sides. Isolde and Winston had made friends and enemies, both sets carried markers of debts to be paid.

Now, Winston was calling in some of them.

She answered on the third ring, just to make him sweat. 'Are you having a rough night, Winnie?'

'You have no idea. I could probably outlast the food and the conversation, the perpetual handwringing and such, but tonight... whoever had the brilliant idea of putting a drug addict here should be shot.'

'So you *are* at the Convo.' Isolde studied her fingertips with a smile.

Winston suddenly realized the trap that he'd just walked into. 'Okay, yes, I'm at the Convalescent Center. And if you ever wanted to know what the seventh circle of hell is like, this is it. The druggie went crazy and attacked the staff and guests with a knife. I think one of them might die. A murder! I was witness to, at the very least, an attempted murder!'

'Did you try to help? Did you step in?'

'I wanted to,' Winston said, 'but I wasn't quick enough. Some of the others had already intervened. The risk would not be worth it.'

Isolde rolled her eyes. 'And the risk to those people. Those commoners?' Her sarcasm was only thinly veiled.

117

'This is not the time to get into a moralizing 'what-if,' Isolde. Now, I need you to do something for me.'

'It's 11:00 at night. I'm not going to...'

'Listen to me,' Winston's voice tightened. 'Speak with Senator Forsythe, as soon as possible. Call him at 5:00 in the morning. He's an early riser. Explain to him what's happening out here. Do what you do best – exaggerate.'

'I don't exag...'

'Isolde, please.'

Pouting, Isolde laid back in the bed. 'What do you want me to say?'

'Tell him... tell him that I'd be willing to be transferred to another Convalescent Centre. It's not as if I'm shirking my moral duty or anything, but my life is at risk here!'

'Transfer... shirking moral duty... life at risk. Got it.'

'Thank you, my friend. When I get out of here, out of any Convo, I'll be taking you out for a night on the town. No expense is too much.'

She smiled. 'I'll look forward to that.'

'Now, contact Quentin as soon as possible.'

'I will.' She hung up.

Taking a long, luxurious breath and stretching her hands high above her head, Isolde Howard rolled to her right and nudged the sleeping form next to her.

'Quentin, I have a message from Winston Faraday III. He wants me to let you know as soon as possible.'

As the call came from dispatch, Tom glanced at his partner Albert. His jaw clenched. If only Steve Cranmere's pickup had not been jacked in the gate, none of this would have happened. They could have been back to the hospital saving a man's life rather than racing back to a crash site.

Jumping back in the ambulance, Tom and Albert flipped on the lights. Whipping the steering wheel to the left, they careened back out onto the road and tore back to the road to Cloud End.

'Do you have a weird feeling about this?' Albert asked.

'Yeah. Yeah I do.'

'Those guys couldn't have caused the crash, could they?' Albert rubbed his head with his gloved hand.

'I can't see how.'

'But it's so...'

'Yeah.'

Taking one more left, they raced up the last road until they saw the Cloud End gate in the distance.

Steve Cranmere's pickup was no longer there.

'What the...'

Tom pulled the ambulance up short, tires crunching the gravel. 'Quick, go open the gate.'

Albert leapt from the vehicle and raced to the gate. The flashing lights created an eerie scene. Albert's orange suit was a mobile hazard sign. He stopped at the gate and shook his head. Tom leaned his head out the window.

'What is it?'

'It's locked!'

'What kind of lock?'

'What difference does that make? We can't get through!'

Tom pondered what their next move would be until he saw headlights behind them. It was Igor's police car.

Hopping out from the driver's side, Tom ran back to Igor who was stepping out of the car. 'Igor! Get your bolt cutters. The gate is locked.'

'Just slow down, Tom. We can't go trespassing on Government property. Especially as it's... you know... a special circumstance.'

'Igor! A helicopter crashed over there. We have to move fast.'

'I understand that,' Igor put his hands on his hips, 'but there are things up there that...'

'Those helicopter pilots may have given up their lives to try to save one of them,' Tom pointed at Cloud End. 'We need to help if we can.'

Sighing, Igor nodded slowly and opened the trunk of his police car. Retrieving the bolt cutters, he walked casually to the gate, and after studying the lock, cut it. Tom and Albert ran back to the ambulance and waited with impatience while Igor pulled the gate back.

Stepping on the accelerator, Tom felt a casual glee that some gravel sprayed up in Igor's face.

As the ambulance tore up the drive, Tom could see in the distant lights illuminating Cloud End. Spotlights glowed on the sign, and others lit the lower half of the siding. It seemed like a glowering troll pulling itself from the ground. About two hundred yards along the road, Tom veered right and began to drive across the grassy field towards the cliff.

There was smoke rising from below and wafting out over the field.

'You see the fence, right?' Albert asked.

'I see it.'

Stopping just short of the fence, Tom and Albert jumped from the cab and strode quickly to the fence.

'Are you going to look, or am I?' Albert said.

'I'll go. Update dispatch and tell them that the chopper is wrecked at the base of the cliff.'

'Right.'

Tom began to shed his protective suit.

'What are you doing?'

'I can't crawl over the fence in this. I'm likely to get it snagged and I'll stumble over to join the chopper.'

'But what about...' Albert jerked his finger toward Cloud End.

'I'd rather catch the Halovirus than fall that far into the burning wreckage.'

'Okay. Good thought.'

Once free of his protective gear, Tom climbed the fence gingerly and stepped over. The cliff, less than ten feet beyond the fence, was disorienting. Where the land gave up, the mesmerizing night sky started. Dropping to his hands and knees, Tom crawled to the edge. Just as he reached it, his hand slipped over.

Almost miraculously, his right shoulder caught on the edge of the cliff keeping him from going over. Adrenaline pumping, heart racing, Tom inched his head out.

No one could have survived that kind of wreck.

Jack and Kylie stood nervously beside Dr. Chandruth.

The priest was unconscious. Dr. Chandruth had consulted the internet just to make sure of the dosage for the anesthesia. It had been a long time. A very long time. The patient's face and body were covered by a makeshift sheet leaving only the abdomen exposed where the ghastly wound still suppurated.

'Okay, people, it's all hands-on deck. Let's go.'

While Jack and Kylie assisted, Dr. Chandruth probed the wound layer by layer. As he continued going deeper, he held his breath. This was the difficult part. Had the knife penetrated the peritoneum, the membranous tissue that surrounds the organs?

As his fingers wandered along the peritoneum, Chandruth felt a huge sense of relief.

'Peritoneum unscathed,' he said.

Jack and Kylie smiled behind their masks. 'Excellent,' Kylie said.

'Let's get him stitched up and see if we can find a blood donor in our midst.'

Just as they were about to begin stitching, there was a commotion in the foyer. Shouting. Then the door to the infirmary burst open and two hazmatted figures appeared.

'Who are you?' Chandruth asked.

'We're the paramedics.'

'A bit too late now, isn't it?' The doctor went back to stitching the patient up.

'There were obstacles to getting here.'

'Well, everything is under control. We just need some blood.'

121

'Type?'

'O negative? Did you bring any with you?'

'Yes,' Tom responded. 'Dispatch sent us with blood because of the stabbing.'

'Go get it.'

Albert walked briskly from the room and returned with a cooler.

Dr. Chandruth finished stitching and moved to the sink where he removed his rubber gloves and began to scrub his hands vigorously with soap and water. To be working with the Halo patient's blood – that had been a threat to his own life. As he washed, he turned his attention to the paramedic. 'What took you so long?'

'There was a car broken down in front of the gate.'

'Are you serious?'

'Yes. So, dispatch sent for a helicopter.' Tom's eyes darkened. 'Do you know what happened?'

Swithin thought about the sharp retorts and then the explosion. It didn't make any sense. 'The helicopter crashed?'

'That's right. No survivors.'

'Rescue on its way?'

'A boat has been sent, but in these conditions, it will be almost impossible. They may have to wait until morning.'

'That's too late,' Chandruth said.

'It was already too late.'

'What are you going to do now?' Chandruth moved back to where Kylie was beginning to administer blood through an IV.

'If you want, we can take the patient back with us to the hospital.'

A long pause ensued. 'Do you believe it's worth the risk?'

Tom's similarly long pause was telling. 'Is the patient stable?'

'At this point, yes. We'll give him a tetanus shot and monitor vitals, but I think he's lucked out.'

'What happened here?'

Jack jumped in. 'A druggie. She ran into the...'

12

'Jack,' Chandruth warned, 'the others are here.' He motioned to the other room where Alonzo was stationed.

'Okay,' Tom said with finality, 'we'll return to the hospital.'

'You'll have to sanitize your suits,' Chandruth warned.

'We have been doing this for a while,' Tom responded testily and motioned for Albert to follow him.

```
VIDEO FEED HIJACK - CE
29 October 2031
22:10-22:17
```

```
Emergency Minutes Joint Pandemic Committee
29 October, 2031
23:04-23:43
```

████████████, █████████████████████, ████████

Attendance: ██████████████, ████████, ██████████████████
████████, ███ ████████████████████████
████████,

██████████ enquired what had occurred. ████████████████████
informed the committee of the violent attack by subject 13. Subject 6
was seriously injured, in need of hospitalization and possible
emergency surgery. Subject 11 required stitches but does not need
hospitalization.

Unfortunately, one of the CECC staff members, ████████████████ was
injured in the stabbing. Her protective gear was torn. A red light will
appear on her Halo Detector.

████████████████ cautioned the group about hasty reactions. ████████
████████ was angry and expressed a concern about aborting Project Green
Light.

Subsequent to the video footage, a helicopter from the Capitol arrived
on scene but crashed near the landing site. Reasons for crash unknown.
Rescue operation unsuccessful. Recovery will take place in days.
████████████████ has asked for a full report on both the stabbing and
the crash. Results will be available for next joint meeting.

Encoded message #9083424
30 October, 2031
01:14

Government device sent: CVH4580387

Government device received: SRC9022289

Be advised, situation at CECC is spiraling out of control. The stabbing
and emergency situation has heightened the anxiety in both subjects and
staff. If ███████████████ cannot control the situation, suggest more
drastic measures.

Encoded message #9083428
30 October, 2031
01:19

Government device sent: SRC9022289

Government device received: CVH4580387

Have notified the committee. Recommendations will come soon. Watch and
record. Take precautions. Will inform you when and if changes to the
project need to be modified.

13

Director Reed-Conway lifted her coat collar to keep the wind from her neck. As she sat on the bench in the cold sunshine, hungry pigeons flitted and scrabbled on the cement in front of her.

That morning, just after six, ten minutes after her first cup of coffee, her AutoCom buzzed. Though not a rare thing, the feeling was still unwelcome. She was constantly on guard, prepared for anything, but she knew that this perpetual state of heightened awareness was taking a toll on her health. One of these decades she'd have to take a vacation. Maybe she'd even turn her AutoCom off. But probably not.

The message was from Senator Forsythe.

Today. Front of Senate chambers. 2:00.

Cryptic, yes, but it wasn't a shock to receive the message. Although everything about Project Green Light started well, there was no overcoming the human element. Ever. Humans reacted differently to stress and trauma, and their susceptibilities to suggestion had as much to do with their makeup as their setting. It was never a guarantee that Green Light would work. It had only been two weeks. There was much more to do.

During her tenure as Intelligence Director, Reed-Conway thought she had seen it all. From wars to riots, uprising to espionage, Stella believed she was prepared for anything. Unfortunately, pandemics were an entirely different kettle of fish.

When Allan Membree approached her with the original plan, it was intended to take place in a psychiatric ward. Then, when the Halovirus reared its beautiful head, new plans were made with mostly-sane people.

As the country followed the Convos with morbid curiosity, with something akin to entertainment, most attention was focused on the Convos near cities. Cloud End was the perfect hiding place.

Almost stereotypical of a Hollywood spy movie, Allan Membree sat on the bench next to the Intelligence Director. In his hands he held a bag of breadcrumbs, and he strew them at his feet where the pigeons suddenly flocked.

13

'Is your AutoCom disabled?' he asked.

'Yes. Yours?'

'I rarely have it on anymore. In fact, I was thinking of getting rid of it,' he grinned ruefully.

'I had that same thought.'

They were quiet while Senator Membree continued to throw crumbs. 'Amazing birds,' he said after the silence was up.

'Pigeons?'

'Of course.'

'What's so amazing about them?' she asked.

'They're quick and smart. They watch for the perfect time to dart in. They can fly a long way from their home and return at any time from anywhere.'

'Analogy?' Stella reached her hand out for a few crumbs which he gave her. She watched as the birds' heads bobbed and weaved, their happy cooing, raucous.

'One of these days, we might have to fly home, back to the way things used to be.'

Alarmed, she turned to him. 'What are you getting at?'

'Governments make mistakes, this one not excluded.'

'Are you saying Green Light is a mistake?'

'No, that's not what I'm saying. Not yet. But we should be ready for the eventuality. If this operation goes awry, I will have your back, that's all I'm saying.'

Warily, Stella turned back to the birds. 'What happened at Cloud End?'

'An incident. Not entirely unexpected. That's what happens with addicts.' She waited for him to fill in the blanks. 'She stabbed a few other Halos, one more severely than the others.'

'Which one?'

'The priest.'

She smiled and squinted ahead. 'At least it wasn't a kid.'

'At least. I'm not sure we could have survived the PR from that.'

'Does the press know?'

He shook his head. 'Not yet. We love our violence, you know. Makes for good headlines.'

'Can they connect anything to Green Light?'

'Not that I know of, but we've got a window of deniability. And, perhaps, we could move to another Convo.'

Startled, she turned again. 'What would we do with Cloud End, then?'

'There are contingencies.'

Suddenly feeling out of control in a dangerous place, out of the loop, she needed to be back in. Intelligence Directors should not be without intelligence. 'Which are?'

'Let's just say we have two people inside Cloud End giving us intel regarding what's really going on.'

'Two?' she was shocked. She knew about the psychologist, but who was the other?

'Dr. Boeder-Mankins seems to think the subjects will be pliable within the next few weeks, but the other, not so sure.'

'Who is it?'

Senator Membree scrunched up his paper bag. 'It's better if you don't know. Deniability, remember?'

Angered, Director Reed-Conway pointed a finger at his face. 'Take care of this, Senator Membree. There's no Convalescent Center in hell for people like you.'

He laughed ruefully and walked away.

The white rat nosed in and around the room poking and prodding for bits of food. Although Oswald fed it well, the rat never seemed content.

'Does that thing have any diseases?' Pasqual asked.

'Probably got rabies,' Oswald said with a laugh.

'Or Coronavirus?'

13

'Maybe even syphilis..." Oswald grabbed the rat. It squeaked as he cuddled it in his arms.

'What's syphilis?'

Oswald shrugged. 'Beats me.'

Pasqual wandered around Oswald's room. As soon as they entered, Os took off his protective gear. The two boys, roughly the same age, had developed a steady friendship in the two weeks since the Drapers arrival at Cloud End. While Titus joined them occasionally, Gina and McKayla had taken to spending more time away from the boys. This was met with great joy from both sides.

'When do you think we're going to get out of here?' Pasqual asked.

'I hope not for a long time.'

'Yeah, me too.'

'You don't want to go home?'

Pasqual shrugged. 'I guess I like my house, and it would be nice to have my toys, but it was no fun to do school online by myself. At least here, you and me can sit in the same room and ignore the teacher together.'

Os laughed. 'It's kind of stupid that they expect us to learn anything, especially when the teachers aren't even there to answer questions.'

'I know.'

'Too bad we can't go back to real school. At least there, we can play outside, and run around and stuff.'

'We can do that here, you know?' Os said.

'But you're supposed to wear your stupid gear.'

Os rolled his eyes. 'Only until they can't see us.'

'Do you think you're going to catch the Halo, like us, because you're not wearing your suit?'

'Who cares,' Oswald replied and handed the rat over to Pasqual.

'Do you want to go outside and run around? Let's go to the fence. Maybe we can even see the helicopter wreckage!'

Oswald nodded. 'Maybe we'll see some dead bodies.'

'Cool.'

It had taken a day for the Halo Detector to be installed in Radiance Morrison's room. Because she'd been a close contact, the St. Croix's had no choice but to move her into the hotel, into her own private room on the lower floor, for two weeks. If the little green light stayed on, she'd have no worries.

Carl and Nancy watched her sympathetically as the device was installed high in the corner of her room. Although she'd been in these rooms many times, never had she assumed she'd be there without her protective gear. And yet here she was, hating her colleagues' pitying looks, reclining fearfully in an uncomfortable green chair, staring out the window towards Herzfeld.

'Okay, Radiance, everything's set. It will take about half an hour to get a full reading.' Carl tapped the box. 'Let's hope it stays green.'

'Let's hope,' she mumbled.

'I'd give you a hug if I could,' Nancy said.

'Don't worry. I'll be back to work as soon as I can.'

'Just stay healthy.'

During the interminable time of waiting, waiting, waiting, hoping for a negative result so she could get back to her life, Radiance passed the time on her phone scanning her social media. She was shocked by how many ads had appeared. Each one showed how well the Government was dealing with the crisis. When she checked international news, there wasn't much out there. It seemed like the world was just getting on with life. Hopefully it would be the same here.

Every ten seconds, her eyes jerked up towards the box. Each time she saw the green, she breathed a sigh of relief. Maybe the drug addict's attack hadn't been enough to let the virus into her suit? Maybe the other guests were nearing the end of their infection? Maybe...

She looked up.

Red eye.

Damn.

As the autumn colors transformed the valley into a cratered blanket of oranges, reds and browns, the mood at Cloud End was similarly changed. Though the guests wanted to return home, the general sense was one of contentedness, not resignation. Genuine friendships began to form, and residents spent more and more time outside their rooms to gather in the atrium or throw open the door for chilly walks outdoors. Books were splayed open in laps as friends walked by. Knowing that they were all in the same, inescapable boat, they escaped what could have been tedium by understanding their neighbors. The differences in backgrounds seemed to be the icing on the cake rather than the wedge separating them. For the first time in years, many felt a sense of restful peace. When the next group session occurred, almost all Cloud End residents attended.

They bustled through the door, two or three at a time, like entering the safety of the ark as the floods rose outside. Laughter, notes of hilarity, a slap on the back, physical contact, which was surprising at first, but welcomed later – it almost felt like a new world had been revealed.

Even though the St. Croix's did not attend the sessions, they were pleased to watch Wallis and Dorothy speaking quietly as they stood near the entrance of the theater. Monica and Damian, beyond Sydney's baleful gaze, chatted animatedly. The children, though, refrained from entering. The boys dashed through the atrium dodging tables and avoiding arrows and bullets from their imaginary war. The girls sat by the waterfall, side by side, staring into their phones. As Claire and Donald turned, the last ones to enter the room were Alonzo and Chantelle.

Alonzo had recovered nicely from his cuts. Only needing stitches and recovery time, he was up and available for conversation and beer at any time of day. He'd really taken to Sam, Chantelle and Gavin, the same ones who had helped on that fateful night. Daily, he visited Lawrence who was in the latter stages of recovery. The dissolvable stitches had almost disappeared.

Seraphim Wyman, once out of the deepest hell of her withdrawals, had apologized to everyone. All but Radiance accepted the apology. When the session began, Seraphim sat in the back row of the theater by herself. Dorothy Draper had asked her if she needed company, but she rejected it.

The lights came on again and Dr. Boeder Mankins appeared behind her traditional glass wall. 'Good morning, everyone? How are we feeling?'

Strangely, most everyone felt relatively calm. Relaxed. Monica reported that they'd been socializing. A few played cards, or games; some read books or watched movies. It was almost as if they were on vacation.

If one were to ask Gavin Matthews, he would have been honest in appreciating the time away from all the anger directed at the police over the last years. In here, at Cloud End, he was just another person. He was quite happy that there weren't fights, or thefts, or rapes, and thank God there hadn't been any more attempted murders.

Damian and Sydney had called a ceasefire on their marital war. Even though they didn't spend any time together (Damian spent more time with Monica than anyone else), at least there had been no more screaming.

As for Chantelle Ingram, this cloistered space had been perfect for her streetwalking soul. Even though she suffered from panic attacks and a constant sense of displacement, she was happy to close her door at night and not hear the inevitable knocks, the desperate wanting to get in.

'I'm feeling really good today!' Monica finished.

Jane nodded. 'And everyone else?'

'Yeah, me too,' Alonzo agreed. 'It's weird. After the... you know... what happened that one night, it seems like things have calmed down now.'

Seraphim sank lower in her seat.

'My family is doing well,' Dorothy said. 'Our kids have made friends; they're doing their schoolwork...'

'Kind of,' Sam's interjection brought laughter.

'... and it feels like we've found a rhythm of life. Don't tell this to anyone, but I think the Government has figured out how to take care of people,' Dorothy said.

More laughter.

'That's very interesting, Dorothy.' She glanced in Radiance's direction. 'And you?'

Radiance did not answer. She huddled in her chair, arms crossed. Alonzo had tried to reach out to her earlier in the week, but she was in no mood. Now that she had the virus, she scowled incessantly, and her once bright mood had turned sour.

'Today,' Dr. Boeder-Mankins continued, 'I'd like to return to something we started a few weeks ago, some pictures of world events. Has anyone been checking out news sources?' All hands raised. 'That's good. Help me translate this outer world news to our inner world here.' A photo of the front page of the Post appeared on the large screen behind her. A specific news article had been enlarged.

(Reuters)

Even as global cases of the Halovirus increase, National Health Organizations continue to update the media on successes. Though many original cases remain, some Convalescent Centers are sending people home already.

A photo had been inserted in the middle of the article. A smiling couple, bags in hand, waving to the masked photographers as they were released from their captivity. In the background, a Governmental car waited to take them home.

While still in the early stages, these successes show the Government's solution to combat this deadly disease is working. Across the board, politicians have received public acclaim for their handling of both restrictions and individual cases of the Halovirus.

'Well, what do you think?'

'Sounds like things are looking up?' Sydney said. 'We might be able to go home soon.'

'Yes,' Monica's voice sounded despondent.

'What's wrong, Monica?' Jane asked.

'Nothing... well, it's just... this has been such a nice change. And the people here have been great. I miss my family and all, but another few weeks might be nice.' Others who were feeling the same way looked around guiltily.

'We're not there yet,' Gavin responded loudly enough for everyone to hear. 'Until that red turns to green, we're still stuck,' he said with a smile.

At that point, Radiance stood and pushed past a few legs out into the aisle and from the room. She covered her mouth and her tears as she left.

'Poor thing,' Monica said.

Dr. Boeder-Mankins refocused them. 'Now, back to the newspaper article. What conclusions can you draw?'

'Sounds like everything is going well! People are safe.' Dorothy's voice rang out.

A smile played and disappeared quickly on the psychologist's lips. 'Anyone else.'

Suddenly, Alonzo frowned. He thought of Lawrence and the last time they'd been in this place, doing this very thing. He scanned the article, and then the pictures. Suddenly, his eyes alit on another small phrase in the corner of the newspaper that read, *The Government keeps people safe.* It was all but hidden, somewhat bleary, but he could see it. Lawrence would have said that the coincidence was too large. What was it about those two words: Government and safe?

A worm of suspicion wriggled in the back of Alonzo's mind and he tucked it away for another discussion with Lawrence. He liked the feeling of safety here at Cloud End, but something wasn't adding up.

'I'm so glad that we're doing well,' Jane said. 'Keep up the good work, everyone, and we'll see you next time.'

As the stage lights turned off and Dr. Boeder-Mankins retreated into the shadows again, Damian yelled out, 'Who's up for drinks?' A round of laughter and hands in the air greeted him. Although it was only 11:00 in the morning, they were quite happy to have the happiest hour in the safety of Cloud End.

```
CECC Server Activity Analyzation
1 November, 2031
07:30 - 22:30
```

Subject 1
        38 minutes sports app, 64 minutes social media, 32   minutes Fox
        News, 133 minutes YouTube
Subject 2
        74 minutes social media, 83 minutes shopping sites
Subject 3
        323 minutes BeMe, 134 minutes PhotoBend
Subject 4
        186 minutes Minecraft
Subject 5
        0
Subject 6
        45 minutes Bible Gateway
Subject 7
        38 minutes social messaging
Subject 8
        97 minutes sports websites, 45 minutes sports gambling
Subject 9
        246 minutes social media, 108 minutes PhotoBend
Subject 10
        440 minutes Archer business
Subject 11
        0
Subject 12
        153 minutes sports, 48 minutes pornography, 65 minutes social
        media
Subject 13
        0
Subject 14
        244 minutes news, 87 minutes social media
Subject 15
        378 minutes social media, 125 PhotoBend
Subject 16
        426 minutes law online, 48 minutes YouTube

14

By nature, Edgar was a jittery person. When bartending, his custom was to pace back, laughing uproariously at his own jokes and the antics of drunken customers. Yet few would have seen Edgar quite as nervous as that night.

It had been the talk of Herzfeld. Few things carried as much excitement as death. Although the gossip of drunken driving or domestic disputes sent tongues wagging, and car accidents brought out the amateur forensic scientist in every last citizen, these things were seen as deviations from the norm. The helicopter crash was different, though. From senior citizens to seniors in high school, people were talking, using their hands to show trajectory and speed and the eventual crash. Speculations ranged from inebriated pilots to rotor-diving seagulls to Halos throwing rocks at the chopper. No one was inclined to believe any one of these things, but everyone was inclined to behave as if their opinions were the gospel truth. Many conversations started with, *You know what I heard...*

In the coming days, Government police sent a salvage boat to retrieve what was left of the helicopter. Piece by piece, they picked through the wreckage at the base of the cliff. Perilous work, many said, and a few stood along the cliff's edge, not on Cloud End property – that would have been too dangerous, but at the edge of the town park which under looked Faucini cliff. As the salvage continued, Igor's binoculars were focused on the Government's work as he sat in a lawn chair balancing precariously on shifting stones.

Finally, they located the bodies.

That was Edgar's edgiest night. Twice, he spilled drinks. One near Rector Falkirk and the other for Renata Lerner who had parked herself along the bar for a night of information gathering.

When the drink slipped from Edgar's hands and over the bar, cascading down the cliff and splashing the rocky ice on Renata's feet, she chewed him out. 'For Pete's sake, Edgar,' she said, 'just relax.'

He grumbled an apology and refilled her glass with another rum and Coke, easy on the Coke. She took a sip and glanced to her left at the rector who watched her bemusedly.

'He's pretty jumpy tonight,' Falkirk said as Edgar disappeared into the back.

'He's always like that, isn't he?' Renata asked.

'Not like this. You'd think he was waiting on the lottery.'

'What's his problem?'

Magnus shrugged. 'He didn't say. Must be something with the crash. Everyone's still upset about it. Have you seen Tom and Albert? They're really cut up.'

'Why?'

'Because it should have been them in there. They were called to the scene, but they couldn't get in to Cloud End?'

'Why not?'

Falkirk scooted his stool closer after sneaking a glance at Edgar who now was serving another town member. 'Tom told me that they couldn't get into Cloud End because Edgar and Steve had broken down in front of the gate.'

'What?'

'Steve's truck was parked in the middle of the road so the ambulance couldn't get past.'

'What were they doing out there so late at night?'

'According to Tom, they said they were making sure there were no escapees, but weirdly, when the ambulance came,' he lowered his voice even further, 'they couldn't move the car. Yet, after the crash, when Tom and Albert went back, this time with Igor, Steve's truck was gone, and the gate had been locked.'

'So much for the truck being broken down,' Renata said.

'Interesting, isn't it?'

'What does that have to do with the crash?'

'Nothing... probably,' Rector Falkirk responded slowly, quietly. 'But it is a strange coincidence.'

'So, Edgar's nervous that people think that he had something to do with it?'

'There are rumors.'

Renata shook her head. 'There are always rumors, and rumors about rumors. Poor Edgar is going to have a coronary.' She shook her head.

'I didn't start the rumor. I'm only passing it on.'

Edgar finished serving drinks and placed his hands on his hips. 'Does anyone else need another round?' When no one raised their hand, he pushed the swinging doors into the kitchen where Steve was working in the office.

'I need to talk to you,' Edgar said.

'What about?' Steve didn't look up.

'About the other night,' he whispered.

'What other night?'

'You know...'

Steve sighed and put down his pen. 'We agreed not to talk about it anymore. What's done is done. It was an accident.'

'Are you serious?'

'Of course. If the Halos wouldn't have taken to knifing each other, the ambulance wouldn't have been called out.' Steve peered over his reading glasses at his partner. 'Let me remind you that this act of violence threatened Herzfeld's safety. It was the Halos' fault. We were justified in doing what we did.'

'But two people died!'

Steve suddenly pushed his chair back, shot up and struck Edgar across the face. Edgar recoiled, feeling his face suddenly grow warm. Shocked, Edgar's mouth flopped open.

'Get a hold of yourself,' Steve hissed. 'If you continue acting this way, people will keep talking. We need people to stop talking.'

'But they're all talking, Steve,' Edgar pouted. 'Falkirk, Renata, Liz. They're all talking.'

'Well shut them up, then.'

'How do we do that?'

'I don't know. But tonight, you need to calm down. Okay?'

'Okay, Steve. Okay. We'll think of something.'

Edgar backed out of the office, through the swinging doors and returned to the bar. Joining Falkirk and Renata at the bar was Igor Kovschenko.

The three of them were staring directly at Edgar.

Father Lawrence winced. His abdomen was healing, but not quickly enough. Most everything that occurred on the night he was stabbed was a blur, but in his dreams he could still see the knife coming at him. Slowly, jagged, like a giant shark's tooth. Sometimes the knife stabbed him in the side. Sometimes he could see it coming at his eye, or his throat, or his heart.

While Lawrence reimagined the nightmare, Winston Faraday III made a surprise visit. When he showed up at the door of room 2, Lawrence didn't know what to think. Lawrence had liked Winston Faraday the II very much, but The Third seemed to be... lesser. Faraday was dressed in navy blue suit pants, a long-sleeved pink shirt with white collar and white tie. His five-hundred-dollar brown leather shoes seemed recently polished.

'May I come in?'

Lawrence winced as he tried to get up.

'Please, don't. I can stand in the doorway if that's easier.'

'No, no. Come in. Come in.' Lawrence was dismayed to see how messy the room was.

After entering, Winston remained awkwardly positioned in the short hallway just beyond the bathroom door. 'How are you feeling?'

'All right.' He was actually miserable but complaining seemed to make it worse. 'How is Radiance?'

'Who?'

'The housekeeper. The other one who was attacked.'

'Ah.' Winston had forgotten about her. 'Seems fine. A little upset that she's one of us, now.'

'As you would be.'

'As I am,' Winston responded.

There was an awkward silence until Lawrence smiled. 'What can I do for you, Senator?'

'Please, call me Winston.'

'All right, Winston. What can I do for you?'

'I was wondering if you'd thought about what you'll be doing?'

'Pardon?'

'What you're going to do next? Any thoughts about bringing charges against the woman? It seems like you could get a pretty big settlement from both Cloud End and the Government. Why...'

'No. I'm not going to bring charges against her or them.'

Winston blinked rapidly, his face a whirlwind of confusion. 'But she... I... if you need, I know some good lawyers who could...'

'I'm not pressing charges,' Lawrence said firmly.

'But why not?'

'Because she was not in her right mind. She was in pain.'

'And her pain has become yours. That's not fair. That's criminal.' Winston crossed his arms.

Lawrence had gone through this scenario many times already. Yes, of course, the logical thing would be to send the addict off to jail, but the *good* thing to do would be to help Seraphim. Maybe she needed a break. 'Well, life isn't fair sometimes, but we can be merciful.'

'That's your religion talking.'

Lawrence pondered the politician. 'Haven't you ever encountered mercy before?'

'It's not a particularly popular arrow in the Government's quiver,' Winston responded with a rueful laugh. 'We err on the side of justice.'

It was Lawrence turn to snicker. 'Justice,' he repeated derisively.

'What's so funny?'

'To be just and to work for justice are two very different things.'

14

'Enlighten me.'

Lawrence shifted in his seat. 'What would be the justice in pressing charges against Seraphim?'

'Is that the stabber's name?' Winston asked.

'Yes.'

'Strange.'

'Perhaps.' Lawrence waited for Winston to respond.

'The justice of this situation is: a woman attempted to kill you and two other people, perhaps three, if you include the male nurse. If his suit had been ripped, he'd be in the same situation as... what did you say her name was?'

'Radiance.'

'Serving time is the only way for these people to learn. And, possibly, to dry out. Then, with some coaching and a few breaks, she might get a job, work hard, buy a house, pay taxes...'

Lawrence ground his teeth. 'Let's assume for the moment your definition of justice is good. Now, what is the *just* thing to do?'

'I don't understand the difference.'

'Politicians rarely do.'

Winston felt his face flush and anger creep up under his collar. 'You're dancing close to self-righteousness.'

'One of my failings,' Lawrence said with a shrug. 'But the *just* thing to do would be to work at the source of Seraphim's issues, not the result.'

'You mean drugs.'

'Not just drugs. Those are probably a symptom of a greater ill.'

'Like poverty.'

Lawrence waggled his hand tiredly. 'Yes and no. Society doesn't pay attention to people like Seraphim. They see her as a convenient excuse for their overindulgence. The average person is addicted to so many other things, the internet, food, caffeine, money, themselves – socially acceptable narcotics,' the corner of Lawrence's mouth curled up in a wry smile, 'that, if these were illegal, they would be locked up for life. But Seraphim, whether by choice or by force, has already been imprisoned in the life of a drug addict. People are relieved to point fingers at her: she's the problem with society. She's the dirty one, the disgusting, needle-marked lowlife. 'Throw her in jail,' they say. 'Teach her a lesson.' And if she is gone, they can feel comfortable in their own overindulgent addictions.'

'That's a little judgemental from someone like you.'

Lawrence rolled his eyes. 'Convenient, isn't it? Assume that my faith should make me toe the line while those without, or on a different journey of faith, are not held to the same standards.'

Winston frowned, ignoring his last statement. 'She doesn't have a job, but she's obviously got money for drugs. She should learn...'

'Learn what?' Lawrence responded firmly. 'Learn from her mistakes by forcing us to compound them? We should punish her while she punishes herself? Should we ship her off to an island, along with all the other drug addicts, alcoholics, shoplifters, extortionists, pervs, and then what? Would all us *good* people be happy? Feel better about ourselves.'

'Yes! Of course. Exile them until they learn better.'

Lawrence shook his head. 'Did you know that's what they say about us?'

'What?'

'Us 'Halos.'' Lawrence motioned with his head towards the Halo detector. 'We obviously did something wrong, and there are many, even those in the village, I'm sure,' Lawrence pointed towards the south, to Herzfeld, 'who would send us to an island to be safe from us diseased ones.'

'Ridiculous. We did nothing wrong. How could I, a senator, be the same as an addict?'

'Viruses don't care about your politics or your history. At our very core, we are all addicted to something, and if we got what we really deserved, we'd all be shipped off to an island.'

'That's still your religion talking.'

'And that's why you'll never get it,' Lawrence said quietly.

Offended, Winston took a step back into the shadow of the hallway. He wanted to leave, but he hadn't finished his business. 'I came here to help you.'

Sadly, Lawrence shook his head. 'You came here to help yourself.'

'Excuse me?'

'You want me to sue this place and the Government in order to shut the doors on Convos. Isn't that right?'

'Preposterous.' Faraday took another step into the hallway, almost out of sight.

'What you don't understand is that these Convos,' he said with a wince as he tried to motion around him, 'might be more than just a place to recover – they might be a place to heal.'

'I don't even feel sick,' Winston argued loudly. 'I just want to get out of here. I want to return to normal life to do the work of the people.'

'Hopefully soon,' Lawrence's eyes darted to the red light.

Faraday's eyes followed. With irritation, he spun on his heels and stormed from the room. Why was it such a bad thing to want to go back to the way things used to be? And what did he mean that Cloud End was a place where people could heal? It was a Convalescent Center. People were supposed to get better there.

Winston's AutoCom buzzed and he checked the message. Isolde had delivered his thoughts to Senator Forsythe. Hopefully, Cloud End was about to change.

Not long later, there was another knock at Father Lawrence's door. He had been near sleep. The pain pills, though taking the edge off, left him unable to focus. Thus, he found himself startled from his near nap to hear Radiance's voice in the hallway.

'Come in.'

After Radiance entered, Lawrence was surprised to see how haggard she looked. Dark rings shadowed her eyes like grapes and her hair had been tucked messily into a bun at the back of her head. She wore grey sweatpants which matched the sallow color of her skin. She was barefoot, toenails unpainted and badly in need of a trim.

'Hello, Father.'

'Please remember,' he motioned to a chair beside him, 'you can call me Lawrence.'

She sighed, relieved. 'It's so much easier to do that. It's hard to call someone who is not my father, 'father.''

Lawrence laughed. 'I know what you mean.' He paused. 'Are you feeling sick?'

She nodded. 'I think so.'

'You think so?'

'My throat hurts a little bit and I've got a headache, but I'm not sure that's from the virus or... something else.'

'What would that be?'

'I've got a hangover.' Her smile was pinched. 'It seemed like the best avenue.'

'You're still angry?'

She waited for a moment before replying. Radiance wasn't sure why she had come to see the priest. 'This feels like a confession.'

It was Lawrence's turn to laugh. 'That's completely up to you, but this is neither a confessional nor am I on active duty. I'm on vacation, you know?" His smile was warm and welcoming.

'How do you do it?' she asked.

'Do what?'

'Stay sane? I mean, this place, it's beautiful, but you're trapped.'

'And you aren't?'

'I wasn't. At least not until the druggie slashed my protective gear. Now, I'm just like everyone else.'

Lawrence shrugged. 'Seraphim might have done you a favor.'

'Fat chance at that. Now I'm stuck here until that little red light turns green.'

Lawrence glanced out his window to the grassy knoll where children and seagulls were playing. Sometimes freedom is given away, rather than taken. 'Can I tell you what I think?'

'I think that's why I knocked on your door.'

'That little red light in the corner of my room is a symbol of what's happening in our world. Believe me, the red light's been glowing for a long time – much longer than you or I have been around.' Their eyes strayed in the Halo Detector's direction. 'Supposedly, that box can sniff out the Halo virus and let us know if we're clean or not. But to be honest, it will never turn green. We'll always be sick.'

'I hope you're not going to talk to me about sin. I'm not a religious person.' Her eyes fell. 'Maybe this is a confession.'

'No, I'm not talking about sin, even though there might be, to some extent, an application of that. What I mean by that red light is: Outside these walls, the entire world is a Halo Detector and it's primed to pick up the scent of weakness or fear and blink madly at the smallest sign of stepping out of line. Believe me, that red light out there will keep you up all night.'

'I don't understand,' Radiance said.

'The real virus, Radiance, is not a microbe, it's unforgiveness.'

She shook her head. 'That's ridiculous. The Halovirus is what's making...'

'Radiance,' he interrupted gently, 'the Halovirus is the light which has exposed what's really wrong with humanity. Unforgiveness is what's killing us. Wars, murders, suicides, endless online verbal assaults that cannot and will not be won. It's all because we can't forgive each other. We're infected by anger and outrage, always spotting the wrongs of others and how we've been slighted, or shamed, or worse. Even if we think we can be inoculated, we refuse on grounds of personal choice. 'My body, my choice. My ego, my choice.' We've moved far past the symptoms and now we're in the latter stages of organ failure. It won't be long before the world collapses in its unforgiveness.'

Radiance raised her eyebrows. 'Wow, that's, uh, not what I was expecting.'

'What were you expecting?'

'That I would come in here and you would tell me everything is going to be alright. You'd tell me to buck up and get on with it, a little pep talk, you know? But this... I'm not sure I was ready...'

'You have to forgive her.'

Radiance's jaw twitched and her eyes closed. 'She's ruined my life. From now on, I've got the virus inside me. I'm an outcast.'

'No, no,' Lawrence said softly. 'The mask is off. The blinders are gone. You can see clearly.'

'I don't want to forgive her.'

'Nobody ever does. There is power in being the victim.'

'That's really offensive,' she said.

'Is it untrue?'

'No, but...'

'Then free yourself. You won't be able to trust Seraphim again, but you'll be free of her actions. Then, find a different path.'

Radiance stared at the red light. 'I don't think that's going to happen. Not until I'm virus-free.'

Lawrence nodded. 'As you wish.' He leaned back in his chair and crossed his arms feeling the stitches pull.

'Thank you for your time, Lawrence,' Radiance said as she pulled herself from the chair. 'I feel like I should be crossing myself, or something.'

Lawrence smiled sadly. 'You watch too many movies.'

Without answering, Radiance left the priest's room. As she approached the railing, she saw Seraphim below her slowly walking with a blanket clutched around her shoulders. For as disheveled as Radiance appeared, Seraphim looked as if she'd been through a nuclear war. Her jaw clenched again.

'Welcome to the great unmasked society.'

Startled, she turned to see Alonzo approaching her.

'Mmhmm.'

Alonzo stared down over the railing to where Radiance was looking. 'She looks even worse than we do, doesn't she?'

'She deserves it,' Radiance mumbled.

His eyes narrowed. 'I'm not so sure about that.'

'Don't tell me the priest has gotten into your mind, too.'

Alonzo shrugged.

'I think he's got some pretty old-fashioned ideas.' Radiance continued watching Seraphim slowly wend her way through the tables toward the library.

'I'm a bit of an old-fashioned man myself,' he said.

'How is that?'

'Well, if I see a pretty lady, then I'm likely to compliment her.'

'Don't see many of those around here,' Radiance said.

'There are a few.'

She turned to him. 'Look, I'm not in a great mood, and getting hit on in a Convo is not exactly romantic.'

Alonzo took a step back. 'I was talking about someone else, but if it helps you, I think you're pretty also...' He laughed and held up his good hand.

'Oh, dear,' Radiance covered her cheeks, 'I've really put my foot in it this time.'

'It's all right,' Alonzo replied. 'Just wipe 'em on the carpet outside your room. That'll clean 'em off.'

'Forgive me, please. I'm not feeling well. Maybe the virus...'

'Think nothing of it,' Alonzo said magnanimously. 'You're forgiven.' He turned slowly and began to walk back toward his room, hand on the railing, eyes below.

'Thank you,' she whispered. Strangely, Radiance felt a little freer.

```
CECC CCTV Analysis
3 November, 2031
17:30 - 23:59
```

Subjects have begun to separate into cliques. Subjects 3, 4, and 5, have joined with CE children. Footage reveals movement through yard and towards Faucini Cliff.

Subjects 8, 11, 6 spend multiple hours eating and drinking together. Subject 6 and 11 have almost completely recovered from injuries sustained in stabbing.

Subjects 7, 13 and 11 spoke to each other while 13 recovered from withdrawal symptoms.

Subjects 1, 2, 4, 5, 6, 11 eat dinner together.

Subjects 15, 16 Dined together then separated to go to separate rooms.

Subjects 12 and 14 have not connected with anyone else.

15

Behind glass walls, frosted to hide attendees from any prying eyes outside the meeting room, Emery's voice rang out. 'Halo '29 cases are diminishing.' The others around the conference table, in differing states of agitation, glanced around at each other.

'That's great news,' Monica Portney responded. 'Isn't it?'

'To a point,' Renfroe said as he massaged his forehead. 'But we need to keep the Convos open for a while longer. We need more data. The results so far have been...'

'Inconclusive,' Senator Forsythe interrupted.

Renfroe closed his eyes, then opened them. 'They've been there for four weeks. It's time for subliminals. It's time for night messages.'

'Four weeks is not nearly long enough.' Director Reed-Conway said. 'They're only beginning to...'

'It's been long enough for a stabbing, a fatal helicopter crash, and one of the staff to be exposed to the Halovirus.' Senator Membree's mouth pursed. 'We need to look at aborting this thing. If this gets out, our necks are on the line.'

'It's not going to get out,' Reed-Conway insisted with a brief glance towards Senator Forsythe. 'Stabbings happen everywhere in this country every day. The Halos all survived. Yes, it's terrible that the staff member was exposed, but there was no assurance that she'd remain negative even if the incident hadn't occurred.'

'The what-ifs are irrelevant,' Membree responded testily. 'The fact of the matter is: Cloud End is basically an asylum rather than a Convalescent Center. Who knows if the virus is going to go away?'

'That's what the Halo Detectors are for,' Donaldson said with a smirk.

'Be that as it may,' Renfroe's eyes darkened, 'the chosen few are prepped and ready for the next phase. Dr. Boeder-Mankins has given us favorable reports regarding the propaganda, *'The Government is keeping us safe.'* As of yet, only the priest, the gravedigger and the businesswoman are posing any kind of resistance.'

Senator Membree studied the eyes of his fellow conspirators. 'Apparently, some are wondering whether the virus has any effect. They think its potency has waned and they should be allowed to go home regardless of what color their Halo Detectors are.'

'We need to start pumping the message in at night. Monica,' Membree turned towards the ruby-haired woman, who fidgeted nervously with a pen, 'you'll start tonight.'

With a pained expression, she scoured the circle for any naysayers, but there were none – at least none who were publicly against. 'All right,' she answered quietly. 'What do you want their devices to say?'

All eyes focused on Renfroe.

Beware. Your neighbor is watching you. Beware. They are looking for reasons to keep you there. Renfroe noticed the pressure rise in the room.

'Let's hope there aren't any more stabbings,' Membree said.

Elizabeth Happel held the meat cleaver in one hand and the chicken in the other. She'd arrived at the store early. Although many people were shopping before their own work began, some took some time throughout the day to take a break from the monotony of working-from-home. They would take their time shopping (it was one of the only reasons they were allowed outside the house), pausing beside the broccoli or loitering at the deli, a freshly brewed cup of coffee in hand, mask pulled down to drink, to describe how difficult the restrictions were. *Staying at home was such a hardship*, some would moan. *To be locked up, imprisoned, was beyond unconscionable. How could the Government do this to its own citizens?*

And Elizabeth would nod, her mask ceaselessly causing her glasses to fog over. *Yes, of course, how terrible it must be for you*, she would say, but the virus would never stop them from doing their shopping. And if they had an hour or two to spare chatting with people, that was to keep up their mental health, right?

The increased earnings had been wonderful, but Elizabeth wondered if the excess hours were worth it. Yes, she had more money, but she had no way to spend it. More than once, Elizabeth wondered if she should take off her mask and wander up to Cloud End, knock on the door and enquire about getting the virus so she could take a few weeks off.

Those were crazy thoughts, of course. Simply getting sick wasn't going to fix what was happening inside her, nor what was happening in Herzfeld. People were angry and frightened. Paranoid. They pointed out their neighbor's failings, sometimes publicly, but always with a smug sense of self-satisfaction. Self-righteousness, Rector Falkirk named it in his most recent weekly online sermon.

Rector Falkirk might be the most hypocritical of the lot, like a noisy cymbal, clanging and pounding the 'safety' drum. *We wouldn't be in this situation if people would just follow the Government's guidelines,* he declared at another town meeting, yet she had seen him wandering the streets of Herzfeld pausing theatrically to bless people as he pulled down his mask. *It's for the sake of the children,* he would say.

Elizabeth brought the cleaver down with a loud *thunk* which severed the drumstick from the thigh. Things were going to get worse before they got better.

'Liz,' a voice called out from the front, 'are you there?'

Wiping her hands on her apron, Liz emerged from her chopping area and saw Bridgette Priveto standing at the counter. 'What can I do for you?'

'I'd like to get three racks of lamb and ten sirloins.'

'I'll see what I can do. I'm not sure I'll have enough for a whole row.'

Bridgette leaned over the counter. 'Are you running low?'

'Have been for weeks. Customers have these guilty looks on their faces as they buy a quarter of a pig or sixty pounds of beef. They know they're hoarding, but they don't want to be caught short.'

Bridgette looked down guiltily, a gesture that Elizabeth spotted. 'This is for the hotel,' she lied.

'Sure.'

As Elizabeth traipsed to the cooler to get the meat, Gemma Cranmere appeared at Bridgette's side. 'You've seen the news, I suppose.'

Bridgette nodded.

'Apparently, the wreckage is being pieced together.'

'I guess that's what forensics are for, right?' Bridgette tapped her foot impatiently, unconsciously. Gemma Cranmere was not her favorite person. Her election campaign smeared another member of the town. No one had actively sought to fact-check Gemma's statements, but it was on everyone's social media feeds, so it had to be true.

'I wonder what happened.'

'I'm sure they'll figure it out.'

Gemma attempted to move farther into Bridgette's vision. 'I've been wanting to talk to you about our visit to the Capitol. Do we have your support?'

Bridgette turned. The shorter woman's head barely reached her chin, but her eyes were determined and powerful. 'To be honest, Gemma, I'm not sure what you're trying to accomplish.'

'We want to elevate our voices. Protest, if we have to.'

'Who's going to listen? The rest of the country doesn't care. In fact, they're quite happy that Cloud End Convo is near Herzfeld. That means they can avoid thinking about the fact that sixteen rational, normal people are locked away – maybe even wasting away – while they go about their daily business.'

Gemma's eyes flashed above her black mask. 'The Government will listen. I'm sure of it.'

'Because you'll stamp your feet and complain?'

'We might have to break a few things so they pay attention. We may be small, but Herzfeld is mighty.'

'When did breaking things ever change anything?' Bridgette muttered. She really wished Liz would hurry up with her meat. 'During all those riots ten years ago, when that guy got killed, what did it change? It seemed like it just gave people free reign to vent their love of destruction.

And,' her voice raised, 'it only destroyed the livelihoods of other innocent people.'

'You're wrong. Lots of things changed, and for the better, if you ask me.'

'Name one.'

Gemma's eyes narrowed. 'You're not getting soft on this proposal, are you? We need Cloud End to end.'

'Why don't you just let them be? They aren't harming us.'

'But they *could*, Bridgette.' Accompanying Gemma's insistence was a grip on Bridgette's arm. It was one thing to force one's opinions on others. It was another to lay a hand on them.

'Don't touch me!' Bridgette hissed as she yanked her arm away.

A slow, wicked smile crossed Gemma's face. 'I see how it is.'

'Liz, how close is it?' Bridgette yelled out and took a step away from the mayor.

Gemma sneered. 'Just you wait, Bridgette. When the Halo comes for you, you'll be the first one I recommend getting sent to Cloud End.'

Chantelle's gaze was drawn from the vision of Seraphim in the infirmary to movement outside, to the east, where Cloud End children were playing happily. The five kids stared at something in the grass. Or, more to the point, the boys huddled over the object while the girls stood back, hands over mouths avoiding whatever it was.

One of the boys jumped causing the girls to soundlessly scream. Obviously, whatever they had cornered had snapped at them. Streaking for the cliff, the five young people ran with abandon. Nothing in the world could catch them.

'Why are you here?'

Her reverie broken; Chantelle pondered Seraphim who was rubbing her eyes. 'I don't know.'

'You could be anywhere, doing anything else – watching a movie, eating something – and you sit in that chair staring at an addict.'

Chantelle ignored the suggestion of leaving. There was always time for a movie or eating, reading a book or going for a walk outside, but Chantelle was finding something soul-shifting about caring for someone else.

They had some things in common. Although Chantelle's own drug use was part of her story, she had not been overcome or undone by it.

'Sometimes, life takes turns you never expect.'

'You seem pretty well-adjusted.' Seraphim grabbed her water bottle and began to drink lustily from it.

Chantelle regarded the woman with the purple bags under her eyes, the sunken cheeks and the loose-fitting hospital gown. An IV had been inserted into the veins of her hand. Her elbow had too many needle prints already.

'In this case, the adage – 'looks can be deceiving' – fits very appropriately.'

'What did you do?'

'I gave up.'

Seraphim rubbed her eyes. 'What does that mean?'

'It means I stopped looking for the good in the world. Life is but a dream, right?'

Seraphim snorted. 'Only on drugs. So, I'm not the only one who wonders what went wrong?'

'No, not in the least.'

'I started after high school. A guy I know...'

'It always starts that way, right?' Chantelle said.

For the first time, Seraphim tested a smile. It felt strange, to pull her lips across ragged teeth, yellowed from poor eating and narcotics. Smiling was as foreign to her as sobriety. 'We were at a concert and the boy says to me, 'I know how we can make this party last longer.'' She touched her face. 'Oh, how naïve I was. To want to please a boy. So stupid.'

15

Chantelle was surprised at the tears which appeared in her eyes. Pleasing people. That was what she was born to do. Everyone but herself. And the more she wandered through the rabbit holes of gratifying the desires of other people, the more she disgusted herself. Yet, she buried her disgust and kept plodding along. Floating. Bobbing along in life as if somehow the waterfall was always going to be around the *next* bend. 'Maybe being here is the best thing for all of us.'

'How did you get it? Your Halo?'

'A guy.'

'It always starts that way, doesn't it?' Seraphim copied.

'How about you?'

'Who knows. Could have been anyone. Could have been anywhere. To be honest, I don't remember much of anything.'

At that moment, Alonzo peeked his head through the doorway. He was surprised to see Chantelle. He waved awkwardly and tapped the door frame. 'How's the patient?'

'I'm fine,' Seraphim's head pushed back into the pillow. 'I... I'm... sorry.'

'Just a flesh wound,' he responded with a grin. 'Doesn't even hurt.'

'I don't remember any of it, if that makes you feel any better.'

He studied his fingernails for a moment and then shrugged. 'I remember it well enough for both of us. Glad you're okay.' Turning slowly, he prepared to leave, but Seraphim stopped him.

'What's your name?'

'Alonzo Turner. And you?'

'Seraphim.'

His smile widened. 'You're an angel with the Halo.'

'Believe me,' she called out, 'no one has ever said that before.'

After he left, Chantelle watched Seraphim's eyes. 'Just be careful,' she said.

'It always starts with a boy...' Seraphim mused.

Gemma Cranmere held her pizza in one hand while staring down at her AutoCom on the other arm. It had been a long, but productive day. Her encounter with Bridgette had been as revealing as that with Renata. The banker had been able to control her frustration better than Bridgette, but Gemma knew she had struck a nerve. And the same nerve, at that.

Part of Gemma's masterplan was to shape the town of Herzfeld into a modern-day Garden of Eden where like-minded, healthy and wealthy people would become the Utopian tourist: staying, outlaying and paving the way for more and more to visit once this whole Halo thing blew over. What they didn't need were a few bleeding-hearts arguing against what was best for the community. That was the antithesis of the new world.

Gemma looked up from her AutoCom long enough to see her husband blowing on a hot bite of pizza through his lips. Too hot. He spit it out and it dropped onto his plate. Her lip curled in disgust. 'Nice one, Steve.'

'It was hot.' He plucked the mushy, saliva dripping piece, blew on it and popped it back in his mouth and grinned.

She shook her head and noticed a message from the Government. *Your audience with your senator has been denied. Due to Halo restrictions, all correspondence and messaging must be online. We apologize for the inconvenience, but these are trying times for everyone. We're all in this together.*

She swore.

'What'sa matter?' Steve asked through his pizza-filled mouth.

'The Government won't see us.'

'Because...?'

'Halo restrictions. It's always Halo restrictions. Can't build the roads? Halo. Can't pipe the fuel? Halo? Can't visit the dying. You guessed it.'

'Halo,' Steve filled in the blank. He had pizza sauce smeared on his chin.

'We've got to do something about this, Steve.'

'I know. I know. Cloud End needs to go.'

'What do you mean?'

15

He shrugged and raised his eyebrows.

'Steve...' her voice was threatening.

'Let's just say there could be contingencies in place if things don't go the way that they should.'

'Please don't do anything irrational. The last thing we need is more drama. The helicopter crash was bad enough.'

His face reddened.

'Besides,' she continued, 'we need to figure out how to...' she went silent.

'What? What are you thinking?' Steve's mouth remained open. His pizza was displayed underneath his tongue.

'If a few prominent citizens from Herzfeld ended up at Cloud End, it might help our cause. We could then petition the Government on safety concerns. They couldn't refuse us then.'

He grinned malevolently. 'What are you thinking?'

Gemma glanced at the Government's message again. She had a plan.

All residents of Cloud End were unaware, as they slept, of a subsonic message which emanated from the boxes that contained the evil crimson light.

Beware. Your neighbor is watching you. Beware. They are looking for reasons to keep you there. The only way to be safe is to trust the Government. Beware. Your neighbour is watching.

Many stirred uncomfortably during the night, and when they woke up, something felt...

Unsettled.

16

'**Come on, over** here!' Gina Draper called out to the others streaking across the grass towards the fence. They'd been across the yard so many times, a path had been worn down to the dirt. The children's faces were lit with excitement. Pasqual did not wait for Titus who complained bitterly about having the shortest legs. McKayla led the stragglers. Soon, they reached the place where Gina stood. Gina pointed at the sky above them.

'Look, it's a drone!'

They noticed the small craft lazily circling fifty feet over their heads. The girls waved to the cameras. It descended briefly, but then returned a little higher.

'Where is the operator?' McKayla asked.

They scanned the surroundings. It was Pasqual who spotted the two figures on the other side of the Cloud End boundary. Both heads were covered by hoods and mouths hidden by masks.

As soon as the operators saw they were spotted, the drone turned to the south and made its way to the figures. The kids followed the flight, disappointed that they could not watch the drone any further.

'What do you think they were doing?' Pasqual asked.

'Probably Government spies,' Oswald suggested as his rat poked its head from his jacket. The rat sniffed the air and retreated back to the warmth of Oswald's body.

'What's up with the adults this morning?' Gina asked. 'Did anyone else notice how grumpy everyone was?'

'Maybe they're getting tired of each other,' McKayla responded. 'I know my grandparents keep checking everyone's Halo Detectors. One of these days, they're going to turn green. And then everyone will be free as a bird.' McKayla wasn't so sure how she felt about that. It had been wonderful having the Drapers staying with them.

'But not until our lights are green!' Titus shouted happily. 'I hope we stay here forever!'

'Did you see that married couple at breakfast?' Gina and McKayla drew away from the boys who had decided to throw things over the edge of the cliff.

'Yeah, I know. I thought they were going to start fighting.'

Gina giggled. 'I wonder how they'd handle that? Would Gavin need to step in?' She mimicked the sound of a CB radio. 'Officer Gavin, this is base. We've got a 378 domestic happening at the Cloud End Convo. We need you to step in.'

McKayla played Gavin's part. 'Roger, base, but, uh, what do I do with them once I've handcuffed them.'

'Officer Gavin, be advised that a makeshift jail has been set up in the library. Make them read for a while.'

'Maybe,' McKayla laughed loudly, 'we could stick them in front of our Zoom Gender Studies class. That would be a horrible punishment. They might even try to like each other, then.'

Like boxers in separate corners, Damian and Sydney Bellows were taken to their respective rooms by Sydney's lawyer, Wallis, and Damian's new best friend, Monica Xiao. They had not yet paused to be embarrassed as both were still hot under the collar. It had been Sydney's comment, 'I can smell his deodorant – that always drove me nuts,' which had sent Damian over the edge.

'You always nag!' he bellowed. 'First, it's the lawn, then the car, then the food when I took you out to eat. Can't you ever just be happy!'

'With you? Never.'

Damian had placed a finger dangerously close to Sydney's nose which she irritatingly tried to bite. Instead of focusing his fury on his soon-to-be ex-wife, Damian turned to the table next to them and hurled a chair all the way across the room where it struck a glass display case. The glass exploded, shards flying in all directions, while the objects inside suffered the same fate.

'Whoa, there, fella,' Gavin said as he quickly pulled himself away from his bowl of oatmeal and intervened. 'Nothing to be gained by doing that.'

Carl and Esther hurried from the kitchen. Spotting the damage, Carl radioed Nancy who arrived soon afterwards in a breathless huff.

'Sydney,' Wallis warned, 'I'm not sure what you think you're doing, but you need to stop.'

Sydney pointed over Wallis' shoulder angrily. 'He started it. He wore that stupid deodorant, or cologne, or WHATEVER IT IS!'

'SHUT UP, SYDNEY! SHUT UP!'

Wallis pulled Sydney towards the stairs and led her to her room. Once there, Wallis sat Sydney on the bed and stood in front of the television. 'Now, tell me what's going on.'

'Damian, I just know it, he's cheating on me. That... that...' Sydney was going to say *Asian woman* but caught herself just in time. 'That prostitute.'

'Chantelle?'

'What? No! That speeder. You know, Monica.'

'Aaah.' Wallis was always stunned by jealousy. No matter when or how it happened, no matter how little one liked one's partner, jealousy always had venom. 'At this moment, Sydney, you'll simply have to calm down and let that one go.'

'I can't let it go. It's one thing to be a jerk, but another thing to cheat on *me*. Me!' she placed her hands on her chest as if she was truly shocked that such a thing could happen.

'I just want you to understand this. No matter what kind of cologne he wears, or what kind of clothes he puts on, whether or not he stays faithful to you while you're getting a divorce, it is irrelevant. Let's make it through our court time and then you can hurl whatever insults you want at him afterwards, okay?'

'But... but... he's out to get me. Everyone's out to get me.' Sydney pushed out her bottom lip.

'He's not out to get you. He's just... a man seeking a divorce from someone who's fallen out of love with him.'

Sydney looked up into the lawyer's eyes and crossed her arms and pouted. 'You're out to get me, too. You want him to win. I wouldn't be surprised if you want me to stay here, in this terrible place, surrounded by awful people. Can't you see I'm dying in here?'

Wallis' face turned to stone. 'I'm not out to get you. No one is out to get you. I'm trying to help you.'

'Leave me alone then.'

Words to my ears, Wallis thought.

Next door, in room 9, Monica attempted to defuse the time bomb that was Damian Bellows. Unable to sit down, he stomped back and forth pacing in front of the window waving his hands wildly at thought of his wife in the room next door. Gavin guarded the short hallway to the door while Monica approached him like a lion tamer.

'Damian. Damian,' she said calmly but firmly. 'It's me, Monica.'

'I know who you are,' he responded angrily. 'I'm upset, not stupid.'

'No one says you are. You are a strong, intelligent, vastly misunderstood man.'

Gavin raised an eyebrow. In his experience, seeing men like Damian Bellows, day after day living out their rage by pulling the triggers on video games or doing it in real life, these men were physically strong, but extraordinarily weak when it came to understanding or controlling their emotions. Gavin had seen boys as young as eight, enact their rage-filled fantasies on the unexpected. It was literally the worst thing in the world to have to knock on the door of another teenager's parents to let them know that their son or daughter was in the wrong place at the wrongest of times doing the wrongest of things.

As Gavin pondered Damian, he sensed the man's immaturity despite his financial success. Having indulged his desires indiscriminately, Bellows was a keg of gunpowder perpetually placed near a flint factory. His wife was a live spark to say the least. It was a minor miracle that Bellows had not exploded beforehand.

Damian continued to pace back and forth, but the speed had slowed. Monica drew closer and tentatively reached her hand out. At first, he recoiled, but gently she finally found his forearm. It was pulsing with power and energy. 'There you go, Damian. There you go.'

Finally, he stopped moving. 'Sydney is ruining my life. She's out to get me. Always has been. Even when we were first together. She never stopped finding ways to cut my legs out from under me.' The words tumbled out faster and faster. 'And then, and then,' he waved a hand to her room, 'we're put here. Together. I'm sure it was that weaselly lawyer of hers who dropped the virus on both of us. I'm sure of it. Probably on purpose, too.'

'Relax. Damian.' Monica glanced over her shoulder towards Gavin. 'I've got it from here. You can go now, *officer*.' The last word, she spit out. Throwing him a disdainful look, Monica turned her back on Gavin. Shrugging his shoulders, Gavin left the room. Deep down, Gavin knew that leaving her there was going to cause more issues, but what did he care? If she wanted to ruin her own life, that was on her.

As the door clicked shut, an eerie silence settled in the room. 'I'm not against you,' Monica said. 'At least not yet.'

'What's that supposed to mean?'

She moved in closer and pressed her body to his. 'Now, I'm against you,' she said suggestively.

Damian's eyes widened. 'What about your family? What about your kids?'

'What happens at Cloud End stays at Cloud End, right?' She boldly touched his chest. 'Now, how can I help you overcome your pain?'

Without much thought other than, *My wife is in the next room*, Damian turned his eyes from the wall to the woman in front of him. 'You can certainly help me...' A wicked smile crossed his face. 'There is one thing that will certainly make me feel better.' He touched her arm and sat her down on the bed.

When Sydney heard the door shut and steps move down the hallway, she was glad their fight was over.

She sat back down on the bed, lonely. She pondered the things she and Damian had been through. Had she been a good wife? A good housekeeper? A good manager of their money? Of course she had. Was he a good husband? Well, there were times when he took care of her, and certainly they'd had a few fun moments. Vacations and spontaneous dinner nights tumbled through her memories. As she flipped through them like a photo album, she was interrupted by a strange sound coming through the wall of her husband's room. These were sounds she'd heard before.

Muffled laughter.

Muted talking.

A low moan.

He was seducing her.

The bastard.

Pulling herself from the bed, Sydney approached the dividing wall, the ultimate and final separation between her and him. 'HOW DARE YOU, DAMIAN! I WILL GET YOU FOR THIS!' She pounded on the walls, punishing them with the force of her anger. Her fists cracked the plaster, yet she still shrieked. Once her hands hurt, she kicked at the barrier. One of her feet put a hole near the baseboard. Without thought, she stalked out into the hallway and stopped at his door. Banging on it, she blew her top. 'YOU CHEATING, LYING BASTARD!' Every person in the courtyard, from Jacquelyn to the priest, the gravedigger and the two parents, stared up at the second floor as she ranted.

Behind her, the final sounds of ecstasy emanated through the door.

Sydney knew he was doing that on purpose.

Monica's eyes widened as the pounding on the door intensified.

'Keep going,' Damian urged. 'Finish.'

With one last gasp, Monica let out a fake moan and then covered her mouth. As she watched Damian from the chair studying the door and smiling broadly, Monica felt a twinge of guilt about deceiving Sydney. When Damian told her he wanted her to fake the sounds of sex, she was disappointed at first. To do that elicit thing would be a helpful release and, if truth be told, an enlivening thing for her life. As the chains of matrimony had become heavy, she longed for excitement. Now that Damian had entered the sphere of influence, and even better, they were beyond the sight of cameras, she dreamed of a small foray into adultery – it needn't be sex, just... cheating a little.

But Damian couldn't get past his wife. He only wanted to hurt her, not start something new with Monica.

So, she had made the bedsprings creak and moaned a little bit. All the while, Damian's face was a mixture of hatred and anger. It frightened her, but Monica didn't think it would really hurt.

'Those kids saw us,' Edgar said.

'It doesn't matter. They're just kids. We had our faces covered anyway.'

As Steve and Edgar drove back towards Herzfeld along the gravelly path, Edgar pulled down his facemask and took a drink of water. 'But if they recognized us...'

'Yes, if they recognized us, they could tell someone that they saw a drone flying overhead and two people outside the gates. I'm sure Igor would be all over us for that one.' Steve pulled down his own mask and rubbed his nose furiously. His moustache had grown too long and was sticking up into his nostrils.

'I don't know why I let you talk me into these things.'

'Yes, you do,' Steve responded as he turned right narrowly missing the curb. 'You like the adventure, the risk. We don't get a lot of that in Herzfeld.'

'Sure we do. There's Monday night tennis and Thursday night happy hour at the Tavern. Those are always fun. And then trivia nights!'

'Edgar. Calm down.'

'Shut up, Steve.'

Steve raced through a cross walk and missed a pedestrian by a few feet. She yelled at him to slow down, but he didn't pay any attention. 'It doesn't matter. We've figured out how to get our point across to the rest of the town.'

Edgar crossed his arms. 'Don't you think what we're doing is kind of hypocritical?'

'No.'

'Think about it. We accidentally shot down a rescue helicopter carrying people who were trying to help the Halos because we didn't want the virus to escape, and now...' Edgar waved a hand back in the direction of Cloud End. '... And now we're seriously contemplating...'

'There are always sacrifices, Edgar. If I've said it once, I've said it a thousand times, when all is said and done, our actions, although they'll never be revealed, will emphasize that we did the right thing in time of war.'

'But this isn't a war,' Edgar contradicted.

'*Yes*, it *is*, Edgar. We're always at war.'

'Maybe I don't want to be a soldier anymore.'

Steve hit the brakes and pulled the car up short. 'You listen to me, Edgar Post. Desertion from this army will have dire consequences. You might end up like one of them.'

'You're threatening me?'

'Yes.'

Edgar did not know how to respond.

'Now, tonight,' Steve continued, 'you're going to meet me in the park and we're going to walk up to Cloud End. Tomorrow will be a very new day. A beautiful day in Herzfeld.'

Edgar was not so sure.

Winston Faraday III had had quite enough of everything and everyone. To start with, the disturbance in the atrium was disgusting and the ensuing shouting match was enough to drive him to distraction. It was bad enough that a divorcing couple was thrown into Cloud End with him, but to have them directly next door was entirely beneath his position as a member of the Senate, a junior member, notwithstanding. He'd cornered the owners about moving to the penthouse, a turret-like room on the northeast corner (the owners said it had been turned into storage), or at the very least a suite, but they were adamant that nothing was vacant. Faraday's eyes narrowed as he wondered whether they were holding out on him, but it was not the moment to shove his weight around.

Yet.

But that moment was rapidly approaching. After the shouting match, and cornering the St. Croix's about another room, he found a way to separate Jacquelyn Archer from the rest of the Halo herd. Surely, a successful businesswoman like herself could understand the predicament they were both in.

'How are you doing?'

Jacquelyn studied the senator. Everything about him bespoke someone of privilege and silver-spoon upbringing. From the way he wore a suit, to the way he carried himself, rigid, erect, nose held high, eyes studying from the lofty heights of his elitism. One could tell that Winston Faraday III thought very highly of himself and very little of everyone else.

Jacquelyn had not voted for him. 'I'm doing well, surprisingly.'

Faraday raised an eyebrow and sipped at his coffee brought to them by Esther Fields, who was now doubling as cook and barista after Radiance's bad luck. 'You're enjoying this?'

'You're not?'

'Please, Ms. Archer, while we are penned up here, the world is getting on. People are making choices and decisions. People who need people like us to lead. Not to be caught up in here like a rat in a maze.'

It sounded rehearsed. 'Or,' she said slowly, spoon stirring her coffee, 'it could be that the time we're here gives us an opportunity to rethink what is most important in life.'

'What could be more important than leadership?'

For the last week, Jacquelyn had pondered that very question. After turning the corner on fifty, she had felt good, prepared to take on the next challenges as if she was still twenty. But now, even after a small amount of time away, she had become aware of a different kind of clock ticking. Not a stopwatch, but an hourglass. 'Maybe the feel of the breeze on my face or the taste of a nice coffee on a beautiful afternoon?'

'But we're *here*,' he stressed. 'In a Convalescent Center with all the other convicts. We're all frustrated.'

She shrugged. 'Not everyone is frustrated.'

'Name them. Give me their names. Did you not hear the rampaging couple outside our rooms? I would definitely say they are frustrated.'

'And you don't think they were frustrated before they came?'

Faraday knew that she had scored a point, but he needed her on his side. 'Granted, but who, here, is 'enjoying' themselves, as you say.'

'The kids.'

'Kids don't count.' Faraday's face scrunched up with irritation.

'Why not?'

'Because... because they move on from everything quickly. They have no demands on life outside. School is delivered to them. Food is given to them. Everything is paid for.'

'What about you?' she asked.

'What about me?'

'Do you cook? Who pays your bills? What things do you do for yourself? I bet you don't even drive your own car. What about travel? Who pays for that?' She smirked and noticed people were gathering in the room for dinner. Father Lawrence, the Draper family, the policeman and Chantelle had pushed a few tables together and were sitting down like a very strange re-enactment of the Last Supper. At another, Sydney and Wallis were sitting across from each other. Wallis seemed distracted as the woman continued ranting about the poor treatment she'd received.

'That's unfair. I can't control the fact that I work long hours and have little time to cook or clean for myself. It's one of the perks of the job. And as far as everything is paid for, yes, full disclosure, I have a stipend, but I spend it on necessities.'

Both knew that this was not true, and he had failed to mention travel. 'Look at that,' Jacquelyn motioned with her head at the tables pushed together. 'I'm going to guess that those eight people are not too frustrated about being here.'

Faraday followed her gesture. They did seem to be enjoying themselves. The police officer was beaming. The mother was smiling gratefully at her youngest son who was pointing at something in a book to the priest. 'They're shirking their responsibilities. They should actively be seeking out a solution to leaving this place and retaking their position in society.'

'And what is that position, Mr. Faraday?'

He stammered, 'As citizens of the economy, producing goods and services, paying taxes so that the schools and the military and... and... the rest of the world can continue progressing into the future!'

Jacquelyn snorted. 'And here, I thought their place in society was as a family, enjoying life, spending time together.'

'Don't tell me you buy into that Hallmark Card crap. You should know better, Ms. Archer. The world must continue to produce.'

Jacquelyn had had enough. She took one more sip of coffee and stood up. 'Thank you, Senator Faraday, for this enlightening conversation. If you don't mind, I'm going to a table with a little more Hallmark Card crap.' With that, she walked slowly towards the table of eight where, just before she arrived, the priest motioned for her to pull up a chair, which she did.

Meanwhile, as Sydney and Wallis sat apart, Damian and Monica walked into the room together. When they took their seats, Sydney loudly proclaimed that she'd lost her appetite, and it was time to go back to her room.

'Sit down, Sydney,' Wallis whispered. 'You can't run away every time he walks into the room. You'll only be letting him win.'

'He's humiliated me. With that...' she left the last adjective off.

Once again, Wallis quieted her. 'Let's just sit here as we eat our meal together. We're not going to pay any attention to what others might be doing.' Wallis wistfully let her gaze fall on the table of nine and wished that she had been invited to that one instead.

Strangely, as her thoughts remained on the table, a shadow appeared in the corner of her eye. When she turned, she saw that it was Damian.

Sydney, prepared for a fight, to arm her rockets for a new salvo, felt Wallis' hand on her arm.

'What can we do for you, Damian?' Wallis asked.

'I was wondering if I could sit with you for a little bit.'

'We have nothing to talk about,' Sydney hissed. 'Why don't you go back to your floozy?'

Damian smirked. 'She's actually a pretty nice person.'

'I'll bet,' Sydney sneered.

Wallis repeated her question before Sydney could release the mushroom cloud of her indignity.

'I wanted to come over and... well... I actually don't know. The thought simply jumped into my head.'

'I'm not sure this is the best time for you and Sydney to converse,' Wallis frowned.

'Maybe you and I can talk, then.' Damian pointed back and forth between himself and Wallis.

Sydney harrumphed and crossed her arms.

'About what?'

'About your job.'

The statement surprised Wallis. 'In what way?'

'Divorce.'

'Really, Damian, I'm not sure this is appropriate. Sydney is my client, not you.'

He leaned forward and put his chin in his palm. 'I only have a few questions. She's perfectly welcome to listen.'

Wallis looked towards Sydney who had taken out her phone. 'I'll answer to the best of my ability.'

'Why do most marriages fail?'

'Excuse me?'

'You've been in the business for a long time, right?'

'Yes. Twenty-five years, give or take.'

'And in that time, you've been separating people, how...'

Wallis interrupted. 'Let's get one thing straight, Mr. Bellows. *I* haven't done the separating. I've only been part of the polishing off, as it were.'

'Okay, whatever. Semantics. But in the quarter century that you've been polishing, what's the reason most people divorce. Money? Cheating?'

Wallis stifled her smile.

'What's so funny?' he asked.

'People don't 'cheat' in a marriage.'

'I don't understand.'

At this point, Sydney glanced up from her phone but didn't say anything. 'In a marriage, people stray, not because of the absence of sex, or the sex is not good enough – it's usually because they haven't been loved, or they're neglected, or they feel rejected. Cheating is not an end, in and of itself. It's a protective measure.'

'Okay...' he responded slowly. 'How is it a protective measure?'

For years, Wallis had pondered the reasons why couples didn't last. Why did people get divorced? Was it sudden, or a gradual, continental drift that couldn't be reversed?

'Did you know that some researchers believe that love only lasts for two years, and then after that, it's mere stubbornness, those are my words, as to why people stay together?'

'Sounds about right,' Sydney intoned. Damian and Sydney had been married for five, together for seven. At the end of their second year of 'being in love,' they tied the knot, but it began fraying soon afterwards.

'Yeah, that was about right, wasn't it?' Shocked, Damian realized that this was one of the first things they'd agreed on in a very long time. 'So, what happens?'

Wallis shook her head sadly. Year after year, she found couples seeking something to replace the emptiness that 'being in love' used to fill. Instead of loyalty and admiration and respect from their spouse, they chased after the old emotion – the zest of conquest.

'Men don't lose their sexual virility, but they lose their virility in the *relationship*. Instead of looking out for his spouse, or girlfriend, or whomever, he begins to look for love in all the wrong places, as the song goes. Work, sports, addictions, and sometimes the embrace of other people.'

'Why is that?' Sydney spoke sarcastically as she leaned forward, mimicking her soon-to-be ex-husband's posture.

'It's not just the men, it's the women, too. In my experience, couples who divorce, have a distorted picture of who it was that they married.'

'And that is?' Sydney asked.

'The fairytale - Disney Princess, happily-ever-after - is that love doesn't change.'

'That's a good thing, right?' Damian asked.

'Nope. It's fatal for the relationships.' Wallis was intrigued that both were listening intently. Even as the other party across the room became raucous with laughter, the table of three seemed to be intent on something different. 'When people can't love the person the other is becoming, they're doomed.'

'I don't understand,' Sydney's face screwed into a question. Behind thick, fake eyelashes, Sydney's eyes smoldered. Wallis knew that beneath the makeup and the extra time it took to look beautiful, and behind the pouting, self-absorbed front, was a tender-hearted young woman who desperately needed reassurance of being more valuable than the collective of her physical assets. Unfortunately, Damian did not take his wife seriously. He did take her for granted, though. That much was obvious.

Wallis sighed. 'This is a paraphrase of every couple I work with: 'I wish that we could still be like we were when we first started dating.' Yes, the feeling is real, but the reality is different. If people don't fall in love with their spouse for who they *are becoming*, rather than who they were, they can only be trapped in yesterday.'

'This sounds like a Nicholas Sparks novel,' Sydney said.

'Who's Nicholas Sparks?' Damian asked.

'Exhibit F of why we're getting divorced,' Sydney rolled her eyes.

Wallis blew air through her lips. 'If you want my honest opinion, you guys aren't getting divorced because you don't love each other. You're getting divorced because you're in love with the wrong person. You don't love the one in front of you today. You're still holding on for a resurrection of the one from your wedding day. But that's not going to happen. You have to love the person they're becoming.'

'That sounds like a bunch of psychobabble,' Damian said.

'Be that as it may,' Wallis retorted, 'you asked for my professional opinion, and I've given it to you. Do with it what you will.'

'But I can't love him the way he is now,' Sydney complained. 'I mean, he just slept with that woman. And we're still married!' she lifted her ring finger, the glittering band and two carat diamond sparkled in the dim light.

'What are you talking about?' Damian demanded with a glitter in his eye.

'I heard you. You and that tramp,' she pointed to Monica. 'You can't honestly think that I don't know what was going on up there.'

'Oh...' he said with a smirk.

'Disgusting, Damian. Revolting. How could you do that to me?'

'I didn't do it to *you*,' he said with a laugh.

Sydney gasped with horror. 'I can't believe you. And here I was starting to... to... ugh... think about you differently. You know, like Wallis was talking about, and then you go off and do that.'

Damian did not contradict her, even though he could have and probably should have.

'Please, you two. It might be better if you went to your own corners. We still have to coexist.'

Sydney stood and flipped him the finger. Damian received it with a grin. He'd wounded her.

After Sydney left, Wallis frowned at him. 'Why do you do that?'

'She starts it. I like to finish it.'

'Did you ever love her?'

He shrugged.

'Even if you won't answer that, just keep in mind that she is a human being with hurts and haunts from the past. Just be kind, okay?'

Damian snorted. 'Hurts? She is the spoiledest woman on the planet. Her parents did everything for her. Little rich girl who doesn't get her way? Likes to stamp her feet and whine about how unfair life is, while at the same time she doesn't see that the floor on which she stamps is part of a million-dollar house, three cars and a boat in the garage, overlooking the ocean. While she files her nails at home, I work my ass off.' He stood. 'Your words should be meant for her, not me.' He turned to walk away. 'Kindness,' he muttered under his breath, 'she doesn't deserve that.'

17

'**Do you see** them?' Donald asked Claire as he pulled back the curtains from their downstairs apartment. 'They look different. Like they're getting better.'

'But the virus. Red light, remember? They're still registering positive for the Halo.' Claire peeked one eye out.

'Technically, yes. But just because their red lights are on doesn't mean they're all sick. In fact, I'd hazard a guess, most of them look better now than when they got here.'

'They should,' Claire responded as she shut the curtain, 'they've been on vacation. Well fed, well-looked-after, and all that. It costs a fortune.'

Donald shrugged. 'The Government is paying us. We just have to hold up our end of the bargain.'

'And what is that? What is our end?'

Donald moved toward the kitchen and turned the kettle on. 'To provide for their comfort and to help them recuperate.' She raised an eyebrow. 'What? We've done exactly as they asked. We've taken on Dr. Chandruth and Dr. Boeder-Mankins, no questions asked. And then the nurses. They are wonderful, aren't they?'

Claire wasn't sure about that. She had her reservations about the nurse named Jack, and there was something creepy about Dr. Boeder-Mankins. She didn't connect with anyone, not even Nancy, who seemed to be agreeable to everyone else. Carl, though, was able to have a few conversations with the psychologist, and reported back that the sessions were going well.

'I'm ready for them to go, Donald,' Claire said.

'The guests?'

She nodded. 'And the extra staff. We need our home again. We need to get back to the old normal.'

Donald pondered the grassy expanse leading out toward the cliff. Although the light was dim, only moonlight penetrated sparse clouds at this time of early evening, he knew this stretch of land like the back of his hand.

His property. His hopes and future, and that of his family. For McKayla and Oswald, Cloud End was their future. But to be restricted to the house, and the protective gear and schooling online, and... and... and... This weird ol' world was churning out *another* generation of perpetually phobic children. Soon, there would be no one to work. There would be no one to serve. There would be no one to take care of the older folks.

There would be no one to care.

'I agree. We need our home back. But McKayla and Oswald have really connected with the Draper kids. That wouldn't have happened if we'd had seasonals. They bring their Land Cruisers and their 1.3 kids, engrossed in their AutoComs, insisting on more entertainment, more culture, more food, better this, better that, and we're run off our feet trying to acquiesce to every whim. And their kids, even if they do get their heads out of their screens, are so spoiled, they'd have nothing to do with our McKayla and Os.' He sighed. 'I hope they're sick for a little longer.'

'Donald!' Claire chided. 'What a terrible thing to say.'

'I know. I know,' he responded glumly as he turned back to her. 'But it's how I feel. They're getting better. We're getting better. But it doesn't feel like a virus.'

'They need to go to their own homes and be part of their own communities.'

Donald was hesitant about sharing his next thoughts. As he watched the guests, Radiance and the grandchildren without their protective gear, he realized that no one was displaying any symptoms other than a sniffly nose and a scratchy throat (*Those were the first signs before death!* he'd been warned), and most were re-engaging in life. But on a strangely new, and novel, traditional way: they were eating together and talking together.

While Donald and Claire ate with the grandchildren, and sometimes interacted with the staff personally (but more often via text messaging), Donald longed to shed the protective suit and mingle. Thankfully, the Government had told them restrictions were about to ease. Social distancing space was set to decrease, mask requirements would soon exclude the outdoors. What Donald most desired in life was to sit side by side with a guest, raise a pint, and talk of things from other places and other times. No Halovirus. No restrictions. Just talk of what makes humans tick.

'Sometimes I want to move to another community,' he said.

'Don't start that again, Donald.' Claire moved towards the door where she began to don her protective gear.

'I'm serious. I'm tired of this. I want to live again.'

'Well, then, go for a walk. Get some fresh air.'

'In my protective gear? That's not living. That's dying while inhaling.'

'Don't be melodramatic, dear.' She adjusted her helmet and turned on her inner light illuminating her face. She looked like an astronaut. 'We can stop wearing these outdoors very soon.'

'That's what the Government said a couple months ago, but then someone got a new version of the old Halo and suddenly, we're back to square one.'

'It will soon be over,' Claire promised.

'Yes, it will.' Walking to his wife, he touched the side of her helmet and smiled lovingly.

Donald pulled on his protective suit. He felt the familiar constriction as it fitted to his legs and arms. It smelled of sanitizer and sweat, coffee and plastic. Fitting the hood over his head, he once again heard his breath resound like an echo chamber. He adjusted the microphone across his mouth, tested it, to which Claire gave him a thumbs up, then clipped the helmet into place. Once secured, he covered his hands with sterile gloves. Holding them up in front of his face plate, he noticed the hair and green veins through the semi-transparent rubber. It looked as if he hadn't seen the sun in years. He was an albino earthworm desperately seeking the eye in the sky.

Now appropriately protected, Donald used his gloved hand as an ushering guide towards the door. With despondency, he allowed her through first.

After traversing the dining room between guests, Donald reached the podium and rang a dinner bell which slowly silenced the gathering.

17

'Congratulations,' he said. 'You've survived over four weeks of Convalescing!' The conjoined tables burst into applause while Winston Faraday III appeared resentful.

'For a little bit of fun tonight, we've organized a dance.'

A few appeared excited. Most, not so. Dancing had been outlawed by the Government two years before.

'I know. It sounds as if we're breaking the law, but as of today at noon, group dancing is allowed as long as there is no touching. The Chicken Dance, it is!' A few people laughed. 'If anyone wants to forgo the dance, the movie Wall-E will be shown in the theater. I've been told that it is appropriate for all ages. An oldie but a goodie.' Donald was quite aware that most movie theaters, because of heavy handed restrictions, had gone out of business. 'So, if you want an old-school cinematic experience, tonight is the night.'

Donald motioned for Carl to come forward. As usual, Carl's self-assurance and professionalism was on full display – even in his full protective gear. 'Tonight's meal will be steak and vegetables, or vegetables alone for the vegetarians. Combined with mashed potatoes and your drink of choice, you'll feel like you've never left the outer world.'

'Now, enjoy the night, the company, and, with luck, this will be your last day as guests at Cloud End.' He bowed and made his way to tables to take orders.

Winston Faraday felt like an outsider. It was a strange place for him to be. Yet, here at Cloud End, that's exactly what he was. A loner.

Frustratedly, he watched the infected Halos from his isolated table while the remnants of his cooling, half-eaten steak sat in its own juices on a sparklingly white plate. By all measures, the food should have been delicious, but because of his isolation, it tasted like ash. *Those people over there, laughing and toasting each other as if the convalescent center was a Michelin-rated-restaurant rather than a simulation, they should be acting sick. The police officer was well on his second lap past sober, and, oh, for Pete's sakes, one of the younger women, whatever her name was, was tapping the priest on the shoulder in time with the music, as if somehow, the old man had been able to pull them all out of the doldrums and into festivities.*

He listened intently while they spoke of mundane things – the weather, the outside world, what was happening with their families. *Yes, yes, everyone was fine, but they missed us...* Winston rolled his eyes... Of course they miss you, idiot! Like children at show and tell, they projected photos and videos of their loved ones onto wireless screens on the back wall. *Here is my brother. Here is my niece. Here is my home, and my stuffed animal, and my...* Winston almost shouted at them, 'Remember where you are, people! You're sick, sick, sick!' But he refrained.

After the nauseating slideshow, punctuated by the smallest boy presenting a three-dimensional video of his dog, one of the women stood and began to confess something to all of them: 'I just want you all to know how wonderful this night has been, and how much I've needed to laugh and smile.' She glanced at the now-empty table where the shouting couple had been. 'But I wanted you to know that I've had this weird feeling that... oh, I don't know how to put this...'

'Quickly,' one of the others suggested with a laugh.

'Okay.' She put a hand to her chest. 'Over the last few days, I've had this sneaking suspicion that I just need to get away from people. Do you know what I mean?' Corresponding looks, eyes downcast, cheeks blushing – she had tapped into a truth. 'I keep thinking someone's going to turn me in for doing something wrong. Or that if I sneeze, or cough, or have a sore throat, someone will tell the St. Croix's and I'll end up under house arrest, in a room by myself.' She touched her chest. 'And if I dance tonight, I'll get a text message that I've been fined.'

'It's strange,' the married man said guiltily, 'I had that same feeling. It's odd how being separated from society does that to us.'

'It's a good thing we're still connected,' she pointed to her phone. 'I've been able to talk to my family, text them, send vlogs, and some great memes while I'm here. I'm sure that helps them.'

The gravedigger was the next to stand. 'I think if we stick together, we'll make it through this thing just fine.'

It made Winston Faraday want to gag.

'They make a fine circle, don't they?'

The voice made Faraday jump and he looked to his right where the maid, or cleaner, or whatever she was, the one who got the Halo from the psycho druggie, stood.

'It's interesting,' Faraday responded, holding his cards close to his chest.

'Do you mind if I sit down?'

Winston was surprised by her request but motioned at the chair next to him. As she sat, he noticed how attractive she was: brown hair, an angular, but well-proportioned face, hazel eyes and a trim figure. She wore a green blouse with blue jeans. Whether eyeshadow or tiredness, the dim light made her eyes dark.

'What do you think of all this?' she asked.

'All of what?'

She motioned at the gathering of infected souls lifting glasses to each other.

'Ah,' he nodded, 'I suppose we should be grateful they're making lemonade from lemons.'

'But are you?'

'Am I what?'

'Grateful that they've made lemonade.'

He ground his teeth. 'Not necessarily.'

'I think it's pitiful. Sick people in a sick place pretending to be healthy, playing happy holidays in this haunted house.' She frowned resentfully at them.

'You don't approve?' he asked.

'Are you stupid?'

Her vitriol aroused his anger, and at that moment he wanted to push his chair back from the table, take his sweating, two fingers of scotch, and retreat to his bedroom where he could take out his frustration on his AutoCom. But she was too attractive. If she would have been ugly, yes.

'I am decidedly not stupid.'

'Then you just weren't listening.'

'Maybe,' he said as he sipped his scotch. 'I've been feeling a little bit off. Maybe it's the Halo...' His voice trailed off into the vastness of the room, drowned out by the noise of the table across from them.

'You probably don't even have the Halovirus anymore, or at least you're immune to it now.'

'My Halo Detector would say otherwise.'

She harrumphed and glanced around the room. Finally, her eyes fell on Nancy who, for a moment, caught Radiance's eye, but then looked away ashamedly.

'Do you see the staff here?'

'What about them?' he asked.

'They're all nervous. They loiter in their protective gear, faces covered, hands gloved, air filtered, fears worn on their sleeves, hoping beyond hope that they can avoid the lunatics who might rip a hole in their suits, so they don't end up trapped like me.'

'Aren't they trapped like you anyway? Aren't they stuck here?' He pointed at Carl who stood cross-armed along the wall waiting for orders.

'I suppose,' she agreed, 'but they could leave if they really wanted to.'

'Could they? Where would they go?'

'Into Herzfeld, or beyond. They could travel,' she said.

'I'm not sure about that. The Government has pretty much grounded air travel, and even if the planes were flying, the hoops people have to jump through make it almost impossible, and certainly cost-prohibitive.'

Radiance pondered the senator. His hands were manicured and stuck out from an expensive pressed shirt (he must have been ironing in his room) and his face was clean shaven, unlike the other Halos.

'Maybe you could do something?' Radiance suggested.

'What could I do?' he responded disingenuously.

'Surely you've got some contacts in the Government. There are always people with power and motivation. Don't you have any IOU's?'

He was slow to respond. After spending the day wearying almost everyone he knew calling in favors, chits, shelling out promises like Monopoly money, he realized that Isolde still might be his only contact with clout.

And that made him nervous.

She was a beautiful, canny social-climber able to curry information from important people simply by batting her eyelids. She was no half-wit, though she could play one if necessary. No, Isolde never sold anything low nor bought anything high. Though he'd asked her many times how many people in the Government owed her a favor, she smiled like the Cheshire cat. *That* information would have cost him.

He and Isolde had met at a Capitol dinner many years before. Isolde was dressed to impress. Her hair was styled on top of her head revealing a long shapely neck and graceful shoulders. Her green eyes were her greatest asset. No one could have guessed that this gorgeous woman was as dangerous as a great white shark. And if pressed, Isolde Howard could have taken down tiers of senators if they threatened her.

The first night he approached her, his father was present, head bowed in concentration, listening to the wife of another senator. Winston III shook his head. He shouldn't be sharing air with these people. This woman was using her husband's prestige and funds to accentuate her own guilty sense of moral superiority. The Third was sure of it. No one was that altruistic. Instead, his father should be making deals, cornering the market on information to pass important legislation for the party.

While his father wasted his time, Winston III caught Isolde's eye and raised his champagne flute to her. She met him in the middle of the dance floor.

'Senator,' she smiled knowingly.

'Not yet,' he said.

'But soon enough.'

'How do you know?'

'Because people talk,' she scanned the room. 'They say things that they shouldn't and drop hints when they should be picking them up.'

'Are you a woman who picks things up.'

Coyly, she placed a hand on his arm. 'I'm picking up a hint from you.'

Winston III felt butterflies launch in his stomach. He glanced at his father who shook his head once disapprovingly. *Who was this woman?*

'My name is Isolde Howard.' She held up a hand to dance. Winston took their drinks and set them on a table near them. Another Senator was not happy about her table being treated as a dish tray, but Winston did not care.

'And what is it that you do, Isolde Howard?' he asked.

'I make connections. Put people together that need to meet.'

'And who do you think I need to meet?' he placed his hand on her waist.

She purred like a cat. 'No one, tonight. Only me.'

Winston Faraday III was not naïve to think that this engaging, desirable socialite only had eyes for him, but she could be useful. Very useful.

He knew, or at least suspected, that Isolde was generous with her favors. But she would also need a downpayment from him, some kind of information which would curry goodwill among other senators.

'Perhaps I know a few people,' he said slowly.

Seeing the look in his eyes, the wariness, pushed Radiance to go further. She moved closer to him and touched him on the leg. 'If you could swing a free pass for two, I'd make it worth your while.'

Now she had his attention.

Later that night, while the Halo's danced and sweated and breathed on each other, while they broke the rules – some of them touching each other, maybe even a lingering embrace - outside Cloud End, a solitary figure crept through the front gate, over the dewy grass towards the wraparound porch. In the cloudy darkness, very little could be seen. He tripped once and sprawled on the ground. After cursing his clumsiness and the darkness, Steve Cranmere stopped.

His gaze was drawn to the large, arched windows on the ground floor. Flashing lights played out into the darkness, while thumping music pulsed from within. Cloud End seemed alive, electric. Momentarily, Steve felt an irritating jealousy. While everyone else in the world was restricted by social distancing, facial masking and various untenable (and inane) rules, these Halos were breaking every safety requirement. This perspective solidified Steve's resolve and he quickly took the steps onto the porch. Doing a quick search, he found what he was looking for.

Retrieving plastic bags from his black shirt, he grabbed two empty soda cans and two glasses placing them into the bags and sealing them shut. For good measure, he dug through the trash near the front door and extracted a handful of used tissues, weighty with snot. He was careful to use tweezers to stuff them into another bag.

Grateful that no one had exited the building, Steve leapt down the steps and took one last look behind him. When his eyes rose to the second floor, he noticed one curtain open. A small face peered out at him. Pressed against the window, the little eyes stared over the expanse, perhaps straining to see the cliff, or maybe just longing for freedom. Thankfully, it didn't appear that the little boy saw him, so Steve trundled off quickly through the grass back to the gate. Two hundred yards down the road, he started his pickup and drove back home.

Titus Draper, meanwhile, wondered why there was a moving shadow outside. He glanced down at his arms where a new friend sat. It was a baby rat. The progeny of Oswald Ashford's rodent. He cuddled the white, pointy-nosed animal which sniffed twitchily around him. Titus smiled and patted the little thing.

It was hungry.

```
Intercept Text Message
3 November, 2031
22:24
Subject 14 #0590232 to #0566356
```

Are you awake?

Winnie? How are you doing?

You need to talk to him. I need to get out as soon as possible before someone else is killed.

Somebody died?

Two helicopter pilots and the priest almost bled to death. Stabbed.

That's terrible.

It is terrible. Now talk to him. Plead with him. Do whatever you do best but make this happen. I need to get my life back.

Who?

You know.

Him. SF.

Are you embarrassed to write his name?

This is not a secure place to be writing anything. Text messages are too easy to intercept.

You're getting paranoid in that place. (eye roll emoji)

I know how the Government works. Believe me.

I do. What do you want me to do?

Call me.

18

Bridgette Priveto, Hotelier and leading citizen of Herzfeld did not feel well at all.

It was the dreaded nightmare. The slight tingle of skin, a pain in the chest, swollen sinuses, an annoying cough which made her clear her throat time and time again. Bridgette knew that the Halo had settled on her.

The virus couldn't have come at a worse time. People were starting to travel again. Tourists from all over the country were making reservations. Finally, she'd be able to inch toward the black. Even though she'd received Government payments to keep afloat, she was tired of floating. She wanted to sail.

But Bridgette knew that if she showed her face in public, or worse, *didn't* show her face in public, there would be rumors. A cough would bring suspicion. A blown nose would cause people to draw away from her. A sneeze would certainly bring people in orange suits. But if she took the test, she might be the next one with an indefinite reservation at Cloud End.

Stumbling down the hallway, Bridgette opened the bathroom and flicked on the light. The mirror revealed what she already knew. She was sick. And sickness with Halo was almost worse than the kiss of death. You were shunned, avoided like the... plague. If you had cancer, at least people didn't avoid you, but with the Halo? Welcome to the leprosarium.

Bridgette pounded her fists on the bathroom sink causing the faucet to drip. Opening the medicine cabinet, Bridgette grabbed a vial, popped the top and swallowed two pills to keep her fever manageable. Then, with a trembling hand, she punched in a phone number and waited for the answer.

'Hello?'

'Renata. It's Bridgette.'

Silence.

'Renata?'

'Why are you calling?'

'I... well... I wanted to talk to you?'

'About what?' Renata asked suspiciously.

'Oh, you know, about scenarios.'

More silence.

'Can you hear me?'

'Yes,' Renata said, but then she did something that made Bridgette sit up straighter.

Renata Lerner coughed.

'Are you sick?' Bridgette asked.

'No, of course not.' Another cough. Then a profanity.

'Can I tell you something?'

Renata covered her AutoCom, turned her head, and tried to clear her chest. 'Yes, but I'm not in the mood for a long conversation. I think I've got hay fever.'

Bridgette frowned. 'I think I've got the Halo.'

If Bridgette could have seen Renata's face, something like relief washed over it. 'Do you have the symptoms.'

'Yes.'

'Did you take a test?'

'No. I don't want to. I don't want anyone else to know.'

'How did you get it?' Renata asked.

'I have no idea. I haven't seen anyone different in weeks. There have been no leaks from Cloud End. It's like it spontaneously generated. But if I get sent away, I'm finished...'

A small moan escaped Renata's mouth. 'I have it, too.'

'What do we do now?' Bridgette asked quietly.

'I suppose we have to let the authorities know.'

Bridgette stifled her sob through a snort of dark laughter. 'Turn ourselves in.'

'We're outlaws, now,' Renata joined her.

While Bridgette and Renata commiserated, Gemma Cranmere furiously packed her suitcase. She had long since stopped asking Steve for his opinion on her apparel. His general response was, 'That's good,' or 'That'll do.' This was accompanied by a distracted focus on his fingernails, or swinging feet, or something outside the window. His apathy toward her appearance was frustrating, and slightly disappointing, but that was the way things were. The closer they approached middle age, Gemma was thirty-seven and Steve, thirty-five, the less they had in common.

Until the Halovirus.

With surprising vehemence, Gemma and Steve had found a common battle ground. Daily, the two would start the morning with a steaming cup of coffee, brewed in their expensive, coffee-grinding machine, updating their thoughts regarding new restrictions, new amendments, new ideas of how to turn the virus in their favor. It wasn't as if the Cranmeres were particularly nasty, or they didn't start out that way, it was simply their own form of self-protection and false sense of immortality. Control others to protect yourself.

When the helicopter crashed, Gemma wondered if Steve had anything to do with it. That was a particularly silly, nasty thought. Surely, Steve would not have the guts nor the wherewithal to do something so heinous, and yet... he'd been acting strangely, twitchy, as if expecting someone at the door at any moment.

She glanced in his direction as he sat on her hope chest while she packed. 'What are you thinking about?'

Steve's jittery eyes focused from his nail-chewing to hers. 'Nothing.'

'Come on, what is it? What's eating you?'

'Nothing,' he stressed. But when she stared him down, he relented. 'Okay, so you know how, after that meeting, Bridgette and Renata were putting their heads together and trying to undermine us?'

Gemma would have used stronger terms but nodded.

'Well, I wondered what it would be like if the two people who seemed to be a little less, how should I say it, less *worried* about this deadly virus, were to contract the Halo.'

Gemma stopped her packing entirely. 'What did you do?'

His mouth flopped open and shut like a dying fish. His first thought was to deny what he'd done, but he knew eventually he'd tell her anyway.

'I... uh... well, I think we can safely be assured that the two of them might not be feeling so well very soon.'

Crossing the divide between them, Gemma positioned herself in front of her husband, hands splayed on hips. 'Tell me.'

'The other night, I snuck over to Cloud End...'

'You did what!' she exploded. 'Did you expose yourself to the virus?' She reared back to attack him and he winced. Controling herself, Gemma took a step back. 'You idiot! You've undone us! You're going to get sick. I'm going to get sick. This town is going to die because of your stupidity!'

'No! NO!' he held his hands out in front, surrendering, or begging his wife to understand. 'I took precautions.' When she paused, he continued. 'I simply grabbed a few Halo infested items and brought them back, and then I transferred the virus to highly accessible, handy parts of their belongings.'

'Such as?'

'Handles on their front doors, car doors, steering wheels, mailboxes. I thought it might help us in the long run.'

'Do you realize that anyone who touches those handles, might get the virus too? Once it's out, all of us will get it! Many of us will die! Oh, for heaven's sake, Steve. Do you have one brain cell in your head?'

'I thought you'd be happy. Renata and Bridgette...' he pouted. 'We talked about this, remember?'

She took a deep breath and lowered her voice. 'I understand why you did it, but I wish you would have consulted me first.'

Steve's jaw clenched. She always made it sound as if she was the final authority on all matters. He was supposed to consult her about everything: expenditures at the pub, what they were having to eat at night, what brand of pork 'n beans he was supposed to buy. Frankly, he was tired of justifying everything he did, but in this case, he knew she was probably right. He should have said something to her before doing it. In a strange way, he wanted to please her. He wanted to be useful.

'Well, I didn't,' he said stubbornly, 'but you will thank me once this whole thing blows over.'

Closing the suitcase, Gemma zipped it shut angrily. 'I swear, Steve. Sometimes I wonder...'

'Wonder what?'

'Nothing. Forget it. Just don't do anything stupider while I'm away.'

He jutted his jaw out wanting to say something, but the look in her eye deterred him. 'I'll be a good boy,' he said sarcastically.

'You better be.' Gemma checked her AutoCom and picked up the suitcase. 'If you need anything, message me.' She pointed at her arm.

Steve didn't have an AutoCom. Gemma thought it would be broken, or worse, unused. So, he continued with his iPhone 21.

With a huff (and without a kiss), she turned from the room and descended the stairs to leave the house. Steve stood at the front windows watching her pull out from the garage and reverse down the driveway. She was going to pick up Rector Falkirk and Selina Lomiller, the baker of Herzfeld, Unsurprisingly, Steve felt a sense of relief as his wife's car vanished from sight.

His phone dinged from a text.

It was Edgar.

Oh, wow.

Igor saw them coming but couldn't understand why Bridgette and Renata were wheeling suitcases down the main street. As they strolled under the awnings on the other side of the street, Igor saw Bridgette pause at the door of her hotel while Renata waited outside. Renata's arms were crossed and her foot tapped impatiently. She appeared to be cold, shivering. Indeed, the autumn was certainly setting in, but Igor thought it strange that these two were packing up for an ill-advised vacation to warmer climates, or so he supposed.

Bridgette appeared moments later with a computer bag slung over her shoulder. She said something to Renata who nodded, and they stepped down off the curb to cross the street. A few cars were parked in front of shops, but for the most part, the town was empty. From his perch in the police office, Igor had only seen a dozen people including Edgar and Steve, who were slinking towards the Saloon, and Reverend Falkirk, Gemma and Selina who were driving in Gemma's older 2027 electric Ford Zing.

Igor sat up straighter when Renata sneezed. Bridgette reached to her and patted her on the shoulder while Renata shook her head and wiped her eye.

What in the world...

They stepped into the shade of the awning on his side of the street. Renata's face was flushed. Bridgette reached for the handle of the police office door. As it swung outwards, the hinge creaked. Strangely, they stopped outside the door.

'What can I do for you, ladies?' Igor asked.

'We need to talk,' Bridgette said.

'Well, come in,' he motioned for the chairs across the desk from him. He quickly scanned the room for any sensitive documents, but all had been shoved recklessly in manilla folders and stuffed into drawers. Behind him, on a corkboard, news stories about the helicopter crash were pinned with various strings linked to other ideas. Igor was old school that way. He liked to visibly see the interconnections.

The women paused, looking at each other.

'What's the problem? Is my office too messy?'

Bridgette cleared her throat. The rasp in her voice sounded painful. 'Renata and I... we... I think...'

'Spit it out,' Igor said frustratedly.

'We've got the Halo,' her words, frightened and loud, made her cringe.

Reactively, Igor touched his mask and leaned back in his chair. 'You took the test?'

They nodded.

Igor blew out a long stream of air. *It's here.* 'Okay, okay,' he searched around the desk for something that might look like a protocol. Police departments across the country had been briefed about these eventualities, but Igor had hoped his own thick sheaf of Government directives about the pandemic with the title, *Halovirus: How to Control the Panic*, would be unnecessary.

'What do we do?' Renata asked.

'Do you need to go to the hospital? How sick are you?'

It wasn't lost on Bridgette and Renata that he had not moved from his chair. He was fastened to it unable to arise.

'We wouldn't want to endanger any other lives,' Renata responded.

'That's good,' Igor said, but the thought, *Only mine*, sprang to his mind and he squelched it quickly. 'The first thing I have to do is get suited up. Then we'll have to call Gemma...' the women shared a quick glance. They seemed afraid. 'And then,' he swallowed, 'I'll drive you out to Cloud End.'

Resignation and apprehension was writ across their faces. Still in the doorway, Bridgette nervously adjusted the computer bag on her shoulder, while Renata turned her face to the side and coughed. That was enough to get Igor moving faster.

He had to get his hazmat suit on.

Fast.

Gemma saw Igor's phone number show up on her AutoCom while driving. Frowning, she tapped her ear enabling the implanted cell phone receptor to pick up the call. Falkirk, who sat in the front seat, watched her while Selina's head was reclined on the back seat. She had fallen asleep almost immediately after leaving Herzfeld.

'This is Mayor Cranmere.'

'Gemma, we've got a problem.'

'What is it?'

Igor's voice rang out in her ear. When the news came, Gemma's face registered multiple emotions: anger – the twitch in her jaw; fear – arched eyebrows; satisfaction – the slight sneer; determination – eyelids lowered.

'Okay, we'll have to deal with it.'

Igor asked her a question.

'We've talked about this. The protocols say, either the hospital, or...' she glanced nervously at Falkirk, '... Cloud End.'

Falkirk's eyes widened in surprise. He turned in his seat to see if Selina was listening, which she was not, and waited impatiently for her to finish the phone call.

When Gemma did, tapping her ear twice, Falkirk licked his lips and raised his eyebrows. 'Who is it?'

'Bridgette and Renata.'

'Both?'

She nodded.

'How horrible,' he ran a hand through his thinning hair.

'Yes,' she answered slowly, 'but the information might be a blessing in disguise.'

'The Halovirus cannot possibly be a blessing, especially when two prominent figures of Herzfeld...'

'With all due respect, Magnus, Bridgette and Renata have just taken one for the team. We can now tell the Government they have brought the Halo to us.' She tapped the steering wheel and an evil grin spread across her face. 'We're going to sue them!'

Falkirk shook his head. 'Even if we could sue them, and even if we could prove that the Halo came from Cloud End, what good would it do? We're still in the same predicament. We've got to get those people out of Cloud End and onto an island.'

She turned to stare into his close-set eyes. 'Even if Bridgette and Renata are shipped with them.'

Falkirk took a deep breath and stared through the windshield. Finally, he nodded. 'Even with them.'

18

Emergency Minutes Joint Pandemic Committee

5 November, 2031
19:11-20:18

Attendance:

████████████████████████████████ convened meeting. According to intel,
video logs, █████████████████ and ██████████████████, the subjects
were not changed by subliminal messaging nor overt psychological work.
Due to stabbings and the tragic helicopter crash, these two traumatic
events seemed to be galvanizing the subjects, not tearing them apart to
seek safety with the Government.

███████████████████████ became suspicious and made enquiries into
Governmental sources (████████████████ did not divulge identity of
source), regarding methods of release from CECC.

███████████████████████████ told the committee that two citizens
of Herzfeld had been infected with the Halo 29 and had, without
authorization, dropped them off at CECC. Measures needed to be taken.
█████████████████ suggested shutting off all internet access so that the
Herzfeld citizens would not relay messages to the nearby town.

██████████████████████ will be stepping up the psychological modification
program. New data needed.

Intelligence Director Reed-Conway called an emergency meeting.

As the conspirators filed in quietly, she studied their eyes. Emery Donaldson looked bemused, while both Senators seemed concerned. Monica Portney's dark eyes darted around the room. Monica clicked the pen in her hand. In. Out. In. Out. Soon after, Director Renfroe shut the door behind him. He was carrying a briefcase which had been chained to his wrist.

Cloud End's demise was picking up speed. Although the subjects had only been interned for a little more than a month, their informant had notified them of two strange things. First, the majority of Halos were resisting the influence of the nightly messages. Not only was paranoia openly spoken of, the informant said that they'd even begun enjoying themselves. Second, the Halos were talking amongst themselves about wanting to stay, even after their lights turned green.

Excluding Senator Faraday.

He was not a happy camper.

In fact, Quentin had revealed to the others (but not his own source, Isolde) that Faraday was becoming suspicious. While the average recovery time from the Halovirus was just over two weeks, Winston had not had symptoms for ten days. Isolde attempted to mollify him, but he was angry and beginning to reach out to other powerful people to push for his release. If he got out, the entire mission might...

'There's been an incident,' Reed-Conway started.

'We already know about the helicopter accident,' Donaldson crossed his arms. He looked unperturbed. Nothing was out of place. Not his hair. Not his tie. His clean-shaven jaw jutted out slightly.

'And the stabbing is old news,' Renfroe added.

'It's worse,' she said.

'How could it be worse than that?' Senator Membree asked.

'The virus is out.'

Donaldson rolled his eyes. 'How is that news?'

18

Director Reed-Conway's lips pulled back in a snarl. 'Herzfeld. Two leading citizens were infected.'

'So?' Renfroe lifted his arms in exasperation.

'Without telling us, Dylan, the town citizens forced the infected people into Cloud End.'

'What?' Senator Membree exploded.

'There are two new Halos at Cloud End.'

Angry conversations started at the same time. Raised voices. 'What were they thinking? How will this affect the mission?' Senator Forsythe calmed them with his hands. 'Please, be calm. Focus. We need to ask the right questions.'

'What are those questions?' Membree asked.

'Does this really matter?' Forsythe started.

'Of course it matters,' Renfroe said. 'The Halos were chosen strategically as a cross section of the country. If outsiders are thrown in, who knows what could happen?'

'And what are the possible outcomes?' Forsythe asked.

'They could actually *give* the virus back to the participants.'

'So...?'

Donaldson raised his hand like a schoolboy. 'What if they tear the place up?'

'Why would they do that?' Monica asked.

'Because they're angry. Wouldn't you be angry?' Donaldson's mouth twisted into a wry smile. 'If they destroy the place, maybe they'll be taken home, put under house arrest.'

'No, they wouldn't do that,' Renfroe replied testily. 'The more likely scenario is that the town will be in an uproar because the 'virus has escaped.' Did you hear about the Herzfeld delegation on the way?' They shook their heads. 'Supposedly they're going to try to influence us to move the Convo somewhere else. I heard they were planning to sue the Government.'

Senator Membree snorted. 'What good will that do? Even if they win, we'll just raise taxes.'

Renfroe ignored Senator Membree. 'Be that as it may, we need to shut off the internet at Cloud End immediately. No information in or out that does not come from us or is first filtered by us. It's bad enough that Faraday is a loaded cannon but imagine these two from Herzfeld delivering inside information to other citizens. They might even try to burn it down.'

'Let's not get ahead of ourselves,' Reed-Conway said with a sidelong glance at Membree who held her eyes momentarily. 'I agree with Senator Membree. We need to move ahead. Once the internet is manipulated, it's her turn.'

Around the circle, worried faces peered at each other. They hoped Dr. Boeder-Mankins was prepared.

19

Sam Draper's head was pounding. As he peeled open his eyes and gazed towards the thin edge of light bordering the drapes, he was aware that it wasn't just his head that hurt, but his entire body. Noticing the Halo Detector's still-red color, his first worry was that the virus had returned in full force, but then he remembered what had transpired the night before. Although the pain was real, so was the pleasure of remembering.

It had been a long time – years, perhaps – since Sam and Dorothy had experienced the spontaneous kind of enjoyment, they had the night before. Sam was unsure how it started. Someone had connected to the 3D television to bring up live videos of 1980's and '90's music. Still amazed by the technology, the revelers were able to dance and party the night away while Michael Jackson, U2, Pearl Jam and MC Hammer played for them. When Richard Marx popped up for 'All those couples out there' (Alonzo Turner had proclaimed this over the PA), people, whether couple or not, connected happily. Though the Drapers were the only permanent 'couple,' many partyers danced. Some touched and remembered what it was like not to be afraid of human contact. Father Lawrence danced chastely with Chantelle Ingram. Wallis Takamoto jived with Alonzo. Damian Bellows and Monica Xiao were quite adept at Hammer Time. Sam and Dorothy clung to each other while their children ran around the makeshift dance floor staring up at the faces of musicians who were now (if not deceased) quite geriatric.

During the night, the bar had been flung open. Kylie and Jack doubled as bartenders serving basic drinks and the random crushed-ice concoction. Sam wasn't sure how much alcohol he had consumed. But it was enough for Dorothy and him to loosen their inhibitions and, ultimately, when they staggered back to their bedroom giggling like teenagers (their children in tow wondering what-in-the-world-is-going-on-with-their-stumbling parents), the married couple fell into bed and made love for the first time in a very long time.

The Halovirus had taken its toll on them, not just on their sex lives, but their perspective about marriage. Constantly bombarded by social-distancing messages and measures, unconsciously, the two began to grow apart. Dorothy, after wearing her mask continuously while taking the kids to school, then shopping, then returning home from her work at the craft shop, then picking up the kids from day-care and school, then preparing dinner and waiting for Sam to arrive, did not want to embrace her husband for fear of contracting the virus and putting him out of commission. Not only was their love-life stilted, but so was their conversation. The Déjà vu of Coronavirus was almost overwhelming. Yet they had done the best that they could. They could see what the constant fear had done to their children. Gina, already socially awkward, had become almost entirely disconnected from the physical world. She spent most of her time on BeMe, the social media platform which allowed kids to connect in the digital realm as they wanted to be seen, but in Hologram. Gina did not tell them about her digital personality, a 23-year-old Influencer with enhancements to match, but Dorothy was waiting for the right time to confront her. Pasqual was struggling with Math and English. Without a live teacher to hold him accountable, he daydreamed during the lessons. Titus, on the other hand, had excelled with online learning. He had never known a life without fear, panic, social manipulation. Titus had just learned to adapt.

Since their quarantine at Cloud End, Sam and Dorothy realized something beautifully strange. The Draper family was spending less and less time online and beginning to enjoy real time in the real world. The kids were running around outdoors. They were making friends with the St. Croix children, and the adults were mingling with other people – different people who had different backgrounds and different interests. Asking questions and hearing stories about Jacquelyn Archer's biography and her rise to the heights of business; reveling in Alonzo Turner's gravedigging episodes; even Seraphim Wyman's personal tragedy and recovery was transformational for Sam. Not that he was conscious of it, but Sam had, over the years, simply connected with homogenous people, and he had been the poorer for it.

He was surprised how diverse his fellow Cloud Enders were. They were a true cross-section of society.

19

And now they were coming together as an odd kind of Addams Family: sick but surprisingly content.

Sam sat up and groaned. Dorothy did not move. Her breathing was deep and her hair was splayed behind her on the pillow. A dribble of saliva sat at the corner of her mouth and her t-shirt was bunched up over her belly. He pondered her in such a state, feeling a glow of love for her.

After standing unsteadily, Sam staggered to the bathroom. He relieved himself and moved to the window to pull back the shade. The bright light stung his eyes. Wincing, he shaded them with his hand and felt the pressure in his head rise. When his pupils finally adjusted, he saw his children running in the cold morning air towards the cliff's edge.

'What time is it?' Dorothy groaned as she placed her forearm over her forehead.

'No idea.' Sam checked his phone. 'Almost 10.'

'Wow,' she moaned, 'when is the last time we did that?'

'Which part?' he smirked.

'All of it.'

'A long time.' Sam shut the drape again and shuffled back to bed. Slowly, he slid down and waited for the pounding in his head to subside. 'How are you feeling?'

'Like I've been inside a dryer for the night.' She smacked her lips together. 'Dehydrated and hungover.'

'Me too.'

Dorothy reached to the side of her bed knocking the lamp but not upending it. She grabbed her phone then the water bottle. 'Quite the night, wasn't it?'

'Yeah.'

'It felt good. Kind of like it used to be, before the viruses and all that.'

'Did you see Alonzo dancing? It looked like his pants were on fire.'

Dorothy laughed once, then stopped and held her head, groaning. 'The kids were good, too.'

'Yes. How weird is it to say that they've had a good time here?'

'*We've* had a good time here,' Dorothy responded quietly. 'It's opened my eyes to some things.'

Sam grunted and waited for her to continue.

'Out there, we don't go anywhere. We stay at home, watch our movies, entertain ourselves – disengage, I suppose. Gosh, the kids are getting big, and we're getting older. We haven't done much in the last few years.'

'We haven't been allowed to,' he responded. 'With Government regulations, and all the extra requirements, even if we wanted to, it was against the rules. Nobody wants to go camping in a plastic tent, wearing masks, and distanced from everyone else.'

'Maybe after we get out of here, we should pack up the tent and go for a drive. The kids would love it. *I* would love it,' Dorothy said with a smile. 'We could stop in the forest somewhere and just be outside. Just us.'

'That sounds nice. But we still have to wait for restrictions to lift.'

Dorothy frowned. 'We might be senior citizens by the time that happens.'

Sam shrugged. 'Maybe we'll sneak out.'

While the Drapers plotted their eventual escape, the newest residents of Cloud End, Bridgette and Renata, huddled miserably in the corner of the atrium, coffees before them, leaning in to have a quiet discussion. There had been a party. Renata and Bridgette were appalled by the severe lack of restraint from these sick people. But what made it worse was they were feeling miserable.

'You'd think they'd be trying to get better, to get out of here,' Bridgette said.

'The irresponsibility they showed. No masks. No distancing. Dancing! Touching! It's no wonder they're still here.' Renata frowned.

'It's worse than we thought. We'll have to message Gemma, and maybe Igor, about what's going on.' Bridgette sipped her coffee and swallowed painfully. 'This kind of activity should get them shut down.'

As they quietly executed their judgement, Alonzo noticed them and pulled out a seat at the next table. 'Good morning,' he croaked.

Bridgette nodded, but Renata stared cautiously.

'That was a fun night last night. Too bad we didn't see you out there on the dance floor.'

'We thought it best not to be too close,' Bridgette responded tersely, 'considering that a pandemic is raging around us.'

Alonzo continued to smile as he leaned back in his chair. 'Well, we've already got it, so I guess we're not going to catch it again. Might as well make lemonade out of lemons.'

'Is that what you call this? Lemonade?'

In spite of the condescension, Alonzo continued. 'Yeah, I suppose so. What, are we going to live out the rest of our lives in fear? Sounds a bit like not stepping on cracks or refraining from whistling in a graveyard.'

'It's just common sense,' Bridgette sniffed, then coughed. 'If we want this pandemic to finish, we're going to have to work together.'

'What do you think we've been doing?' Alonzo asked. 'Do you think we've just been twiddling our thumbs?'

'I bet you haven't even been vaccinated.'

Alonzo's mouth scrunched up. 'Ah. You're one of those.'

'What's that supposed to mean?'

'Nothin.'

'Are you insinuating something? I'm just protecting the vulnerable from people like you. People who disregard the rules for their own selfish interests. I wear my mask. I socially isolate as much as possible. I make sure others do the same...'

'And yet here you are,' Alonzo interrupted smugly. 'Sick as a dog, right?'

'This virus is no joke, if that's what you mean.'

'Sure. Sure. People have died from it. Some are still sick, but look around. We're all supposed to be sick, or that's what the little red light says. But somehow, I haven't heard anyone cough, or sneeze, or ache for a good two weeks, other than you.'

'How come you're still here, then?' Bridgette asked.

'Lucky, I guess.'

Renata coughed. 'You must be joking.'

He shrugged again. 'You haven't been here long enough to see what's really happening. There are people here whose lives are changing for the better. Halo has opened a door. Now that we're all recovering, the thought of re-emerging back into the septic flow of what culture has become, that's more frightening.'

'I think the virus has scrambled your mind,' Bridgette said testily. 'Out there,' she pointed to the front door, past the empty library and its external bookshelf, 'is a world of opportunity. In here, this is prison.'

Alonzo knew that there was nothing he could say to convince these two. He believed they had swallowed enough media to poison their perspectives, so he remained mute.

'Out there,' she continued to gesture, 'is work and meaning. I own the hotel in Herzfeld and there are scores of people who are waiting, just for a little while longer until it's safe, to flock to Herzfeld and the amazing people.'

Alonzo wasn't quite certain about the 'amazingness' of the citizens as displayed by these two, but he held his tongue.

'And then, as we get back to normal, we can go about our business, raising families, working jobs, paying taxes, traveling... Doesn't that sound nice?'

'Sure,' Alonzo agreed.

'Then why wouldn't you want to get out of here as soon as possible?' Bridgette pushed.

'Because I found friends in here.'

'And you can't make them out there?'

For Alonzo, this was a primary question of life. Finding anyone to interact with him had been a struggle. It wasn't simply his role which turned people off. No, it was the way of the world. Most people younger than he spent most of their time on BeMe. The older ones invested their time in social media chats – old school tech like Instagram and TikTok. It was like they couldn't really move past the past. Alonzo's problem was that he was an anomaly, an analogue avatar in a digital world. While everyone else was speaking in binary code, he was much more interested in sounds and sights – sensory stuff. But finding others who wanted to do that, especially after two pandemics, nuclear scares, a world completely paralyzed by fear, was like trying to find a diamond in a tub of broken glass.

'People don't even know what friendship is,' Alonzo responded.

'Perhaps you'd like to enlighten us?' Renata motioned between herself and Bridgette.

'Uh, you don't seem particularly receptive to me.'

Renata waved the idea off. 'No, we're just interested in what you have to say. Everything you've talked about so far has been, how shall we say, fascinating?' Bridgette nodded her condescending encouragement.

He studied their eyes. 'I've spent the last ten years trying to figure people out. Nobody, and I mean nobody, wants to get together anymore. The bars are drying up, sports stadiums are half-full, cafés are full of snobby computer geeks staring at their AutoComs, and we don't even have cinemas anymore. Do you remember what those were like?'

They nodded.

'Now throw in the fact that we're being watched every moment of our lives, recorded, processed, programmed. You can't go outside without some alarm going off to tell you you aren't where you're supposed to be, or how many steps you've walked, or how many calories you've absorbed. We talk to our cars and they spit us out to park, but nobody goes together. That would be too dangerous.' He rolled his eyes. 'I feel lonely because I may never get to experience friendship, at the very least, and love, at the most.'

'Oh, come on,' Bridgette said, 'that's an incredibly bleak picture of an exciting world. We can go anywhere online and be who we always wanted to be. We can meet exotic people without having to go through the expense and time of meeting up. It's just easier, wouldn't you agree?'

'You're missing the point,' he insisted. 'The human experience is about interaction and learning to live *with* each other, not learning to live *without* each other. When was the last time you went for a walk and held somebody's hand?' He noticed their reactions. 'I bet it's been years. But if you touch somebody's hand, you touch a nerve in their soul.'

They frowned.

He reached his hands out to them and they recoiled. 'Come on, grab my hand. Hold it. You're not going to get sicker. I promise.'

They studied his hands as if they were spiders.

'See, you have no trust.'

'But why would we trust you? We know nothing about you?' Bridgette did not move.

'I bet you'd be willing to have a conversation online with someone you don't know. In fact, I bet it happens every day.'

'Yes, but we don't have to touch them.'

'Physically, for sure, but if we weren't affected by the things people wrote about us, the world would be a happier place.' They both looked away guiltily. 'Look, I know you're afraid, and you're not feeling your best, but this place,' he glanced around the room, '*heals* people.'

'See, when we arrived, we were just like you: distanced, wary to the point of paranoia. But our close proximity, as uncomfortable as it might have been, was as therapeutic as the distancing was outside. I'm not one of those people who believes in a Government conspiracy. I know they were doing their best with the data they had, but we all know mistakes were made. Panic makes people do hasty things and hasty things often turn out bad.'

Even though his hands were still outstretched, Bridgette and Renata remained fixed and confused. Each one wondered about the truth. Like a strange dream, they remembered what it was like all those years ago, growing up before the Coronavirus pandemic, riding bikes, playing with iPads, eating a meal with their parents. But everything changed.

'We can't change the fact that you're here,' Alonzo continued. 'Despite your best efforts, the Halo found you. But you're not going to die, at least not from the Halo.' He laughed, but they frowned. 'When I'm out there in the world you say is so amazing, I'm around people who are grieving their dead loved ones. They shake their heads and sob, it's sad, and often confusing, but should we be that surprised? No one escapes this place with their life, so...' he paused, wondering how to finish the thought. 'Shouldn't we live before we die? Do you call what you were doing out there living? Or just existing?'

'Living,' Renata responded uncertainly.

'Come on,' Alonzo said with frustration, 'you can do this! Remember!'

'But I'm frightened,' Bridgette admitted. 'What happens if we start... touching... people again and we keep getting the virus?'

'But what is the virus?' he asked. 'What is it that's really killing us? Is it this germ that multiplies in our bodies, makes us feel bad for a couple of weeks, and then we get better? Or is it something bigger. More...' Alonzo knew the word, but he couldn't bring it to the tip of his tongue.

'Infectious...' Renata said. She inched forward drawing closer to the gravedigger.

'That's a great word!' He lowered his voice. 'I was talking to the priest the other day and...'

Renata suddenly drew back. 'Don't tell me this is a religious conversion technique.'

'No! No! He wasn't talking about religion or conversion or any of that stuff. He was saying the *true* infection is distrust and unforgiveness. It spreads faster than the Halo and it lasts longer too.'

'Still sounds like a sermon to me,' Renata said distrustfully.

Frustrated, Alonzo pushed on. 'When you get a virus on your AutoCom, what do you do?'

'Take it to the store.'

'And because it's embedded in you, it's like a surgeon has to remove it before you can use it again.'

'Okay,' Renata's voice lowered.

'When is the last time you didn't feel distrustful? When is the last time you thought to yourself, 'I think I'll go hang out with my neighbor?'' He noticed them thinking. 'Exactly. You're infected by a cultural virus that has almost completely destroyed humanity. We look at everyone else and think,

205

'This person has the ability to kill me,' instead of, 'This person has the ability to change my life for the better.''

'You're starting to sound like an infomercial,' Bridgette said, trying to deflect him.

While his arms were outstretched, he put his head between them. 'You can do this. You can get better. You can get rid of the real virus. Just grab my hands.'

'Are you some kind of shaman?'

'If it will help you reach out, then, yes. You can call me whatever name you want.'

Renata glanced at Bridgette. Neither needed to, but both wanted to. They wanted to see what it would be like. Perhaps he was just another cracked pot on the broken shelf of society. But if what he said was true, if he could actually help them remember...

Bridgette reached out first. Alonzo did not move. He did not want to scare her. As his brown eyes encountered her fearful ones, he encouraged her with his smile. Finally, their fingertips met. Bridgette gasped and pulled back. Although she had accidentally bumped elbows with people, and occasionally ran into others at the hotel (but with a quick hand wash and shower when available), the feeling was nothing like this. To actively choose to touch someone else's hand, even one as rough as Alonzo's, was electric.

'It feels...' Bridgette was unable to put into words what had just happened.

'...good,' Alonzo smiled. He wiggled his fingers for Renata to try, and when she did, the same thing happened. Alonzo grinned widely. 'See what I mean? That's what we've encountered over the last few weeks. It wasn't immediate. It's not like we walked in here and people were acting like it was hug factory. We just started needing something different.'

'Does everyone feel this?' Bridgette asked.

He shrugged. 'I don't think Senator Faraday feels like this.'

'He's a bit standoffish?' Renata wanted to reach out again but didn't want it to be creepy. There was something decidedly wonderful about this man. 'Well, that generally happens with politicians don't you think?

'I suppose.'

A bell rang. Bridgette and Renata appeared concerned, but Alonzo brushed it away. 'It's time for Group.'

'As in therapy?' Renata asked.

'Supposedly it's good for us. We get to talk about our feelings and stuff.'

'And you like that?'

His eyebrows arched and his mouth pinched. 'I guess I thought it was a bunch of malarkey before we started, but it was the beginning of us coming together. Once people start to trust, the virus starts to die.' He stood and held out a hand to Bridgette. 'Do you want to come with me?'

Renata looked surprised and slightly rejected that the gravedigger did not extend a hand to her. But the thought brought her back to reality.

'I... don't... I don't think I'm quite healthy enough yet,' Bridgette responded without taking his hand.

Alonzo nodded sadly. 'Well, if you change your mind, we're in the cinema.'

While the menagerie of humans, in various states of sleep deprivation or hangover, began to stagger towards the cinema, an ever-growing anger infused Winston Faraday III. *Enough of this.* For a month, his work had been stifled by this facility and these people. The virus had minimally affected him, but everyone else he interacted with was free to roam. They'd had the Halo, suffered, then gone about their lives grateful to be done with it. But here he was, a successful and popular politician, with sway over a large contingent, reduced to clickbait. That morning, Winston had searched for anything – anything at all – about his missing presence in the senate, but he only found a few conspiracy nuts theorizing his abduction, his incarceration, or worst of all, his death in a Southeast Asian drug house.

These people at Cloud End were loony. Dancing and drinking as if it was November of 2019. The night before, he had attempted to stifle the noise on the dance floor with his pillow. Once he had called reception - no answer, of course, because they were probably serving drinks in the atrium. He blamed his tiredness on the parasitic masses below him, those common people who, though necessary for his re-election, were an irritation to his noble-minded work.

When the bell rang for group therapy, Winston debated whether to attend. Previously, it only took ten minutes before people started crying. They'd exposed parts of their skeletons which should have remained safely in the closet. After a roll of his eyes and an exhalation of disgust, the senator rose, straightened his tie, and harrumphed from the theater. That kind of exhibition was the last thing he needed.

Sighing loudly, Faraday studied himself in the mirror and adjusted the cuffs of his dress shirt. He had decided not to wear the sport coat, though he felt naked without it. His eyes caught momentarily on his Freedom Outfit, as he called it, a white suit with vest and shoes. This would be his clothing when the Halo Detector turned green – when he was released from the hellhole.

With practiced austerity, Winston Faraday opened the door and stepped into the corridor narrowly avoiding the missiles shot by one of the small boys. Not stopping to apologize, the older boy, with a makeshift gun made from sticks and masking tape, screamed, and hid behind a potted plant. In his other hand, he held a grenade – a fist-sized ball of rolled up duct tape. Shoving a finger to his lips, he *Shhhh*ed the man, making it clear to Senator Winston Faraday III that he did not want his position revealed to the enemy.

Soon, the enemy rounded the corner at exactly the same speed as the stick-gun, tape-grenade wielding boy at his feet.

'He's right there,' Faraday pointed at Pasqual and turned away from the angered boy. Titus smiled gratefully, aimed his gun at Pasqual and killed his brother.

Faraday held his head high passing the gravedigger's room, then the police officer's and finally Wallis Takamoto's, where he descended the stairs to the atrium. The gravedigger and the two most recent arrivals, people from Herzfeld, were strolling to the cinema. Others joined the stream speaking happily as if attending a wedding.

Once again, Dr. Boeder-Mankins sat in her traditional spot behind the glass, notebook in hand, sipping from a glass bottle of water. She appeared nervously uncomfortable.

Faraday took his seat in the rear of the theater, above and beyond everyone else. The others sat next to each other in the front half. Even the murderous drug addict.

As the lights dimmed slightly to signal the session was beginning, Dr. Boeder-Mankins adjusted her microphone and began to speak.

'Welcome, everyone. I hope you are feeling better than you have in ages.' A few residents clapped their hands. 'This morning, we've got a special treat.'

Faraday was highly suspicious of what was about to happen next.

20

While Senator Faraday suspiciously studied the psychologist, Gemma Cranmere, Selina Lomiller and Rector Falkirk waited in reception to visit with the Intelligence Director, Stella Reed-Conway. As Gemma rifled through her social media on her AutoCom, Rector Falkirk imagined the conversation about to take place. Throughout his professional life in ministry, it had been his practice to immediately distrust a woman with a hyphenated last name. To his mind, the hyphen designated the woman as a women's libber, which in turn meant she was a misanthropist, which of course meant he would not be listened to. Thus, before Rector Magnus Falkirk met Stella Reed-Conway, he already disliked her. She was probably divorced, anyway. Sinner.

Stella Reed-Conway's secretary, a young man in his twenties, with glasses and physique to make most men jealous, rose to greet them and allow them entry into Ms. Reed-Conway's office. Falkirk pulled himself up taller and ambled beyond the secretary into an expansive room with a million-dollar view. As they waited for the young woman standing in the window to finish her AutoCom conversation, Falkirk reflected on their journey.

The trip from Herzfeld to the Capitol had been informative, at least from the rector's perspective. Although he disagreed with Gemma on many points, including her conclusion regarding the need for worship services to be suspended indefinitely, he held his tongue and allowed her to ramble her way from topic to topic. Race. Religion. Social media. Identity politics and especially the news of Renata and Bridgette's sicknesses. Falkirk was impressed, and slightly concerned, that Gemma was more opinionated than he had known.

Selina was a good traveling companion. Even though she knew little about political things, and was ignorant about other worldly matters, she laughed heartily when necessary. She dressed gaily, decked out in flowery, knee length dress and white gloves, with which she touched the sides of her mouth when her mask was pulled down to drink. As the conversation floated back and forth, more than once, Reverend Falkirk wondered what

Selina really thought about Gemma's rambling. Masks made reading faces much more difficult.

The highway to the Capitol was bereft of traffic. Even when they approached the city, only a few large trucks, construction vehicles and delivery vans were motoring madly from here to there. Now that it was November, the leaves were changing hues giving the skyline a new beard. While Gemma prattled and Selina laughed, Magnus reclined enjoying the scenery yet paying attention to the conversation.

The closer they approached the Capitol, the more drones he spotted. They looked like mosquitos as they hovered above houses and businesses dropping off their goods and whizzing back from where they had been sent. Falkirk reminisced about the days of deliverymen who dropped packages off on porches and then stopped to chat for a little bit.

Finally, they arrived at the Capitol, unpacked their bags, and stayed the first night at a hotel. Gemma ordered out for food, confident that her extra precautions would be helpful. It was from a local fast-food restaurant where the only option was to order via AutoCom/phone code and have it delivered by drone to their waiting arms. When they awoke, Magnus prepared himself for the fight to come, donning his perfectly ironed, black clerical shirt and collar, grey slacks, and shiny black shoes. Even if the world did not take religion seriously, they would think twice about disregarding him.

Now that they had entered Stella Reed-Conway's office, Magnus was surprised to see a young woman, recently returned from her AutoCom conversation, now sitting behind a desk, safety shield planted squarely between them. She seemed dainty, almost weak. Her shoulder length hair hung loosely to her shoulders, but away from her face revealing dark eyes and prominent cheekbones. She had not covered her mouth and nose with a mask which showed red lips tilted slightly to the side, bemused. Magnus half-bowed to her. Gemma did bow and planted herself squarely in front of Stella's desk and shield, arms crossed.

'Thank you for seeing us, Ms. Conway.'

'It's Ms. *Reed*-Conway,' Stella corrected. Falkirk smirked. He was right. Man-hater.

'My apologies.' Gemma did not correct her mistake but launched into Herzfeld's issues. 'With all due respect, we recognize the difficult position the Government is in. With so many cases of Halovirus, the floundering economy, negative optics from the press, you're in a tight spot.'

Stella's face tightened, but she did not respond. Her AutoCom buzzed, but she did not pull her eyes away from Gemma who was wearing a dark business suit with hair pulled severely to the back of her head.

'I'm sure you can appreciate, though, the desperate place you've hopefully unknowingly put the people of Herzfeld in. Without consultation, without any thought of the danger brought to us, two of our leading citizens have been taken to the Convalescent Center, Cloud End, the very Convo that you unilaterally decided to set aside, you've...'

Stella held up her hands. 'Excuse me, Ms...'

'Mrs. Cranmere. Gemma Cranmere.'

'Mrs. Cranmere. I'm sorry you feel that this has been personally done to you. I *can* appreciate the struggle that many towns feel, including...' the name failed her.

'Herzfeld.'

'Of course. But if I could give you a little perspective. Millions of citizens are infected with the Halovirus. In the Capitol alone, thirty percent of the populations has, or has had, Halovirus. Businesses are shutting down. Education is becoming more and more difficult. I'm sure you can appreciate why we've...'

'I'm the mayor of Herzfeld,' Gemma interrupted. 'I'm sure *you* can appreciate the delicate position *we've* been placed in as opposed to the Capitol which seems to have moved along without much damage to the Government or to its subsidiaries. Everything seems to be humming with all the taxes...'

'We've delivered stimulus packages,' Stella replied testily.

'Thank you for that,' Selina's happy voice leaked from her mask. 'Why, we've been able to...'

'At whose expense?' Gemma interrupted. Selina's eyes widened and she stopped speaking. 'Who is going to pay for that?'

'Eventually it will be absorbed into the national debt and we'll...'

'It's people like me, Selina and Rector Falkirk who will be paying this money back. Not you, nor your Governmental friends, but us, the little guys.'

Stella took a deep breath and stood but didn't approach beyond her glass wall. 'Before we travel down this rabbit hole, I need to know the purpose of your inquiry, Mrs. Cranmere.'

'We want Cloud End to close. Now. It's too dangerous.'

The director's eyes shifted to the rector who smiled. Selina was completely ignored. 'Yes, Ms. Reed-Conway. Or is it Missus?' She didn't answer so Falkirk continued. 'Why Herzfeld?'

'As detailed by various press releases, it wasn't just Herzfeld, but both Government and national interests decided that remote areas were better locations for isolation.'

'Why not islands?' Falkirk asked.

'The expense of the Convo itself is onerous. To situate one on an island, with transport, staffing and supply – the cost would be unbelievable. We're barely making ends meet with those we've started.'

'And yet somehow the Government has no issues with its own standards of living,' Falkirk said with a smile as he waved out the window of her office into the wide blue expanse of the city. Restrictions had been eased in the Capitol. Masks were no longer needed outdoors and children's face coverings were no longer mandatory. Not so in Herzfeld.

Reed-Conway blushed. 'We're doing everything we can. We're working hard to solve the nation's problems, but there are costs. Sometimes we have to make difficult decisions.'

Gemma snorted and rolled her eyes.

'What exactly is it that you hope I can do for you, Mrs. Cranmere, and...'

'Rector Magnus Falkirk.' He wanted to extend his hand for a firm shake, but the glass partition blocked that option. Selina only blinked as she was conveniently ignored.

The brief given to Dr. Jane Boeder-Mankins was straightforward. The current residents of Cloud End were to be inundated with massive amounts of both subliminal and overt messaging reminding them of two things: 1. That they needed the Government's protection and handouts and 2. That their goodwill for each other was a mirage.

After last night's spontaneous celebration, the psychologist's task had grown much harder. In spite of the mission's worst intentions, altruism had increased and inversely, paranoia decreased.

As an accomplished psychologist, Jane should have admitted to herself the truth of what was happening. These people were lonely and starved for attention. If they had come to her individually in the outside world, she would have advised them to put down their electronic devices and re-enter the physical world. Go for a walk with someone. Visit the café. Have a conversation. Join a volleyball league.

But at Cloud End, she was to prescribe the exact opposite. Though paid handsomely for her work, Jane felt a stab of guilt. *Do no harm* had transformed into *Do no* permanent *harm.*

'It's nice to hear the pleasant buzz,' she started as the last of the stragglers took their seats in the cinema. 'We have some difficult things to chat about this morning.'

As silence settled over the auditorium, Jane noticed that Senator Faraday had leaned forward in his seat. 'Across the country, Halo Detectors are beginning to turn green. That's great news, isn't it?' The residents turned to each other unsure of what the announcement meant for them.

'We need to start preparing you for the eventuality of your departure.' Dr. Boeder-Mankins took a deep breath and exhaled. 'What you've experienced here is most likely an anomaly. When you return to your homes and your jobs, things will look remarkably different. Even with the recent lifting of restrictions, there will still be fear and anger and sadness; a constant state of panic, for some. Very few have returned to the office. The desire to work remotely has replaced the need for contact. Because, as we now know, it is physical contact which is imperilling the world.'

Jane noticed the frowns staring up at her from the seats. 'Once you leave this place, I have to warn you – and you won't like to hear this – but these people you've befriended will once more become a threat to your safety.'

Angry murmurs. Monica stood. 'I think you're overstepping your role, Dr. Boeder-Mankins. You're supposed to help us mentally recover, not send us back to where we were.'

Jane nodded and held up her hands. 'In some ways, you're right, Monica. But I can't, in good conscience, send you like lambs among the wolves believing that what you *think* you found in *here* will be representative of what it *will be* like out *there*.'

Winston Faraday unsuccessfully stifled a grin. The door opened. Dr. Chandruth and Carl, the house manager, emerged from the darkened hallway. They positioned themselves along the wall like bouncers. Jane was happy for their presence just in case things got out of hand.

'Even in the time since you've arrived, the world has changed.' The curtains behind her parted, the lights darkened, and images appeared on the screen. The first, a protest, showed unmasked figures throwing rocks or bottles at police officers. 'Brussels. Anti-vaxxers enraged by vaccination mandates, which will save lives and keep the vulnerable safe, are protesting their personal rights.' Slide change. 'A birthing ward. A new variant of the Halovirus is emerging which might be more virulent for pregnant birthing mothers and newborns.' The word *might* was slightly disingenuous, and there was no way the Cloud End guests could have known that the photo was taken two years previously.

Slide change. 'Office buildings all over the world are vacant. People are rightly afraid of entering enclosed spaces which quickly could become superspreader events. Unfortunately, with companies moving to working-from-home models, economies are crashing. And the only way forward seems to be trusting the Government to prop us up long enough until we can figure out the future.'

Slide change. 'Schools are shutting down permanently. For the safety of teachers and their families, for the safety of students, for the safety of all involved, the world, for better or worse, is moving to online learning. Yes, we've been doing a hybrid model for years, but the Government has made the call to keep everyone safe.'

The repetition of the word 'safe' and its connection with 'Government' was imperative. These people needed to believe that they could be kept from harm.

'But our kids aren't learning anything,' Dorothy Draper said. 'They can't read and write. They don't know their mathematics or basics of anything. Kids are falling through the cracks.'

Boeder-Mankins raised her hands again, not in surrender but to quell the thought. 'It will be difficult, but there will be more emphasis on parents being involved in teaching.'

'How are we supposed to do that?' Dorothy responded angrily. 'We've both got jobs. What do we know about teaching? That's what our taxes go towards, supposedly.'

Jane glanced over at Swithin and Carl who stared impassively across the gathering.

'Please, I want you to know that I, too, wish we could go back to the way things were fifteen years ago, before Coronavirus, when the world seemed so easy and carefree. But we can't go back. There is only forward.'

'What's going to happen to us?' Chantelle called out. 'Who's going to take care of us?'

It was the question Jane hoped would arise. 'Thankfully, the Government is doing its best to make sure that all who have been placed in Convos will return to society anxiety-free because they will be writing more stimulus checks, more debt forgiveness, more help to the vulnerable. Rest assured; you will be taken care of.'

Alonzo broke the short silence that followed her statement. 'I don't want to be taken care of. I want to take care of myself. And my new friends, too.'

'That will be the sound of music in the ears of the Government. They want us to get out there to work, pay our taxes and live our lives.'

'Why don't they just leave us alone?' he asked.

Silence settled over the room. Jane's mouth dropped and she shut it. The question sounded so simple, so easy to answer. Before she could say anything, Winston Faraday III broke the uneasiness. 'Because,' his deep voice resonated in the theater, 'it is the Government which has the ability to do what *you* cannot. *You* cannot build roads, protect cities, create infrastructure for free trade. *You* cannot see to national protection, immigration systems, power networks. *You* cannot do this because you do not have the skills to govern.'

'And *you* do?'

Alonzo's questioning of Winston's authority was angering, but the senator controlled his outrage. 'I've been working in politics for years working hard on *your* behalf. We've been passing laws to keep people safe. We've been creating opportunities for equity and justice. We've been building a society which will thrive in a strange new world while *you* reap the benefits.' Winston didn't mean to jab a finger at the gravedigger, but it happened.

Alonzo stood, faced the politician in the back row far above the rest, and copied the jabbing gesture. 'With all due respect, when you go back, your suffering will be over. Our taxes pay for *your* salary, *your* travel expenses, *your* cost-of-living increases. What benefits are *you* talking about for *us*? A thousand-dollar subsidy?' Alonzo *pbbbb*ted his lips scornfully. 'Yeah, that'll last me for... oh... a good week, or so.'

Damian Bellows hollered out his *Amen*, while Jacquelyn and Wallis smirked. Though they, like Faraday, would suffer no economic ill-effects after their return, they had no love-loss for the senator. His smug arrogance and distance had been all-too evident and irritating.

'All right, all right,' the psychologist called for order, 'there is no need to attack our distinguished guest.' In truth, Dr. Boeder-Mankins needed the chaos to continue. It would break down the good feelings and rebuild walls of distrust.

'Distinguished?' Damian questioned. 'How has he distinguished himself? While we've been trying to get better, what has *he* been doing? Sitting in his room? Are you sending messages to the Government? Reporting on us? It wouldn't surprise me if he doesn't have the Halo at all.'

Damian's conspiracy theory was a foundation stone to build on. 'The Government is not our enemy, Mr. Bellows,' Jane said. 'Now, if everyone could sit back down again, I think we can continue...'

'With what?' Chantelle asked. 'If we're about to get better, let us enjoy our last few days here. Let us spend the time enjoying life. That's what you said.'

Once again, Jane caught Swithin Chandruth's eye. He looked frightened. If anything, the psychologist should cease the session before someone got hurt.

'Just a little more discussion, please,' she said. Carl shifted towards the door as a few residents restlessly decided whether to stay or go. Unfortunately, Senator Faraday's patience and ego had reached its limits. Stomping down the stairs, he readjusted his silver cufflinks, and with a brief glare at the other residents, he raised his head haughtily and brushed past Carl to leave the theater.

As he left, the tension in the room decreased.

'Now, where were we?' Jane laughed nervously.

No one else did.

'Cloud End needs to be shut down *now*,' Gemma's voice was hard. She'd had enough of Stella Reed-Conway and her petty excuses.

'Please, Mrs. Cranmere. That is simply not an option. For the greater good of...'

'I don't care about your damned greater good! Your greater good is a greater evil for the people of Herzfeld. Since Cloud End opened as a Convo, two innocent medical personnel have been killed in a helicopter crash, multiple people have been stabbed by a deranged druggie, and members of my community are beginning to get sick. All because of YOU!'

'How did you know about the stabbings?' Stella asked.

Gemma stammered, so Magnus stepped in. 'News in small towns travels fast, Ms. Reed-Conway. One person listens to the scanner. That person calls his or her friend. Soon there are rumors, and they stay that way until they are substantiated. You can't expect something as traumatic as a helicopter crash or a stabbing to go unnoticed.'

'But how did you know there were stabbings?'

'We're quibbling over sources of information,' Magnus responded. 'Our real contention is with the Convo itself, not necessarily with what is occurring there.'

Stella's eyes narrowed. It was apparent that the cleric was much cagier than Herzfeld's mayor. 'Even though there is nothing I can do, I'd like to hear your ideas.'

'I think we should just get going,' Selina said as she attempted to mollify the situation. 'We'll survive, won't we?' Her eyes moved from Rector Falkirk to Mayor Cranmere and back again. Falkirk closed his eyes and shook his head slightly. Then, Magnus checked Gemma who motioned for him to continue.

'Move the Convo off the mainland. There is an island – Pendulum Island, a mere eight miles into the ocean – which could house a considerable number of, how shall I put it delicately, *diseased* people, thus protecting the sick and the healthy.' He touched his chest. 'This solves the problem for everyone.'

'What about costs? Who is going to pay for that?'

'Instead of issuing stimulus checks, let the healthy return to normal. Make a living. Earn a wage. Spend the money on the Convos. We'd gladly be part of that.'

Stella frowned. As logical as it sounded, moving Halos to an island wouldn't sway any voters. But free money? Anyone with a pulse was moved by the sound of that. 'I'll have to speak to people with greater influence than I.'

'You do that,' Gemma said.

The statement, just three words, perturbed Stella more than anything else Gemma could have said. Stella's patience was redlining. From the cadre of politicians and their maneuverings to these small-town upstarts strutting around the Capitol like stiff-combed roosters, she'd had enough of people patronising her, and frankly it was time to push back. 'Mrs. Cranmere, you do realize the precarious situation you're in, don't you.'

'Maybe you should explain it to me.'

'These 'dangers' you spoke of – at Cloud End – the stabbing, the helicopter crash, the town's immunity compromised. They are a direct result of your own failings.'

'How dare you...' Gemma's jaw clenched.

'Not as a leader. From what I hear, you are a perfectly acceptable mayor. Social. Pliable. A perfect politician. Love the one you're with.'

Gemma made a move towards Stella, but Magnus intercepted her. 'Easy, Gemma,' he said.

'If you weren't a Government stooge, I'd have your head on a platter,' Gemma threatened with a pointed finger. Stella's wry smile stopped Gemma short. 'What aren't you telling me?' Gemma asked.

'You have nothing to stand on,' Stella remarked quietly. 'Whether or not you want Cloud End to remain a Convo, there's nothing you can do about it. And if you throw up a stink, we will destroy you. Ask your husband.'

Gemma Cranmere's mouth dropped open. As did Selina's. Only Magnus Falkirk was able to control his shock.

Senator Allan Membree received the call through his secretary. She was used to clearing his calls and sending them through to his

AutoCom, but this call, which came via an indirect emergency channel, was one that he would have to answer himself. And quickly.

He touched his temple to activate the microphone for his AutoCom. 'Senator Membree.'

'Green Light is failing,' the voice said.

'What do you mean?'

'They're revolting against the measures. Dr. Boeder-Mankins barely made it out of the session today without revealing our intentions.'

Membree swore. 'What the hell is she doing? I thought she was the best in her profession. These people should be sheep. How did this happen?'

'The Halos – they've bonded together and seem to think they can continue after they leave.'

'That would be the worst-case scenario, wouldn't it?'

A pause ensued. 'Yes. If they were to continue their connections outside... it will come out.'

Membree touched his hair and wheeled towards the window behind him. Around the Capitol, tourists, some in full protective gear, others only in masks and rubber gloves, a few tedious rebels wearing no protection at all, wandered aimlessly across the grounds taking photos of buildings and allowing themselves to be tracked mercilessly through the Capitol grounds via cameras. Digital scans would show that at least a third of the people were infected with the virus.

'What can we do?' Membree asked.

'The next phase needs to be implemented as soon as possible.'

'I really wanted to avoid that. To cut off all outside communications, phone, text, internet... What will the Halos do?'

The voice cleared its throat. 'We knew this was a possibility, Senator. We either move forward or...'

'Or what?'

'Abort.'

The word rang in the senator's ears. To abort would mean failure and a forfeiture of millions of tax dollars. If any of this leaked, the least of the senator's worries would be public shame. He would be facing jail time. Maybe worse.

'Let's take this one step at a time. Hopefully, cutting off contact will be enough.'

The voice at the other end took a deep breath and exhaled. 'Very good, sir. I will see to it quickly.' The line disconnected.

Allan Membree very much needed to call an emergency meeting.

Encoded message #10215525
7 November, 2031
23:26

Government device sent: CVH4580387

Government device received: SRC9022289

███████████████ is unable to bring about any reasonable success in
driving a wedge between subjects during group therapy. Although a few
seemed more agitated than normal, during the day, they rejoined.

Another wrench in the works are the subjects from Herzfeld. They have
been making noise with friends in the town. Although their time here
has not been positive, the town itself might put more pressure. Please
advise.

Encoded message #10215539
8 November, 2031
00:21

Government device sent: SRC9022289

Government device received: CVH4580387

See attached file. Open only when directed. Sensitive.

(ATTCH: 13 files MP4 vid 13.2 GB)

21

Each member of the group received the message simultaneously via their AutoComs. Although encrypted, most of them hid their arms from snooping eyes. Monica Portney was aghast to see that they had been summoned again. It could only mean things were not going well.

Dylan Renfroe chuckled. Somewhere deep inside, he had known that Cloud End would be managed by screwups. Even the owners were live wires. Though the St. Croix's were not in on the details, they had been briefed, for the sake of national interests, to control the Halos as if they were hostages. Obviously, they had failed.

Emery Donaldson felt a cold, sinking feeling in his stomach. Nothing about this operation had gone according to plan, and if this emergency meeting was any reflection of what had already occurred, he felt as if nothing short of a nuclear blast would make it go away.

Director Reed-Conway closed the door behind her and moved swiftly to the front to position herself before the screen. The lights darkened leaving only the glimmer of ovate LED lights embedded in the table to reflect the worried faces of the group.

'What's going on?' Senator Forsythe asked as he stared back and forth between Membree and Reed-Conway.

'Just a little damage control,' Membree said.

'What damage?'

Membree nodded to Stella who turned on the screen behind her. 'Yesterday, three citizens of Herzfeld came to the Capitol to protest the Cloud End Convo. As you are all aware, we've prepared for these kinds of disagreements. Two prominent members of the community came down with the Halovirus.'

'So?' Dylan challenged. 'It's two people, so what? There's probably two people per second who get sick in the Capitol.'

'Yes,' Stella said calmly, 'but the media and, to be fair, the Government has been slightly overplaying the severity of the virus since its inception as a matter of national safety.' Each person in the room knew that this was a half-truth. Safety was a priority, but not the ultimate one. Control. Every part of society sought control.

'What did they want?' Emery asked.

'They wanted the Convo to be shifted to an island off the coast. Their reasoning was quite logical.'

'We can't do that! We've invested everything in this Convo.' Senator Forsythe's face turned red.

'I know that,' said Stella calmly, 'and we won't have to.'

'How can you be sure?'

Stella brought up the images on the screen behind her. 'Firstly, Dr. Boeder-Mankins has assured us she is making headway. According to her, the session today was close to bearing fruit.'

'You said, 'firstly,' Stella,' Emery said, 'what's the 'secondly?' How can you be so sure?'

Grainy video footage appeared on the screen behind her. It looked like a camera in a cockpit. 'This is the footage from the fateful emergency helicopter crash at the base of the cliffs at Cloud End. When the authorities salvaged the wreck, our agents acquired the video.' The camera was focused towards the Convo. 'You can see here that the helicopter is about to land. It's roughly fifty feet from the ground. Here,' she pointed towards house, 'is where the stabbing victims were to be brought out, but notice this.' She paused the video and used the laser pointer. 'South of the Convo, at the end of the lane, there is a gate. What do you see there?'

'It's a car,' Monica said.

'A pickup, actually,' Stella corrected. 'And standing outside the pickup are two figures.'

'Who are they?' Monica asked.

'We'll get to that in a moment, but follow the video.' The action continued when suddenly, the helicopter's windshield shattered, and the video began to spin. Stella stopped it.

'What happened?' Dylan asked.

'It appears that the pilot was shot.'

'That's outrageous!' Membree shouted.

She rewound and went frame by frame. 'The camera shows the two figures, there is a flash of light – five of them, actually, in quick succession – and the chopper starts to veer backwards and downwards. The audio feed is of the co-pilot yelling that something has struck the windshield and hit his partner.'

'Shot down,' Monica covered her mouth and gasped. 'How terrible.'

'Whose pickup is it?' Forsythe asked.

'Our techs were able to enhance the video and focus on the license plate. It belongs to a man named Steve Cranmere. He's from Herzfeld.'

'So? Throw him in jail for attempted murder.'

Stella shook her head. 'We're not going to do that, Quentin.'

'Why not?'

'Because Steve Cranmere is the husband of the mayor of Herzfeld. The very person who visited us this afternoon.' Stella filled in the last blanks. 'A little bit of blackmail goes a long way. If the mayor backs down, her husband stays out of jail.'

'But those poor medical personnel,' Monica intoned.

'Whose murderers will come to justice once we're done with the Convo,' Emery inserted, following Stella's line of thought. 'Once we've determined how to use our findings from Cloud End, a quick note to the authorities will be perfect.'

Donald St. Croix's frustration had reached its maximum. As he watched the tide's turning of the resident's emotions, he began to feel them, too. Stifled behind his protective suit, his mask, hell, even his constant handwashing and handwringing, Donald wanted to be free.

He sat in the kitchen, hands gripping a sparklingly clean knife and fork, delicious looking food positioned in front of him, but he had no appetite. No matter how much he wanted to slice a small piece of steak and let it marinate in his saliva, he couldn't produce the energy to cut, stab and bite it. He sighed and stared through the windows of the swinging kitchen doors. What he wouldn't give to be sitting out there, out with the rest of the mob who were laughing and clapping each other on the back. They were supposed to be the sick ones, but Donald was the one who felt ill.

'What's the matter, Don?' Claire asked. 'Not hungry?'

'No.' His morose tone caused her to frown.

'Did you have too many cookies this afternoon?'

He shook his head and sighed again. 'I want to eat out on the porch.'

'Then go ahead.'

'I don't want to put on my protective gear to walk through the house.'

Claire calmly set down her knife and fork. 'It's only for a little while longer. The news stations are reporting that the Halovirus is almost done, and...'

'So what? The Halo Detectors at Cloud End are still registering red. The people are still ill. I thought this was just going to be for a few weeks, but now we're well into our second month. What if the Government sends more infected people? What if this is how we have to live for the rest of our lives?'

'Don't be so pessimistic,' Claire responded. 'Besides, there is good money to be made. If it lasts a year, we can retire to the mountains, or the oceans, or wherever we want.'

'And then what? We live happily ever after? What will we do? Despite the world's desire to 'return to normal,' enough damage has been done by COVID and now Halo, humanity's ability to be... human... is over.'

'Desperate times call for desperate measures.' She pointed her fork at him. 'Now, if you want to go eat on the porch, put your gear on and go do it. Stop moping. You're making me depressed.'

Donald studied his wife as she dug back into her meal. At that moment, he did not want to be near her. Not in this way.

He pondered her last statement. *Desperate times call for desperate measures.* He felt desperate. Without thinking, he grabbed his plate and utensils, and stood.

'What are you doing?' Claire demanded.

'Something desperate.'

'Donald,' she warned.

Wheeling quickly, he walked towards the swinging doors. Just before he pushed them open to reach safety, Claire shrieked. 'Carl! Nancy!'

Carl was the first to arrive. In protective gear, Carl pushed open the door from the outside and encountered Donald carrying his food. 'What's happening?'

'I'm going outside. Get out of my way.'

Through the plastic visor, Carl looked at Claire.

'Carl, Donald has gone crazy. Stop him, please.'

'I'm sorry about this, Donald.' Carl grabbed him by the arm. Donald resisted, so Carl held tighter. Because of Carl's strength, Donald was unable to free himself.

'I just want to be free,' he mumbled.

'We all do, Donald.' Carl swung his boss around to the table. Suddenly, Donald shoved Carl with his shoulder and Carl lost his grip. While Carl fell into the prep island, pots and pans crashing and clanging about, Donald dashed for the door. Nancy entered and Carl yelled out for her.

'Stop him!' Carl screamed. Nancy, unsure of what was happening, reached out for Donald but he slithered past her. Streaking into the bar area, he navigated quickly through the bottles, the sterilized cups, through the door, and took a large breath. It had been such a long time since his nose had tasted freedom. The room smelled of grilled things, steak and vegetables. The sound of the waterfall was unfiltered. It sounded delightful. Instead of plasticky streaked faces, Donald found himself in the presence of the newest Halos, Bridgette and Renata. They shied away from him, but he shook his head.

'May I have lunch with you?'

'We're... sick.'

His smile was warmer than it had been in the last month. 'It's not you who are ill, it is us.' He turned to see Nancy and Carl stalking towards him. Their faces were aghast. What Donald had done was unthinkable. To

228

expose himself to the deadly virus was an invitation to endangering the lives of everyone who was still healthy.

'Go away!' Donald screamed at his workers. 'I'm having lunch.' He glanced down at his plate and only then noticed that he had left a line of grilled vegetables across the floor. *Like the breadcrumb trail behind Hansel and Gretel,* he thought bemusedly. Bridgette and Renata pushed their chairs back.

'Don't!' He shouted. They recoiled again and he realized the volume of his voice was too high. It had been stuffed inside a suit for too long. 'Don't,' he repeated quietly. 'I don't want to eat alone. I *can't.*'

Carl grabbed his boss and yanked him backwards tipping over his chair. He landed on the floor with a thud. Carl began to drag Donald across the floor. He resisted and his legs knocked against other tables spilling the drinks.

As Donald was hauled kicking and screaming and sobbing back to the bar area, the children entered the atrium. McKayla saw her grandfather and shouted. Racing to him, she reached out and tried to pull him from Carl and Nancy, but Carl pushed her to the side, knocking her to the floor.

Enraged, Donald struggled even more, but he was unable to reach his granddaughter. 'Just let us be!' he shouted one last time before being hauled through the bar and back into the kitchen. As the doors swung shut behind him, the last thing he heard was McKayla calling out for help.

Carl and Nancy dropped their boss on the kitchen floor. When he looked up, he saw his wife's figure looming over him. Through her protective equipment, he saw a riotous, outraged, angry confusion on her face and a prediction of the next month: she was going to be alone, and he was going to be sick.

After Donald was ingloriously dragged into the kitchen, Bridgette and Renata listened to a teenage girl wail at the top of her lungs because her grandfather had just been victimized by his own staff. At the end of the long line of disturbing things which had accosted McKayla's world, this sight could have been the worst of all. McKayla was old enough to know that the world was a generally rancid place. She was becoming sick – sicker than just a Halo – soul-sick. It was as if her genes now had a permanent fear receptor and whatever was docked in them was there forever.

Curled into a fetal position, McKayla wailed, waiting for anyone to attend to her. Certainly, the psychotherapist or doctor should have been the second to arrive (her grandmother being the first), but neither diplomaed member of staff felt entirely at ease treating the teenager. She'd been running around with the rest of the diseased residents.

Thus, it was left to Lawrence who hurried from his room and descended the stairs quickly to where the girl was lying. As he reached her side, he noticed other residents were circling the proceedings from above. Monica recorded everything on her phone, but when Father Lawrence frowned at her, she guiltily stopped.

Soon, Chantelle and Seraphim appeared at his side, and he took a step back. As they squatted beside McKayla, other Halos began their descent like angels on Jacob's ladder. Within moments, most of Cloud End's residents had circled the young girl in a protective cocoon. The front door swung open and Oswald, noticing the commotion, ran towards the group. Gavin held him back from his sister, but when he struggled, he let him go.

Oswald's eyes were wide with terror. 'What happened to her? Is she sick?'

No one knew how to answer that question.

Then, finally, Lawrence knelt down in front of him. 'She's had a shock. She saw something she never should have seen. We're going to take her to the doctor's office, okay?'

'I'm coming with,' Oswald stated as he pulled his white rat out from a pocket and began to stroke its hair furiously.

'Yes, yes, of course,' Lawrence responded gently.

Chantelle lowered her mouth to McKayla's ear. 'We're going to take you to the doctor's office, sweetheart. Alonzo is going to carry you.' She looked up at Alonzo who nodded. Gently, he reached down to pick her up in his arms. Many times he had seen the limp body of the dead, but never had he been called upon to carry one.

Dorothy Draper covered her mouth with fright. If this kind of thing could happen to Donald and McKayla, it was not a long thread of narrative to suggest that it could happen to any of them. At any time.

Carefully, the gravedigger lifted the girl, and the entire congregation of residents, sans Winston Faraday III, followed Alonzo Turner to the infirmary.

Where was Winston?

He was sitting at his window staring out over the waving grass towards the cliffs beyond. His AutoCom was lit up and the voice he heard via the implant was filled with yawning disinterest.

'How are you doing?' Isolde asked him.

'I need to get out now. Not tomorrow. Not the next day. Now! Don't tell me to be patient. March over to Forsythe and tell him get off his ass and get me the hell out of here!'

'Winston,' she teased, 'you sound positively anxious. I've never heard you like this before.' Isolde was studying her fingernails as her AutoCom projected the news ahead of her in 3D. Not surprisingly, there were riots in Africa, despots in Southeast Asia, and a certain megalomaniac in Russia who needed more worry than Winston's discomfort.

'The people here are going crazy!' he shouted. 'The owner has had a psychotic episode and wandered out into the atrium to eat lunch with our newest inmates.'

'That's his choice, isn't it? His body, his choice,' she snickered.

'Don't give me that crap, Isolde. Nobody really has a choice when the world's safety is at stake.'

'You're starting to sound like a Socialist.' She changed the station and found an old rerun of Survivor. Always drama.

'Don't start with me. I'm angry enough the way it is.'

'Oh, pooh. Don't be such a grumpy pants.'

'Listen to me, Isolde Howard. I've already promised you the world, but now I'm going to promise you the universe. Rich beyond your wildest dreams. I've got inside information into all sorts of deals which I'm willing to trade for my freedom.'

Her attention was refocused from an Immunity Challenge, where two small teams were attempting to wrestle each other for supremacy, to Senator Faraday's pledge of unlimited financial gain. 'I'm listening,' she said.

'I need to know *exactly* what it will take to get Cloud End shut down.'

'Wouldn't you just be moved to another Convo, then?'

'According to the news, they're closing down everywhere, but not this one. Why is that?'

'I don't know,' she said.

Winston Faraday III ground his teeth. 'That's what I want you to find out.'

'What do you think will happen to the rest of the people there?'

Faraday noticed a fox's red tail dance just above the grass. Obviously, it had pounced on an unsuspecting mouse. 'I don't care. I'm sure the Government will take care of them somehow.'

'You're positively heartless, Winston.'

'That's why I love you,' he responded with as much sincerity as possible.

You don't love me, she thought. 'Okay, Winnie, I'll do my best. Give me a day or two and I'll get back to you.'

'One day, Isolde. One day.'

'Gotcha.'

On the screen in front of her, a wiry young woman had tossed her opponent from the ring and lifted her hands exultantly.

22

Isolde Howard called Winston at 11:00 p.m. two days later. The information was not particularly difficult to retrieve, and she'd held on to it just to make Winston squirm.

Forsythe never meant to divulge the information but his resistance to her wiles was futile. After dining-in at his Capitol-provided residence, a five-bedroom, five-bath house on the edge of the city, the two lounged on the sofa. Scantily clad, Isolde twirled a cherry stem in her mouth and waited for him to answer the question.

'I'm not supposed to talk about the Convo.'

She pouted. 'You've talked about it before. I've never told anyone anything.'

'This is different.' Forsythe wore a red golf shirt and khaki pants. He swirled a snifter of brandy in front of him.

'How?'

'Because things have changed. My reputation is at stake.'

Isolde found that amusing. Politicians always seemed to be worried about their reputations, but his affair with her had never been an issue. 'Why are all the other Convos closing?' she asked forwardly. 'If the virus is still rampaging like the media tells us, certainly it's in the best interest of everyone involved to keep them open.'

'Funding issues.'

His curt answer was not rewarding. 'Doesn't the Government have unlimited access to resources?'

'So naïve,' he said.

Isolde passionately hated to be patronized and swallowed her irritation. 'Enlighten me, Senator.'

His eyes sparkled over the rim of his glass. 'The Government's ability to raise funds is limitless, but only during post-election times. We all run on platforms that limit taxation, but what that really means is, we'll limit taxation to the boundaries of a fat budget. During post-election times, we'll pass a national budget that is far too healthy. Then, when we trim the excess fat, it looks like we're giving the average citizen a break. In reality, we're just raising taxes a notch below what seems obscene.'

'Obscenity will be achieved the next time a budget is passed?'

He winked at her. 'Now you're getting the hang of it.'

'But what does this have to do with the Convos?'

Forsythe leaned his head back against the chair and gazed upwards to the crenelated molding topping the walls. In the middle of each room's ceilings were elegant glass light covers which separated light casting a warm glow across the expansive rooms. Large windows exposed the twinkling night Capitol skyline. Lights blinked on and off. Electric cars and the newest fad, personal drones, raced here and there. Forsythe knew the world was beginning to pick up steam as it left behind its masks and vaccinations. 'Once people start testing negative, they can go back to their normal life.' He swallowed. 'The virus's power is waning, Isolde, and that's not a good thing.'

Her eyes expressed shock. 'What do you mean that's not a good thing?'

Forsythe weighed his words carefully. To express the entire truth would be playing Russian Roulette with her. 'Look, people getting sick and dying is a bad thing. But to be brutally honest, when pandemics occur, the average citizen puts their hope in the Government, and when that happens, we can get things done. We can pass spending bills that would never have gone through during non-pandemic times. People get fear-crazy and are easily manipulated into believing that we can solve all their problems: health, financial, psychological. Amazingly, some people think the Government should be *more* involved in education, and we tip our hats to them and say, thank you very much, because indoctrinating children is one of the next steps in creating a society totally reliant on Government handouts. And Government handouts mean more power. It's an amazing circle.'

Isolde felt physically ill by the way his mind worked. The Government's first responsibility should have been public service. They were elected to lead, not to dominate. For the common citizen, one vote was all they got, though most of them believed elections were already predetermined, rigged media popularity contests. She ruefully wondered if elections were not dissimilar to Survivor. Outwit. Outplay. Outlast. Whether or not the winner was the best candidate was often debated. But the camera and the producers had a show to create.

'What does that have to do with the Convos?' she repeated.

'I really shouldn't be telling you this...' his words were beginning to slur. Unbeknownst to the senator, Isolde had diluted a small amount of sodium pentothal in his drink. Though the effects weren't always perfect (she had used it on Winston once with mixed results), the drug allowed her at least some access to the part of Quentin that *wanted* to let her in on the details.

'You can trust me, Winston,' she said.

Shocked, he held her gaze. 'What did you call me?'

Realizing her error, and the danger she had put herself in, she moved closer to him and put a hand on his leg. 'You're being paranoid, Quentin.'

He sighed and relaxed again. 'We did set up numerous Convos for purely humanitarian reasons. We truly wanted to take care of those in our country who were suffering greatly from the pandemic. But one...' he raised a shaky finger in front of his face, '...one Convo was set up to... understand the psychological effects of pandemics and how a Government could, in fact, benefit... er... no, that's the wrong word... I'll retract that. How a Government could learn from the mistakes of the past.'

'Cloud End?' Isolde continued to caress his leg.

'Cloud End,' he substantiated. 'It's the perfect spot. Away from everything and everyone else, perched on the side of a cliff, run by financially-pressed owners who needed the Government to do something.'

'Do they know what's going on?'

He shook his head. 'Nothing. They're part of the experiment, too.'

'Experiment?'

Like a patient revealing secrets to a psychologist, Forsythe leaned back on the sofa putting his feet up on Isolde. Placing an arm over his forehead, he sighed deeply. 'Cloud End was set up as a testing place for group manipulation. We control the environment, the social setting, who is involved, the messages they receive, to understand how, during the *next* pandemic, and there will be one, we can assist the citizens of the country to work together. To really see that we are all in the same boat.'

'Unfortunately, Cloud End has been an unmitigated disaster. No matter what we've tried, whether psychological manipulation or social pressure, in spite of all the fear we've pumped into the place, from worrying about Halo Detectors to subconscious suggestions, the residents have found a common ground and refuse to bow to whatever we try.'

'That's a good thing, really.'

'Try running a country of selfish egomaniacs.' Forsythe's blind spot for hypocrisy was apparent to Isolde.

'What about the Halo Detectors? How do you manipulate those?'

The senator's eyes opened wide and he wondered if he'd shared too much. The Halo Detectors were the key to the entire thing. 'I've said more than I should. I like you, I really do. But there are some things that must remain unsaid.'

Isolde's jaw clenched. He had almost given her the key. 'Okay,' she pouted, but then meandered up his leg with her fingers. 'But I'm so intrigued. Just give me a hint. A little hint?' Her lascivious eyes held his as she made the journey up to his chest and placed her lips an inch from his.

'The Halo Detectors. Red. It doesn't mean what they think it means.' The last of his words were cut off by Isolde Howard's kiss.

She got enough out of him to be set for life.

McKayla struggled to return to awareness. It wasn't until her grandfather showed up by her side, when she heard his voice, and felt the actual skin of his hand, that she made her way through the murky darkness back to the light. The sight of him being dragged away, as well as some heartless resident recording it on her phone, had stripped away her soul and all she felt was pain. It was this pain which dropped her over the cliff of consciousness.

'McKayla,' her grandpa called out, 'you can come back now. We miss you.'

'Yeah, even me,' her brother said.

Gina Draper appeared on the other side. 'I'm so scared,' she said. 'Can you open your eyes, or something?'

McKayla fought with a strength she'd never known to make her eyelids flutter.

'It's working,' Chantelle said.

'Keep talking,' Father Lawrence encouraged.

It had been three days since the incident. Donald, after being hauled out of the atrium, had been taken to a separate room where, after a day of isolation, watched his Halo Detector turn red. He had checked his phone multiple times, but Claire had refused to speak to him, even by phone.

Ironically, once the Halo glowed red from his infection, he was given free run of his own house. Without protective gear. When he emerged from his isolation, multiple people were there to greet him with hugs and well-wishes. Fortunately, though, Donald was feeling no ill-effects from the sickness. Just some bruising from being manhandled by his staff.

Jacquelyn sat him down and told him about McKayla's condition. Donald wanted to go to her quickly, but they restrained him. He had to wait to see if Halo symptoms would flare up. Certainly, in McKayla's tender state, he wouldn't want to pass anything on to her.

He waited impatiently, yet with something nearing contentedness. The residents had taken him in, treated him as an equal, shared conversation, ate and drank with him. It was beautiful.

The nights were the hardest. As he pulled the covers up over his face, his eyes focused on the single, malevolent red eye pinioned above him, Donald wished that he could reach out to Claire, to hold her, to hear her speak. The isolation was smothering. Twice during that first night it felt as if he might suffocate. Anxiously, he wondered if he had the Halo: shortness of breath, rapid pulse, body aches. Breathing deeply, he calmed his nerves and eventually fell asleep.

On the second day, Oswald took him by the hand. As they walked past the rest of the residents, Oswald waved like a small child. They were going outside. When Oswald opened the front door, Donald shaded the sun's light with his hand. Strangely, the power of light and the sun's heat was both rejuvenating and tiring. Oswald tugged on his arm and they strolled out onto the porch where Monica and Damian were sitting in the swing rocking back and forth. They were not speaking, only swinging. A breeze had come up from beneath the edge of the cliff. Salty air wafted past his nose and Donald inhaled deeply. A handful of seagulls played in the drafts. Grass swayed back and forth in front of them.

Oswald tugged his arm. 'Come on, Grandpa, I want to show you something.'

They stepped down from the porch and onto the lawn. Weeds had sprung up everywhere and the last few dandelions dared to track the sun with their aging old faces, their white hair and beards puffing in the breeze.

'What is it?' Donald asked.

Pointing ahead of him towards the cliff, Oswald smiled happily and dropped his grandfather's hand. Cavorting like a young lamb, he gamboled through the waist-high grass to the beginning of a trail. 'This is where we always start,' he said.

'Who?'

'Me and Pasqual and Titus, sometimes the girls come with.' A brief spasm of sadness passed over his face, but it was gone in an instant.

'How long have you not been wearing your masks?'

Oswald didn't answer. He raced ahead and waved for his grandfather to hurry up. Donald did his best, but the physical exertion of walking to the cliff, slightly uphill, through grass and hidden stone proved difficult. The air was so refreshing it hurt his lungs, but he continued to gulp it in like a man who'd suddenly realized he was dying of thirst.

Every twenty steps, Donald stopped to peruse his surroundings. Here, a daisy. There, a tiny sapling which had sprung up from nowhere. To the right was a small copse of spiny trees struggling against the elements. To the left was a vast expanse of unsettled land. The extent of Cloud End went on

238

another half a mile, but Donald, for the life of him, couldn't remember a time when he'd explored it.

Another twenty paces onwards and after another impatient hand wave from Oswald, Donald stopped to tilt his head back to the sky and its bushy fleece. The sun played hide-and-seek in the sky's fur.

Finally, with ten steps left to the fence and the boundary of all things beneath, Oswald dashed back to re-grab his grandfather's hand and yank him forwards. Donald's first instinct was caution, but because of the invigoration he felt, he discarded it and raced with his precious grandson towards the white fence.

For a moment, the two stood staring out over the vast, aquamarine expanse of the ocean. Oswald had been doing this every day, but it had not lost its glorious wonder. To do this, to stand at the cliff's edge, was to experience all of life and its gifts, pleasure and pain, fear and exhilaration, worry and wonder. It was a marvel of childhood. The freckles on Oswald's suntanned face sparkled in the morning rays and his lips stretched across gappy teeth revealing short, sharp stumps of oncoming reinforcements. Oswald's hair streamed in the breeze and he spread his arms wide. He was chilly and shivered. Nestling into his grandfather's side he hugged him.

'It feels like we're flying with the seagulls, doesn't it, Grandpa?'

Donald nodded.

'You have to do it. Spread your arms like this.'

Studying his grandson, Donald copied the gesture and tilted his head back to look over his cheeks at the sparkling reflection of the morning sun on the shimmering surface of the ocean far below. Perhaps a mile out from shore, a lonely island jutted from the watery world. It was a rocky island with only a few trees sprouting from the top. It looked bare and cold, very much like Cloud End must look like to the rest of the world.

'I want to go there someday, Grandpa.'

'Maybe I'll take you.'

With great joy, Oswald squeezed his grandfather's middle. Donald rested his hand on Oswald's shoulders. If only Claire could have joined them.

The thought of his wife, cloistered inside the Convo, behind a skin of non-permeable plastic, made him sad. Donald wished they could have shared this moment, grandparents and grandchild, new life and teetering life, at the edge of the world, staring out to the vastness beyond.

'Keep talking,' Father Lawrence said. 'I think she's coming back.'

Gina continued. 'The wi-fi isn't working anymore,' she said, 'that's why I need you to come back. I'm lonely.'

The others laughed uncomfortably. Yesterday, the wi-fi had ceased to function and all contact with the outside world, apart from the television news, was done. Strangely, many of the residents had not missed it. Just the kids, and they weren't even that upset because it meant that they didn't have to 'attend' school. Now they were on unofficial school holidays.

McKayla's eyes fluttered again. Like an engine sputtering, they finally caught and she kept them open. She spotted Father Lawrence and Oswald. Gina, of course. But then, right before her very eyes, was Grandpa Donald.

'You're alive.'

'Yes, yes, sweetheart.'

McKayla's mind couldn't quite connect the dots. 'But you're not wearing your suit. Did you test positive?'

He smiled. 'Red light and all.'

'Does that mean you get to stay with us?'

'I guess so.'

She reached out for him, and he hugged her.

McKayla looked past her friend and the others who had gathered around. She found Dr. Chandruth's hooded face above the rest. His arms were crossed, and his smile was enigmatic. Happiness but... fear?

'When can I leave?' McKayla asked.

'We'll get you to eat a little bit and then see how you feel.'

McKayla nodded. 'Now, tell me what's going on with the wi-fi.' She reached for her phone and felt an immediate sense of fear when she couldn't locate it. 'Where is my phone?'

Oswald handed it to her. 'Chill out, McKayla.'

'Shut up.' McKayla noticed her brother's white rat. 'That thing is hideous.'

'So are you.'

McKayla swatted pathetically at him, but she smiled nonetheless. She, along with everyone else in the room scanned for wi-fi access, but for all intents and purposes, they were marooned on an analog island.

The Government Cadre's isolation of Cloud End from the rest of the world began with a metaphorical flick of a switch but not until two important conversations took place. The first was Isolde Howard's revelation to Winston Faraday III regarding the shocking news about Halo Detectors. And the other was a scrambled text between Stella Reed-Conway and a worried-faced Cloud End Insider who was getting spooked by the plan's slow demise.

The phone buzzed in the Insider's pocket. Checking it, the Insider frowned at the message. It was 7:04 p.m. and what was being asked was dreadful, something not wished upon an enemy much less people who were suffering already.

But that was why Carl Van der Hoven was being paid double what the other staff were. Carl had been tasked with relaying information and intel back to the Cadre in real time. After the stabbing, Carl had been available to assist, but had also recorded the scene through his protective mask so that the Cadre could have first-hand knowledge of the struggle. When the helicopter crashed, Carl had run to the cliff, climbed over the fence and precariously dangled his phone over the edge to video the wreckage. When Donald St. Croix had been dragged through the house in sight of his granddaughter and other residents, Carl had felt a twinge of discomfort as he retained the visuals on his device.

Other than Director Reed-Conway who'd recruited him, Carl did not know who made up the Cadre, and he didn't care. He assumed they were high level politicians. Thus, the inherent secrecy. The hubris of what they were working towards was disgusting, but for Carl, the long-term benefits outweighed his heavy conscience, so he'd agreed.

Sighing, the house manager pocketed his phone and strolled from his small office to a nook in the kitchen. As he walked past Esther, who asked him if everything was okay, he smiled and said that everything would be fine eventually. Esther took this as a sign that Carl was tired and bid him a good evening.

At 8:30 p.m., an announcement came over the loudspeaker telling the residents to gather in the atrium for some exciting news. For many, this was the moment they had hoped for. But strangely, they also hated the thought of their freedom arriving. Sam and Dorothy stopped their nightly rhythms. The boys had already crawled into pajamas and Titus had a dribble of toothpaste drying on his mouth. The family dragged themselves from their corner suite and down the stairs where they met Seraphim and Jacquelyn. Seraphim appeared nervous, as if her landlord had knocked on the door and she was two months behind on her rent.

The almost-divorced Bellows had seated themselves on opposite sides of a table. Surprisingly, they were weathering the storm of each other's company. Wallis no longer had to be the referee. She was seated with Alonzo and Gavin who, because of the celebratory nature of the night, had grabbed a bottle of high-end scotch and poured some into snifters.

Lawrence and Chantelle, along with Monica and Radiance, were the last ones to arrive. Their faces were the same mix of hopeful happiness and pre-sadness. Renata and Bridgette appeared happily and situated themselves near the back of the room. Even though they'd only been at Cloud End a short time, they were expectant about returning home.

By the time Claire St. Croix walked across the dance floor towards the podium at the front of the room, the only ones who hadn't arrived were Senator Faraday and Donald St Croix. But the latter shuffled in by the time

22

Claire took her position in front of the residents. Donald studied his wife sadly and smiled. She did not return it.

Along the back wall, the house staff, cleaner, cooks, psychologist, nurses and manager stood sentinel in their protective suits.

Just as she was about to begin, Senator Faraday's door opened. Many of the residents glanced up to see the immaculately dressed politician approach the railing. Not deigning to grace the rest with his presence, he motioned with his hand for Claire to continue while he stood above them. Behind her, the three-dimensional projection lit up and cast an eerie glow. The nightly newscast. In the dim light of the evening, the hologrammatic faces of journalists seemed otherworldly. Though the newscast was mute, the intent was pure. Small, circular representations of the Halovirus malevolently danced in the background.

'Welcome, everyone,' Claire began as the microphone in her protective mask squawked. 'I hope you are all doing well.' Her eyes fell on Donald who couldn't quite bring his up to look at her. 'It's been a long slog. We've had our hiccups, but by and large, I think we've done pretty well.'

She placed her hands on the unnecessary podium in front of her. 'I think we've seen a miraculous resilience in our little community. We entered as strangers and we'll leave as friends.'

'Although you wouldn't have known it due to the internet disruption, the Government has released a date by which most restrictions will finish.' A few people wanted to interrupt but she smiled and shook her head. 'If you'll allow me to finish, I'll answer any questions after.' Hands lowered.

'By next weekend, masks will no longer be mandatory outdoors. Distancing requirements will diminish from sixteen square feet to four.'

'Does that mean we can start kissing each other?' Gavin asked to a chorus of laughter.

Claire smiled and her gaze was drawn to Donald. 'What you do with your lips is your business, but make sure that you are standing at least a meter from your beloved when you kiss them.'

Groans.

'I'm sure all of you are wondering when you will be able to escape here...'

Anxious faces stared at her.

'That, though, has not been relayed to me yet, but I'm sure that very soon, you all will be on your way home.'

'Wait! Wait!' Monica called out. 'What good is an easing of restrictions when we're still locked up?'

Claire held up her hands. 'The Government is working hard to fix this, but we have to be patient.'

'I'm tired of being patient. I want to go home. I want to see my husband. I want to talk to my family. I want to get out of here!' Monica shouted.

'As do we all,' Father Lawrence said with less sincerity, 'but I think we can handle a short time longer.'

From above, Winston Faraday spoke. His voice, low and powerful, resonated in the large room, but everyone could hear each word. 'You have been deceived.'

People below strained to catch sight of the man above.

Like an actor capturing the audience with a dramatic soliloquy, Faraday walked slowly along the upper floor, hand running along the railing, gesturing and speaking as he went. 'Yes, it's true. You've all been deceived. Not that you had much choice.' His face was momentarily hidden behind a support beam and then he moved into the light again. 'This place, this... convalescence,' his face registered distaste, 'is a lie.'

He paused at the top of the stairs. 'How do I know this? Because I have sources outside of this place. Not just family and friends who, though they might miss you, and wish you were back,' he made a sarcastic face, 'but powerful people who *know* things and can *assist* with getting us out of here.'

'This Convo was based on a premise, an idea, that we can be manipulated from the outside. Subtle messages, daintily wrapped gifts of 'safety' and 'protection' while we recover. It's all rubbish. You are guinea pigs and I'm about to expose the opening from this inescapable maze in which you've been trapped.'

As Faraday took the first step down, his hand on the banister, the residents' eyes swiveled to Claire whose mouth had dropped open.

'It is not entirely shameful that you should be so deluded. Throughout your lives you have been quickly mesmerized by sound bites, trailers, swiping left, right, up and down, all the while your subconscious dines on advertising and translucent messages of need and greed. You entertain yourselves to a mind-numbing, semi-conscious state while corporate raiders violate the ark of your psyche. You succumb to the zeitgeist of the current age, constantly whimpering and complaining about your trivialities – an omnipresent narcissism – while the real world passes you by.'

'And so you have been deceived in your diversion. As you look away, the thief sneaks up behind you and robs your future blind until you finally check your pockets for what was important and bemoan the fact that nobody told you the thief was there. And,' he stopped, 'you can't remember what you had in the first place.'

'You were sent to Cloud End because of this. You were not alone. We've all been similarly deceived and yet you were chosen.' He smirked halfway down the stairs.

'You mean it hasn't hit you? Look around. You're all different. You're all suffering from different traumas or dramas, moved like sheep under the pretence that you are sick and need to be isolated for recovery.'

He snorted derisively. 'You had the virus, yes, but you don't have it anymore. They're keeping you here to change you.'

'What are you talking about?' Damian called out. 'None of that makes sense. We're getting better and soon...'

'And soon what?' Faraday interrupted as he stopped two steps above them. 'You'll go home?'

'Yes.'

Faraday nodded. 'Yes, you'll go home, and you'll spread the disease to your friends and family.'

'We've already done that in one way or another,' Dorothy Draper said.

'You've infected people with the Halovirus, but the disease is not a microbe, it's...'

If Winston Faraday III would have been paying attention to the house manager standing in the shadows, he would have seen Carl sigh deeply and press a button on his phone. This button hijacked the 3D video screen where the news had been playing. Suddenly, an eerily real, life-size video of Winston Faraday III appeared. This caused the real senator on the stairs to cease his monologue.

The hologram began speaking to a beautiful woman in a green chiffon dress. Her hair was coiffed neatly above her head and a string of pearls dangled gorgeously to her cleavage below.

'It's a big night,' Winston's hologram said.

'It certainly is.' The woman turned her back. 'Can you zip me up?'

Winston's hands worked quickly, but remained on her nape, just for a second. 'Tonight is the night I take my first leap into what I've always wanted.'

'What's that?' the woman asked as she turned to him and placed her hands on his chest. She smiled up into his face. It seemed that the question was unnecessary. She already knew the answer.

'Power, of course.'

'Your father will be devastated.'

'He'll get over it,' Winston said with a smile.

She tapped his chest and took a step backwards. 'Some will see this as heartless. He is a good man.'

'There's no such thing,' Winston said. 'There are only opportunities. Men grab them. My father dropped the ball. He believed the Government's primary role was to look after citizens, but it's not, Isolde.'

'What is it then?' She began to clip on pearl earrings.

'To rule.'

'You're not a king, you know.'

He smirked. 'Not yet. But when I am, this country will be in much better shape. We'll do away with the society's parasites. Criminals and homeless people will be shipped off to permanent detention facilities. People on welfare will be awarded a one-way ticket to an exotic destination of their choice, South Seas or Indian Ocean, and there, we'll give them a phone and they can screen away the rest of their lives, voices quiet, minds numbed. Those that deserve to live in safety and freedom, with hard work and a dedication to the advancement of the country, can do so without having to pony up for the lazy and the incompetent.'

The woman's face registered disgust but she hid it quickly. 'You've thought this all through?'

'Politicians have to have plans.'

The real Faraday stormed across the floor to the podium and pointed a finger in Claire's face. 'Turn it off! Shut it down! What are you doing? How did you get this video? My privacy has been invaded.' His eyes turned towards the other residents where many had crossed their arms looking insulted.

'She did this! She did this! It's not even me! It's fake! These kinds of videos can be faked! That's an AI algorithm. She's trying to destroy me because I've spoken the truth.'

Claire appeared as surprised and disgusted as everyone else. Faraday twirled around but couldn't find the right words. Finally, his eyes landed on Claire again. 'You'll pay for this,' he threatened.

As the last spittle issued from his mouth, a figure came from nowhere. It was Donald St Croix. Essentially kneecapping the senator, he bowled into him knocking him from his wife. Falling to the ground, Donald wrestled with him. 'Don't you dare talk to my wife like that, you bastard!'

Before getting one last slap in, Alonzo grabbed Donald and pulled him off. 'Easy, boss.'

With rage, Faraday pulled himself to his knees and then stood. Straightening his vest and jacket before adjusting his tie, he shouted at Donald. 'I'll have you arrested for assault. It's unconscionable what you've done.' Seeing Gavin, he frowned. 'You saw what he did. Arrest him.'

Gavin raised his arms in surrender. 'I'm on vacation.'

'Have we all lost our decency?' Faraday asked the empty air.

Behind Faraday, a new video began to shimmer. Beginning as a grainy image, it slowly solidified. The perspective appeared like that from a security camera on a building. As it focused in on the alley below, two figures emerged, one in a suit, the other in a short, colorful dress. Once in the alley, they stopped and the man began to paw at the woman. From the height of the camera, it was apparent that the man was about to have his way with her.

Suddenly, the video showed the woman push the man back. Surprisingly, he didn't become enraged, but reached into his coat pocket and pulled something out.

Transfixed, the residents watched as the woman reached out and grabbed what was in his hand and then slowly, as if suddenly changing her attitude, began to...

'TURN IT OFF!' Chantelle shouted. 'Please,' she begged, 'no one needs to see this. Especially the children!'

But the image was not cut short. Claire searched diligently for a power switch, but she'd never had to stand at the podium before, and certainly she'd never set up the video equipment. 'Carl!' she shouted, 'where is the switch?'

Turning slowly, Carl shook his head. For this was ultimately his doing, or at least he was a pawn to it. Carl Van der Hoven knew exactly where the power switch was: in the Capitol. Unfortunately, the Government had decided these people truly needed to know who was in control. Not them and their interesting, new relationships, but a big, bad world which continued to sink its teeth into the unsuspecting.

The Government recorded everything. The Government watched and waited, listened and prepared for the time when information could, and would be used, outside of a court of law, to condemn any who would stand against them.

In abject horror, every adult watched as their worst nightmares, those things which had been done in secret, were displayed in public. Though they wanted to leave, somehow, they couldn't. They had to know. They had to understand what the true nature of their fellow sick people was. It didn't matter who they were now, or how beautiful they'd become, it was their past and their dirty little secrets.

A fifteen-year-old video of a much younger looking Father Lawrence Haskins surfaced where he'd spoken to a trusted friend about his bias against people of Asian descent.

Gavin Matthews was caught by a police car security camera roughing up a teenager who had swung first.

The image switched swiftly to an early twenty-something Monica Xiao returning from a trip to China. No one had known she was a pickpocket.

With every revelation of darkest secret, each stared with horror at *that* particular moment in life which had been captured by the camera's unblinking and unforgiving eye. For Jacquelyn Archer, this was a secret conversation about disposable employees.

For Alonzo Turner, this was a drunken escapade in college which ended up in a sexual harassment charge.

Damian Bellows had spent a lot of time perusing disreputable websites.

And the Camera did not blink. It never shut its non-objective eye. It recorded the events, but not the context, and regurgitated without remorse.

Sydney Bellows had committed arson in a local church which supported a traditional view of marriage. As she splashed the gasoline near the darkened black stairs, it was apparent, by her sign language, how much she detested the thought of religion.

Wallis had wanted to walk out, right then and there, but the image shifted to a recent meeting with a client, in this case, Sydney Bellows. Directly after Sydney left the room, Wallis unleashed a tirade of verbal abuse against Sydney that would have ashamed even the hardiest of sailors.

Sam and Dorothy Draper were shown to be unsupportive of their local school. In a private meeting, the Draper's went after Gina's teacher, a respectable, but tough, English educator. After calling him every name in the book and threatening him from sideways to Sundays, they left the room where Dorothy immediately smeared the teacher on social media using a fake account.

And finally, as the images swirled to reveal an unconscious Seraphim Wyman lying prone in the street next to the dregs of society, sobs could be heard around the room.

Mercifully, the video footage cut, and the room was left in stunned, horrified silence. Afraid to look around, most stared at their hands as if wondering how these two tools could have done such evil. The Draper children, unspared from the sins of their forebears, stood back from everyone. Little Titus six years old, was crying softly underneath a table. The kids wanted to go to their parents, but something held them back. Something dark and terrible.

They had *seen* what adults were like. They had seen what adults *were*.

Claire St. Croix had no idea what had just happened. Dumbfounded and terrified, she stood, like a petrified sculpture, hand over masked mouth and waited for something else to occur.

'It serves you all right,' Winston Faraday III said through the despairing semi-darkness. 'You wanted to revile me for what happened with my father, but you've done worse than I. You are pathetic,' he spat. 'Hypocrites.'

'Where... How... What just happened?' Sydney asked. 'Did you do this?' she asked Claire. 'Why would you...?'

Claire held up her hands. 'I had nothing to do with this. I... have no idea. No words.'

'Then who? Who did this?'

Along with Sydney, many of the others wanted someone to blame. The revelation was perpetuated by someone, and to pin this despicable act felt right, and a way of erasing some of the shame they felt. If they could blame someone, or something, they could refocus this outrage and anger and destroy it. To blame someone else was, at the very least, an attempt to shift the attention away from their actions.

'You're sick,' Sydney pointed a finger at Father Lawrence.

'Easy, Sydney,' Alonzo spoke. 'What you did is not any better.'

'But mine was justified. For intolerant people like him and those he represents, they deserved it.'

'Intolerance?' Monica said. 'You don't even tolerate your husband. You should be ashamed of that as much as what you did to the church.'

'Ah, the thief speaks,' Sydney sneered. 'You're all alike. All you Asians.'

'How dare you!' Monica erupted from her seat and charged Sydney. Gavin stopped her but she wheeled on him.

'Get your hands off me, pig! I'm in here because of you, and now my life is ruined. Ruined! This is going to be plastered on social media. It will be a public assassination.' She wrestled herself away from him, and with great effort, returned to stand beside her chair.

Wallis Takamoto stood. Sydney's unfortunate comment only reinforced her own feelings about the young woman, but as a professional, she had to be better. As Wallis walked to the podium, she felt a tear drip from the center of her eye. It had been many years since she had cried. Being a divorce lawyer had numbed her against the pain of others and her own recorded outburst was a result of this cultural anesthetic. They were all numb. They had become immune to the pain of the world around them. Each of the illicit videos had shown each one of them compromising goodness and kindness for shameful release. Instead of seeking common ground, they had burned bridges.

Taking a deep breath, Wallis nodded to Claire who moved back into the shadows. 'I suppose I should be apologizing to Sydney, first.' Her eyes caught Sydney's who seemed satisfied that justice was about to be done. 'But I can't. Not yet. Obviously, that scene was not meant to be viewed by anyone. Not just my scene, but yours, too.' She sighed and wiped another tear. 'The illegality of what has been done is incontestable, yet here we are, exposed – naked before each other, souls bared, in some cases, not just our souls.' Multiple people, including Damian and Alonzo turned away.

'We've all done private things and said public things we're not proud of. If I do some soul-searching, it wouldn't take much to find that this kind of thought pattern and activity is unfortunately common for me. I'm not one for making excuses, but I'll offer a plea anyway.'

'For as long as I've been a lawyer, I've listened to clients prepare their case with half-truth and insinuation. They want to build their case on emotion rather than facts. But what's really happened is, two people have ceased to see the other person as valuable.' She touched her forehead as if probing for a thought. 'Maybe that's what has happened in every horrific video tonight. I don't know why it was done, only that I can't unsee it. But what has arisen in me is, perhaps, not what they'd expect. Whoever 'they' is.'

Wallis Takamoto straightened her spine and her clothes. 'Each of us has failed to see the value in the other. We can't go back. But we can move forward. The past is past. We are not the same people now as we were then. The Halovirus has changed us. If they could have recorded the way we've become now, I think they would see a different humanity.'

She turned to Sydney. 'On the day this video was taken, my father had a heart attack. In fact, it occurred about two hours before our meeting. But I decided to attend to you instead. When you came in, angry, frustrated, complaining about your husband, his habits, me, and the slowness with which the trial was moving, I swallowed my anger. The video obviously didn't show that. And after I let that venom out, I took a deep breath and went to see my father. He died a week later.'

Sydney's brow furrowed.

'Whoever edited these videos had a purpose, and it was to destroy our resolve to help each other.' Wallis glanced at Father Lawrence who tried to hold her gaze but couldn't. 'Lawrence, your statements are not rare. When the Coronavirus broke out, I, along with people of Asian descent, were reviled simply by the look of our eyes. I don't know how these viruses begin, but I know what they do. They make us act in ways, and say things, we wouldn't do and speak in normal times. The pressure of mortality is on us all. Again.'

'That being said, it hurts every time someone looks sideways at me, or uses an Asian slur, or makes 'Chinese eyes,' or any number of ignorant racist things. Yet I feel like I have to keep my mouth shut or face the ubiquitous, 'See, she's one of *those* Asians,' as Sydney pointed out.' Sydney's face turned red with shame.

'But with you, Lawrence, I've only found gentleness and courage.' She turned her attention to the others. 'The things that Lawrence Haskins said many years ago are not the things Lawrence Haskins says today. Even though you weren't talking about me then, it affected me, but I choose to forgive the thing that I saw. I forgive you, Lawrence, and I hope you can forgive me for disliking you, even for just a moment.'

Slowly, Father Lawrence Haskins unfolded from his chair and stumbled to the podium, tears streaming down his face, where he knelt in front of her and begged for forgiveness. She raised him up and hugged him tight. Though she only stood to his shoulder, her act of forgiveness seemed a Titan-like action.

Behind them, people began to stir. What seemed both painful and cathartic at the same time, hurting people finding other hurting people, became a ritualistic purging of the last viruses infecting them.

Hatred and unforgiveness.

Seraphim wrapped Chantelle in her arms. Gavin and Monica faced each other. Though Monica launched into an attack, Gavin accepted it with humility and begged her for forgiveness. She was tempted to withhold it, but Gavin was already free. Damian and Sydney came together. Damian's embarrassment at his behavior and Sydney's shame at what she'd done cauterized a few of the wounds from their past.

While the people below him mingled in teary reconciliation, Winston Faraday III threw his arms up with scorn. These people were morons. They'd just had their worst moments revealed very publicly and shamefully, and now they were hugging each other. He glanced at Jacquelyn who, as of yet, stood on the periphery of the proceedings. She stared at him offering no consolation or accusation, only a look of pity.

He sneered. She had no right to look at him this way. Her own business practices were unethical. In fact, Faraday made a mental note to have her investigated after he left Cloud End.

If he would have searched the room, Faraday would have noticed the house manager walking slowly towards the bar. There was something misplaced about the strident way he walked. Faraday shook his head. The people below him were dying, perhaps already dead. They had no lives to go back to. When any one of them decided to reveal to the real world who the others truly *were*, there would be no turning back.

As he reached the top of the stairs, he pondered the window at the end of the hallway which overlooked the back grassy area towards the cliff with the ocean below.

A thought occurred to him, one that carried significant risk, but if it worked, Cloud End would be closed permanently. And when that happened, he could go back to his life and his freedom. It only required a small bit of destruction.

Encoded message #10215976

9 November, 2031
02:05

Government device sent: CVH4580387

Government device received: SRC9022289

It is done. Project Green Light has failed. Subjects gathered after revealing videos and commiserated rather than tearing each other apart.

Recommend Erase.

23

'They aren't buying it.'

'Carl, you've made a mess of this,' Stella said.

'If you want, you can try to do it better. These people have found something they never expected here.'

'And what is that?'

'Immunity.'

Reed-Conway snorted. 'They have the Halovirus.'

'They might have it, but they aren't sick. They look healthier than anyone I see on television.'

In her office overlooking the river, Stella Reed-Conway leaned back in her chair. It creaked. Her eyes fixed on the afternoon joggers and lovers laying on flannel blankets. Though growing cold, people were happy to be outside.

Ducks paddled in the river and lazy clouds floated overhead. The late autumn weather seemed to be stuck in a wrestling match. The sun, though lower in the sky, stretched its yellowing rays to the grey granite buildings of the Capitol where the light was absorbed and muted. Stella was glad that she lived in the Capitol, but she missed her monthly trips to her country estates: one, a lake house two hours from the Capitol, and the other, a mountain chalet half-way across the country. She'd occupied neither one during the Halovirus pandemic except for three or four vacation weeks. Oh, yes, and one out of every six weekends as a reward for her long hours. And then, of course, the public holidays.

'I don't understand. How could we have been so wrong about this? The guidelines were established to control the virus.'

'Perhaps you underestimated the power of the human collective,' Carl countered.

'Don't give me any of that touchy-feely crap, Carl. You were given a directive and paid handsomely for it. You've failed.'

Carl's jaw twitched. Outside his room, he heard people returning from the purging. 'Perhaps the blame should be leveled at Dr. Boeder-

Mankins. Certainly, she should have...'

'We don't have time to point fingers,' Stella responded testily.

'Yet, that's what you're doing.'

'I'm frustrated, that's all. Now, what are we going to do?' she asked.

Carl shook his head. 'I'm afraid my part in this has run its course. There is nothing else I can do.'

'Carl,' Stella warned, 'if word of this got out, you would be in a lot of trouble.'

He snorted. 'Do you really think I would be a scapegoat for you. Social media loves a Governmental conspiracy theory.'

'You signed a non-disclosure agreement. You cannot speak of this to anyone.'

Carl shrugged. 'We'll see. I might go to jail for it, but I won't be the only one.'

Stella felt her blood run cold. She hadn't expected this reaction from Van der Hoven. 'Let's just take a step back from the ledge, here. This is what I want you to do. Go back to the Halos. We'll send some more videos. Jacquelyn Archer herself has dozens of shady dealings which would destroy her if they...' She stopped and looked at her AutoCom. It was blank.

Carl Van der Hoven had hung up on her.

Night fell quickly over Cloud End. Seagulls finished their wind-dancing as the sun lowered in the west, behind the residence which cast an imposing, house-shaped shadow over the yard leading to the fence and cliff beyond. Autumn's cooler temperature had chilled the insects which had ceased their chirping. Only rodents and predators were left wriggling in the browning grass.

Into this darkness, Senator Winston Faraday III crept outside. No one stopped him. They had no reason to. In fact, most wished he would stay away.

Treading quickly to the unlocked shed, he entered and used his AutoCom to illuminate the dirty space. It appeared as if it had not been straightened for years. Rusty equipment, hammers and screwdrivers, a spare wrench, homeless sockets and a number of plastic buckets were strewn everywhere. Carefully, he stepped past an overturned wheelbarrow and around an unused lawnmower and searched the wall for that which he sought.

A handsaw.

Delightedly, he found it hanging by a nail. Its wooden handle was cracked and the teeth were rusty. He cringed at the thought of cutting himself with it. Winston couldn't remember when his last tetanus shot was. Retrieving it from its perch, Winston found his way back to the door and shut it noiselessly behind him. Carefully, with just the moonlight to illuminate the track underfoot, he stepped through the grass and made his way to the fence.

It was a gorgeous, cool night. Winston felt the slight breeze on his face and neck and shivered. He was wearing the only non-suit clothes he owned: a designer tracksuit with expensive tennis shoes. To be without collared shirt and tie, cufflinks, and leather shoes, was like a soldier without his body armor.

Winston stared up at the skies above him. It was a cloudless night. The stars, bereft of light pollution, twinkled merrily billions of miles away from this egocentric politician.

In Faraday's mind, it would only take a slight accident, nothing fatal, of course – just a scare – for Cloud End to be shut down. Winston could then resume his chase for the brass ring. Where Sisyphus failed, Senator Faraday would not. He would grasp the ring and people would applaud. They would follow his lead. His name would go down in the annals of Government as the greatest politician – nay, president – of all time.

Winston bent down and leveled the saw at the base of one of the fence posts. The sawing was difficult. Even though the wood had been abused by wind and rain and briny spray, it stood solidly. Soon, sweat broke out on his face. His hand and fingers began to hurt. Blisters appeared on his palm. Finally, he cut within half an inch of severing the post. If anyone leaned on it, it would break but it would still be connected to the thin metal fencing. Just to be certain, Winston fought through the pain and sawed through one more post.

Seeing his work done, Winston stood and hurled the saw over the edge of the cliff. The roar of the waves so far below drowned out the sound of the saw hitting the rocks or water, but the evidence of his deed was gone, swallowed with the tide.

He turned and quickly retraced his footsteps back to Cloud End.

If he would have looked up, he would have noticed a small face watching him. Pasqual Draper wondered what in the world that grumpy old man was doing.

'**What did you** do?' Gemma Cranmere screamed at her husband.

Steve cringed and avoided her swing. 'What are you talking about?'

'The helicopter crash, idiot. What have you done?'

'Nothing! Nothing!' he lied.

'You better not,' she threatened. Stomping towards the living room, she stopped just short of entering and turned back. 'I swear to you, if you have something to do with that craziness, I'll send you out on your ear so fast you'll beg to be transported to the hospital, not Cloud End.'

Steve attempted to control the fear in his eyes. It was enough to accidentally take down the helicopter. Bridgette and Renata were acceptable casualties in a war against the Government. They were just getting in the way.

'I'm sorry,' Steve replied.

Wheeling on him, she turned, face blanched. 'You *did* have something to do with it.'

'I... no... it was just... it was an accident. We were just doing as you told us.'

'*Us?* Who else is involved? Who else knows?'

'Edgar. That's it. Just Edgar. The night of the crash, we went out to block the gate. You didn't want the Halos brought to the Herzfeld hospital, so we blocked the ambulance. Pretended to have a flat battery. But they called the Heli flight and we didn't know what to do. To let that disease get out of there would have been terrible.'

'You moron. The Heli flight would have taken the injured into the city, not Herzfeld.'

'You don't know that,' Steve whined.

'Yes, yes I do!' Her eyes were wide open, scared.

Her shouting hurt his ears and he cringed. 'Relax. Nobody saw anything.'

'What did you do?'

'I just sent a few warning shots across its bow. Nothing serious. The pilot must have got scared and accidentally hit something. It was an accident.' Steve had replayed the event over and over in his mind until the lie had become true. *Really, they were warning shots and the pilot overcorrected. Poor guy. Should have trained better.*

'Oh, God, I can't believe it.' Gemma put a hand on her forehead and began to pace.

'You told me to do it,' Steve insisted.

'Are you joking? I never said shoot a helicopter out of the sky. We only discussed the danger they posed to Herzfeld if they escaped Cloud End and showed up in town.'

'Same thing.'

Gemma rounded on him and slapped him. 'You listen to me, Steve Cranmere. You better fix this. None of this will ever get out or you will burn.' She stepped back, face flushed. 'And my career will be finished.'

'I'll fix it, Gemma.' Steve felt the hot wash on his cheek where she had struck him.

She studied him for falsehood, but he hid it. 'Very well,' she said dismissively, 'but from now on, if you're going to do anything stupid, you need to clear it with me.'

His eyes narrowed. Something cracked in his mind. Over the years of absorbed abuse, layers and layers of physical and emotional beating, he had patched these cracks with self-pity; after the verbal assaults on his intelligence, the financial control over the tavern, where she never worked, the nagging and slapping, the incessant gossiping about him, he'd had it. As the fissure of sanity yawned, he saw a frightening way out, one that would define him forever. Yes, this would erase any knowledge of his part in this last month. *Of course*, he thought, *it would require an immense act of bravery, but he thought he could do it.*

'Gemma,' he said, his voice lowered evilly, 'I've decided to do something stupid.'

The morning sun seemed to prise up the bedroom shades and peek through the windows on the east side of Cloud End. For those in rooms 4-8, this was both welcome and detestable. That it was already 6:30 a.m. and they still had not been released was frustrating. That they were still alive and feeling healthy filled them with gratitude.

The Drapers, in room 1, slept in. It had been an exhausting night of terrors, of being revealed in such a way that painted them as intolerant and aggressive parents. The children had recoiled from them, not so much by what they did, but because of what they didn't. The parents had not protected the children from all the preceding videos – the anger and rage, pornography, drug abuse. The moment the videos began, they should have pulled them away, but it was the way the world worked. Parents were unable to pull themselves and their children from moving pictures. Unfortunately, parents usually placed the device in the kids' hands and said, 'Have fun, but don't do anything you'll regret.'

Pasqual had gone to bed early. Whether from shock or exhaustion, he barely made it between the sheets before passing out. It took Titus, a constant worrier, a lot longer to get to sleep. Dorothy sat beside him rubbing his back slowly. Once they were out, she kissed them both, flipped the switch and left the bedroom. Sam was sitting at the table cradling a glass of whiskey in his hands.

'Are they asleep?' he asked.

'Yes, thankfully.' Dorothy found a twin glass and poured before sitting down. 'It's been a horrible night.'

'You're telling me.'

'Can you believe what happened? It feels like... I don't know... we walked into someone else's nightmare. I guess I knew that we're always being tracked, but I had no idea that it could be so callously and spontaneously reproduced.'

'You're not that naïve, are you, dear?'

She smiled sadly. 'I guess I wanted to be. I wanted to trust the Government, but...'

'Do you think it's just the Government?'

'What do you mean?'

Sam took a big swig and set the glass down to look at his wife. 'This is not a Government thing, but a planetary thing. Can't you feel it? The whole world's gone crazy. We've built so many borders and boundaries between us that everyone is the enemy. I can feel it. We're constantly being manipulated by something. Someone.'

Dorothy sighed deeply.

'We fight over oil and grain and money. Hell, even toilet paper. We don't share anything. Instead of taking care of each other, we kill each other, all in the name of almighty self-preservation. If I can just outlast the last guy, I'll finally be okay.'

'Has the world really come to that?' she asked.

'I believe it has.'

'Then what do we do?'

Sam shrugged. 'I don't know. I really don't know, but if I had to guess, it would start with something like what happened after the videos tonight.'

The scene of forgiveness flashed in front of both their minds. 'We do and say stupid things, but that doesn't mean we are stupid. Momentary lapses, old biases, the ancient human problem of ego comes out everywhere, but it doesn't mean that we can't live together. And I'm not talking about co-existing, that's just a synonym for tolerance.'

'What's wrong with tolerance?' Dorothy asked.

He lifted his glass again. 'It's a wolf in sheep's clothing. Tolerance says that I am accepting of your behavior, but I hate you, and we're just not going to talk about it.'

'And what does tolerance have to do with co-existence?'

'Nothing. Nothing at all. We're not meant to co-exist; we're meant to care for each other. Care for the planet and the people, for the climate and animals – for all of it. It has nothing to do with politics or governments, but it has to do with us as a human village. We've got to tear down the walls and see the people on the other side.'

'That's beautiful,' Dorothy said.

'And it's not how I've been acting.'

'*We've* been acting,' she stressed.

'And now our children have seen us at our worst and we'll have to live with that. But we can only make it better. Once we get out of here, we'll go directly to Mr. Amundsen, and we'll apologize to him for our...' Sam searched for the correct descriptor.

'Unforgiving nature,' Dorothy inserted and lifted her glass for a toast.

'That's a good way of putting it.' He clinked his glass with Dorothy's, and they drank together.

Now that it was morning, Pasqual was up early. Before he went to sleep, he'd seen the old man, the one who was always angry, coming back from the fence. Pasqual wanted to know what the man had been doing, so he slipped his clothes on and laced his shoes. Grabbing his rat gently, he stuffed it inside his coat and opened the door quietly. Padding out onto the balcony, he scanned other rooms for traces of life. Finding none, Pasqual raced towards the stairs and took them down two at a time. He could feel his rat's claws dig into his shoulder, but he didn't want to be spotted.

Pausing outside Oswald's door, Pasqual knocked softly. Three times. Then, he shuffled his hand along the outside. Three more knocks. After a moment, Pasqual heard the soft sound of footsteps and then the door was pulled open in front of him.

'Hey,' Pasqual smiled.

Oswald smiled back and hefted his own white rat. 'Hey, back.'

The two boys, instead of crossing the center of the atrium where they might be seen, walked in the darkness underneath the balcony. They passed by the staff doors. They knew that Nancy would already be starting her first loads of laundry and preparing supplies for the daily rounds. The boys could hear Esther and Carl in the kitchen preparing the menu for breakfast. As they walked past the psychologist's room, they knew she'd be sleeping until at least eight. Grandpa St. Croix said this was because her brain was tired of analyzing everyone, but Oswald wasn't sure that was possible.

Once at the library, the boys sprinted to the front door and quickly opened it, exposing themselves to the beautiful, cold morning.

The fresh wind from the south blew the scents up from Herzfeld village. There was the bakery and café, hints of bread and caffeine, and the diesel exhaust of the brave truck drivers who had arrived early to bring supplies to the gas station, the hospital and the grocery store. If they listened carefully, they could hear post-dawn laughter from free citizens of Herzfeld who were connecting with each other. Since restrictions had eased, they could safely talk to each other face to face. *Those diseased people at Cloud End could bring it all down*, citizens might have said, but they were happy that they didn't really know what was going on. There were rumors, of course.

It would be later that the sounds of the ambulance would echo throughout the town. The siren was not rare, but it always brought rubberneckers. People would theorize who it was and what happened. Probably a geriatric fall or maybe a pubescent skateboarding accident.

But the siren wasn't sounding yet.

Pasqual and Oswald raced each other to the fence. Once there, they breathlessly stood next to the fence feeling the sea air blow up the side of the cliff and wrap them in its briny scent.

'It's awesome today,' Oswald said as he set his face into the breeze.

'Yeah.' Pasqual began to search around the fence.

'What are you looking for?'

'I don't know,' Pasqual responded as he searched through the grass.

'What do you mean you don't know?'

'You promise you won't tell anyone?'

Oswald rolled his eyes. 'No.'

'Well, don't tell any other adult, okay, but last night I saw the guy who wears the suits out here.'

Snorting, Oswald began to climb up on the cliff fence. He wanted to get a better feel of the wind. 'Why would the suit guy be out here in the dark. He never comes out. He's like a vampire.' Oswald climbed up another step. He was unaware of the post next to him which was beginning to cant outwards toward the cliff. Just slightly.

'Even vampires have to go out and bite people.'

'You think he was out here biting people?' Oswald laughed.

'No, but he might have been destroying evidence.'

Oswald climbed another step. He almost lost his balance but caught himself. The force, though, caused the post to crack. Unfortunately, the wind covered up the sound. 'What kind of evidence? Do you think he killed someone?'

'Probably,' Pasqual said.

As Oswald climbed up the last wire step, Pasqual took that moment to turn around. It was then, that Pasqual noticed the bottom of the post and how it was listing outwards, towards the cliff face. If it broke, Oswald would be sent over. 'Oswald!' he cried out.

Oswald's face radiated happiness. In the innocence of youth, it would have been plausible to believe that a young boy like him could have sprouted wings and begun to sail with the seagulls and soar with the albatrosses. Far from his consciousness was the big bad world and its viruses and its hatred and its self-absorption. No, it was just a young boy and the wide-open expanse of his future.

But when Oswald saw his friend dive towards the fence, Oswald jerked his legs backwards, the motion causing the post to break. From Pasqual's perspective, everything seemed to move in slow motion. Unable to stop Oswald's motion outwards and towards the vastness, Pasqual leaped for him. Hands outstretched to each other, they just missed. Due to Pasqual's momentum, he crashed into the now collapsing fence and followed his friend over the cliff edge.

Alonzo Turner poured himself a cup of coffee and sat on the veranda enjoying the peaceful serenity of the early morning. With a steaming cup in front of him, Alonzo sat next to Chantelle who stared desultorily at her shaking hands. Alonzo asked if he could put a hand on her hand. She appreciated the gesture, and it felt good to be next to a man who was completely different than the one that appeared on that horrible video. Chantelle remembered that encounter. It had been the same as every other one, but that guy... she shivered, and he squeezed her hand until it passed.

'Why does the world have to be this way?' she asked quietly.

'I'm not sure,' replied Alonzo, 'but maybe we can reshape it differently after this pandemic.'

'Nothing's gonna change.'

'Ya never know. Sometimes traumatic things bring people together. Maybe this is one of them.'

'Nobody is going to want anything to do with me after this.'

Alonzo felt guilty. His own conscience had capsized on his own video, but he tried to remind himself that bygones had gone by. His guilt and guilty memories were powerful motivators for not returning to the place Alonzo used to be. 'If it's possible, I've got a few spare rooms in my house, if you need a place to stay.' His face reddened. It had been a long time since he had asked a woman something so forward. 'I asked Seraphim, too.'

Chantelle frowned, but felt relieved. If it had only been her, she would have expected that eventually, even a kind person like Alonzo Turner would expect 'payment.' But with Seraphim, perhaps his motives were altruistic after all. 'What did she say?'

'She'd think about it.' He paused. 'Well, at first, she eyed me like you're doing now, as if I'm some kind of weirdo. But if you have somewhere to stay after this, not a problem.'

'Where do you live?'

'In a small town about five hours from here. You'd never have heard of it.'

'Tell me about it,' she said.

While he sipped coffee that morning, a Thursday, listening to the birds transact the last of their business before the cold winter winds forced them indoors, Alonzo sat up straighter. He thought he heard screaming.

Setting his mug down, he stood. There it was again. It sounded like kids.

Kids near the cliff.

Hurtling himself from the porch, he raced through the tall grass towards the fence. By the time he got within fifty feet, he could see what had happened.

The fence had broken outwards, and two sets of tiny hands were holding onto the fence as they dangled over the edge.

'Hold on!' he shouted.

The boys continued to scream. Their terrified voices carried up and outwards.

Alonzo turned back to Cloud End, and he began to shout at the top of his voice for help. Whether or not reinforcements were coming, he made a decision. Crawling out over the mangled mess of the fence, he attempted not to dislodge the boys. As his body neared the edge, Alonzo felt a queasy sense of disorientation. The rocks below were so far away.

The boys' terrified faces peered up at him through the wire holes of the fence. 'Please! Help us, Alonzo!' Pasqual called out.

'I'm coming.' He crawled out a little farther, but the fence began to slide.

The boys screamed again.

Somehow, Alonzo inched forward without moving the fence.

'Hurry,' Pasqual whimpered.

With a slow movement, Alonzo leaned slightly forward and with one last surge, he grabbed one hand of each boy. In his vice-like grip, he held on for dear life. Turning his head, he screamed again for help. No one could hear him.

'It hurts,' Oswald said. 'My wrist hurts.'

'I'm sorry, buddy, but I've got to get one of you up first. You're not light.' He tried to smile.

'Please...' Oswald begged.

Alonzo's arms were beginning to burn. If he didn't do something soon, he wouldn't have the strength to bring them up. 'All right, I'm going to hold on to you, Pasqual, and hoist the other boy up.'

'His name is Oswald.'

'Okay, Oswald. On the count of three, we're going to do it, okay?'

He nodded.

Alonzo tried not to pay attention to the extraordinary drop underneath the boys' feet. If the fence shifted any further, they'd be in big trouble.

'One...'

Pasqual's face was a complete mask of fear.

'Two...'

At that moment, Oswald's white rat crawled out of his pocket and up his arm towards Alonzo's hand. Surprised, Alonzo flinched. There could have been no worse thing. With the abrupt movement, the fence shifted and slid further out over the edge. Fortunately, Alonzo's feet were caught in the fencing, but it wouldn't be long until they slipped again.

Alonzo swore as the rat scampered up his arm and over his shoulder to the safety of the ground behind him. But their situation had drastically worsened. There was no way Alonzo was going to be able to hoist them one at a time. He'd have to attempt both simultaneously. But there was a new realization. If he did so, there was no guarantee his feet would hold. The odds were, he would sail over the edge to the precipitous drop to the rocks below.

His face twisted in anger and pain, shoulders beginning to strain, Alonzo gritted his teeth. 'Okay, boys,' he said, 'I'm going to bring you both up at the same time.' He stared at their little white hands in his dark ones. 'You're going to be okay.'

'One...'

'Two...'

Summoning the reserves of his strength, Alonzo jerked the boys upwards and over his shoulders onto the fence behind him. As they sailed upwards, Alonzo felt his feet dislodge from the fence. With a horrified feeling, Alonzo knew he was going over. As the fence broke, he looked up to see the boys clamber to safety.

Alonzo sighed.

He hoped the end would be quick.

On every other day of the year, Tom and Albert would have driven the ambulance with utmost speed to Cloud End. Even though they would not have been able to retrieve the body, they would certainly have been on hand to deal with the shock of the situation, especially for the two little boys who sat huddled in blankets, petting white rats while the adults stood over them chewing fingernails and wondering what it was and what it could have been.

As it was, Tom and Albert were called to Mayor Cranmere's residence. When they arrived, they found a distraught Steve Cranmere being consoled by his best friend, Edgar Post. Already, Igor Kovschenko was next to the body. There was nothing he could do. There was nothing the paramedics could do either. Gemma Cranmere's head was twisted at an awkward angle at the bottom of the stairs. By her head was a broken whiskey glass. The contents were spilled everywhere.

As Tom and Albert rushed inside the house, Igor exited the house. Onlookers gathered across the street. Some were people he knew well, people who frequented the tavern, but others were gawkers who simply wanted to see what all the commotion was.

'What happened?' Igor asked Steve.

'This is how I found her this morning.' His wild eyes were red and ringed with tears.

'Where were you?'

'Are you accusing me of something?' Steve screamed in Igor's face, who took a step back.

'No,' Igor said conciliatorily, 'I just wondered how it came to be that you found her this late in the morning at the bottom of the stairs. You didn't hear her fall? I assume it was last night judging by the whiskey glass.'

'I stayed at the tavern last night. I do that sometimes.'

'What for?'

Steve ran a hand through his thinning hair. 'Because we'd been arguing, and when Gemma argues, I lose. So I left.'

'When was the last time you saw her?'

'This morning, when I walked in,' Steve answered.

'I mean the last time she was alive.'

Steve pretended to think hard. 'I suppose it was about seven o'clock last night. She'd just returned from the Capitol and decided to have a few drinks. When she drinks, it's worse than normal. So, I left.' Steve tried to add as few details as possible.

'And then you went to the tavern.'

'That's right.'

Glancing behind him, Igor saw Tom and Albert stabilising Gemma's body and lift her onto the stretcher. 'Okay, well, I'm sorry, Steve. Really sorry.'

'Thank you.' Fresh tears started. Steve was surprised he could summon them. Maybe he would miss her - eventually.

Moments later, Tom and Albert wheeled the mayor of Herzfeld out the front door to the ambulance. Just after they opened the back door, their

AutoComs lit up. Albert looked down and then up at Tom whose eyes were widened. He was staring at Igor.

'What is it?' Steve asked.

'Trouble.'

There was nothing anyone could do. Not even a professional climber could have scaled Faucini Cliff to where Alonzo Turner's corpse was bashed by wave and rock. It seemed patently unfair to the rest of the residents of Cloud End that someone as kind and gentle as Alonzo Turner would be the one to fall. And to save the boys, he was a hero.

Only Father Lawrence had the courage to crawl to the edge and peer over. Thankfully, it was too far down to see the wreckage of Alonzo's body. When he stood up, he shook his head sadly and felt the first of his tears start its journey down his face. A terrible thought occurred to him, one that he wanted to retrieve, and he asked God for forgiveness. *Why couldn't it have been Winston Faraday III?*

As they consoled each other, Senator Faraday stood to the side. His face was ashen. He seemed highly shaken.

When Herzfeld's police officer showed up in full protective gear, the residents seemed resentful. Why had he been delayed? Where were the paramedics? Shouldn't a rescue boat be on the way?

'I'm sorry, folks,' the officer said with his voice amplified through his mask, 'it's been a tough day.'

'Not tougher than Alonzo's,' a woman said.

'There was a death in town last night.' The police officer defended himself.

'Not good enough,' the woman said.

The police officer's jaw twitched behind the mask. 'Please take me to the site.'

Donald St. Croix stepped forward. His own pale face displayed the horror of what he knew would be forthcoming. Constable Kovschenko followed him to the site of the accident where Igor studied the surroundings. He frowned. 'Tell me again what happened.'

'The boys, one of them is my grandson, were playing out here this morning when the fence broke. The boys were able to hang on until Alonzo – Mr. Turner – arrived. He saved their lives by sacrificing his own.'

Igor's frown continued. 'Has the fence ever broken before?'

'No,' Donald insisted. He glanced out over the vast expanse of the ocean. 'We check it every six months to make sure there is no rust or wood rot. We told the boys not to play on the fence, but their weight, even for ones so small, must have been too much.'

'Who has access to this area?'

'Everyone. We don't keep people locked inside. This is not a prison.'

'It wasn't an accident,' Igor said.

'What?' Donald's startled eyes widened. 'What do you mean?'

Igor pointed down at the post. 'Someone sawed through that.'

Donald had not noticed. How long had it been like that? 'Someone was trying to kill the children?'

'I'm not sure they were trying to kill children, but the kids might have simply been in the wrong place at the wrong time.' He paused. 'We can't let your people go until I've asked a few questions.'

'Yes, of course. But be gentle. They've all suffered a great tragedy here today.'

Igor nodded but didn't speak. The day was going to get even worse.

```
Encoded message #1037883
11 November, 2031
10:24
```

Government device sent: CVH4580387

Government device received: SRC9022289

Be advised: Subject 11, fell to his death early this morning. The other
subjects are in shock. The local police have arrived. I checked the
site myself. Two of the posts have been cut. It was not an accident.

Did you do this?

```
Encoded message #103785
11 November, 2031
10:26
```

Government device sent: SRC9022289

Government device received: CVH4580387

The Government claims no responsibility for this action. We want to
know who did it. Find out.

```
Encoded message #1037887
11 November, 2031
10:28
```

Government device sent: CVH4580387

Government device received: SRC9022289

One of the children claims that he saw Subject 14 leave CECC last night
and enter the shed, leaving with an object in his hand. He claims it
was a saw. I doubt the truthfulness of his words. He's just a boy.

Things are getting out of hand.
```
Encoded message #1037890
11 November, 2031
10:31
```

Government device sent: SRC9022289

Government device received: CVH4580387

It is apparent that Project Green Light has reached an ultimate
decision. Await confirmation for Erase. Do you understand?

```
Encoded message #1037887
11 November, 2031
10:32

Government device sent: CVH4580387

Government device received: SRC9022289

I have ceased to be comfortable with final contingencies.


Encoded message #1037888
11 November, 2031
10:33

Government device sent: SRC9022289

Government device received: CVH4580387

Will $1,600,000 change your mind?


Encoded message #1037883
11 November, 2031
10:24

Government device sent: CVH4580387

Government device received: SRC9022289

Proceed.
```

24

Faraday's profanity was horrible. Isolde had to turn down her AutoCom and focus on the sight outside the window. The Capitol's lights twinkled merrily. The festive season was approaching, not that many celebrated religious festivals, but all enjoyed the days off work.

'If you're going to talk to me like that, Winston, I'm going to hang up and you can call me when you've calmed down,' she said as the lights of a plane merged with the skyline, descending into the Capitol.

'You don't understand what's happening here,' he hissed. 'Today, a man fell to his death. Apparently, one of the posts in the fence had been cut.'

'So?' Isolde countered. 'Who cares? It might even get you out of there quicker. Insurance companies are going to be throwing a hissy fit over it.'

He stated slowly, 'I'm being blamed. For some reason, a stupid brat has it out for me.' He stopped pacing. 'I almost wish it was the little kid who went over.'

'Who died?'

'You're not going to believe this, but a gravedigger. He saved the kids.'

'He's a hero?'

'I suppose.'

'Why did he accuse you? Have you been naughty?' she laughed.

'This is not humorous in the least, Isolde. I am a Senator, a politician of good repute, and to have my identity impugned is beyond repugnant.'

'It's just a kid...'

'That doesn't matter. In the current way our media works, it could be a mongoloid and I'd still be found guilty in the court of media.'

'You shouldn't say that word,' Isolde responded. 'It's offensive.' She picked her teeth with a fingernail.

'I don't care if it's downright nasty. Right now, I need help, and you're the only one who can give it to me.'

'What can I do for you, darling?'

Faraday paused his pacing and looked out over the grassy area. Lights had been set up and yellow police tape surrounded everything. The police officer was still out there staring out over the ocean. 'I need you to talk with Quentin Forsythe. Can you get near him?'

'Yeah,' she smiled.

'Tell him I'm being wrongfully investigated for a tragedy and to preserve both my dignity and Governmental status, I need immediate – not tomorrow, or the next day, or whatever timetable you think you have – transfer out of here.'

Isolde studied the piece of food which she had prised from her teeth. 'And what will you owe him?'

'Owe him?' Faraday blustered a tirade of more non-repeatable words. Isolde muted him until he was finished. 'I'll owe him lunch. I have a feeling he was part of what happened to me here. It would be difficult for him to deny if I made an accusation.'

'Without evidence?'

'It doesn't matter, does it?'

'Touché. It does if Forsythe sues you.'

'Then,' Faraday's exasperated voice cracked, 'convince him I'm serious.'

The police tape fluttered in the wind, a ceaseless and abhorrent flapping sound that made Chantelle want to rip it off and chuck it over the cliff. Chantelle, as well as Seraphim, had both struggled to sleep. Seraphim begged Dr. Chandruth to give her something – anything – to stop her from thinking about what happened to Alonzo. She couldn't stop her mind from re-enacting what had happened with the boys and ultimately the freefall to the rocks below. Unfortunately, Chandruth reminded her that any kind of drug would push Seraphim off the wagon again. At that moment, Seraphim didn't care if she was run over by the wagon, as long as she didn't have to feel anything.

Chantelle and Seraphim were not the only ones feeling the intense grief of Alonzo's death. Father Lawrence, too, was in shock. More than the others, Lawrence could feel himself folding inwards like an armadillo being attacked by a predator.

The family St. Croix felt impending doom approach. Not only were they shattered by the fact that someone had deliberately cut through the fence, but Pasqual was blaming Senator Faraday. Sam and Dorothy attempted to shush him. *Little people always needed to place blame,* they said. Faraday denied the accusation vehemently and had controlled his outrage. So far.

The next day, the Halos warmed themselves by the heat of the fireplace in the corner adjacent to the theater. Huddled together, they sipped coffee and cocoa, nibbled on cookies and chips, and whispered short, clipped sentences. No one wanted to go to the scene of the accident.

During breakfast, the Draper family sat together but away from the others. Gina pushed her eggs across the plate while Pasqual hunched in his chair. He stared at his hands and wrists, the marks of the fence, and Alonzo's grip, still apparent. Titus seemed to be the only Draper with an appetite.

'Everything will be okay, sweetheart,' Dorothy said as she touched Pasqual's arm.

'No, it won't.'

'Someday.'

'It won't be okay for Alonzo, will it?' His eyes brimmed with tears.

'Pasqual, I'm so sorry.' Dorothy desperately wanted to protect her son from the pain, but ever since the Coronavirus pandemic, the world had been in a constant state of pain from which no mothers could completely rescue their children.

'It was him,' Pasqual stubbornly insisted.

Sam and Dorothy shared a look but did not say anything.

Father Lawrence approached. 'Can I sit with you?'

Sam held out a hand in invitation to the empty chair.

'I didn't want to be alone this morning,' Lawrence said.

'I suppose that's part of your existence, isn't it?' Dorothy asked.

Nodding sadly, Lawrence bowed his head to pray. When finished, he picked up his fork and took a bite of his scrambled eggs. His lanky grey hair hung over his furrowed forehead. He looked haggard, drawn too thin over a tired soul. 'I've never been able to get used to it, though.'

'It must be very lonely for you.'

'Constant rejection of both person and ideology has a weathering effect that I could not, even in my earliest days as a priest, begin to imagine. When the Coronavirus hit, corporate faith was essentially wiped from the planet. I heard the refrain all too often – 'There is no God. If there was a God, then none of this would be happening. There would be no virus.'

He took another bite of food. 'Interestingly, it was during COVID that the world completely distanced itself from the spiritual world. Though they didn't know it, they found their god – and it was not a virus.'

'That doesn't make sense,' Gina said.

Lawrence smiled kindly at her and pointed his fork in her direction. 'It's not a microbe, young lady. It's what you're holding in your hands.'

Gina glanced down at the phone. 'That's something old people say.'

'I suppose,' he shrugged. 'I grew up in a world that didn't have mobile phones and somehow we survived. But you haven't had that experience. You've always had them. And the virulent, addictive device has infected the last few generations.' He looked around the room. 'Notice all the AutoComs?'

Almost half the Halos had the devices embedded in their arms and ears. 'My guess is,' Lawrence continued, 'that even though the internet is still not fixed, most of them are watching or listening to things they've saved on their AutoComs.'

'What's wrong with that?' Gina asked. 'At least we don't have to think about what happened to Alonzo.'

'Why wouldn't you want to think about that?' Lawrence asked.

'Because it's sick and horrible. I want to feel happy.'

'And you'll feel happy by watching a movie?'

'Yes,' Gina responded as she unconsciously put her phone down.

24

The priest felt a twinge of irritation at this common refrain. *I just want to be happy.* 'Will that help your pain and fear?'

'For a while.'

Lawrence took a sip of his orange juice. 'And then after you've finished that movie, what next?'

She shrugged. Everyone knew the answer. *The next movie. The next binge. The next social media event. The next avoidance...*

He sighed. 'How long before you will feel ready to talk about Alonzo's death and how it affected you?'

Sam, noticing Gina's discomfort, coughed politely. 'Lawrence, I'm not sure...'

Gina, clutching her phone, tipped the chair backwards and left the table.

'I didn't mean to offend, Sam. I was just trying to...'

Sam, shaking his head, pushed himself away from the table to follow Gina. With an exasperated sigh he said, 'Come on, family. Let's go.'

'I don't want to go,' Pasqual said.

'Me neither,' Titus echoed.

Holding Lawrence's eyes, Sam said, 'Please don't upset the boys, too.'

'Understood,' Lawrence responded.

After their father left, Pasqual swirled his sugary cereal around in his bowl while Titus bounced in his seat. He was humming. 'Do you believe me?' Pasqual asked quietly.

'Would it help?'

The boy frowned. The answer was not what he expected and certainly not helpful. 'Why don't adults believe kids?'

'Do you want the truth?'

'Well, I don't want you to lie to me.'

'Me either,' Titus repeated.

Lawrence smiled wryly. *Why don't people believe kids.* 'I suppose adults don't trust kids because kids are fairly absorbed in their own perspective.'

'What does that mean?' Titus asked.

Lawrence was about to respond when Pasqual answered first. 'He thinks kids can't see what's going on.'

'Is it true?' Lawrence asked.

'My eyes are better than yours.' Pasqual's jaw jutted out.

'No doubt.'

'It's not like adults are great at hearing other people's opinions.'

'That, also, is beyond doubt.' Lawrence chewed his eggs and then swallowed. 'What do you think you saw?'

Pasqual frowned. 'That's just an adult way of saying, 'Tell me what you saw, but I've already decided not to believe you.'

'You're a smart young man.'

'Then don't treat me like I'm stupid.'

'I'll rephrase the question, counselor. What did you see?'

Pasqual spooned some cereal into his mouth. Some milk dripped down his chin and he wiped it with the back of his hand. 'I couldn't sleep. Maybe it was because I hadn't played Minecraft for a few days, I don't know...'

'I miss it, too,' Titus added.

Pasqual ignored him. '...and I was staring out my window when I saw a person walking back towards the house and he was wearing dark clothes.'

'How do you know it was Senator Faraday?' Lawrence tried not to emphasize *senator* too much.

He rolled his eyes. 'We've been in the same house for a long time now. He has a funny walk, like he's got a stick shoved up his...' Pasqual mimed where the stick was.

'Up his bebop,' Titus started laughing.

'He walks stiff, not like other people,' Pasqual finished.

'Even if it was him, that doesn't mean he cut through the fence.'

Pasqual frowned. 'I saw him throw something over the cliff.'

'What was it?'

'A saw.'

Lawrence's eyes widened. 'You actually saw the saw?'

Pasqual looked away, just briefly. The admission of falsehood was quick and apparent. 'No, but, what else could it be?'

The priest nodded. 'And therein lies why it's hard to believe kids.'

Face reddening, Pasqual felt tears come to his eyes. 'I'm telling the truth, that's why you have to believe me.'

'It's more likely that he went out for a walk to get some air. Maybe he was throwing rocks over the edge. People still do that.'

'I saw him! It was him! I saw what he was doing.' Pasqual's voice interrupted the other Halos dining quietly. Tears spilled over onto his cheeks. Embarrassed, he pushed his bowl away slopping the cereal and milk over the side and spilling onto the floor in front of him. Running from the table, he stumbled up the stairs.

Titus stared up at the priest with large brown eyes. There was no guile in them, only a need to understand.

'I'm going now, too,' he said simply.

Lawrence did not answer, but as Titus left, he cupped his chin in his hand and moved his gaze to the front doors. *How could they prove if Senator Winston Faraday III was involved in a murder?*

Senator Faraday's hands shook. He clenched them but they seemed to have a mind of their own. Even though it was only ten o'clock in the morning, Winston poured himself a finger of scotch and downed it in one gulp. The immediate heat brought some calm, but he couldn't stop thinking about what happened to the gravedigger. It was one thing to suffer the indignity of an accident, but for him to lose his life because of Winston's selfishness...

The child had laid the blame, but thankfully, no one believed him. Everyone *wanted* to believe politicians. Unfortunately, politics had become a teenage popularity contest. Around the world, movie stars, comedians, professional wrestlers, even a sax-playing governor had become leaders with varying degrees of success or failure. For Winston, now after the accident, he would need more than his Hollywood-steely-blue eyes and patrician nose to get him through these dark times. No, he needed his wiles and quick-thinking.

And, he needed Isolde to reveal what she'd learned about the Halo Detectors. The last time they had spoken, she only said that the Halos were the key. As if he needed another reason to distrust some of his colleagues, Isolde implied that there was something special about Cloud End, something about a social manipulation and that the Halos were guinea pigs.

Long had he suspected Dr. Boeder-Mankins and her head-shrinkery. There was nothing she could say or do to make him swallow the Kool-Aid, but the Halo Detector?

Faraday spoke his command to the AutoCom to call Isolde and touched his cheek. He waited only a few moments before her silky voice answered.

'Winnie...'

'Isolde.'

'What can I do for you?'

Frustrated, he smiled through gritted teeth at his AutoCom. 'Haste, dear. Haste.'

'I thought you might say that,' she said. It was apparent, even through the AutoCom, that she was smiling.

'What have you found out?'

'Oh, Winnie, tell me how you're doing, first. How are things at...'

'Isolde!' he shouted, 'I'm not in the mood. I need to know, right now, what Forsythe said about Cloud End. What is it about the Halo Detectors?'

Then, without preamble, she spoke. 'They have nothing to do with the Halovirus. They are engineered to pick up the signals from phones, or AutoComs, in your case.'

Faraday felt the blood drain from his face. 'Pick up the signals? Why?'

'Because it's through your Halo Dectector that the Government can send subliminal messages. They can manipulate everything that comes to you while you're sleeping, or even awake, I think, so you begin to believe certain things. Whether it's ultimate trust in the Government or swaying voting for a particular party, I'm not sure. They're trying to understand if they can get people to believe anything. The Government knows that no one goes anywhere without their devices, so that when the AutoCom or phone is inside a room, the Halo Detector will begin to transmit.'

'Good God.'

'According to Forsythe, Halo Detectors only turn green when there is no device in the room.'

'But I've got an AutoCom! It's embedded in my arm.'

'I'm sorry, Winnie, but it looks like you'll be stuck there forever, then. You'll always test positive.'

Furiously, Faraday tried to think his way out. Even if he couldn't get his Halo Detector to turn green, perhaps he could show the others. If he could...

'Winston? Are you still there?'

'Yes, I'm just thinking.'

'There's one more thing.'

'What is it?'

'They don't want you to leave. You're too dangerous. A loose cannon. They actually hope...'

'Hope what?'

Isolde cleared her throat. 'That you get sick and die from the Halo while there.'

Faraday was infused with righteous indignation. 'That's monstrous.'

'I'm sorry to be the bearer of bad news.'

'Thank you, Isolde. I'm going to fix this.'

'How?'

Strangely, as she asked the question, Winston had a sneaking suspicion Isolde was playing both sides. He sensed her duplicity. 'I'll let you know after it's happened.'

'Oh, Winnie. Please?'

By the time she finished pleading, Senator Faraday had already hung up. There was a knock at the door. And it was not a person he wanted to see.

Igor Kovschenko, dressed in full protective gear, bounced nervously from foot to foot. He seemed contrite, apologetic, to be standing in a senator's doorway.

'Senator Faraday, I'm so sorry to do this, but is there a chance we could have a cup of coffee and discuss a few things?'

'I'm sorry, that's entirely inappropriate, especially without legal counsel.'

Sheepishly, Kovschenko glanced to both sides and refocused on Winston. 'It will only take a minute. I just want to clear a few things up before I move on to someone else. There are obviously other people here who could have done this deed – perhaps the druggie? She's already lost her cool once.'

Faraday nodded. 'Yes, yes, that's probably who did it. You can't trust addicts.'

Igor breathed a sigh of relief. 'If you would be so kind, we could have that cup of coffee and then I'll be out of your hair.'

Faraday knew that in no way should he be doing this, but to not do it would invite even more suspicion. 'Let me grab my jacket. I'll meet you downstairs in five minutes.'

Igor nodded and Faraday shut the door behind him.

Before heading downstairs, Faraday glanced around his room. Everything seemed to be in order. He'd hidden the clothes from last night in the hamper to be washed later that afternoon. Taking a deep breath, he glanced up at the Halo Detector and frowned. Later in the day he would approach one of the lesser-well-offs who may have only had an old iPhone 19. He would test Isolde's hypothesis.

24

While Faraday and Igor waited for someone to wait on them, Father Lawrence knocked on Radiance Morrison's door.

When it opened, it was obvious that she'd been crying. The streaked mascara under her eyes and blotchy cheeks stood in stark contrast to her pale skin.

'What do you want?'

'Can we talk?'

'About what?'

'I have a favor to ask of you. A professional favor.'

Immediately suspicious, she closed the door slightly. 'I don't know what you mean.'

Lawrence looked over his shoulder. The town police officer in his protective gear and Faraday were standing at the bar.

'Do you still have keys?'

'Keys to what?'

Lawrence lowered his voice. 'To guests' rooms.'

Suspiciously, Radiance tilted her head. 'Why?'

'The police are investigating an accusation that...' he motioned with his head towards Faraday, '...could have been involved in the, uh, murder.' He winced when he said the word.

'Are you serious?' Her eyes widened. Stepping back, she finally allowed the priest to enter. 'Who accused him?'

'Pasqual.'

'Who is that?'

'One of the boys who almost went over the edge.'

She touched her chest. 'I can't even imagine what those boys are going through. Are you sure? What did he say?'

'He said he was watching out the window and he's sure he saw Senator Faraday retreating from the fence.'

'And you think that it's Faraday? That's dangerous.'

He cleared his throat. 'Which is why I'm coming to you with such secrecy.'

'And you want me to let you into his room? What are you looking for?'

'Something. Anything. Nothing. Whatever will bring the truth to light. I can't imagine that a senator would have anything to do with this, but if you could have seen the boy's eyes, he was so sure.'

She nodded. 'Trauma can do that. It can change our memories, right?'

'Yes, maybe, but... if it's true, if Senator Faraday did this, everything about this place, the Government's role – everything – changes.'

'But if it's not...?'

'No one will know the difference, Radiance.' Lawrence's eyes held hers.

Radiance wrestled with what to do.

'Radiance,' Lawrence said kindly, but impatiently, 'time is of the essence.'

She turned quickly, grabbed her keys and followed the priest under the balcony to the central stairs. 'You go up first,' Lawrence said, 'and I'll follow you in a minute.'

Radiance ascended the stairs quickly. In the balcony above, the two teenage girls sat on cushy chairs in the hallway staring morosely at their phones pleading with them to reconnect to Wi-Fi. One of the boys fidgeted on another chair in another hallway window as he pondered the freedom of the outdoors. He looked sad, defeated.

Walking quickly, Radiance found Senator Faraday's room and inserted the key. Thankfully, because Cloud End was an old residence, the keys were still made of metal, and the master key which fit them all had been left with her. With one last check to see if anyone was watching, she opened the door slightly, then walked back to the stairs where Lawrence met her.

'What are you doing? Didn't the key work?'

'Yes,' she whispered, 'but I don't need to wait at the door for you. I've left it ajar.'

'How will I know if he's coming?'

She shrugged.

'Can I give you my phone number and then you text me if he starts up the stairs.'

'I think I've done enough already.'

'Yes, you've done enough.'

Radiance was bothered by his troubled face. He was trying to do the right thing, trying to bring about justice, the kind of which was so rare in this world. She sighed. 'Okay, okay. I'll do it. Give me your phone number.'

He did, thanked her, and moved quickly across the balcony towards Faraday's room, staying out of line of sight.

Lawrence turned briefly at the door. Radiance was moving slowly down the stairs. The girls were still on their phones paying no attention to him, but Titus saw him and waved. Lawrence smiled uncomfortably and entered Faraday's room.

'**Where were you** two nights ago, the night before the... accident?' Through plastic facemask, Constable Kovschenko scanned the senator's eyes.

'I was downstairs, then I came up to my room.'

'If we check the security cameras, would they tell the same story?'

A dark cloud passed over Faraday's face. 'Of course.' Faraday knew that there were no security cameras in the rooms, and to check the ones downstairs... *The camera by the front door.* 'I hesitate to tell you this because all sorts of things are implied by it, but I'm happy for full disclosure. I left for a breath a fresh air, I'm not sure what time.'

Kovschenko's eyes raised slightly.

'If you give me that judgemental look one more time, I'm calling my lawyer and we'll wait while I finish 'convalescing' here.' The constable's jaw hardened. 'I'm trying to do the right thing, yes?'

Igor nodded but said nothing.

'I felt ill after supper. It could have been the stunt that Cloud End pulled. Everyone was in shambles.'

'Tell me about that.'

'Someone has been finding skeletons in our closets. We took turns watching the worst of our lives played out before us. The things the prostitute and druggie did... And that police officer! Even the 'nice, little family' isn't quite so nice.'

'You mean someone recorded you without your knowledge?'

Faraday was frustrated, angry and worried. 'What century were you born in? Everything is recorded. It's inescapable. You walk down the street, somebody is watching and waiting for you to screw up. You ride in the elevator. Watching. Supermarket. Recorded. About the only place that isn't recorded is in the Government's Capitol headquarters.'

'And why is that?'

'Because the information spoken there is too sensitive for common citizens.'

Faraday's smugness caught Igor off guard. 'Nothing in the Capitol is recorded?' Igor asked.

The senator snorted. 'Not like here.'

'It must be rough being at Cloud End,' Igor said sarcastically. 'What dirt did they show on you?'

'None of your business, constable,' Faraday responded brusquely. 'It would make no impact on the investigation, or whatever you're calling this.'

'I'll be the judge of that.'

Leaning forward, Faraday pointed a finger in his face. The senator's eyes were alight with fury. 'You have no idea what you're doing or who you're messing with. This whole thing – this distraction, and the words of a boy to discredit me, an influential lawmaker - is a sham. Because I'm a high-profile person-of-interest, they've sent you from a village somehow 'confident' that someone with your talents, you who probably deals with, what, three traffic violations per day and a domestic in the evening? Would be able to investigate someone like me? I'll have your badge for breakfast and toss *that* over the cliff.'

Amazingly, Igor Kovschenko held his tongue. Though he was a small-town police officer, he was not stupid. And certainly, he'd been around enough lawbreakers to know that those who vehemently and angrily deny accusations were usually guilty of something. Faraday's outburst was concerning. 'Threatening me solves nothing, Senator.'

'Likewise, Constable.' With that, Faraday pushed his chair back from the table and made his way towards the central stairs where Radiance Morrison was texting someone furiously on her phone.

As quickly as possible, Lawrence searched the senator's room. Everything seemed to be in place. The remote control was positioned on the small table beneath the antique plasma television secured to the wall. The small desk in the back right corner of the room held a laptop computer, a notepad and an old watch. Faraday turned it over in his hand. *To my son. Time brings wisdom.*

It was a beautiful, old wristwatch. Timex, nothing extremely valuable, but priceless to the senator who displaced his father.

Lawrence repositioned the watch in the same spot and looked at the pad of paper. A cheap plastic pen with partially chewed cap sat next to it. The top page had been ripped off, but the imprint could be seen on the next pages. He wrote hard, it appeared. Maybe he was nervous?

Looking in the wastebasket, Lawrence hoped to find a note with a phone number or name on it, but there was none. Lawrence did not even attempt to mess with the computer. Senator Faraday wouldn't dare to store anything on it. The digital world was one big room with an infinite number of doors and countless master keys.

Lawrence checked his phone. He needed to hurry.

Dropping to his knees, the priest searched under the bed. A discarded sock was lodged beneath the sheet. Circling the bed, he checked under it until he reached the side closest to the closet. He saw himself reflected in the mirror. A red-faced old man on his hands and knees, greasy hair falling over his glasses, recklessly searching for evidence that would be highly circumstantial and illegally attained. After checking under the bed, he turned and saw something that made his heart race. Certainly, if he would not have been on his knees, he would have missed it. But there were particles of something, and a small trail leading to the closet.

Sawdust.

Quickly, Lawrence opened the closet. An army of suits were hung carefully above an arsenal of shoes. There must have been ten suits, blues and blacks, one full white suit with vest. Ties of muted colors were stashed on a tie tree. Obviously, he'd come prepared for a lengthy stay. Deeper into the closet, the darkness covered the thing which he sought.

The clothes hamper.

Moving farther into the closet, he reached into the hamper and carefully pulled out what felt different than the fine fabric of Faraday's suits. It was a black, designer jogging suit. Grabbing it, he delicately pulled it into the light.

More sawdust.

Lots of it.

Oh, Lord, Lawrence thought. *Could he actually be guilty?*

Suddenly, the priest's phone chimed. It was Radiance.

He's coming.

Before reaching his room, Faraday knocked on Jacquelyn Archer's door. When she opened it, Faraday invited her into the hallway.

'I need to talk to you.'

She studied his handsome eyes. 'What would you like to speak about?'

'I've got some information which will get us out of here.'

Her heart jumped. If for no other reason than to escape the trauma of last night's revelations, she was willing to listen.

'Okay.'

They walked along the balcony towards his room.

He's almost there!!!!

Lawrence's heart sank. In his hands he held the circumstantial evidence of a senator's betrayal, but he was about to be caught. And if he was, the evidence would be lost. Frustratedly, Lawrence peered around the room for a place to hide. Only the closet offered scant defense, but if Faraday stuck his head in the closet...

Moving the suits aside, he crammed into the back corner and ducked down behind the clothes hamper.

It would have to do.

Faraday opened his room door and allowed Jacquelyn to enter first.

'Ms. Archer, Jacquelyn, I'm offering this information to you for a small price.'

'That's an interesting way to begin a conversation,' she responded as she motioned for him to move farther into the room. The last thing she wanted was for him to be blocking her path to the door. 'What, exactly, is the price I need to pay for this 'secret' information?'

'A willingness to vouch for my whereabouts two nights ago.'

She frowned. 'That sounds ominous. Where were you two nights ago?'

'I *was* outside getting some air, but I had nothing to do with the gravedigger's accident. No matter what the rumors are, people are always out to get those who have power, am I correct?'

'I'll concede the point, but if you didn't do anything, you have nothing to worry about.''

'You and I both know, Ms. Archer, that innuendo is as much a verdict of guilt as holding a smoking gun.'

'Go on,' she said. 'I want to hear the information before agreeing to the terms.'

'No, I can't do that. Once I tell you, you'll use it and escape without me.'

Jacquelyn was smart enough to know that agreeing to these terms would be dangerous, but certainly, she wanted to leave 'I agree to your terms.'

Faraday tried to stifle his sigh of relief. 'Over the last six months, Halo Detectors have been placed in houses and business across the country. Once the light turns red, whoever is closest to it is deemed untouchable – sick.'

'There's nothing new in that information,' she said.

He pointed to the Halo Detector. 'But these are different. They aren't detecting the Halovirus. They turn red when a phone, or digital device, is within the proximity of the room.'

'That's ridiculous. Why would they need to track if anyone has a phone?'

Faraday leaned in closer and pointed to his head. 'Think. They've convinced the world that these 'Halo Detectors' are keeping us safe, but here, at Cloud End, they're actually keeping us imprisoned to see how we hold up under constant psychological manipulation. When a device is in the room, the Detectors emit a subsonic message which only our subconsciouses can pick up.' He shook his head with derision. 'It's clever. No one is ever without their phone or AutoCom. Hell, *we* literally cannot go anywhere without them.' He touched his arm.

'But why would they do that?'

'They want control. More than anything else, they want control.'

Jacquelyn's face blanched. It all made sense, up to a point. 'Who is they?'

'The Government. I'm pretty sure Dr. Boeder-Mankins is in on it. It's obvious that during our sessions, we were fed some pretty steady Government propaganda.'

'I noticed that, too. Nobody is that stupid, are they?'

'Are you kidding? If you put something on a screen, people believe it.'

'I thought we'd evolved past that.'

Faraday shook his head. 'We have *devolved.* The only sense we use anymore is our sight. We disbelieve our ears, taste, touch...'

'So what do we have to do, then? How can we get out of here?'

'Disable your AutoCom. Rip it out of your arm if you have to.'

'Why haven't you done it, then?'

He swallowed. 'I need to contact people on the outside, power brokers who have helped me with the information.'

'They've corroborated this? If we just shut down our phones, we can leave?'

'And the truth will set you free.' Faraday held his breath.

Jacquelyn looked down at her AutoCom. Since its invention, she had been one of the first to have the device embedded in her arm and ear. It had made communication easier and more accessible, but it had also brought on a pervasive tiredness, always aware that a message *could* be coming, or information *needed* to be received. Many times, she wished that she didn't need it, but her business was run from her arm and ear. To get rid of it would be paralyzing. And yet, how nice would it be...

'Okay,' she said.

'Okay, what?'

'If this turns out to be true, I'll stand up for your whereabouts.'

Faraday released his breath. 'Thank you.'

Inside the closet, Father Lawrence Haskins could not have been more surprised.

25

By the time Igor Kovschenko returned to his office in Herzfeld, stripped from his protective gear and sat down at his desk, he was overwhelmed. In one day, he'd witnessed the demise of a significant member of Herzfeld, a tragic, presumed-murder of a Halo at Cloud End and interviewed a person of interest who happened to be a prominent member of the Government. In his wildest dreams, Igor had never dreamed of having a 24-hour period like this one. And yet, here he was, his mind working overtime on all three simultaneously.

While yawning, he opened his email. Most were follow-ups from various agencies, a few bills, numerous complaints and finally, buried a page down, was a message from the Coast Guard.

After scanning it, his eyes widened. He was well aware of the implications. The helicopter crash was not an accident. According to the retrieved black box from the helicopter, the last video was of multiple bullets cracking the windshield.

What the... Igor played the video multiple times and felt the sinking sensation in his stomach with each. *Another murder.*

In his seventeen years as constable of Herzfeld, Robert Kovschenko had never, not once, investigated a murder. There were accidents and many instances of bodily harm. People were angrier than they used to be. And unfortunately, were more distrustful of police. But everyone had stopped short of ending life.

Until Cloud End had opened as a Convo.

Igor peered up and over his computer at the corkboard. Did the helicopter crash and the man dropping over the cliff have anything to do with each other? And then another thought entered his mind.

What about Gemma's death?

Drinking that early in the morning?

What seemed to connect them all?

Steve Cranmere.

Swigging his cold coffee he cringed at the bitter, sawdusty texture. He swiveled in his chair and began to piece together a 'what ifs' on his corkboard. As he continued to draw the lines, the sinking feeling in his stomach morphed into a trepidatious descent into a terrible reality.

Dammit.

The call was both unexpected and unwelcome. For Steve, the reality of everything which had transpired had snowballed into an avalanche of deceit. So many lies. If only the Halovirus hadn't shown up. If only the Government hadn't restricted people to the extent it had. If only Edgar had said, 'Steve, put the gun away.' If only Gemma had not gone to the Capitol.

At that moment, Steve believed that it was everyone else's fault. He was just a pawn on the chessboard of powerful people. If anyone should be pitied, it was him. If Gemma had been a little more lenient, compassionate, the medical personnel would still be alive. As much as he hated to do that thing to Gemma, she had brought it upon herself, really.

'Hello?'

'Mr. Cranmere.'

'The only time people call me that is when I owe them something or I'm in trouble.'

There was a brief silence at the other end of the line. Then, the woman's voice came through. 'This would be both,' she said.

'Who is this?'

'Someone who knows what you've done.'

Adrenaline coursed through his veins. 'I'm about to hang up.'

'If you do that, we'll go to the police, Mr. Cranmere. We know you shot the helicopter down. We know you intentionally infected people with the virus. We know about your wife.'

Steve had difficulty swallowing. 'You don't know anything,' he said unconvincingly.

The woman ignored him. 'If you do as we say, Mr. Cranmere, we'll make it all go away.'

'Who are you?'

'People with power.'

'Let's say your information is correct, and I'm not saying that, but what are you asking me to do?'

'We will send someone to bring you to us. In person. No recording. No phone. No cameras. Is this agreeable?'

'How can you guarantee that? Everything is recorded?'

'Not everywhere,' the voice said mysteriously.

It took three hours for Winston Faraday III to leave his room again. In that time, while in the stifling, airless space of the closet, Father Lawrence Haskins crouched in the cramped space, his back and legs spasming, waiting for the politician to leave his room. At various points, Lawrence could hear him scribbling or typing. Then, almost an hour into his stay, Winston made a phone call.

'Isolde.'

———

'I'm going to get out of here.'

———

'I'm going to turn off my AutoCom.'

———

'Yes, yes I can.'

———

'I'm *not* sick. As soon as I turn it off, the light will go green, and when it does, I'm out of here.'

———

'Because I needed to line up a few ducks before I left. Diverting attention elsewhere while darting out the back door...'

———

'I need you to set up a meeting with Forsythe. There's going to be some serious retribution.'

——

'How can you say that? I won't reveal you as a source, obviously, but what he did to me...'

——

Faraday was silent, thinking. 'Maybe you're right. I could use this information against him later.'

——

'As soon as I hang up with you.'

——

'You won't. I'll contact you. As soon as I get back to the Capitol, we'll reconnect.'

——

'Me too.'

The conversation went silent.

Lawrence had to get out. He had a lot of things to share. But he had to get the others out first. With his ears still pricked, Lawrence waited with bated breath. There was a deep sigh, some beeping noises, and then silence. After a few moments, there was growling.

'Dammit!' Winston shouted. 'She told me! She told me that the Detector would turn green when my AutoCom was off! It reads mobile signals.' Slamming his hand against the desk, he raged.

While he did, Lawrence Haskins prayed to God that the senator would not rethink his assessment that the only mobile device in the room was *his* AutoCom.

Radiance assumed the worst.

After Senator Faraday and Ms. Archer entered the room, Radiance felt nauseous. Coughing into her hand, she retreated downstairs and went back to her room to await the inevitable discovery. She hoped the priest would not reveal her, but in positions of stress, one never knew what would happen.

When no alarm had been raised, Radiance felt her tension ebb. Opening her door, she scanned the courtyard. Ms. Archer was among those eating lunch. Perhaps not so strangely, the residents were scattered across the atrium eating separately. Even though there had been a genuinely peaceful resolution and a promise of forgiveness, there was no such thing as forget-ness. No matter how much Radiance knew the extenuating circumstances regarding their public sins, she couldn't erase Chantelle's evening escapades or Monica's... it didn't matter. They were islands on a cliff.

After ninety minutes, Radiance peered from under the balcony towards Faraday's room. He still had not left. Radiance began to fret that something had happened to the priest. Maybe Faraday had disposed of him, too?

To bide her time, Radiance ordered some chicken wings and brought them to the table where Sydney sat. Surprised, Sydney looked up to see Radiance.

'What do you want?'

'Company.'

'Go find someone else. I'm in a bad mood.'

Radiance flinched. She wanted to go sit with someone else, but Sydney's table had the best view of Faraday's room.

'I'll sit quietly, I promise.'

Sydney shook her head, but didn't say anything, so Radiance sat. Eventually, the quiet became too much.

'What will you do when you go home?' Radiance asked.

Sydney frowned.

'I mean, when you get out of here, do you have family? Do you have a nice house, or pets, or...' her voice faltered.

'My parents live up the street from us.'

'Oh, that must be nice.'

'Sometimes.'

'Which times?'

Sydney pushed her food around on her plate with her fork. 'Why do you want to know?'

'I just need to hear other people's voices.'

Sighing, Sydney's head dropped, and when she brought it back up, a tear had formed in the corner of her eye. 'You don't have to be nice to me.'

Surprised, Radiance leaned back in her chair.

'I know what kind of person I am. I'm exhausting. I'm spoiled. I get it, but you don't have to feel sorry for me.'

'My dad used to tell me I was spoiled, too,' Radiance admitted.

'Was it true?'

She shrugged. 'I got my way, but I didn't always get things. My parents didn't have much money, but they were good at loving me.'

'Sounds wonderful,' Sydney responded. 'Mine were just the opposite. I always got everything, but not always love.'

'You're right. That sounds hideous,' said Radiance.

For a moment, Sydney didn't know what to say, then she began to laugh. At first, it was a tearful snicker, as if the silence would stifle it and let sorrow continue to hold power over the room. But then, somehow, one hiccup, turned into a guffaw, to a roar. She couldn't stop. The *hideousness* of the past, her parents' protectiveness which, in many other families would have been considered a blessing, was now funny.

Though confused, Radiance chuckled with her.

'My parents were rich. My dad was a consultant for political action groups who protested climate change. He made a lot of money and a lot of enemies. My mother was a lawyer for the same company. Together, they could afford anything but time. And so they bought me anything, anything at all. Anything that would keep me amused. I had the newest phone and digital equipment. I begged my mother for the earliest AutoCom which she gladly gave to me. I was only twenty, but it seemed like everyone who was anyone got one.' She looked ruefully at her wrist. 'But I can see the pressure it's put on me and Damian.'

'And then, when Damian got a little handsy with women at his own work, I blamed him, as I should have, but I told my parents about it, and they shamed him. How could their baby girl be treated so unjustly? They pressured him, made life difficult for him.'

Sydney glanced up to his room. 'He's a good man, really. He's more than I deserve.'

'And you still live near your parents?' Radiance still kept an eye on the rooms above.

'They engineered it to keep an eye on me. Theoretically, though, they never took their eyes off.' Once again, she tapped her built in device. 'I can never escape them.'

'I thought about getting one,' Radiance said, 'but I couldn't afford it.'

'Don't!' Sydney's face looked shocked. 'Don't do it!'

'Okay,' Radiance responded unsteadily.

Above them, Radiance saw Faraday's door open. Heart leaping to her throat, she waited. It was only Faraday. He looked flustered.

'Uh, I have to go.'

Puzzled, Sydney stared at her. 'Did I say something wrong? I said something wrong, didn't I?'

'No, no. I have to make a call.' She touched her pocket where her phone lay nestled like a sleeping bird.

Sydney's face fell. 'Okay. Maybe we talk some other time.' She paused and then smiled. 'Thanks for making me laugh.'

'Likewise.'

Radiance watched Senator Faraday descend the stairs. His suit seemed immaculately pressed and he was rubbing his wrist. She could tell he was muttering something under his breath while studying his AutoCom.

He passed her at the bottom of the stairs. Angrily, he brushed past her, then stopped and turned on her. 'Have you seen Jacquelyn?'

'No.'

With a curse, he turned back from her to stomp into the courtyard.

Radiance texted Lawrence.

Where are you?

Moments later, the reply came.

I'm hiding in his closet.

Radiance typed:

He's gone. I'm watching the room. Come out now.

Shortly, Faraday's door opened and the priest exited. When he turned to Radiance and peered over the balcony railing, his face was white. Pointing to the front door, he mouthed the words, *I'll meet you outside.*

She nodded.

Not long after, she was outside waiting on the porch. *What did he find out?*

Constable Kovschenko ran his hand through his hair.

Although he was not greying yet (*after this, he wouldn't be surprised,* he thought), his hair felt middle-aged, thick around the middle and a little weak at the extremities. If the revelations of what he was thinking were true, the ramifications would set Herzfeld on fire. But who could he talk to? Who had the information? Gemma was dead and he didn't want to alert Steve. The Coast Guard would only have scant details on what had happened. He would have loved to talk to Bridgette or Renata, but they were both holed up at Cloud End.

Igor thought of Magnus Falkirk. He had traveled with Gemma to the Capitol.

After putting his hat on, Igor left the station and turned left. As he walked quickly to the church, masked citizens avoided him. Although the restrictions had eased, the health directives stated that wearing a mask would still lower the odds of contracting the Halovirus. Igor smiled wryly that before the pandemic, people were required to take their masks off before entering all premises for the sake of identification, but now? Well, better to get robbed than get the Halo.

When he reached the church doors, Igor found a sign which read, WORKING FROM HOME ON SUNDAY SERMON. IF AN EMERGENCY, PLEASE CALL THE RELEVANT AUTHORITIES. I WILL BE BACK IN TOMORROW FROM 9:00-11:00 AM.

Igor crossed the street to where the parsonage sat, squat and brooding. Although the house seemed dark, it had recently been painted and new furniture was situated on the porch. Igor rubbed his hands together to work the blood back into them. It was getting colder.

After climbing the steps, Igor knocked on the front door. Moments later, an irritable reverend unbolted three locks and opened the door.

'Yes, Robert?'

'Can I ask you a few questions?'

Magnus glanced behind him to the darkened interior of the house. 'I'm quite busy.'

Igor noticed the sleep marks on the side of his face. *Busy napping.* 'It will only take a few minutes. It's about Gemma.'

Magnus' eyes narrowed. 'Ah, yes. Tragedy. So young.'

'Please, Reverend,' Igor motioned for the front porch. Magnus grabbed his mask. It was almost second nature to wear it now, even outdoors. He situated it snugly over his mouth and nose and settled into a deck chair.

'What do you want to know?'

'Tell me about your trip with Gemma to the Capitol.'

Magnus tried to read the officer. 'What does that have to do with her death?'

'I'm just trying to get a picture of what Gemma's last mood was before her death.'

'Because of the alcohol?'

Igor said nothing. The silence was implication enough.

'They were condescending. We had petitioned to have the Convalescent Center moved from Cloud End to Pendulum Island, but they seemed less than excited about that option.'

'What did they say?'

302

'Financially speaking, it would have been difficult. Although we put forth our best case, they denied it.'

'So she was upset?'

Magnus stared out over the street. 'I suppose. She was trying to protect her community the best way she could. She and Steve were determined to do whatever it took to keep the Halovirus out of town. But it was always going to get here.'

'How were they going to go about keeping it out?'

'You know as well as I do, Robert. Restrictions upon restrictions. Close the town's borders. Keep out all undesirables, all foreigners. Only allow goods in. Accept Government money to keep us afloat and keep people safe. It was a shame about the helicopter crash, but in the end, it probably saved an outbreak here in Herzfeld.'

Igor's frown deepened. 'Did the Government say anything about the helicopter crash?'

Magnus's eyes narrowed. 'What are you implying?'

'Nothing, really. I'm just trying to line up the events from the stabbing at Cloud End, the Heli crash, the Herzfeld outbreak...'

'It was only two people,' Magnus interjected.

'It only takes two people to be a superspreader event. We were just lucky.'

'Would Renata and Bridgette feel like they were lucky?'

'No, I suppose not.'

'Then I suppose you'd better change your rhetoric.' Hypocritically, these were the same words Magnus had used in his congregational message just weeks before. *No matter what we do, we have to keep the vulnerable safe. Ultimately, we'll work with the mental health aftermath, but we can't control death. Let's stay separate so we don't spread it.*

'Point taken. Now, with Gemma's death, do you seen any reason why she would be drinking that early in the morning?'

It took a moment for Magnus to respond. 'I think things weren't great at home.'

'Between Steve and Gemma?'

'I'm not sure who else it would be.'

Igor stifled his irritation. 'What do you think they were fighting about?'

'I am not at liberty to share that information, but I think it's safe to say that it's been a stressful time during the pandemic. I'm sorry. I don't feel comfortable walking on the grave of a highly respected citizen.'

'I'm not asking you to walk on her grave, Reverend Falkirk. I just need to get to the bottom...'

'I knew it,' Falkirk hissed as he stood up suddenly. 'You're working for them, aren't you? Trying to insinuate things, evil things, about Gemma and Steve. No, they weren't perfect people, and the way Steve...' He stopped his voice short and waggled a finger at Igor. 'But you should be ashamed of yourself. Who have you been talking to?'

'Who should I be talking to?'

'If you want to know about the night of the crash, talk to Tom and Albert. They were the ones who weren't able to get to Cloud End.'

'The paramedics?'

'What kind of police officer are you? If I, a lowly cleric, know more about what happened at an accident, that says something about your abilities, doesn't it?'

It took Igor Kovschenko's entire focus not to mention the sleep lines on the reverend's face as a dereliction of duty, but he contained himself.

'Thank you, Reverend Falkirk. I'm sorry to have upset you.'

Falkirk was gone before Igor could finish the sentence.

While Constable Kovschenko left Reverend Falkirk's home and strolled to the hospital to interview the two paramedics about the night of the helicopter crash, Father Lawrence met Radiance Morrison outside Cloud End.

'You're not going to believe this,' he gasped, as they stood on the front of the porch taking in the cold air coming up over the cliff.

'He did it?'

'I don't know, but I found some sawdust on the floor and on his clothes in the hamper.'

'Oh, my,' Radiance responded as she placed a hand over her mouth.

'Do you think you could sneak into the laundry, grab his sweat suit and socks, and put them in a plastic bag?'

'Evidence?'

He nodded. 'If the sawdust matches the post...'

'I'll see what I can do. I'm sure Nancy wouldn't mind me helping a little bit.'

'Especially now that you're healthy.'

Radiance's eyebrows creased. 'What? I'm not. My Halo Detector...'

'It doesn't detect the Halovirus. It's worse.'

'What you're talking about.'

'The Detectors respond to digital stimuli. They're designed to pick up the presence of mobile phones or, in many cases, AutoComs.'

'But why?'

He told her. 'It started with Dr. Boeder-Mankins, but subliminal messages are sent out during the night through the Halo Detectors.'

'Who is doing this? Who else could it have been?' She asked.

'Certainly not the St. Croix's. Did you see Claire's face? She was appalled.'

'So, the Halo Detectors...?'

'Turn red when a phone or AutoCom is in the room. The Government created a restriction that if your Halo Detector is red, you have the virus, thus keeping whomever they want in protracted confinement.'

Radiance paced the porch agitatedly. 'I can't believe it. Then how do we defeat it? Just break the box?'

'No, we have to be without our phones.'

'Like leave them outside the room?'

'I don't know. I hope that's all it takes.'

Radiance moved her eyes towards her room. 'Should we check it out?'

He nodded.

They re-entered Cloud End and walked to Radiance's room. A few eyes followed their journey. Oswald and Pasqual both cradled their rats in their arms as they sat by the railing. When they reached her room, Radiance handed over her phone and entered. Staring up at the Halo Detector, she shook her head. 'Still red.'

'Maybe we have to destroy it,' he said from outside her room.

Turning to her left, she looked into his eyes. The pandemics had taken it out of him, out of them all. She wondered what he looked like in the late teens, before the Coronavirus, before the world went crazy, before everyone started hating each other. Radiance had not even been a teenager at that time. Getting her first phone at six years of age, her first iPad even before that, all those wonderful cartoons and games and learning by screen. But it wasn't until after the Coronavirus pandemic she truly wondered if she missed out on something fundamental.

And then the in between time, from 2025-2030 when the world tried to restart, and everyone talked about getting back to normal, and people started arguing about working from home and the anxiety that came from being pressured to go back to the same space as people. When she got her first job at the hotel, she felt lucky because the hordes were swarming back to vacation spots. People were starting to smile again, until inflation and plane companies and oil companies and tech companies all wanted their slice of the common-person's pie. And then the Halo hit, and everything reverted back to the way it was.

She could sense these things in his eyes even when he asked her to destroy her phone. It was like cutting off her nose or asking her to stop tasting or listening. To be without her phone was unthinkable, and yet with it might be her freedom.

'I... can't,' she finally said. 'I have people I need to contact on the outside. How can I be part of the world if I'm not connected to it?'

'Would it help, Radiance, if I destroyed mine, first?'

'Yes.'

He held out her phone to her which she accepted with something like relief, like an infant who takes her pacifier back.

'What are you doing?' Pasqual asked as the duo stood at the railing.

'Testing something,' Lawrence responded.

'What?'

'Would you like to help?'

The boys were excited to do something other than think about what happened to Alonzo. 'Sure!'

Once outside room 2, right next door to the Drapers, Lawrence handed his phone to Pasqual. 'Now, I'm going into the room. I have a suspicion that my phone is linked to Halo Detectors.'

'That's silly,' Oswald said. 'My grandparents said the Government told them that Halo Detectors detect the Halovirus.'

Lawrence grinned. 'Just hold onto it for a little bit.'

Pasqual accepted the antiquated phone and laughed at it. Only old people had iPhone 16's. In seconds, Pasqual had activated it without Lawrence's permission, but the priest only rolled his eyes as the boys took a few selfies on the phone.

'Now,' Lawrence said as he stared at the Halo Detector above him, 'the light is red.'

'See,' Oswald said, 'you've got the virus.'

'Pasqual, I want you to smash my phone.'

The boy's eyes widened. 'Are you serious?'

'Yes. Throw it over the edge of the railing as hard as you can. Smash it on the floor below. And if it doesn't break, go get it and do it again.'

Pasqual stared at the object in his hand. It seemed like such an inconsequential thing, a shiny rectangle which projected light and sound. Yet even with permission to destroy it, Pasqual struggled to bring himself to do it. The phone had done nothing wrong, and there was no guarantee that the Halo Detector would turn green. The priest might go crazy and then tell his parents and blame him. No, Pasqual would definitely not destroy the phone. He handed it to Oswald.

'You do it.'

Oswald refused. 'No way. He asked you to do it.'

'I don't want to get into trouble.'

Pained by the boys' inability to destroy even *his* phone, Lawrence wondered how much they would struggle to break their *own* phones. *If he was right.* It was the only way to freedom. Lawrence approached the boys and held out his hand. 'Give it to me.'

Pasqual did.

With a sudden violence that made the boys and Radiance jump back in shock, Lawrence screamed and hurled the phone as far as he could over the top of the atrium. Amazingly, the phone, flipping end over end, smashed into the water feature, shattering to pieces. As the bits lay strewn about the floor, Lawrence smiled and began to tap dance on the second floor. After Pasqual raced down the stairs and retrieved the pieces from the fountain, he handed them back to Lawrence.

'Drop them on the ground.'

Pasqual did.

Lawrence continued his jig on the remnants of his phone. It snagged on the carpet. The glass, smashed and shattered, appeared like a web – a web of deceit, the greatest of lies. As he danced, Lawrence felt an immense weight lift from his soul. Until that moment, he wasn't aware of the pressure his phone had placed on him. Always at the call of someone else. Always watched. Perpetually jailed by the device.

'Ooh, that felt good,' he said.

'You're crazy,' Oswald laughed.

'Crazy, but free. Go check my Halo Detector,' Lawrence said to the boys.

As they raced into the room, they looked up at the jailor's key, that small black box that kept everyone cornered in fear, and shouted one word.

'GREEN!'

Igor found the paramedics in the hospital cafeteria. Both seemed on edge, especially when they saw the constable nearing them. Albert, the taller of the two, lolled in his chair, feet extended in front of him under the table while Tom leaned forward, his elbows resting.

'Albert. Tom.'

'Igor,' they both responded at the same time.

'Mind if I join you?'

They shrugged, so he sat.

'How are you doing?'

Tom looked at Albert, as if Albert was the spokesperson of the duo. 'All things considered,' Albert said, 'we're doing okay.'

'What do you mean?'

'We haven't had many traumatic deaths for a while.'

'I'm sorry about Gemma.'

Albert shrugged again. 'If not us, then who?'

'Government paramedics, I guess.' The two shared a look. 'How are you feeling after the helicopter crash?'

Albert's jaw flexed.

'You look angry.'

'There wasn't anything we could do, Igor. We couldn't get in.'

'The Cloud End staff wouldn't let you in?'

Albert shook his head. 'The gate was locked and...' he put his head down.

'And what?'

'There was a truck parked in front of it.' Guiltily he leaned his head back. 'If Steve's truck wouldn't have been there, those two paramedics wouldn't have had to fly to Cloud End. We could have brought the patients here. It feels like those two deaths are our fault.'

Igor's stomach sank. *Steve's truck?* 'It's not your fault, fellas.'

'Yeah, whatever.'

'Can I ask you another question?'

'Shoot.'

'Did Steve say why his truck was there?'

Albert studied Igor's eyes. 'It was broken down. He said he was making sure Halos didn't leave.'

'He parked it there on purpose?'

'No, that's not what he said. He and Edgar had gone up to check on Cloud End in case, and these are his words, 'any rats were escaping the sinking ship.' But when he tried to move it, he couldn't start it. We made him try, but it wouldn't. I even gave it a shot.'

'But he got it started later?'

'Obviously,' Albert responded.

'Did Edgar say anything?'

'No, but he's been edgy lately.'

'Any idea what's bothering him?' Igor asked.

'Probably as upset about Gemma's death as the rest of us.'

Igor nodded. 'Thanks, guys. I'm sorry this has been such a difficult time for you.'

'Like I said. Part of the job.' Albert responded.

Sighing, Igor turned, but he had a sneaking suspicion that Edgar Post knew some painful things.

26

When Igor Kovschenko saw the Capitol transport landing just outside Herzfeld town limits, he wondered what was going on. By nature, the Government stayed out of a place like Herzfeld. It offered nothing but taxes, and those sparse collections barely paid for one Senator much less put pavement on the roads. But to see one of the aircraft land here, that was something else. Whatever was happening, Igor needed to see it with his own eyes.

Jumping into his police car, Igor changed course from Edgar Post's house and diverted his attention to the landing site. He stopped a quarter mile from the descending craft. Pulling out his binoculars, he saw three forms get out of a black sedan and walk to the plane. The two on the outside held the arms of the man in the middle as if he was a criminal. Focusing the glasses, Igor was shocked to see that the man in the middle was Steve Cranmere.

As the two Capitol agents guided him up the stairs and onto the aircraft, Steve felt a sickening sense of doom. Ducking his head to enter, he saw another form, a woman. This surprised him – maybe she was the same one who had spoken to him on the phone. She sat stiffly erect, cross-legged in the back of the plane, her face calm and confident. She was beautiful in a masculine sort of way.

'Welcome, Mr. Cranmere,' she said.

'Who the hell are you?'

'My name is Director Reed-Conway.'

'Your name is Reed?'

'I have a hyphenated last name. It's Reed-Conway. My first name is Stella.'

'I'm a little bit pissed off that you've pulled me from my home, especially after my wife's death...'

311

'You seem really torn up about it,' Stella replied evenly.

'I am. She was a good woman. You met her, I assume.'

'Yes.'

'Then you can tell her loss leaves a big hole in my life.'

Stella did not respond.

'You'd better tell me what's going on here before I call the cops.'

Stella shook her head. 'You won't do that, Steve. We're offering something the cops can't.'

'What?'

'Immunity.'

'From what? The Halovirus? Did you guys cook something up in your lab again? Got tired of viruses and now you want to heal people?' His belligerent tone grated on her nerves.

'No, Mr. Cranmere, immunity from prosecution.'

'I'm not persecuted. Everybody in Herzfeld likes me. Me and Edgar run the pub, we make people happy.'

'Not *persecuted*, Mr. Cranmere. Prosecuted. In case you didn't know, the local authorities are closing in on you for the deaths of the helicopter paramedics, intent to do bodily harm by infecting two citizens of Herzfeld with the Halovirus, and now, for the death of your wife. Goodness knows how many other laws you've broken to keep yourself safe.'

The aircraft began to lift off.

'Please, Mr. Cranmere, sit down and buckle up before you get injured.'

He did, just before the craft surged forward and sucked his stomach up through his throat. As the aircraft headed out over the cliff, Steve looked down over Cloud End and noticed the fluttering yellow police tape.

'Now, as I was saying,' Stella restarted, 'the authorities in Herzfeld are beginning to connect the dots starting with the helicopter crash and linking it with your wife's death. She knew about the crash. We think you knew that also, so you killed her.'

'That's insane, I loved my wife. And... and even if I did something, Igor couldn't put the pieces together if it was an eight-piece puzzle. He's a moron.'

'Be that as it may,' Stella said calmly, 'he was watching us depart from Herzfeld just now.'

Steve thrust his face to the ovate window, but they were too far away to see anything. 'I'm not saying anything to you.' He crossed his arms. 'I need a lawyer.'

She nodded. 'You should, but wait until you hear our proposal.'

'Who are you?'

Stella smiled and looked away from him. The trip was completed in uncomfortable silence.

Titus Draper saw the Government aircraft fly over Cloud End. He had a fascination for flying things and often wondered if he'd fly a Government plane someday. As he watched it go, Titus was drawn by the noise inside the house. There were screams of delight. Hustling through the door, he cast it open and saw with amazement people were smashing their phones in the courtyard. Chantelle had a rock held above her head, and she was screaming at the top of her lungs.

'AAAAAAAAAAHHHHHH!' The rock came down with such force that pieces of the phone were scattered throughout the courtyard. The gathering clapped raucously.

Titus found Gina who was clutching her phone closely to her chest. 'What are they doing?'

'Apparently, if you destroy your phone, you escape the Halovirus.'

'That doesn't make sense.'

Gina scowled at him. 'That's what I said. There's no way I'm going to break mine.'

Titus rolled his eyes and moved towards his parents whose eyes were wide and excited. 'Titus, where have you been?'

'I was watching the P24 fly overhead. It was pretty cool. Did you know they launch vertically, like a rocket and then they...'

'Titus,' his mother interrupted, 'I don't care about the silly planes.'

'They're not planes. Their engines are actually more like...'

'Stop it!' his mother shouted. 'Now is not the time for a lecture on aircraft.' She held out her hand. 'Where is your phone?'

'I don't have one, remember?'

She sighed loudly. 'Of course. Of course. I knew that.'

'Are we breaking them all?'

'Yes.'

'Why?'

She leaned down in front of him. 'Because when they are broken, the Halo Detectors turn green.'

'You mean we don't have the Halovirus, then?'

'That's right.'

'Can I break yours?'

Dorothy nodded. Just before she was about to hand the phone to him, she pondered it knowing how much it cost – almost a month's salary – and three people in the family had them. Three months of earnings down the drain if they went through with it.

'What are you waiting for?' he asked.

'Nothing.' Dorothy handed the phone to her six-year-old son and watched him dance delightedly with it over his head. As he approached the indoor waterfall, he stared over his shoulder just to make sure. He knew how much time she spent on it. 'Go ahead,' she motioned and then proceeded to put her hands over her mouth.

Others stopped their own destruction to watch the smallest Halo position his mother's phone on the edge of the rocks and then pick up another rock. With a quick giggle and smash, he left the phone in pieces. 'What should I do with it now?' he yelled at her.

'Whatever you want!' she shouted back.

Titus grabbed the pieces in his small hands and raced out the front doors. A few others followed him with the remnants of their own phones. Charging ahead, Titus dashed through the grass towards the cliff. His mother shouted at him to be careful. Pasqual and Oswald, with their pet rats, eventually caught up to him. They were laughing outrageously at the outrageous thing which had just happened. Past the fluttering yellow police tape, to the edge of the destroyed fence, Titus stopped. The sun was behind them. Even though it was cool, the kids were sweating and breathing hard. They had not run much in the last few days. Now that they were here, at the land's edge, at the cloud's end, they felt euphoric, as if life was truly going to change for the better.

Finally, Dorothy and Sam reached their sons' sides. When Dorothy turned, she saw the others trailing, some slowly, some quickly. Those that had actual phones, Chantelle and Seraphim, Radiance, Donald St. Croix and his wife, Claire, who had shed her protective gear and was walking slowly, hand in hand, with her beloved husband, each carried the shards of their phones.

And behind them came the staff. Dr. Chandruth, Kylie and Jack, the nurses, Nancy and Esther. The only ones to remain were Carl and Dr. Boeder-Mankins.

Standing side by side, the small community felt the chilled breeze lift over the edge of the cliff. The water below was dark and dreadful. Breakers smashed over the rocks sending spumes of mist high in the air.

'I'm going to throw your phone over, Mom!' Titus shouted above the wind's noise.

She laughed and nodded. 'Go ahead!'

Rearing back, he hurled the phone outwards. The breeze was too stiff for his throw and the pieces flew back towards him.

'Try again!' his mother said as she helped him pick up the pieces.

The others, with great joy, hurled their phones over the cliff's edge. As Seraphim threw, she thought with sadness how much Alonzo would have appreciated this moment right now. They were sacrificing their online social connection for a happier life. From digital back to analog, from screens to smiles.

Titus tried again. This time, the breeze captured the pieces in its windy fist and sucked them down below with the rest. He smiled up at his mother who had placed a hand on his shoulder. After the last phone had been hurled, the Cloud End ensemble circled up. Father Lawrence prayed a prayer of thanksgiving for their deliverance from slavery, or that's how he described it. Even those who had no faith were drawn to the simplicity of the ritual and were thankful for it.

'Now,' Lawrence said, 'how about we head back to Cloud End and start packing.' He spotted Donald who was beaming beside Claire.

'Maybe we'll have one last meal together,' Donald said.

Edgar saw the police cruiser approach and felt in his very soul that the end had come. Ever since Steve had shot down the helicopter, Edgar had been waiting, dreading the moment when Igor, or someone else with flashing lights, was going to arrest him and take him away to jail forever.

As it was, Igor did not turn on his flashing lights, nor did he look particularly serious. Maybe it was just a social visit?

'Afternoon, Edgar.'

'Igor.'

'How are you doing?'

Edgar swallowed hard. Despite the cool breeze streaming downhill from Faucini Cliff, beads of perspiration broke out on his forehead. 'I'm all right.'

'You don't look so good,' Igor said.

'Must have a cold, or something.'

'Hope it's not the Halovirus.'

Edgar's mouth hardened. 'Doubt it.'

'Let's hope it's not.' Igor put his hands on his hips. 'Can we have a little chat?'

'I assumed that's why you're here.'

'What do you think I want to talk about?'

Fidgeting, Edgar crossed his arms. 'No idea.'

'I'm here about the helicopter crash, Edgar.'

His face blanched. His vision seemed to be closing in around him, walls crumbling, his façade eroded. 'What did you hear?' Edgar whispered.

'I know about it.'

Edgar turned another shade of pale. 'You... who... was it... Steve?'

'Yes.'

'Dammit, I told him we shoulda gone to you right away, and now he's gone and blabbed. You gotta believe me, Igor. I had no idea he was going to do it.'

'Do what?'

Edgar shut up. 'Wait a minute. I thought you said Steve told you.'

Igor shook his head. 'No, you said it was Steve. I just agreed.'

'Holy...' Edgar turned in a circle rubbing his head through his baseball cap. 'I tried to stop him, Igor. When he pulled the gun out, I thought he was just gonna fire a few warning shots in the air, but he didn't. He aimed right at the dang thing and he musta hit the pilot and then it crashed into the cliff and blew up down below and then there is pieces everywhere. I swear it, Igor. I swear it. This was all Steve.'

Igor ground his teeth. He knew Edgar was not the type to do something that rash, but Edgar should have been able to talk his friend out of it. That's what humans are supposed to do.

'You know I'm going to have to report this.'

Edgar nodded glumly while Igor continued, 'Like you said, if you would have come to me first, we could have worked something out. If it was an accident, well, we could have treated it like that. But now, after you've hidden everything from me, we've got to have a different plan.'

Edgar started to cry. 'I'll tell you whatever you need, Igor. You just gotta know that Steve is gonna kill me.'

'Steve Cranmere is done killing, Edgar.'

Steve Cranmere sat at the end of a very long table staring at a very reflective window. He could only see himself and the person sitting opposite him, Director Reed-Conway, whose face was masked by darkness and fabric.

'Mr. Cranmere,' Stella said, 'you are in a very secure and safe environment. Inside these walls, nothing can hurt you. Everything we say is confidential and cannot be used against you no matter what. There will be things asked to you and of you which, if revealed in the outer world, would bring about your death.' She noticed his pale face. 'I'm sorry to frighten you like this, but it is the way of our world.'

'You're not frightening me,' he squeaked. 'You're threatening me.'

'Once again, we apologize.'

'Who's we? Who's behind the glass?'

She leaned forward and placed her hands on the table, ignoring his questions. 'Mr. Cranmere. We have evidence of some very serious misdeeds. As we've spoken of before, murder, reckless endangerment, interference with a police investigation, fraud... a litany of sickness... you've committed these, yet we've brought you here to ask you to help us.'

'Help you? You're the Government. You don't need any help.'

She smiled and shook her head. 'Alas, the Government's powers are not limitless, yet.'

'What do you want me to do?'

A voice came over the PA. 'Cloud End needs to be destroyed.'

Steve raised an eyebrow. 'Why do you care so much about Cloud End? It's just one of a bunch of Convos littered all over the world.'

'Let's just say we've been keeping a close eye on it.'

'What are you doing there? Experiments on people? Wouldn't surprise me.' Steve's mind was rapidly spinning.

'No, nothing so dramatic. We've just been watching the people there to see how they react to certain stimuli.'

'I knew it. You're treating them like test rats.' He looked up into the reflective glass. 'Are they dying?'

'Not yet,' the voice said coldly.

'But they're about to,' Steve concluded.

'Before we get to what happens with Cloud End, we want you to know the clientele at the Convo.'

318

'Don't need to tell me,' Steve butted in, 'scum of the earth. Diseased. Need to be put somewhere else.'

'Thank you for your opinion,' another voice spoke, 'but included in these 'scum,' as you put it, are a senator, an influential businesswoman and a very popular divorce lawyer.'

Steve almost spit. 'Well, I got the 'scum' part right with the lawyer, didn't I?'

'Also involved are five children, various workers, two who are faithful to the Government's cause, and other adults who had the misfortune of being diagnosed with a virus.'

'So what?'

'You're going to burn Cloud End to the ground.'

The statement shocked Steve to the core. It was one thing to move a bunch of lowlifes onto an island somewhere, but it was a total other thing to light them up. Accidentally shooting down a helicopter and orchestrating a slip for his wife were necessary, but these people were just unfortunate.

'I don't understand,' he said.

'The senator has information regarding our work here that would be detrimental to us.'

'What, like, you mean he could put you all in jail?'

'Mr. Cranmere, we will need an answer.'

Steve's mind raced. To do this thing would be an atrocity. Convos were supposed to be places where people got better. 'I... geez...' he scratched the beginnings of his beard. 'And what did you say I get out of this?'

'Total immunity for all crimes previously committed.' *But not the one he was about to commit.*

'How are you going to do that?'

'We're the Government. We can do whatever we want.'

'Including committing murder, I guess,' Steve said.

Stella broke in again. 'This is not murder,' she justified, 'but we don't want this strain of the Halovirus getting out.'

'Huh? You mean they've got a new virus there? Is it one you made?'

'One of the children, though immune to the Halo, unknowingly created a new, more powerful strain. In only a few days, most of the adults will die. It's only a matter of time until it gets out. And if it does, the world may never recover.' The plausible lie seemed like every other lie people in positions of power told. They only needed gullibility and hope.

'But why don't you just do this yourself?'

'Mr. Cranmere... Steve... The Government's responsibility is to the people – the majority who voted for us. We must protect them, but this kind of action would not be looked on favorably.'

The penny finally dropped. 'So you need a stoolie like me.'

'Just so,' Stella spread her hands.

'How do I know you'll hold up your end of the bargain?'

'Because we will. When the Government says they will do something, it happens.' Stella looked over her shoulder towards the glass.

'I'll need some time to think about it,' Steve responded.

'You have three hours.'

'And then what?'

'If you do not agree, we drop you off back in Herzfeld,' the video screen turned on behind her in the reflective glass where an image of Igor appeared. 'There you'll find a very inquisitive police officer with a very special warrant headed to your very conspicuous pickup looking for a very important gun. And then after that very inquisitive police officer confiscates that gun, he will enter your house with his very special warrant and find all sorts of things that you wouldn't want to be found.'

Steve's stomach dropped. 'How did Igor find out about this?'

The image on the screen changed. A face appeared.

Edgar.

27

The courtyard was arranged with methodical neatness. All tables had been placed end to end and decorated with whatever Christmas finery could be found. Tinsel had been strung up and around the balcony; the kids helped put up baubles and ornaments everywhere. There was a general sense of celebration which hadn't been felt in months, maybe even years.

Esther slow-roasted an entire side of beef and the smell permeated Cloud End. As they went back to their rooms to prepare for the dinner, Christmas music played in the background. A new lease on life seemed a miraculous present.

Radiance Morrison, now deemed healthy by the green light in her room, meandered by rooms to check in on other residents to see if they needed anything. The Drapers raucously packed their belongings while attempting to get Titus to stand still so Sam could put a tie on him. His little suit looked incredibly handsome.

Father Lawrence sat on his bed, hands on thighs, smiling at Radiance as she poked her head in. His eyes betrayed mixed emotions, but Radiance was in too much of a hurry to interpret them.

In room 3, Chantelle studied herself in the full-length mirror. Claire had discovered a dust-covered bridesmaid's dress from the late 90's that she'd kept for special occasions. She never expected it would be the end of a pandemic celebration, but she was quite happy to loan it to Chantelle. Twirling from side to side studying both her figure (which had filled out with good eating) and her made-up face, Chantelle recognized how healthy she'd become. Though men told her she was sexy, it had been a long time since *she'd* felt attractive.

Radiance continued to glide down the hallway where she espied Wallis staring at her arm. It had been bandaged and wrapped. The residents with AutoComs found it much more difficult to destroy the devices embedded in their arms. Not only was there psychological pain of destroying their connection to the outside world, but the physical pain of pulling pieces from their flesh was evident. When they returned to civilization, they would need to have surgery to remove the receivers from their ears.

Wallis had dressed in a black cocktail dress which emphasized her shapely legs. She waved to Radiance as she passed by and went back to picking at her arm.

When she peeked into room 5, she was surprised to see Gavin standing in his parade uniform. Dark blue with an epaulette draped over his shoulder, he was putting on his white gloves. He looked embarrassed when he saw Radiance watching him.

'I don't know why I brought this,' he said. 'I guess it just reminded me of better days.'

'You look very handsome,' she replied honestly. 'It becomes you.'

A spasm of sadness wracked her as she walked quickly past Alonzo's room. The door was closed. The children had decorated it with pictures and cards. The St. Croix's had set up a white board where people could write notes. If it helped the grieving process, so be it.

The only other closed door on the second level belonged to Senator Faraday. No one knew if he was going to join them for dinner. He was staring morosely at his Halo Detector waiting for the green light to come on. Because he hadn't left his room, he had not discovered that only the *destruction* of the AutoCom would release him.

Amazingly, Sydney and Damian Bellows were in the same room getting dressed. Though things had not been completely resolved, the two had sat down during the day to hash out a truce.

And Monica, too, could reset her mind to her own family waiting back at home.

Sydney had, for some reason, brought along an evening gown, a shimmering midnight blue dress with a strap over one shoulder and dark lace along the bottom. Damian assisted her with the zipper while wearing his dapper dress pants and collared shirt. He stopped short of wearing a tie.

It wasn't until Radiance reached Seraphim Wyman's room that she found someone who seemed unhappy. The door was open, but Seraphim was hunched over on the edge of her bed, hands open on her thighs. She had not changed her clothes.

'Seraphim?' Radiance called out. 'Are you alright?'

Tears spilled from her brown eyes. Her face, splotchy from crying, was a well of sadness.

'Is it Alonzo?'

As Radiance entered the room, Seraphim returned to staring at her hands. 'Yes. No. Maybe.'

'I'm truly sorry for your loss.'

She blubbered. 'He was a really good man. I wish I was going to the party with him. I can't remember the last time I went to a party.'

'He'll be with us in spirit,' Radiance responded.

Seraphim frowned. 'That's what people say, like it's supposed to make you feel better, like when all you want is a steak and someone gives you a vegan burger.'

Radiance laughed. 'That's a good analogy, I think.'

'I don't want his spirit to be here. I either want him, or nothing. I don't want to be haunted.'

'You've had a hard life.'

Seraphim responded. 'You don't understand. The last six weeks I've been here, I've had the worst withdrawals. Some nights I'd sit in my room rocking back and forth on my bed. I wanted to die. Now that the drugs are out of my system, I know I can make it, but I have to do it without you people. I'm scared. If I can't fill my need with these relationships, will I go back to using?'

'You can always call...' Radiance said lamely.

'Same thing as saying, 'Their spirit is with us.' Nice sentiment, but it's just another veggie burger.'

'What do you think you'll do, then?'

'Maybe Chantelle and I can find a place together. Get real jobs. A real life.'

'I hope that's so,' Radiance clasped her hands in front of her. 'Now, you should get dressed and ready to party.'

Seraphim remained mute so Radiance moved on to the last rooms in the hallway where Jacquelyn had dressed in a sharp business suit and done her hair up nicely in a bun. She looked relaxed, unhurried, as if the night would be something she'd remember for the rest of her life.

When Radiance finished her tour upstairs, she trekked back down the steps and wandered past Bridgette and Renata's rooms. Although they had not been here quite as long, their Halo Detectors had turned green also. With a sigh of relief, they had wanted to return home, but Dr. Boeder-Mankins had suggested they stay for the party. 'Good closure,' she said with an awkward smile.

Radiance did not know that Jane had received a phone call letting her know she had to keep everyone at Cloud End so that they could prepare an appropriate press release regarding what had occurred at Cloud End.

Or so Jane believed. One always believes what the Government says.

When the chimes rang for dinner, laughter and loud conversation could be heard in every corner of the Convo. Residents stood behind chairs waiting for the hosts to arrive. As the St. Croix's took their spot at the head table, the rest pulled out their seats and settled in for a wonderful Christmas-like dinner. Donald stood again, and after an exultant glance at Claire, whose hair was done up in braids and encircled her head like a grey halo, he rang his glass with his fork.

'Welcome, everyone,' he intoned happily, 'it is a night to celebrate and to reflect. What a journey.' Happy smiles met him. 'Though we mourn Alonzo, we know he would want us to enjoy tonight, so we will.' He raised his glass. 'To Alonzo.'

They toasted the heroic gravedigger.

'We have been through a ringer, you and I – us. From the onset of the virus and its subsequent restrictions, to your forceful relocation to Cloud End. In the beginning, I wondered if we'd make it.'

'Pandemics have willed humanity to break, and break we almost did. Across the world, rumors of rage and protest and wars and fear continue to circulate. Viruses have evolved to attempt to change the very nature of who we are as people, but it has failed. No matter what the Halo has thrown at us, we have repelled it. Our own natural defenses are building an immunity to it.'

'But can we say the same for the real viruses that plague us?' Faces peered up expectantly at him. 'It's fear, isn't it? Fear is a soul killer. It infects all the good things in life, happiness, contentedness, togetherness, hope... and leaves a...' Donald was going to say *corpse* but caught himself quickly at the empty chair left for Alonzo. '... a shell of what could have been. But we've banded together against all odds, against all authorities.' His eye fell on the other empty chair where Winston Faraday III should have been sitting. 'And survived. Maybe even, dare I say, mutated?'

Ironic laughter rang through the dining area.

'As we sit here tonight, a healthy group of people who have not only recovered, we are stronger than ever, we know the virus can't get us any longer.' He raised his glass again. 'Damn the virus, down the hatch!'

The others repeated his toast loudly and downed whatever liquid they had in front of them. Happy faces, some wet with tears, others red with excitement, children staring in wonder at adults whose faces glowed in the Christmas lights and candles, greens and reds, set around the room. If only all nights could be like this.

Steve Cranmere seethed on the return flight from the Capitol. Even while he stared out the window at the constantly shifting colors of the sea, the eternal blues dancing in the light of the setting sun, his mind could not settle. Everything that had happened in the last two months, or perhaps the last ten years, had been orchestrated by the Government. Steve did not consider himself a conspiracy theorist, but now he was beginning to wonder.

Deep inside he knew the Government consisted of well-intentioned men and women who truly had the interests of their constituents at heart. But it only took a handful of public servants to infect the entirety of the Capitol, and suddenly, all politicians were disliked and pilloried. All policies were scrutinized with suspicion and active disdain. All political decisions were seen through the lens of a horribly warped system which sought the extension of the party regardless of whether there was an extinction of the species.

Throughout the last ten years, governments all over the world had diligently attempted to create therapies and cures for diseases. Yet, the media, corrupted with a pervasive fear and fundamental distrust of humanity, insinuated and deflected so much that people believed they *needed* the governments and their policies to keep them safe. And social media amplified the fear to toxic levels.

When was the world going to be freed from it?

Steve finally realized how much he had been played by the media, by the news, by his town and now by his Government. If he didn't step up to the plate, if he didn't do this abominable thing, he would spend the rest of his life in prison. The politicians who'd orchestrated this terrible idea would hide behind denial, shift blame, point fingers until people just got tired of it and moved onto the next circus with its clowns and acrobats and entertaining monkeys.

The ping sounded in the cabin and Steve was brought back to the moment. As the aircraft began its vertical descent, he sighed deeply. He couldn't go back to his house. Igor was probably waiting for him. He'd have to wait for the last of the light and sneak up to Cloud End.

He made up his mind.

He was going to put an end to this.

Constable Kovschenko saw the aircraft landing again. As the craft settled onto the rocky ground, pebbles and stones shot out like bullets in all directions. Igor noticed the Government sedan in the distance waiting for the engines to be shut down. When the craft alit, its doors opened and two serious looking people in black suits exited while buttoning their jackets. Behind them came a scruffy, worried Steve Cranmere.

Turning his binoculars to the car, Igor was startled to see the driver staring at him through his own binoculars. His heart dropped into his stomach when the man held up a Governmental badge and then drew a quick line across his throat.

Governmental authority. Cease and desist.

Suddenly, Igor was very frightened.

The sounds of revelry frustrated Faraday. They were rubbing it in.

They were all Halo negative while he remained red-lighted. Staring up at his Halo Detector, Faraday shook his head. He had watched them smash their AutoComs or mobile phones. Yes, he supposed this might turn the light green, but realistically, how would *he* be able to communicate with the greater world without his device? Wasn't it safer to wait out the Government's directive (as heartless as it was) rather than cut himself off from his sources of information?

As he pondered this reality, his AutoCom buzzed. It was Isolde.

'You need to get out now, Winston,' Isolde said without preamble.

'I can't. My Halo Detector is still red.'

'You don't have the virus. It's a ploy, remember?'

'Yes, of course, but what happens when I'm arrested for dodging restrictions? If Forsythe was vindictive enough, he'd wait until I get back to the Capitol and paste my arrest all over the...'

'If you don't get out now, you'll never get out.'

His eyes widened. 'What are they going to do?'

'Cloud End is going down.'

'How? When?'

'Tonight. They've sent someone to take care of it.'

'What does that mean? Are they going to...'

'We can talk details now and you can go down with the ship, or you can pack your things and take the lifeboat, Winston. It's up to you. I consider you a close friend and I care about you. Warn the others and leave before it's too late.'

'Okay.' He paused. 'Thank you, Isolde.'

'You're welcome.' She smiled as she overlooked the Capitol River where lights twinkled in the darkness like Christmas decorations. 'You owe me.'

Faraday disconnected the call and thanked his lucky stars he had not destroyed his device like the halfwits toasting their good health beneath him. Quickly, he retrieved his bag from the closet and began to pack his things. Without care, he dumped his suits and belongings into the suitcase, shoved his expensive colognes and toiletries in, packed his computer, and then, with one finger in the air, remembering something, he returned to the hamper where his track suit was. But then he remembered that it had been taken to the laundry.

Oh, well, he didn't need that anyway.

Faraday flicked the closet door back to reveal the one suit he was going to wear as he left. It had always been his intention to be spotlessly clean, an in-your-face symbol of his purity, this white suit with white waistcoat, white shirt, and white tie. His shiny white dress shoes sparkled in the light of his room. Quickly, he donned the suit and shoved the remaining clothes in his suitcase, zipped it shut and walked over to the Halo Detector. More than anything, he wanted to wrest it from the wall and hurl it out the window, but an alarm would go off. Thus, he left the Halo Detector in its red-lit glory and dragged his bag to the door.

Quietly he exited his room and shut the door behind him. Quickly, he strode to the back stairs illuminated by a green exit sign, pulled open the door and made his way down. When he opened the back door, he shut it softly behind him. Into the dim light he walked deeper into the grass to avoid any wayward looks from the illumination inside.

When he turned for one last glance at his six-week prison, he saw through the windows the glow of merrymaking. For a moment, he felt guilty that he was leaving them there, but in truth, they deserved it. They shouldn't have destroyed their devices.

He checked his AutoCom. It was almost 7:30. Isolde had not told him exactly what time the danger might start, but it had to be soon. He moved around the house to the front gate bidding the stress of his last weeks goodbye. After climbing over the locked gate, he lugged his suitcase over and slunk his way in the darkness into Herzfeld.

Steve felt the tension in his sinew and bones. The brutal torture of delivering what the Government wanted, but trading his soul for this freedom, this was beyond pain. At 7:00 p.m., well after the sun set, Steve stayed in the shadows as he crept through Herzfeld. He knew Igor was looking for him. He had an intuition that Edgar was also. Steve cursed him as he crept past Bridgette's grocery store and between the bank and post office. They were common places, places where he and Gemma had frequented not weeks ago. Hadn't they been happy then? Hadn't life been easier and complete? Weren't they content in their rustic life in the shadow of the cliff?

And yet he couldn't see himself in prison. Maybe the Government could fix this all. Maybe the Government could erase Cloud End and the evidence of its evil. Yes, they needed him, but wasn't that a fair trade?

Not far from the front gate he heard a noise. Diving for cover, he peered through the long grass and spotted a figure dressed entirely in white. From head to toe, he reflected the faint moonlight as he dragged his suitcase nosily over the gravel road towards Herzfeld. Steve felt his eyebrows pinch. Certainly, this Halo should not be bringing his uncleanness to his town. Momentarily, Steve wanted to rush the man, maybe even strangle him, but that would interrupt the importance of his journey. He needed to get to

Cloud End before any more Halos left. Director Reed-Conway had explicitly stressed this.

As he watched the retreating figure stagger down the gravel road to Herzfeld, Steve checked his pockets for the third time. The lighter. White briquettes. On the ground next to him was the canister of kerosene. Steve wasn't particularly hot on the idea of burning the Convo to the ground, but that's what the Government wanted. Nothing left. No trace of building, appliances or electronics. Nothing.

After the last rolling sound of the suitcase faded into the distance, Steve counted to fifty. Then, he stood and raced to the fence, climbed over, and crawled through the grass to Cloud End. He checked for his quickest escape route. Steve did not want to be around to hear the screams.

When he finally reached the porch, he heard voices raised with laughter. Music was playing, (Christmas music?) and the sound of chattering conversation. Certainly, this was not what he had expected. They should be staying in their rooms getting better. Being silent. Being sad. None of this joyful stuff. That was for healthy people, not the sick.

As he lay at the base of the front porch, he considered his next course of action. He could pour some kerosene, then jog around the side and do the same. Or, he could climb the steps and set fire to the front door itself.

Moving rapidly, he opted for the front door. Grabbing the door mat, he rolled it up and stuffed it with pages of a Stephen King book which had been lying on a nearby bench. He stuffed a lighter brick inside and doused the front door and area with kerosene before moving across the wraparound porch to a side exit. In the same way, he created the kindling for fire. All the while, he kept his mind numb.

As he moved around to the back side of the house, he paused. The sound coming from inside was raucous. A true party. Without thinking, he opened the door slightly to see what was going on.

His senses were overloaded. First, the noise and the smell of a feast. Through the narrow tunnel he saw a snapshot of people standing in small groups, holding drinks, talking loudly, each conversation an attempt to out-decibel the next. Behind the scene, a few young boys ran back and forth throwing a ball of some sort. No one stopped them or even yelled at them. Without conscious thought, Steve felt drawn by a strange gravity. As he took a few steps more, the smell of the meal assaulted him and his stomach rumbled.

A few more steps in and he realized that everything happening before him was a throwback to decades gone past. An older couple had their arms around each other's waists. Four or five others were dancing in the background, hands touching, breathing on each other. Steve looked down at his hands. They were raw and rough from constant washing and scrubbing. When was the last time he had touched anyone else's hand? There were restrictions for that kind of thing.

There were no masks, no protective gear; he couldn't see a single bottle of hand-sanitizer anywhere. Napkins were strewn over the remnants of the food, but no tissues. He cringed. How could these sick people not have a readily available source of tissues nearby? As Steve Cranmere watched them, he wrestled with two basic emotions: jealousy and disgust. At that particular moment, he would have done anything to be invited to the party, to forget what was going on in the rest of the world. It struck him then, there were no phones visible anywhere! No child or teenager was staring vacantly into an illuminated rectangle. There were no AutoComs. In fact, there were almost a dozen people who looked as if they'd wrapped bandages over their arms. What was that about?

His jealousy was almost overwhelming. But then his mind snapped back to reality. He had a job to finish. If they got out...

Suddenly, a face appeared in the doorway.

Renata.

'Steve?'

Like a deer caught in the headlights, Steve froze, mouth open.

'Is that you?'

Suddenly able to move, Steve wheeled back to the door and thrust his way outside. The fresh night air awakened his senses and brought him back to sanity. Steve glanced back through the window. Thankfully, Renata had not followed him down the hallway. With utmost haste, Steve prepared the porch for his purging, atoning fire, poured the kerosene, and without a glance back inside, he flicked the lighter.

It would be an enormous fire.

'Renata,' Bridgette called out, 'what are you looking at?'

'You're never going to believe this,' Renata said as her friend approached. 'I just saw Steve Cranmere.'

'What?'

Renata pointed to the door. 'Steve. He was right there.'

'You must be joking.'

'I don't think I've had *that* much to drink.'

'Why would Steve Cranmere be inside Cloud End. He and Gemma hated the thought of this place.'

Bridgette began to walk down through the hallway towards the door. She squinted. Twinkling light appeared outside the window as if the porch was shimmering. The closer she got to the door, the more she frowned.

'What in the...'

Suddenly, flames began to lick just underneath the window. Bridgette felt her heart drop. 'Renata!' she turned back to her friend. 'Fire!'

Renata met her at the door. Through the window, they could see that the porch was afire, and it was spreading quickly. Not just the planks but also the furniture. Soon, the beams would be alight. They had to do something quickly.

Sprinting back into the atrium, Bridgette screamed, 'FIRE!' The music was too loud. 'THERE'S A FIRE OUTSIDE! WE HAVE TO GET OUT!'

Only then did the realization hit them that Bridgette was serious. Donald unhitched himself from Claire and ran to the sound system to cut the music. When he did, there was an audible groan. Damian shouted, 'Donald, don't ruin my groove!'

'Listen, everyone! Quickly and calmly go to the exits. We need to get people outside.'

27

'What's going on?' Monica asked.

'There is a fire. Please, remain calm.'

Donald was already contemplating how to contact the authorities. No one had a mobile phone. No one had an AutoCom. Suddenly, he remembered the old landline in the kitchen. He wondered if it still worked. It hadn't been used in years. 'Radiance, take everyone to the evacuation area. I'm going to call the fire department from the phone in the kitchen.'

While he was speaking, Sam and Dorothy herded five children together and followed Radiance towards the front doors. When they got there, Radiance stopped them. 'Listen,' she said as calmly as possible, 'the fire is on this side also. We need to move toward the side door.'

En masse, they turned, this time Nancy led them, but as they reached the door, she felt it before opening. 'Oh no,' she uttered loud enough for the closest few behind her. 'It's everywhere.'

They were trapped.

Carl felt an immense fear as he stood next to Jane outside Cloud End. As the flames licked farther upwards and outwards, he wished that there could have been another way. From their position near the shed, they saw Steve Cranmere enter the Convo then hurry back outside to set it alight.

'This is horrible,' Jane had covered her mouth while tears began to pool in her eyes. The firelight was reflecting in them.

'It was the only way,' Carl responded.

'It wasn't,' Jane insisted.

'We signed up for this. We knew that this was a possibility. Just be thankful it wasn't you striking the match.'

'I didn't sign up for this!' Jane pointed at the burning house. 'I signed up for a study of human nature. And...'

'You wanted to be rich,' Carl said with a sneer.

She hesitated. 'But I didn't want to be a murderer.'

'Give me a break, Jane,' Carl's derisive tone was harsh, 'you can't claim a conscience now that we've reached the worst-case scenario.'

'But this is not what we do! This is inhuman.'

Carl shook his head and grabbed her by the arms. 'Wake up! You, better than all people, should know that this is a Darwinian world. Everything evolves. The fittest survive. The weak have to accept their fate.'

'That's fine for you to say,' she shouted in his face. 'You're not facing extinction!'

'Don't you get it, Jane? The fate of the world rests on getting this right. We can't have any more chaos during these pandemics. We have to have order and control.'

She shook her head. 'You really don't understand science, or even human nature.' She pulled away from him. 'Humans are communal animals. They can't function without each other. We've been pulling people apart for so long, they're bound to snap back. Everything in the natural world longs for its own space, but humans need connection. It's the ultimate irony.'

The ultimate irony burned behind them. The flames were now reaching the second story. Suddenly, one of the upper windows exploded. Someone had thrown a chair through it. Carl and Jane spun to see what had happened. Then, something crawled from the window. Then another, and another.

'What is that?' Carl asked.

Jane squinted into the light. 'Rats. White rats.'

Carl smirked. 'The pets. They belong to the kids. Figures. Rats know best when to abandon ship.'

The wriggling animals scrabbled along the roof of the porch attempting to gain a place to crawl down. Inside the window, a face looked outwards. It was Dr. Chandruth.

'Jane! Jane! Help us!'

With one last look of hatred to Carl, Jane ran into the shed. There, amidst the dirty buckets, rusty lawn tools and racks of unused oil, she found drop sheets for painting. Clutching them in her arms, she turned, but only to see Carl's leering face in the doorway as he slammed the shed shut. With horror, she heard the latch close. She was trapped.

By the time Steve Cranmere reached his house, he was a bawling mess. If any of this got out, the people of Herzfeld would never forgive him. Somewhere in town, an alarm went off. Steve's scanner blipped and the message for the fire department was sent. The people inside were going to die, maybe after asphyxiation from smoke inhalation, but sure as the sun would rise tomorrow, Steve knew they would all be incinerated.

Those poor kids.

Those people who were just getting their lives back together.

The vision of the party, the dancing, the closeness, even Renata's face appearing, created a surge of compassion, and suddenly, Steve made a hasty decision.

He had to reverse the horror. He had to go back to help.

Dashing outside the house to his truck, he jumped in and started the engine. Backing out into the street, he peeled out into the darkness and sped to Cloud End's gate. Not slowing down, he rammed the pickup through the metal barrier and drove quickly up the lane towards the house. He was horrified to see the entire first floor engulfed in flames and now the Halos were creeping up to the second-floor balcony. Turning into the long grass, he drove cross country to the side of the house where a sight startled him. There was a man staring up at a window. But he wasn't helping.

Steve brought the pickup to a crunching halt near the man and jumped out.

'What are you doing?' he asked.

The man was nonplussed. He seemed to recognize Steve.

'Help them, dammit!' Steve yelled, but the man remained transfixed by what was happening above.

Then, without warning, Steve heard shouting from the shed.

'Who is that?'

Carl shook his head. 'You started this, Steve. Put your conscience back in your pocket and drive home. You've already achieved your reward.'

'I can't! I can't! This is barbaric. Can't you hear them screaming?'

Carl turned menacingly to Steve. 'Go home, or I call the Government.'

Seeing the evil in his eyes, Steve backed up to his truck. In the distance, the sirens began to wail. Soon, fire trucks, paramedics and the police would arrive. Opening the door, he reached in. When he turned, his rifle was in his hand.

'Back up,' Steve growled.

Carl raised his hands. 'Easy, Steve. Think about what you're doing.'

From above them, screams emanated from broken windows. The Halos were beginning to pour out the window like rats. The children went first, then the women. The only man on the roof at that point was Dr. Chandruth who was organizing the children.

'Help me!' Jane screamed.

Steve, keeping his eye on Carl, sidled towards the shed where he manipulated the latch. Jane burst out, surprised to see Steve.

'You?' Her eyes were questioning, when suddenly she looked over his shoulder. 'Look out!'

It was too late. Carl had swung both of his hands over his head to knock Steve across the crown. Steve staggered, dropping the gun. They wrestled for it, but it was flung into the grass. Jane made a step towards it, but Steve stopped her. With a grunting voice he said, 'Get the pickup under the window. Let them jump into it!'

Jane paused, then ran to the truck and started it. Hurriedly, she drove it under the balcony beneath the window. Unfortunately, the balcony was already on fire. They would have to hurry. She jumped out of the pickup and raced back to the shed. Jane entered the shimmering darkness and grabbed the bundle of sheets, drop sheets and tarps, then raced back to the pickup. She threw them in the bed and looked up.

'You've got to jump! Hurry!'

Chandruth unceremoniously grabbed Titus and hurled him screaming into the pickup bed. He cried out with pain. It was not soft, but certainly it was better than the fire. Flames began to lick up and over the eaves as the next two children jumped. Then the girls. With each thud, Jane felt a surge of hope. She turned around. Carl had won the battle and was sitting astride Steve choking him. It wouldn't be long before Steve's heroic act would be finished.

Leaving her post, Jane ran to the bushes and got down on her hands and knees to search for the rifle. Even if she found it, she'd never shot one before. Finally, her back leg bumped against the cylindrical tube of the muzzle. Grabbing it, she held it in front of her, aiming it at her former colleague whose eyes were full of blood lust.

'Stop! Carl, Stop!'

He didn't. Steve's face had turned purple and he was beginning to stop wriggling.

'I'll shoot. If you don't stop, I'll shoot!'

Carl rolled his eyes. 'No, you won't, Jane. You can't. You don't have it in you.'

'I will.' She held it up to her shoulder awkwardly.

Carl laughed. 'Just put that down before you hurt yourself.'

'I'm going to count to three. One... two...'

Carl released his grip on Steve who sucked in a deep breath. Still sitting astride Steve, Carl lowered his head but glared up at her.

'Jane,' he said calmly, 'in a moment, I'm going to finish what we started. And then, you're going to put down the gun and we'll drive out of here. I will pay you one hundred thousand dollars. Do you understand?'

She shook her head rapidly. With a quick glance over Carl's shoulder, she saw that a few of the women had made it safely down, but the upstairs was now almost completely engulfed. Only a matter of seconds before the men would be consumed.

'I'm going to count to three,' Carl said, 'and then you're going to put the gun down. One... two...' he started to rise from Steve and move towards her. 'Th...'

Before he could finish the word, Jane Boeder-Mankins pulled the trigger.

The retort was so loud Jane's ears rang, but what happened to Carl's gut was worse than a nightmare. With a look of shock, he held Jane's eyes. He wanted to speak, to question her – Were they not co-workers? Were they not co-conspirators? Why had she...

Before the last question could exit his mind, Carl van der Hoven keeled over to the side. The last thing he saw was a white rat staring at him in the grass.

Jane dropped the gun as if it were a snake and ran quickly to Steve's side. Still coughing and spluttering, he sat up. 'Is everyone out?' he croaked.

'Not yet.' Jane pointed up. A few of the men were attempting to spread out on the roof to distribute the weight before it collapsed. All of them were coughing. It appeared that Father Lawrence had already passed out. Damian Bellows neared the edge, but before he could leap, the entire balcony trembled. With a look of immense fear, Damian felt the burning balcony would begin to crumble.

'Damian!' Sydney screamed.

It was too late. As the porch roof crumpled into the fire, the increased air caused a *whoomp* and the flames shot up higher. With a panicked scream, Damian rolled from the porch and out onto the ground. His hair and clothes were on fire. The woman grabbed one of the drop sheets and patted the fire out, but those remaining on the roof knew it was hopeless. They began to leap, but they, too, were on fire. Pain seared their bodies as they crunched into the ground. A few bones were broken, but it was nothing to the searing pain of the inferno.

One by one they leapt.

The only one left was Father Lawrence. He couldn't be dragged. Then, the entire porch had collapsed. Father Lawrence's body was engulfed.

Without thought, Steve Cranmere leapt to his feet and charged the house. Although every part of his body hurt, he hurled himself into the fire. Scorched, he felt the heat crinkle his skin and his hair was singed. The breath he took was too hot and his lungs began to burn. Desperately, he jumped into the fountain to extinguish his burning clothes. Then, with dripping body, he climbed the burning stairs until he found the priest. He jerked him out the window. The heavy body made it extraordinarily difficult. With Herculean strength, Steve tossed the body of Father Lawrence Haskins over the eaves and into the pickup. As Lawrence thumped into the truck, Steve leapt from the inferno and landed awkwardly on the ground. As he rolled, Steve felt his skin crackling.

His legs began to collapse. With just enough strength, he found the reserve to stagger to his pickup. While the rescued Halos worked to drag Lawrence further from the blaze, Steve Cranmere hopped in and drove his vehicle away from the house.

'Stop!' Jane yelled.

He couldn't hear her. He only wanted the cool relief of water. There was too much pain. Too much anguish. Accelerating, Steve drove his pickup towards the cliff's edge and when his tires no longer found traction, Steve screamed. The precipitous drop to the bottom was met by an incredible crunching sound.

Steve Cranmere's last thought was, *'Thank God, the water is cold.'*

28

(Reuters)

What was meant to be a place of healing has turned tragically into a place of horror. Cloud End Convalescent Centre was engulfed in flames last night. Fire fighters labored into the night to extinguish the fire while rescue workers tended those who had been injured. For fear of contracting the Halovirus, paramedics took extra precautions in treating the wounded which, according to Reuters' inquiries, delayed life-saving measures for multiple victims. Herzfeld paramedics claim they simply followed protocols, but according to Government authorities, an inquiry will be made.

Among the casualties was Father Lawrence Haskins, age 62, who died at the scene, as well as police officer Gavin Matthews and a woman, Seraphim Wyman. Owners of Cloud End, Donald and Claire St Croix, were treated for injuries, but have not been able to give any details as to what happened on that dreadful night.

In what has turned out to be a Government nightmare, not only were there casualties from the fire, but one of the employees, Carl Van der Hoven, was found dead by gunshot. Government agencies will be investigating.

In a connected story, Reuters has learned that multiple high-ranking Government officials have been implicated in a cover-up. All charges have been denied. More information will be coming in the next weeks.

With the destruction of Cloud End, all other Convalescent Centres are being closed for investigation.

December 3, 2031

Epilogue

'**Mom, can we** go play outside?'

Startled from her reverie, Dorothy Draper pondered her beautiful son, Pasqual. He had still not entirely recovered from his injuries. He'd lost his eyebrows and his legs had second degree burns. He had escaped the worst of it, unlike Sam, who was still going through skin grafts. For Sam, every day was a trek of torture, but he promised Dorothy they'd make it through.

'Yes, you can go outside, but take your brother with you.'

'Do I have to?'

She gave him the look.

He sighed. 'Titus!' The thundering sound of footsteps came down the hall and the smallest Draper made his way toward the front door.

Once they left, Dorothy sat near the front window with her cup of tea. The heat burned her fingers, but she paid no attention.

Jacquelyn Archer had checked in on her. She'd sent an email.

Dorothy,

I wonder if you're feeling the way I am. Stunned. Jumpy. I can't quite seem to focus. I've gone back to work, but I can't look at people the same way. They see me, but I don't see them. At first, a few of them asked how I was, but now that my hair is growing back, that's stopped. They have returned to staring at their computers, texting on their AutoComs, entertaining themselves to death. They wear masks, but I can't help but believe that the hardest mask to get rid of is the one that keeps attaching itself to people's hands. Their thumbs work like crazy. They don't see the real world, only the algorithmic filtered version of it.

I want to talk to them, to shake them, to remind them that there is something better, but I know they won't listen.

As I stare out my office window at the busy people below me running, endlessly running, through the maze, a rat race, designed to distract us from

341

the realest things: I know that life is tenuous at best and we're only one virus away from losing hope.

I don't know if you've heard much from the others, but Chantelle has moved in with me. It feels right, you know? Helping someone else seemed so foreign a few months ago, but now it feels natural. I've hired her as an assistant in my company. She's not very good (ha ha) but it keeps her off the streets (literally).

Monica is mostly silent. I think she's gone back to the old ways, which is fine, but I'll continue to check on her.

Whether or not it is the right choice, Sydney and Damian are back together. I think they still meet with Wallis, even though she has taken a leave of absence. I'm not sure if she will go back. Wallis seems decidedly disinterested in hearing people complain about those they once loved.

I haven't heard from the senator.

I don't expect to.

I hope you and the children are well and that you continue to stay in contact with the St. Croix's. I almost wish they rebuild Cloud End so we could all go back to vacation there. I wonder if we could handle it?

If you ever need anything, especially with Sam's recovery, do not hesitate.

Love,
Jacquelyn.

Winston Faraday III reclined in a booth at his favorite restaurant, a swanky business on the south side of the Capitol. Sitting across from him was a beautiful woman, long neck and shoulders bared and emphasized by a generous string of milky pearls. When Senator Faraday lifted his finger to the waiter, a middle-aged man in a white jacket and black pants hurried to them. The senator ordered a bottle of their finest champagne.

'It's definitely a night to celebrate, isn't it, Winnie?'

'That it is.' His million-dollar smile had made headlines as the most famous survivor of the fated Cloud End disaster.

'Here's to you,' she raised her glass and let the scintillating liquid reflect in her admiration of him.

'Here's to the future,' he responded and clinked flutes with her.

'Do you have big plans?'

His enigmatic smile appeared after he sipped. 'I've got enough information to make my way to the highest levels of government.'

'Ooh, you bad boy,' she said as she stroked his leg with her foot under the table.

'They will pay for what they did to me.'

She raised her eyebrows. 'What are you going to do?'

He shrugged. 'I'd love to tell you, darling, but...'

'But what?'

'I'm not sure my secret would remain safe.'

Appearing hurt, she touched a hand to her chest. 'I'm sorry you feel that way about me.'

'It's not you, Isolde,' he said.

His eyes glanced up at the video cameras in the corner of the room.

'They're always watching.'

The End

Author's Note

Unfortunately, George Orwell was right. Big Brother is very present and very powerful. The deception was intentional, and whether we knew it or not, we have been swallowing it for a very long time. For decades, Big-Brotherish social media platforms have been gathering information about us, feeding it to voracious algorithms which ingest, digest and spit out the perfect combination of what companies want us to believe and to consume. And all the while, they record us doing it.

This deception is nigh irrevocable. It has divided us, abducted our attention, and transformed us into an angry, outraged and hopelessly tribal humanity. The artificial intelligence employed by social media, and its subsequent surveillance, has brought us to a dreadful reckoning:

Destroy each other, or love each other.

The Government is not out to get you. I promise you this. Though not always generous in public service, they are doing the best they can not only to keep people safe, but to point us to a better future.

COVID was not a hoax. Unfortunately, depending on where you lived and what your prejudices were, social media made you believe one of two things: that COVID was a Government or Chinese conspiracy, or that every person who did not follow the Government's best directives was a Fascist. Either way, we were turned against each other and haven't recovered. Not totally, anyway.

So why did I write this book?

In my role working with young people every day, I ponder the impact that mobile devices have on their present and future. As they are unable or unwilling to tear their eyes away from that small little piece of glass with moving pictures, I can't help but be afraid.

This is the kind of thing that the financially motivated, ethically bankrupt social media companies want us to believe so we purchase more products. The more afraid we are, the more we buy things to insulate ourselves from that fear. They want us to fully associate with fallible, scared people like the Cranmeres, Father Lawrence, Gina Draper or even the

344

Government cadre. Whichever figures we choose, we will be forced to hate the 'other' who does not think like *us*.

In the end, true freedom is to dissociate yourself from the addictive nature of many forms of social media, to set your phone in the kitchen at night rather than on the lampstand in the bedroom, and to live on the edge of life's cliff. Watch the seagulls. Hold someone's hand. Smell the pine trees. Delight in your grandchild's horribly off-tune violin solo. Taste the bitter bite of mustard on a hotdog. In any case, live your life with others and for others.

Acknowledgments

Some incredible work has been done regarding social media's influence on both the physical and mental health of the world today. A truly frightening eye-opener is the Netflix documentary, *Social Dilemma*. Thanks to those involved for their bravery in exposing what is happening in humanity today via the digital world.

I owe a great deal of the final copy of this novel to my daughters, Elsa, Josephine and Greta who read these pages circumspectly, and with an eye to how twenty-somethings might understand it, not just fifty-somethings.

To Christine, who consistently points out the beauty and difficulty of storylines, I'm thankful. Your honesty and your heart are only rivaled by your beauty.

Thanks to Bonnie Doty for her keen love of stories and an eye for cohesion.

CPSIA information can be obtained
at www.ICGtesting.com
Printed in the USA
JSHW010942090723
44219JS00001B/1